Worms That Never Die

Worms That Never Die

A Novel by
Alfred W. Walker

Worms That Never Die

© Alfred W. Walker 2018

This book is a work of fiction. Named locations are used fictitiously, and characters and incidents are the product of the author's imagination. Any resemblance to actual events or places or persons, living or dead, is entirely coincidental.

Copyright registration: TX0005484885

Published by
Lighthouse Christian Publishing
SAN 257-4330
5531 Dufferin Drive
Savage, Minnesota, 55378
United States of America

www.lighthousechristianpublishing.com

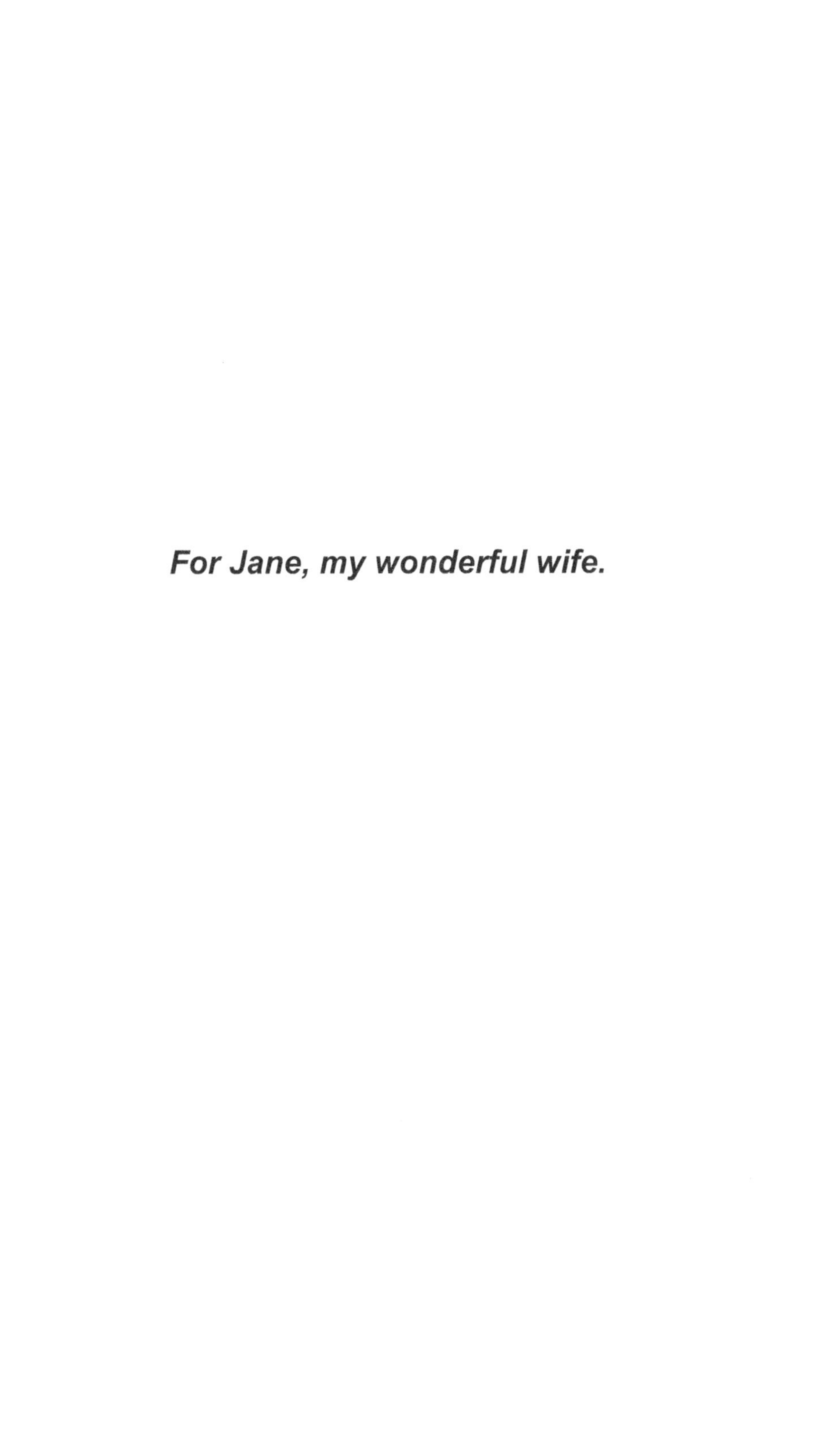

For Jane, my wonderful wife.

Chapter One

The menacing sight of that rattlesnake, purposely slithering towards the old man's face, would probably have shocked most people into muteness. Not Royal Renfro. He had already lost his voice to an earlier horror back in East Texas. And his nervous system, completely numbed by that previous ghastly experience, was incapable of triggering any quivering or cold sweating. So it was that the eighteen year old boy coldly and matter-of-factly raised himself up on his left elbow, unsheathed his .30-.30 rifle and pulled it out from under his dew soaked blanket.

Royal's bed roll, beside that of his father, was under the branches of an ancient hackberry tree, situated on the north margin of "Buffalo Wallow". Before they were eradicated in the 1870's, some forty years ago, the buffalo liked to wallow in the shallow, grassy lake bed, happily scratching their huge bodies, and, for at least a short time, making life miserable for their ever present enemies, the screw flies.

Royal was looking across a narrow, fifty foot wide neck at the east end of the wallow. The target of his fixed stare was a mop of shaggy, gray hair protruding from a bed roll. The hair seemed to furnish a magnetic draw for the killer snake which steadily slithered towards it. The old man had not been there the night before when the saddle weary father and son had gratefully fallen into a deep slumber. Glancing quickly at the mule which was silhouetted against the orange beginning of the West Texas sunrise, Royal surmised that the old man must have come along later on his mule; and, in deference to his sleeping neighbors, had noiselessly bedded down.

Royal also noted that the gray bearded one had taken traditional measures to ward off rattlesnakes. The bed roll, at a distance of about four feet out, was encircled by a lariat rope. Tradition had it that a rattlesnake would not crawl over a rope. The explanation for this claimed behavior was that the snake would mistake the rope for another snake. To this particular rattlesnake, feasting its fascinated eyes on the old man's gray beard, the rope trick was nothing but an old wives' tale. It had long since wiggled over the rope, traveled past the old man's boots and was now paused alongside two feet which were clad in dirty, once white socks, now wet with dew. Incredibly, the snake broke its fascination for the old man's face long enough to invest a couple of seconds in a stare at the socks. After disdainfully shaking its head from side to side, it again fastened its eyes on its target and resumed its journey.

By this time, Royal was sitting erect, following the snake's progress through his rifle sights. Quickly he perceived that from where he was sitting a bullet from his rifle could not strike the snake without also striking the old man. He needed to move about three feet to his left so that he could send his bullet on a line running perfectly parallel with the old man's head and body. Cat-like, he made the necessary lateral adjustment and rolled into a prone position. Just as he got the rattler in his sights again, it drew its head back, swiftly preparing to strike its deadly fangs into the face of the peacefully snoozing man.

It was the loud bam of the .30-.30 that woke the old man. But, since the bullet traveled faster than the sound, the snake's head had already been blown to smithereens when he awoke to the horrifying sight of the bloody stump withering in his whiskers. Bellowing with rage and fright, he erupted from his bed, grabbed his own rifle and leveled it at Royal.

"Stop. Don't shoot." The voice which rang out the words was frantic, but it was also honest and authoritative. It caused the old man to lower his rifle. The voice belonged to George Renfro, Royal's father, who had also been awakened by the shot.

George, walking slowly towards the old man, said, "I don't know what this is all about. I just woke up. But it's not worth anybody gettin killed over. Now, Son, what's goin on here?"

"That's right. Ask him," snorted the old man. "He's the only one who knows what's goin on. I sure don't"

With that, Royal started walking towards the old man's bed roll.

"Where you goin?" the old man testily demanded. "Why won't you speak up? Cat got your tongue?"

"In a sort of a way the cat does have his tongue," George softly responded. "You see, he's mute. He hasn't been able to talk for over eight weeks."

The old man's face immediately softened. "Oh, well pardon me, young fella. I didn't mean to make fun of you."

"It's alright," George assured him. "He understands."

Continuing to the bed roll, Royal picked it up off the ground, revealing the headless snake. Calmly picking up the rattler so as to plainly display the bloody stump, Royal went on to give a clear sign language account of the shooting.

"Well, I'll be a monkey's uncle," the old man responded. Somehow that snake's mama never taught him the West Texas rule that snakes don't cross ropes. Anyway, thank you, Son. I'm sure you saved my life."

Then, plainly giving the frustrated appearance of one who wants to do or say something else but can't quite figure out what it is, the old man shrugged his shoulders, frowned and opened his mouth without emitting a sound. Finally, in a tone of relief, he said, "Look, why don't you boys let me fix you some breakfast. I picked up a bunch of eggs yesterday. How long's it been since you've had any eggs?"

Both Renfros smiled. "Long time," George replied. "Sounds good to us."

The old man chuckled with pleasure. "I guessed as much. By the way, my name is William T. Applegate." Then he quickly added: "But understand, now, I ain't askin for your name."

George gave is face a quizzical twist. "Why don't you want to know our names?"

"Oh, I didn't say I didn't want to know. I just said I wasn't asking?"

"You got me mixed up."

The old man chuckled. "It's easy to see that you haven't been in this country very long. Out here and in Eastern New Mexico you won't make yourself very popular by goin around askin people their names or where they came from. A world of these folks out here are runnin from something. And if they want you to know who they are or where they're from, they'll tell you without bein asked."

George's eyes shone with amusement. "I'll remember that," he evenly replied, "but we don't have anything to hide. My name is George Renfro, and this is my son, Royal. We came from East Texas-Van Zant County, and the fact is that we're running away from something. However, I reckon it would be a waste of our time and yours for me to go into all that." Pausing to hit the old man with a hard-eyed stare, he continued: "You can just take my word that we ain't ashamed of what we're runnin from. What about them eggs?"

Without any sign of nervousness, Applegate chuckled again as his practiced eyes quickly sized up his new companions. The older one, about 40, was one of those dark, leathery, whipcord types with hard brown eyes. He stood just under six feet; and notwithstanding his two or three days growth of blue-black beard, Applegate judged that most women would probably say he was handsome.

Shifting his gaze to the boy, Applegate concluded that all women would no doubt call him handsome. Towering a couple of inches above his father, he too was dark and slim. However, the boy's eyes brought his reemblence to his father to an abrupt end. They were dark blue and seemed to be always be flashing and commanding attention. Applegate had already noticed, when the boy was giving his account of the shooting, that he related the facts with hand signals and body English; but his emotions were communicated through his eyes.

Both father and son wore faded blue overalls with twisted straps which were drawn over the shoulders of new, never washed, blue shirts. Instead of boots, they wore light brown brogans. They stood bareheaded at he moment; but Applegate noticed tat a fairly new black felt hat, with round crown and wide round brim, lay beside each of their bed rolls. The hats seemed to him to correspond to their horses which, in his expert assessment, had seen much more of the plow than the saddle.

Dirt farmers, he concluded to himself. Strangers in a strange land.

Aloud he said, "Ya'll go and do whatever you do this time of the morning, and I'll be gettin our breakfast cooked. Come on back in about half an hour."

When the Renfros reappeared at the appointed time, they found Applegate, knife in hand, picking thick strips of salt pork out of a skillet brimming with hot grease. From a gallon bucket sitting on the edge of the same small fire arose the pleasing aroma of boiling coffee. Pointing to the small black pot sitting on a bed of glowing coals, the old man said, "That bread'll be ready shortly. In the meantime, each man cooks his own two eggs." Noting the signs of mild surprise which crossed his guests' faces, he explained: "I'm a good cow-camp Cook. But you'll find that eggs are scarce out here, and no cow camp Cook with any experience at all is ever gonna take the responsibility of cookin a cowboy's eggs. That's the one thing he's got to cook for himself. If the Cook don't get 'em like the cowboy wants 'em, he'll take abuse ranging from a good cussin to a bullet. But if the cowboy ruins 'em------. Well, "he finished, "I ain't ever heard of one committin suicide over it." He looked up and smiled. "See now, that's your first lesson in special West Texas wisdom."

In response, Royal's eyes lite up, and he immediately began to talk with his hands and walk in a circle. In a short time George grinned and nodded his understanding. But Applegate was clearly bewildered. "What's he sayin?"

George explained, "He says he hopes that bit of West Texas wisdom about cookin eggs works out better than one about snakes and ropes."

The old man's eyes momentarily darkened. Then he slapped his knee and roared with laughter. Pointing to the skillet, he said, "Alright, boy, you are a pretty good hand with a rifle. Lets see how you can handle eggs in hot grease."

Royal let his eggs get much harder than he had intended, but he carefully covered that fact and consumed them with exaggerated relish. With smile lines barely crinkling the corners of his mouth, the old man just as carefully concealed the fact that he wasn't fooled.

Later, as each of them blew across his second cup of coffee, Applegate spoke up. "Uh, I was just wonderin-----. If ya'll are amin to ride along towards where the sun sets, I'd be awful glad to ride along with you."

The Renfros looked at each other and nodded. "Glad to have you," George replied.

"Good" the old man exclaimed. "I'll get my mule packed and be ready by the time ya'll can get back across the wallow and get on your horses. I'll shore be glad to have somebody to talk to."

Walking towards their horses, father and son exchanged good humored looks of mock horror. "Wonder what we got ourselves into," George muttered. "He may talk our ears off."

The old man fooled them though. While

they were riding, he said very little, being content to pay on his French Harp. He was pretty good on it too, and by the end of the long, hot day in June they had enjoyed hearing him play all of Stephen F. Foster's tunes along with just about all of the church songs they had ever heard.

They made camp on the bank of a dry creek, and after a supper of salt pork, beans and biscuits, George complimented Applegate: "We liked to listen to your French Harp playin."

"Well, I appreciate that," Applegate returned. "I learned to play it mostly because it helps me to get a crowd together and keep 'em interested before I start preachin."

"Preaching?"

"Yeah. Did I forget to tell you that I'm a preacher?"

"Yeah. You shore did. I thought you said you were a cow camp Cook."

"Well, I am. But I'm also a preacher and a cowpuncher and a windmiller and a fence builder. Mostly though, I'm a preacher." He paused to deliberately put a strong note of mystery in his voice. "Except right now I guess you could say that I'm mostly lookin for treasure."

The mysterious reference to treasure caused George to immediately jump on guard. Was this shaggy old geezer some king of a con man? Refusing to take the bait, he casually responded: "What kind of a preacher are you anyhow?"

Quickly swallowing his chagrin, the old man proceeded to inundate them with the profuse flow of words which they had anticipated earlier in the day. It turned out that describing his brand of preaching necessarily included a short account of his whole life history.

He swiftly skipped through his barefoot boy days on a farm just outside of Holly, Mississippi. But he dwelled for almost an hour on his wartime experiences at the side of Nathan Bedford Forrest. He well remembered the Sunday night of April 16, 1865 as both the saddest and happiest time in his life. It was then that he heard the news of Lee's surrender, but it was also the night when he "found the Lord and surrendered to preach his word". True to the usual pattern of an old man who lived through a war, Applegate recalled his forty odd post war years in anti climatic tones.

"God called me to Texas after the war," Applegate declared. "He told me to go right then and not to stop for any study or training. He let me know that I was just to speak to people from my heart and that he would put the right words in my heart. And that's just what I've been doin ever since."

He went on to outline his years as a buffalo hunter and later as a ranch hand with the XIT's the Matadors and the Spurs. He had also driven freight wagons out of both Amarillo and Colorado City. And for a couple of years he managed a mercantile store in Clarendon. "Along the way," he matter of factly bragged, "I built up a reputation for being about the best cook in the cow business."

All the while the most important thing, he said, was his preaching. He had preached in a few churches but had never been the pastor of one.

"Mostly," he explained," my preaching has been to whatever crowd I could get together whenever I happened to be on a Sunday morning. And," he added, "any other time if the spirit happens to move me."

"Of course," the old man went on, "I always managed to get in a little prospecting of gold and silver here and there and to sneak a few looks for Spanish treasure."

He paused to pick up a green mesquite stick and poke at the last glowing coals of the camp fire. "Of course," he sadly acknowledged, "I've never hit it lucky. But by the way I'm onto a sure thing this time.

He raised his head, excitedly looking for the Renfros reaction. Their response came in the sound of soft snoozing. Each of them had fallen back on his bed roll, dead to the world. Although Applegate had no intention of sharing any secrets with his new friends, his failure to tantalize them left him feeling cheated. Disgustedly he kicked dirt on the coals; and, joints cracking, unfolded his own tired body on his bed roll. "They'll learn to pay more attention to me before I'm done with them," he grunted to his mule. The next sound the mule heard was one to which it had long since become accustomed--the old man's snoring, deep and rumbling.

Chapter Two

Wide eyed, George Renfro sat up. He looked around and saw nothing out of place. The hobbled horses and mule were quiet, probably sleeping. He heard the far off howl of a coyote, but he neither saw nor heard anything strange or frightening. Since he had gone to sleep, the moon had risen, bathing the whole scene in its light. George guessed that moonbeams striking his eyes must have nudged him out of his slumber.

He cast his eyes on his still peacefully sleeping son. He tensed at the sight of the boy's face, pale in the moonlight. Funny, he thought, that a man's love for someone could sometimes make him ache all over. He wanted to crawl over and plant a kiss on his son's cheek, but he quickly kicked the very thought out of his mind. A man, of course, would never do such a thing.

George was suddenly struck by the irony their present journey. Why, he asked himself, do I keep on pushing us towards that place that has already jinxed my whole family? His wide awake mind started drifting back to the genesis of the jinx. It started a little more than a year ago, on a hot evening in May.

George and Royal had finished bedding down the plow horses and were making their way through the darkness to their share-croppers' house. Suddenly in a soft, croaking voice, they heard the question, "Might you be George Renfro?"

The inquiry came from a figure on horseback silhouetted against the dimly lighted house.

"Well, I might be," George cautiously replied. Then aside to Royal, he calmly but quickly whispered, "You just walk straight on in the house and get your rifle."

However, the shadowy figure promptly cancelled any real or imagined need for the protection of a rifle. Emitting a low moan, he fell off the horse, meeting the ground with a sickening thud. George and Royal ran to the crumpled form. "It's an old man," Royal gasped. "Is he dead?"

"No, he's breathing," George answered, turning the man over on his back. "Lets get him into the house."

By the time they laid him out on Royal's bed, Kate was there, holding high a coal oil lantern. In the eerie light they beheld a gaunt, emaciated man, immaculately dressed in an elegant black suit, complimented with boiled white shirt, stiff collar and black string tie. His deeply lined, ashen face lay in a nest of long white hair. He was laboriously sucking breath through tightly clinched teeth.

"I'm gonna get him out of this hot coat," George announced. "Kate, bring some cool water and a towel. Son, you go tend to his horse."

When Royal returned from the barn, he was surprised to see the strange visitor sitting up in bed, sipping gratefully from a tumbler of water. As Royal approached the bed, the old man smiled, and his brown eyes, feverish though they were, sparkled with pleasure.

He spoke in a deep, resonate voice, using grammatically correct speech patterns which sounded somewhat strange to the Renfros. Addressing Royal, he said, "You must be Royal, George's only son."

"Yes, sir," Royal replied.

Leering intently at Royal, the old man slowly added, "Your features affirm your Renfro blood-black hair, thin lips, strong chin and a tall, slender build. You got those blue eyes from your mother though, didn't you?"

Royal smiled. "I guess so," he answered.

"Well," the old man continued in a louder, stronger voice, "since the entire family is together, allow me to identify myself and state the nature of my business."

Kate protested, saying that he should first take some soup and rest awhile.

"Please," he insisted, "I appreciate you concern, but I am confident that I will not overtax myself, and I will not be able to relax until I have explained my presence here."

Turning to George, he continued, "George, I

am Joseph Renfro, your father's youngest brother."

"The lawyer," George responded.

"Yes, and I come bearing the last fruits of my professional practice. But I'll get back to that in a moment. First, I'll explain that my doctors in Houston have advised me that I have been visited by a tumor which grows larger every day. There is nothing they can do to arrest its growth, meaning that my remaining time on this earth amounts to but a few weeks, at best a few months."

After a fit of coughing, the old man continued. "I have friends, of course, but no immediate family. As a matter of fact, George, I have ascertained after diligent inquiry, that you and yours are my only living relatives. Now, it may seem odd to you, since I had never laid eyes on you until tonight, but I have a deep yearning to live my last days in the company of my own kin, to die in their watch are and to be buried by their hands. Does that sound uncommonly strange to you?"

"Oh, no!" Kate blurted, "that's most natural, and you're most welcome here."

A smile crossed Joseph's face. "I'm not surprised at you reaction, Kate. From what I had heard about you, I judged that I would be welcome here, even if I came empty handed."

"But," he excitedly added, "I did not come empty handed. Royal, did you bring in my saddle bags?"

"Yes, sir."

"Fetch them to me please."

Upon receipt of the bags, Joseph rummaged inside one of them and withdrew a folded document. Unfolding it with a flourish, he triumphantly announced, "this is a deed, conveying to you, George, your heirs and assigns, forever, a full 640 acre section of land in Miller County, out in Northwest Texas. I have already executed it before a Notary Public, and I deliver it now to you. All I ask in return is that you let me live with our family the remainder of my days."

Accepting the deed, George responded, "You'd be welcome anyhow, but we sure appreciate this."

"I have but one further request," Joseph added, "it is that you delay moving to Miller County until after I'm gone. I'm in no condition to make the journey, and I want to die with as little pain as possible."

"Of course, of course," George assured him, "We'll do whatever you want us to do about that."

Joseph closed the scene by smiling, closing his eyes and falling into a deep sleep.

Royal lost his bed to the visitor and was obliged to move to the hay loft. He didn't mind much though. The loft wasn't so bad; and besides that, he liked having the old gentleman around, He had the knack of making Royal feel important, and he captured the boy's wide-eyed attention for hours on end with colorful accounts of his courtroom exploits.

"The deed" put a spark in George's eyes an a spring in his steps. For the first time in his sharecropper's life, he had a dream. As to Kate, she too glowed in the hope engendered by "the deed". Moreover, the old gentleman's presence was a pleasant boost to her ego. She was charmed by his frequent compliments on her personal appearance as well as her cooking.

Joseph, perceiving that George and Kate might be overly excited about their newly acquired land, explained that he had never seen it and that it was undoubtedly undeveloped, droughtly pasture land. He related that the land had been homesteaded back in the late 1880's by four Armstrong brothers, Clarence, William, James and Bert. Each of them had filed a homestead claim on 160 acres, a separate quarter section of the 640 acres section covered by the deed. Each of the Armstrongs, with their wives, built the necessary small house and lived on his quarter section for more than the three years necessary to make it his under the Texas homestead laws. However, several years after perfecting and recording their title to the land, they, for reasons never disclosed to Joseph, moved back to Houston and became successful and wealthy land developers. When they were getting started in their new business, they were short on money, explaining why Joseph had accepted the deed to their Miller County land in exchange for legal services. That had been almost nine years ago.

Mixed with his warnings, Joseph sounded two optimistic notes about what the Texas General Land Office had now officially named the "Armstrong Survey". First, he deduced that there must be a source of water on it, else the

Armstrongs would never have homesteaded it and couldn't have lived there for all those years. Secondly, although the land was now over 30 miles from a railroad, he had heard strong rumors that the some of the of the big ranchers were about to persuade the Fort Worth and Denver Railroad to build a track into the town of Mesa, not more than five miles from the Armstrong Survey.

Joseph obviously enjoyed living with his newly found relatives. Occasionally he would take to his bed for a day or two with a "spell". But most of the time he was up and around, cheerful an openly delighted

to have an audience who hung on his every word. The experience was a good tonic and served to prolong his life several months beyond his doctors' predictions.

Joseph's death in the last week of February, 1914 struck the surviving Renfros with a mixture of sadness and release. They were truly sorry to lose the old gentleman but were also delighted with their material benefits. As is common with others in similar circumstances, they were a bit ashamed of their delight. Happily though, it took only a few days for nature to cause the shame to fade away.

The plan was for George and Kate to sell one of their teams of horses. The other team would pull a wagon filled with the family and all their possessions to the town of Mesa. George was pretty fair "jack leg carpenter" and thought that he and Royal could find work in the building boom that was bound to follow the railroad into town. They would save their money; and using Mesa as their base, would scout out their land and start to develop it.

* * * * * * *

However, as George now ruefully observed, the absence of Kate from the moonlight scene gave stark evidence of the fact that their plan had been abruptly altered. Just then a thick cloud floated over the moon, casting a shaft of darkness over that tiny part of the would and serving to jolt George out of his musings. Mercifully, the weariness in his bones halted the workings of his mind, and he fell again into a deep slumber.

Chapter Three

It was barely daylight when two loud shotgun bams brought both of the Renfros to a sitting position, hands on rifle. They were quickly relieved to hear a happy and excited announcement in the voice of William T. Applegate. From the other side of a plum thicket about 100 feet on down the dry creek, Applegate shrieked, "Yea hoo, I got three, two with one shot."

He shortly appeared from behind the plum bushes, grining and holding his shotgun in one hand and six legs of a feathered species in the other. "We're gonna have prairie chicken for breakfast," he trumpeted. "Have you boys ever had prairie chicken for breakfast?"

"No," George acknowledged, "and not for any other meal either. We ain't ever had prairie chicken a'tal."

"Well then, it's past time. You two build me couple of little fires while I'm dressin these birds and I'll give you something as good as anything you ever ate in your whole lives."

The old man halved the chickens and roasted them quickly in the flames of one fire while the biscuits were baking on the coals of the other. When he pronounced them done, the chicken parts were coal black, causing the Renfros to exchange questioning glances. However, their doubts about the tastiness of their charcoal colored breakfast were dissolved with their first bites. The old preacher was a gifted cook. That much was for sure.

As they had the day before, the Renfros reined their horses down to the lazy gait of Applegate's mule. Applegate gave his mount a pat on the neck. "He's slow, I know, but he's steady. He'll take me from here to California and back if I want him to, and he'll never cause me one minute's trouble. Why he's got more sense than both of your horses put together. Besides that," the old man ended in a defensive tone, "he's my friend."

George grinned. "you don't have to make any more speeches in favor of your mule. We ain't got anything against mules."

"Good. Course I'll admit I'm about the only one that rides one, but you'll notice that more than half of the wagons we see are drawn by mules."

"Yeah. Where are they all goin anyhow?" George wanted to know. "Seems like we're nearly always in sight of a wagon."

"Some are gonna buy small farms on slow notes from the Swenson Land and Cattle Company out in Dickens County. Some will go on to the plains and others on up to the Panhandle. And some of 'em will wind up in New Mexico. You can be sure of one thing: nearly all of 'em are goin after land in one place or the other, in one way and another. You'll notice too," Applegate continued in a complaining tone, "that they're not too good at camping."

"How so?"

"They don't put their fires all the way out like they ought to. That's why I slow down at their campsites. If I see some live fire, I kick dirt on it. A lot of these folks don't have any notion about how grass fires can start with a few live coals in a high wind. And, brother," he finished, "when one of those flaming devils gets started, it can kill or ruin everything in it's path for miles and miles.

"Royal," George said, "your horse is uneasy--keeps throwing his head high. Why don't you let him out for a little while? Go on. I'll stay back with our friend here."

Nodding his understanding and agreement, Royal extended his arms, moving the reins ever so slightly upwards on is mount's neck. Grateful for his new freedom, the horse took off in a lazy lope. Royal let him go for about 150 yards before reining him down to a fast walk.

"I'm glad we can have a little privacy from the boy," Applegate said.

"Why so?"

"I'd like to hear why he's mute. I'd like to know what happened. Maybe I can help him."

"How do you think you could help?"

Applegate shrugged. "I don't know. And I guess I really didn't mean that I might help him. What I really meant was that maybe I could get the man I represent to help him."

George frowned. "Who's that? he demanded.

Applegate cast his eyes upwards and pointed an index finger towards the heavens.

"Oh, I see," George replied.

"Well, come on" Applegate urged, "the boy saved my life, and I want to know all about him."

"Alright," George replied, "I guess it won't do no harm for you to know about it." Then, pointing to that distant point on the rim of the world where the undulating wagon road finally ended, he remarked, "Anyhow, it's gonna be a long day without much to do."

With that as an introduction, George related the story of his Uncle Joseph and the plans which he and Kate had made for their move to West Texas.

At that point in the story, Applegate interrupted. "Hold up for just a few minutes will you, George?" Placing two fingers on his lower lip, he sounded out a loud, shrill whistle. Royal immediately looked back, and Applegate motioned for him to come back and join them.

They were at a place where the wagon road ran along the North rim of a huge rolling canyon which Applegate called the Cedar Brakes. Pointing, he said, "See that trail windin down through them cedar clumps? It goes down to a good little spring. We can lead out mounts down there and get 'em a good drink and get one for ourselves too."

After the water break, they hit the road again. Soon Royal's horse, seeming not to like company, again galloped ahead. Then it was that George unfolded the rest of the story about how his son lost his speech.

* * * * * * *

It was a week after Joseph's death when George mounted the best of the plow horses and rode into Canton, leading the team of older horses. He returned shortly before supper time, highly pleased that the sale of the old horses had brought him $50.00 in cash. It would be enough to take care of them until he could find work in Mesa.

Kate, humming happily, put out an unusually good supper of ham and sweet potatoes, topped off with ribbon cane syrup poured over hot buttered biscuits. They had just pushed back from the table when there came a knock at the front door.

Royal opened the door and immediately grunted with pain and surprise as the barrel end of a double barrel shot gun was roughly thrust into his stomach. A high nasal voice coming from the other end of the gun snarled, "Back up, Sonny." Prudently, Royal obeyed the command.

"Now," the voice excitedly continued, "Renfro, you and the Missus just put your hands up and be still and that way you won't have to see me separate this boy from his guts."

The man giving the orders had a companion. They were dressed almost identically in grayish, once blue overalls, patched at the knees. Their shirts were dirty enough to hide their true color. Their frayed straw hats were pulled down against their ears. The older of them, a man about twenty-five, held the shotgun and issued the orders. The other one looked to be a little older than Royal. He could have been twenty, maybe twenty-two. Each of them had a thin face covered with a short, scrubby black beard. From their striking physical resemblance, the Renfros silently deduced that they were brothers; and the accuracy of their deduction was shortly verified by the manner in which the strangers addressed each other.

"We've come for the $50.00 you got for them horses," announced the man with the shotgun.

"Yeah," blurted the younger one, "We need it so we can go to New Mexico."

"Shut up, you lop eared jackass," the older man hissed. "Now, where's the money?"

Instinctively, George decided to lie. "I paid a debt with it before I left Canton."

The older an roared out a mocking laugh. "You ain't even a pretty good liar, Renfro. We watched you real close. You still got the money alright. Search him, Little Brother."

The younger man quickly checked all of George's pockets. "He ain't got it on him, Big Brother."

The older brother's black eyes hardened. "Alright," he growled, "We'll find it the hard way. Pete, get some rope and tie 'em up sos we can take our time."

Pete, who was holding a pistol, thrust it

inside his belt and went outside. Moments later he returned with a coil of rope.

"Tie Renfro up first."

Flashing a yellow toothed grin, Pete needlessly gave George a shove before he began to slowly and awkwardly bind his hands behind his back.

Squinting over George's left shoulder, the older brother snapped, "Pete, ain't you through yet?"

"Just finished," Pete replied.

During the couple of instants when both brothers gave their undivided attention to George, Kate slyly took a couple of quick steps sideways, to her right, and then froze again. The movement took her almost in reach of Royal's .30-.30 rifle leaning in a dark corner by the fireplace.

In the next few seconds, amid blinding flashes, ear splitting roars, screams and swirling movements, the lives of all those present were sharply and forever changed. Kate lunged for the rifle. Grabbing it, she whirled around and instantly took a shotgun blast in the stomach and a pistol bullet in the heart. Bursting with rage, George and Royal heedlessly hurled themselves into the intruders. Hands bound, George managed to body check the older one, causing him to drop his shotgun. Meanwhile Royal jarred Pete with a hard right fist to the left temple. Dazed but still clutching dumbly to his pistol, Pete fell to one knee.

Shocked by the furiousness of the attack, Big Brother howled, "She done messed us up.

Let's get out of here."

As the panicked brothers bolted through the door, Royal made a dash to his fallen mother and paused to quickly examine her. Then, grabbing the rifle, he made for the door. George, following close behind, hollered "Get 'em, Son. Get 'em."

"Royal shouted back, "I will, Dad, I will.'"

The intruders had mounted their horses, whirled about and started to ride away when Royal came out of the door. He put the stock to his shoulder and took aim at one of the riders, not more than 100 feet away.

'Shoot, Son," George hissed.

But Royal didn't.

"Shoot, Royal, shoot," George shouted in anguish.

But Royal didn't.

Here, Give me that rifle," George demanded as he tore the .30-.30 from Royal's hands. Wild-eyed, George quickly aimed and jerked the trigger. He obviously missed. The riders were now too far away in the dusky darkness.

Eyes blazing, George turned on his son. "Those men killed your mother. Why didn't you shoot?" he roared.

No answer.

George dropped the rifle, grabbed his son by both shoulders and shook him, "Why didn't you shoot?" he hissed through clinched teeth.

Royal opened his mouth but nothing came out but a low moan. Seeing the horror mingled with confusion in Royal's eyes, George slowly removed his hands from his son's shoulders.

"Well," he quietly began "I know Kate is dead. Lets go and tend to her."

When George knelt beside his slain wife, he cried for the first time since he was a small boy. Without putting any restraints on his grief, he allowed the tears to stream down his face onto his shuttering chest. As for Royal, with ashen face, he knelt and lovingly stroked his mother's hair. But not one tear came from his horror struck eyes,

And so it was that after the Renfro men buried their beloved wife and mother, they decided to sell their wagon and household possessions and to ride horseback to West Texas.

****

Finishing the story, George turned to Applegate and said.. "And from the time I took that rifle away from him up to this good day, Royal has never been able to speak a word."

The old ran rubbed his chin. "Real odd. You say he shouted at you right before he got ready to shoot?"

"Yeah. He said 'I will, Dad, or don't worry, I will, or something like that. He definitely spoke to me."

Applegate pressed: "So he for certain talked after he saw what happened to his mother, but he couldn't talk after he was unable to shoot at the murderers?"

"You got it right." George replied.

They rode in silence for several minutes before George inquired, 'Well, do you think you or the one you represent can help Royal?"

"The one I represent can. That's for sure. Now, whether he will or not remains to be seen. Have you given this boy much religious training?"

"Kate did. She and Royal read the Bible and talked a lot about it. I can't say that I ever joined in on that business too much. I'm a sort of back seat Methodist, but I have never gone in very deep on that Church stuff. There's a lot of it I don't understand, so I just kind of keep what religion I have and stay away from the rest of it."

Pointing up the road to Royal, Applegate said, "I got a feeling that you're not the only one around here that gets confused by religion. But I'll tell you somethin else. You don't solve the problem by runnin from it. Would it offend you if I started reading out loud from the Bible every night while We're together?"

George paused to take off his hat and run a bandanna over his face and head before answering. Finally he said, "I guess I'm pretty comfortable with my confusion, but maybe Royal ain't. So. if you think it might help him, I'll go along with it,"

"Fair enough, but there's one thing I'll ask you to do besides just listening."

"What's that?"

You've made it pretty clear that you're not gonna be askin any questions about what I read, and I reckon I can respect that. But the catch to it is that the boy can't ask questions. Least ways if he asks 'em, he either have to act 'em out or write 'em out; and he probably won't do either one."

Impatience ruffled George's face. "What are you drivin at?"

'What I'm sayin is that I want you ask any questions that you think might naturally cross the boy's mind."

George shot a knowing grin at the old man, "You're an old fox aren't you?"

No answer.

"Well, alright, " George thoughtfully concluded, "I'll give it a whack."

Riding northwest, they had left the Cedar Brakes several miles back when Applegate Pointed to some trees in the distance. "It's really too early to stop, but them big cotton woods up there by the side of Turkey Creek make for about the only good camp site we're gonna see for about twelve more miles."

"Well, since we ain't in any big hurry," George responded. Why don't we just stop."

"Just what I was hoping you'd say. And by the way, that creek always runs with a little spring fed stream, so We'll be able to wade and splash around. We can get cooled off and maybe even cleaned up a little bit."

Suddenly Applegate pulled his mule to a stop. "'Stop". he whispered, Then quickly whipping his Winchester from its scabbard, he made it go "Bam, bam."

"Ha. ha, " the old man yelled, "they didn't think I could see 'em."

Returning the rifle to the scabbard, he jumped off his mule and scampered about 100 feet to his right. Returning, he clutched in each hand the hind legs of a tanish colored rabbit. Holding them high, he shouted, "Yah hoo, I got 'em both in the head. We'll eat rabbit tonight."

After they unsaddled and hobbled the horses and mule, the man stripped themselves naked and rolled along the sandy bottom of the shallow stream. They splashed and giggled like little boys, and George's heart was made glad. He saw his son smile with mirth for the first time since his mother died.

After they had sucked the last rabbit bone clean and had sopped ribbon cane syrup from their plates with the last of the biscuit halves, Applegate brought out a surprise. Opening a brown paper package, he passed to each of the others a hunk of dried apples, half as big as his fist. "Now, people usually cook these things. Matter of fact, when I'm settled down somewhere I do too. But when I'm on the trail, I just chew 'em up. Take a bite and see if you don't like 'em."

Each Renfro took a bite off of his brownish hunk and began to chew. And they chewed and chewed and chewed. Finally George said, "You didn't give us some rubber to eat did you?"

"Naw, just keep chewin. That's one of the beauties of not cookin then things. They last a lot longer."

"Anyway," he continued., as he reached for his Bible, while ya'll are chewing, I'd like to read a little from this Bible before the fire goes out." Looking squarely at Royal, he went on, "Your Dad said it would be OK from me to read a little from the Bible and talk about it; and I'm guessing that it's alright with you too, Royal."

Noting with satisfaction that Royal was nodding his head, Applegate raced on. "Now, men, it's the gospel truth that the main story of the Bible--the main message it has from God is love--God's love for me and you and everybody else. But I'm here to tell you that ever since I started preaching out here right after the war, the people who listen to me are, I guess you'd say, pretty ornery. And I found out pretty early in the game that I couldn't get much of anybody to listen very long about God's love and about how Jesus died for 'em and such as that until I first scared 'em half to death with a large dose of hell. That's why I started preachin so much on hell. My first sermon to a new bunch is always on hell and sometimes the second and sometimes even the third."

He stopped long enough to stir up the fire to get a little more light on his Bible. Thumping the old book, he said, "So, I thought I'd start with you like I start with everybody else. I'll read to you some about hell. Bear in mind that hell is mentioned dozens and dozens of times in the Bible--more times than heaven by the way--but I'll just take time to cover two or three passages." Suddenly the preacher snapped his fingers. "Oh, wait a minute. I nearly forgot. One time I went through all this only to find out that the man I was preaching to was already saved--as a matter of fact was a preacher himself, I felt like a sucker. Have either one of you been saved?"

The Renfros shrugged their shoulders. "I guess so," George replied, "we went to church with

Kate almost every month, almost every time the circuit rider came to preach."

"And you think that makes you a Christian?" the preacher gently inquired.

The Renfros again shrugged their shoulders,

"You may be saved. God only knows, But to tell you the truth, it don't sound like you're saved to me. My own notion is that when a person is saved, he feels sure about it. He doesn't go around guessin about it. So I'm gonna go ahead and try to scare you."

Opening his Bible and turning so that the print faced the fire light, he cleared his throat and said, "Now listen to this. I'm gonna read from the 16th chapter of Luke, This is Jesus himself doin the talkin:"

"There was a certain rich man, which was clothed in purple and fine linen and fared sumptuously every day: And there was a certain beggar named Lazarus, which was laid at his gate, full of sores, And desiring to be fed with the crumbs which fell from the rich man's table: moreover the dogs came and licked his sores. And it came to pass, that the beggar died and was carried by the angels into Abraham's bosom: the rich man also died, and was buried; And in hell he lifted up his eyes, being in torment, and seeth Abraham afar off, and Lazarus in his bosom. And he cried and said Father Abraham, have mercy on me, and send Lazarus, that he may dip the tip of his finger in water, and cool my tongue; for I am tormented in this flame. But Abraham said, Son remember that thou in thy lifetime receivedst thy good things, and likewise Lazarus evil things: but now he is comforted, and thou are tormented."

Looking up, Applegate licked his right index finger and turned some pages. Here's something else Jesus said:

"When the Son of man shall come in his glory, and all the holy angels with him, then shall he sit upon the throne of his glory: And before him shall be gathered all nations: and he shall separate them one from another, as a shepherd divideth his sheep from the goats: And he shall set the sheep on his right hands but the goats on the left, Then shall the King say unto them on his right hand, Come, ye blessed of my Father, inherit the kingdom prepared for you from the foundation of the world: For I was an hungry, and ye gave me meat: I was thirsty, and ye gave me drink: I was a stranger, and ye took me in: Naked, and ye clothed me: I was sick, and ye visited me: I was in prison, and ye came unto me. Then shall the righteous answer him. saying Lord, when saw we thee an hungered and fed thee? Or thirsty, and gave thee drink? When saw we thee a stranger, and took thee in? or naked, and clothed thee? Or when saw we thee sick, or in prison, and came unto thee? And the King shall answer and say unto them, Verily I say unto you, Inasmuch as ye have done it unto one of the least of these my brethren, ye have done it unto me. Then shall he say also unto them on the left hand, Depart from me, ye cursed, into everlasting fire, prepared for the devil and his angels: For I was an hungered, and ye gave me no meat: I was thirsty, and ye gave me no drink: I was a stranger, and ye took me not in: naked, and ye clothed me not; sick, and in prison, and ye visited me not. Then shall they also answer him, saying, Lord, when saw we thee an hungered, or athirst, or a stranger, or naked, or sick, or in prison, and did not minister unto thee? Then shall he answer them, saying, Verify I say unto you, Inasmuch as ye did it not to one of the least of these, ye did it not to me. And these shall go away into everlasting punishment: but the righteous into life eternal."

The old preacher paused and deliberately searched the faces of his audience to ascertain if he still held their attention. Satisfied that he did, he went on: "OK, now here's the last one I'll read tonight. Jesus also said this:

"And whosoever shall offend one of these little ones that believe in me, it is better for him that millstone were hanged about his neck, and he were cast into the sea. And if thy hand offend thee, cut it off: if is better for thee to enter into life maimed, than having two hands to go into hell, into the fire that never shall be quenched: Where their worm dieth not, and the fire is not quenched. And if thy foot offend thee, cut it off: it is better for thee to enter half into life, than having two feet to be cast into hell, into the fire that never shall be quenched: Where their worm dieth not, and the fire is not quenched. And if thine eye offend thee, pluck it out: it is better for thee to enter into the kingdom of God with one eye, than having two eyes to be cast into hell fire: Where their worm dieth not, and the fire is not quenched."

"So you see," Applegate began explaining, "if you don't turn from your wicked ways and trust Jesus, when you die, you'll be thrown in a dark place where you'll burn forever."

The old preacher was excited not--as worked up as he wanted his audience to be. With eyes blazing he raised his right index finger; and, wagging it at the Renfros, hissed, "Now, ya'll don't want to go there do you?"

"I've got a question," George coolly announced.

Applegate smiled. "Ask it, my friend."

"What about them worms?"

Applegate's face fell. "What about what?"

"Them worms."

Applegate was plainly irritated. "Well, what about them worms? What do you want to know about them for. What do they have to do with anything?"

"I don't know," George answered, "All I know is that it seems like a person in hell is goin to burn and also be eaten on by worms."

"That's right,"Applegate confirmed.

"And from what you read, those worms won't ever die."

"That's right. So what's your problem. Sounds to me like you caught on to all there is to know about the worms."

George shook his head. "Just one thing I don't understand. Why is it that God throws them poor old worms into hell and lets 'em suffer forever?"

Armstrong spat in the fire. "Who cares?" he disgustedly snapped.

"I do. I care," George calmly replied.

The old man jumped up, tore his hat off his head and slammed it to the grounds scattering sparks from the fire. "Dad gum it, that's about the sorriest, most no-count question I ever heard."

After taking enough time to retrieve his hat, Applegate, in a bit calmer voices continued, "There's lots of good questions you could ask like: Is there really a hell? or Why does God send people to hell? or how can a body keep from goin to hell? Questions like them. But no, "he growled, "you mess up my nest by askin about worms."

Don't get sore, Preacher. I didn't mean to get you all riled up," George soothed.

The preacher scowled as he very deliberately pulled his hat back on. "Not your fault," he muttered. "I'm just mad at myself, You hit me with a question I ain't ever heard before, one I don't know the answer to."

Then sitting back down and slowly pulling at the stubble on his chin, he continued to talk, very slowly thinking out loud. "I guess, uh, I guess that God lets them worms suffer in that heat because they don't deserve no better. They're feasting on sinful flesh. They're makin a living off of people God send to hell." He snapped his fingers before excitedly concluding: "That's it. Them worms are takin advantage of somebody's weakness; and God let's 'em suffer for it. And that's just plain justice. As a matter of facts that's the way things work out right now in peoples' lives."

George broke in. "Could you clear that up a little bit?"

The preacher, speaking confidently now and moving his right hand up and down for emphasis, replied, "What I mean is that a man shouldn't ever take advantage of another man's weakness, If he does, he makes himself like one of them hell-worms, and he'll have to suffer for it. Any questions?"

The preacher's theology caused father and son to roll their eyes at each other, but they held their peace.

Pleased and a bit surprised by his own teaching, the preacher let a smile flicker across his face as he kicked sand on the coals of the fire. And without a break in the silence, the three travelers exhaustedly stretched out on their pallets spread on the clean, white sand of Turkey Creek.

Chapter Four

The next day, as they rode along in the cool of the morning with the sun at their backs, the Preacher asked if Kate's murderers were ever apprehended.

"Naw," George sadly replied, "they got clean away. The Sheriff got up a posse and all of us looked hard for over a week. And me and Royal looked for a long time after that. The Sheriff even got a couple of his Texas Ranger friends to come in and work on the case, but they couldn't do any good either."

"I take it they weren't locals," Applegate ventured.

"You're right. Nobody in Van Zant County seems to have ever seen them before they showed up in Canton on the day they shot Kate. The Sheriff and Rangers asked all over the counties all around us too, but nobody seemed to know anything."

"Well, George, I believe you said that one of the killers said something about goin to New Mexico."

"I did. And the Sheriff wrote to a couple of Sheriffs in Eastern New Mexico and to a couple of others in West Texas, along this very road. He asked 'em to be on the look out and pass the word along. But so far, no good. They just seem to disappear from the face of the earth."

"Hey," the Preacher interrupted," look what's comin over the cap rock."

George looked up and saw in the distance a boiling, rusty red cloud which was tumbling over a high ridge, fanning out into the rolling prairie below and heading their way. His mouth fell open. "What in the world is that?"

"Sandstorm," was Applegate's disgusted reply. He put his fingers to his lips, making ready to whistle at Royal, but the whistle was not necessary. The awesome new twist of nature had caused Royal to come galloping back, instinctively seeking strength in numbers.

The Preacher admonished his friends to wet their bandannas and tie them around their faces. Then, he said "We'll just stop and put our backs to it and hunker down 'til it passes by. That's all we can do. The animals will put their noses to the ground and make it through alright. They seem to be able to take more dust than people can."

Soon they were enveloped in a thick cloud of rust red dust, causing them to close their eyes save for a quick peek every few minutes to check the progress of the storm. Inexplicably, the cloud which had boiled over the ridge and howled down its eastern slope like a mad wolf was now slowly drifting by, meek as a lamb.

Looking to the East, the men could easily ascertain when the storm had passed. The west end of the cloud, towering some 500 feet, was thick and sheer--looked like it had been chopped off from a larger mass by the sharp axe of a giant. And after it passed, Royal, with his hands and eyes, and the others with their voices, openly marveled at the crisp, clear air and beauty of the earth after the passing of the storm.

On the trail again, George asked, "You called the rim up yonder the Cap Rock. How did it get that name?"

"All I know is that all along this part of Texas the east edge of the high plains stops and breaks off and lunges down into the rollin prairies. And where that happens, they call it the Cap Rock. We've been goin up all mornin, and it'll get steeper all along. We'll be lucky if we make it to the top of the Cap before supper time."

As it turned out, they led their mounts up onto the Cap Rock just in time to be bedazzled by the glory of a South Plains sunset. Awestruck, the three men stood still and watched the whole thing, from the time the blazing orange ball first kissed the edge of the world until it had entirely slipped away, leaving only its rosy reflections on a few billowy clouds.

"I never cease to be amazed," the old preacher reverently whispered. "And just think, it was free."

"My Kate used to say that she could see God in a sunset," George softly offered. "What do you think of that?"

The old preacher wrinkled his forehead and thoughtfully replied, "If she said she saw him, I'm sure she did. As for me, the only place where I've ever seen God is in people."

Changing the subject as he stuck his hand up in the steady ten-mile-an-hour wind, George asked, "Does the wind blow like this all the time up here?"

Applegate chuckled. "Yeah, as far as I know, it has never let up. Speaking of wind, you see that windmill over there?" He gestured towards a windmill about a quarter of a mile to the Northwest. That's on the Spur Ranch, but they won't mind if we camp over there."

"Lets go" George responded.

As they got closer, they noticed that the wheel was not turning. And when they dismounted, they discovered that the wooden stock tank was bone dry.

"Huh," the Preacher mumbled, "bet there's nothin wrong

with that mill, It's just been out off. Guess they don't have any cattle running here about."

The preacher then proceeded to mount the rungs on the side of the derrick and climb to the tower where he unlocked the wheel. Seeming to thrill in the ecstasy of release, the wheel softly groaned and gently shuddered before it began to rotate, wild and-free, in the swift breeze. Immediately the whir of the wheel was accompanied by the muted creaking and clanking of the up and down strokes of the pump rod. And soon each downward stroke caused a foot long swoosh of water to come gushing from the end of a two-inch pipe.

Royal's eyes gleamed at the sight of the sparkling, crystal clear water. He tried to bend over the wooden tub and get his mouth to the stream. But the tub was too big, and the pipe was too long. In his disappointment, he saw hanging on a rusty nail on the side of the windmill tower a rusty can. Probably an old tomato can, he thought. The can was hanging by its handle which had been fashioned of rusty bailing wire. The wire had been cleverly wrapped around the top and bottom of the can and then looped back and forth from top to bottom, five or six times, so as to form a sturdy handle.

Royal unhooked the crude mug and bent his gaze down into the rust spotted interior. His head recoiled and his nose turned up in disgust. Then he grinned and shrugged his shoulders and advanced towards the inviting stream of water. Holding the mug at the end of the regular gushes, he allowed it to fill and overflow. Emptying it, he let it fill and overflow again. Then he put his lips to the mug's rusty rim and drank deeply of the cool, sweet water.

"Is it good?" the preacher asked.

Royal's eyes danced as he enthusiastically nodded.

"I was afraid it might be gyppy or salty."

Royal vigorously shook his head from side to side.

"That's good news," the old man said as he accepted the mug from Royal. "Some of these mills have water good enough for cows but not good enough for people."

Later, as they were peering at the last glowing embers of their fire, the old preacher's curiosity got the best of him. "I never did get it straight about were your land is located. You said it was about 5 miles from Mesa, but you never did say which way."

"Well, really and truly it's not five miles," George replied. "Uncle Joseph kept saying 'about 5 miles', but we looked on a new map at the courthouse before we left, and it turns out that this Armstrong Survey is on the official General Land office map, and it shows to be only two miles from Mesa."

"Which way?"

"Due North."

The old man's eyes widened. "You sure?"

"Yeah, the south line of the Armstrong Survey is exactly two sections north of the north line of the townsite survey." George stopped and peered at Applegate. "What's the matter? You look like you just saw a ghost."

"Nothin. I'm alright," the Preacher mumbled, "I--uh--guess I was a little surprised. Did you know there's a road that runs along the west side of your land--on south down to Mesa?"

"Not, but that's good news."

"Yeah," the old man agreed, "but there's somethin else that's not so good news."

"What's that?"

"It's right in the middle of Dundee's South pasture, and he uses that land just like it was his-- probably thinks it is his."

"Well, He'll find out different," George

evenly replied.

"Yeah," Applegate replied as he plied his habit of pulling nervously on his chin whiskers.

"By the way, Preacher, you seem to know an uncommon lot about our land."

"Oh, well, I--uh--guess so, Applegate stammered. "But you see what I forgot to tell you is that I worked for the Dundee Ranch two different times, and I know this country pretty well."

"I see," George responded.

"Hey," the Preacher put in, "I'd better change the subject and get in a little Bible reading before ya'll pass out on me."

"Go ahead and take a shot," George responded, "but I'll tell you right now you didn't scare me much with all that talk about hell."

Surprise crossed the Preacher's face, "Oh, I'm losing my touch, I guess. I thought that anybody who heard about all that fire and all those worms would get seared out of his skin. How about you, Royal. Did I scare you?"

Royal looked up from the embers, some of which burst briefly

into flames, and shot a soft, blue-eyed note of sadness at the Preacher. Then he slowly nodded his head.

Calling for verification, the Preacher pressed him. "You say you did get scared?"

Royal nodded.

"Well, I can't see why," George broke in with irritation in his voice. I've done a few bad things, but I ain't ever done anything bad enough to deserve bein pitched into a pit of fire and worms.

And if I haven't done anything bad enough, you dead sure haven't."

"In other words," the Preacher interrupted, "you think some people might be wicked enough to go to hell, but not you, and certainly not Royal."

"That's right," George defiantly answered.

"How wicked would a man have to be before he deserved it," asked the Preacher.

"I don't know, The men who killed Kate will make it I think, but I don't know who else."

Suddenly Royal thrust his right hand out, palm open and vertical to the ground. Agitatedly, he waved that hand from side to side in the moonlight while he simultaneously used his left index finger to point to himself.

The Preacher smiled with satisfaction. "So you're pretty sure you are a candidate for the bad place?"

Without moving, Royal used his eyes to say "Yes".

"Looks like Royal has already figured out the situation," the old man opined as he licked his fingers and rapidly turned the pages of his Bible, "But I'll have to work on you, George; and I've got just the right tools to do it with."

Presently, having dog eared his well worn Bible in three places, the Preacher said, "I can't read much by the light of the moon, but I won't stir the fire because I just want to read three short pieces; and besides, I know 'em mostly by heart anyhow."

Opening his Bible to the 64th Chapter of Isaiah, the Preacher read Isaiah 64:6, as follows:

"But we are all as an unclean thing, and all our righteousness are as filthy rags; and we all do fade as a leaf; and our iniquities, like the wind, have taken us away."

Pausing to pass to the next dog eared page, he read these words from Romans 3:23:

"For all have sinned and come short of the glory of God;"

Then, flipping to the last dog ear, he read only the first part of verse 23 of Chapter 6 of Romans:

"For the wages of sin is death;"

"Huh," George growled, "if that's the way it is, an ordinary man just as well give up trying to keep out of hell."

"Oh there's an easy way out, a real easy way," the Preacher responded. "But We're tired. Let's discuss it another time."

George opened his mouth to protest, but the Preacher abruptly slammed his Bible shut; and George reluctantly accepted the slamming as an official signal that the conversation was ended.

The men said good night and flopped down on their pallets. George and Royal went to sleep almost instantly, but the old preacher lay staring at, but not seeing, the stars. He was overwhelmed with a sense of loneliness. It was an empty feeling that made unscheduled visits almost every day and night. His melancholy is familiar to men who have no wife, no family, no heirs.

Through the years he had received letters

from Mississippi, first from relatives, then from friends, and finally from lawyers, which in total told him that he now was the sole survivor of the Applegate and Martin (his mother's maiden name) clans. When he died, two valuable blood lines would be forever severed from the human family. It had occurred to him that he might not be too old to procreate,, but he had neither the looks nor the wealth to lure a young woman of child bearing age into a marriage. Moreover, he doubted that his conscience would permit him to pull a young woman into a union solely on the speculation that he might be able to sire an heir.

He recalled with melancholia the belief popularly held by Old Testament Hebrews: He who is survived by heirs lives on, but he who leaves no heirs dies forever. He was haunted by the notion that his unbroken bachelorhood had cast him into a dark pit of quicksand. There was no way out. Not even his excitement over his recent prospects for unearthing a treasure had lessened this particular sadness, On the contrary, his chances for riches had served to enhance it. He looked upon his prospects for riches without heirs with an irony which approached bitterness.

The old man's eyes turned from the stars to his sleeping companions, and they softened with fondness. He was surprised at the great intensity of his fondness for them. After all he had known them for only a few days. He despaired of trying to explain to himself why he felt drawn to George and Royal. But the want of logical explanation did not frustrate him. He had long ago learned that reality is sometimes revealed by what you feel in your guts rather than by the words formed in your brain. And the truth was that he liked this man and his son more than he could understand; and when they parted company, he would miss them more than he would ever admit. George, he thought, could be my son; and Royal could be my grandson. I'm drawn to that blue-eyed boy. I want to help him, not only because he saved my life, but because his eyes tell me that he is especially set apart, one with a noble heart. Then it was that a warm tide came in and rippled over the preacher's body as he admitted to himself that he loved this boy and his father.

The Preacher continued to muse as he pulled at his beard. Maybe there is a way out after all. Suddenly he snapped his fingers and sat up straight. It's the Lord's will, he shouted to himself. I'll pull myself out of this mess by adoption. I'll make George and Royal my heirs! I've lost my roots in the past, but praise the Lord I'm gonna have roots in the future. And with this new hope in his heart, the old man fell to sleep with a smile on his lips.

The next morning, after they hit the trail, Applegate made his initial move towards acquiring some heirs. "George, there's something I need to tell you. I never have told you where I'm headed for."

"You ain't obligated," George replied. "After all, it's none of my business."

"I know, but I need to tell you now because it goes along with a sort of invitation I want to make to you and Royal."

"How's that?"

"Well, I'm headin for Dundee Ranch headquarters. Dundee got me located at Jacksboro last month and sent for me to come on up and he'd give me the cook's job--said I wouldn't have to do anything but cook. Made me a good proposition. However," he went on, assuming again an air mystery, "I'll admit that if the offer had come ten days earlier, I'd have turned it down. But during that ten days, I got some information that made a trip to the Dundee Ranch look pretty good to me. So here I am headin for that cookin job."

"I see," said George, "but what's all that got to do with an invitation to me and Royal?"

"You want to find work in Mesa, save your money and get started ranching, right?"

"Sure," George affirmed.

"Well, the better idea is for you not to stop in Mesa but to go on with me to the Dundee headquarters, I'll guarantee you I can get you on there. They're always needin hands. Somebody's always quittin or gittin fired. And besides that, since you're a carpenter, they'll hire you for sure. The ranch is not as big as some of 'em. but it's big--about a hundred sections--and it has lots of houses and barns and pens to keep up."

"What'll they pay?"

"Top hands get one dollar a day plus room and board. And bein as how you're a man with a skill, Dundee'll pay you top wages."

"But how do you know they need a

carpenter?”

"Thunder, they always need one, And besides, if they don't, you can just turn around and ride back down to Mesa--wouldn't be but about five miles back. What have you got to lose?”

"What about Royal? Would they hire him as my helper?”

"Maybe,” the old man thoughtfully began, “but I've been thinkin about that, and it seems to me that the best thing would be to sell Dundee on the idea of hiring him as a cook's helper with the understanding that when I don't need him, He'll help you. That way Dundee will come more near thinkin that he's gettin his money's worth.”

"How much money is that?” George inquired.

"Half wages. Fifty cents a day. But he already has most of an outfit, and soon as he learns about punching cows, he can move right on up to a cowpuncher job.”

"What did you mean when you said he had most of an outfit. What's an outfit?”

"Dundee won't hire a cowboy unless he has his own outfit. Dundee will furnish the horse, two horses as a matter of fact. But the cowboy must have his own saddle, blanket and bridle. And, of course, he's got to have his own bedroll and clothes. And that takes in boots, spurs, hat, slicker and warm coat. From lookin over your stuff, I'd say he has everything already except the boots and spurs. Not many young men who want to be cowboys start out as far ahead as he is.”

"Yeah. Well, I'll talk to Royal and let you

know."

"That's good. Take your time. No hurry."

After traveling another three or four miles, the riders came to a fork in the road. The road they were on continued almost due west. The other, obviously much less traveled, stretched out in a north by northwest direction.

"Here's where we turn north to go to Mesa," Applegate announced. After they made the turn, the old man fell silent and began to impatiently pull on his chin whiskers. Guessing the cause of his nervousness, George said, "Now don't fret. I'll get around to talking to Royal about the ranch deal, but---."

The Preacher interrupted, "What about doin it right now?"

George chuckled. "OK".

"That's what I wanted to hear," the Preacher said as he put two fingers to his lips to make a whistle.

When Royal heard the shrill Whistle, he stopped his horse and turned around to see his father advancing alone at a gallop. Then, as they rode together, George repeated the preacher's proposition to his son and asked for his reaction. The Preacher watched them from a distance for ten, maybe twelve minutes before he saw George's horse turn and come trotting back.

"We decided to take you up on your proposition," George reported. "And, by the way, we appreciate your help."

The old man beamed. "By the way you're welcome," he said as he struggled to control the wild urge to scream and holler in celebration of his good fortune, He won the contest with his emotions; and with outward calm, he took up his canteen and silently drank a toast to his good luck with some of the sweet water which he had carried from the windmill. Then, shading his eyes and looking to the horizon, he said, "We'll be in Mesa in just a couple more days."

Chapter Five

Amos Dundee and his foreman, Slim Feister, needed nothing more than an occasional gentle flick of the reins to urge their horses up the long, gradually slopping south side of Comanche Hill, the highest point on the Dundee Ranch. Except for the low whines and squeaks of saddle leather and the soft clop of the horses' hooves, there was silence. Both men were totally enveloped in private thoughts. And some of those thoughts were much more similar that either of them would have guessed.

It had been Dundee's idea to ride to the top of the hill. He was always on the look out for an excuse to go to the pinnacle of his property. There, turning in every direction, he was the owner of all the eye could see. He liked that. He liked to warm in the full glow of his power and majesty. He was a land and cattle baron who, without any hesitation or humbleness, recognized the regal nature of his position and arrogantly demanded that others do likewise. He was the heir of his tough but far from regal father who had wrestled the land away from

Indians, rustlers, claim jumpers, droughts and storms, and who had buried three wives and as many still born babies in the process.

Dundee glanced at his foreman and thought, If he ever gives in to Bertha's flirting, I'll have to kill him.

At the same moment, Feister was thinking, If he ever finds out that I'm sleeping with his wife, I've got to know it right off so I can kill him before he kills me.

The irony was that neither of them loved Bertha Dundee. Dundee's conditional vow to kill sprang solely from manly pride--in this case a pride that was also regal--which dictated that no other man could have anything that belonged to him, more especially his land or his wife, As to Feister, he was physically attracted to Bertha. That was true enough. She was not a particularly handsome woman, but she was passionate, alluring and highly available. However, when he stopped to analyze his attraction to her, Feister was forced to admit that it was no stronger than his attraction to several other loose and semi-loose women he had known in Mesa and Amarillo and several points in between. He had easily and quickly succumbed to Bertha's advances mainly because she was Dundee's wife. Dangerous though it was, his possession of Bertha brought him the greatest joy of his life, not because he particularly delighted in her, but because it allowed him to defeat and insult his boss, the object of his choicest hatred for so many years.

Although this strong, but secret aversion

probably began earlier, Feister always dated it to the night of the medicine show in Mesa over thirty years ago. Amos at ten was a rich, spoiled brat. Slim Feister, also ten, was the barefoot son of some poor, struggling homesteaders. Lean and lithe, quick and strong, he had discovered at an early age that he could whip boys two years his senior. His physical prowess was complimented by a coyote-like cunningness and shortly after he started to the one teacher school at Mesa, he firmly established his reputation as a bully. Acutely aware and highly resentful of his poverty, he was a poor, spoiled brat.

In school, the only boy under twelve who Slim did not bully was Amos.

Whipping the rich boy would have presented no real challenge, but he was utterly intimidated by the riches and aloof arrogance of the young cattle baron. He was awestruck that first day when Amos alighted from his black, servant-driven buggy, wearing a black velvet, knee length suit with white ruffled shirt. And from that day forward he had cowtowed to a boy whom he naturally despised. Among the poverty stricken there are some, young and old, who are instinctively overawed by raw wealth. Slim Feister was one of those.

* * * * * * *

On the night of the medicine show, the poor brat found himself shoulder to shoulder with the rich brat in a gang of other kids standing directly below the front of the stage. The stage was a big, flat bed wagon which had been parked in the pasture across the street from the school house. Some of the people sat on the few temporary bleacher seats, but most of them had to stand.

The medicine show, offering a rare opportunity to witness professional entertainment, pulled people in from miles about. There must have been at least a hundred grown people and no telling how many children in attendance. When Slim claimed his standing place, the clown was already warming up the crowd with jokes and fiddle music.

Slim and his companions looked up with eyes shinning and mouths agap. They were completely bedazzled. The rows of gleaming bottles of red medicine lining the front of the stage twinkled with countless reflections of the gently swinging coal oil lanterns which were suspended from a wire high above. The rear of the stage was bordered with two-foot stacks of red and white candy boxes. And most eye popping of all was the backdrop display of prizes for those who would be lucky enough to find coupons in their candy boxes, blankets, dolls, jack knives and flashing jewelry. Slim defended himself against disappointment as poor boys naturally must do in such circumstances. He put a bridle on his enthusiasm and reined it down to a walk. He knew the candy would sell for a dime per box, and he didn't have a dime.

After the clown performed a well received juggling act, the self styled Doctor took center stage and began to extol the multiple virtues of his medicine. It was "Waducalum", compounded according to a secret Indian formula which was whispered to the Doctor by Chief Pink Cloud with his dying breath.

A reverent hush fell over the crowd as the Doctor tightened his oratorical hold. The presentation was climaxed by the reading of at least a dozen sworn affidavits, testifying to the healing powers of "Waducalum, The testimonials covered external ailments ranging from ring worms to cancer and internal disorders from constipation to heart trouble.

The regular price was one dollar a bottle; but for a limited time," in this fine community where people seem to stand in special need of the medicine," the Doctor announced that he was going to "--let you friends have it at two bottles for fifty cents." Then the Doctor and the clown waded into the crowd and started peddling the medicine. Each began with a box containing a dozen bottles; and when he sold that twelve, he raised the empty box aloft and triumphantly shouted, "All sold out!" and raced back to the stage to quickly refill his box. The clown kept up a constant stream of funny remarks, such as "And another soul made happy!" and "Hey baldy, get some for your head; it even grew hair on my tongue." Again and again the crowd guff-hawed. Business was brisk.

Medicine sale over, the Doctor and the clown regaled the audience with a skit. And then came the candy sale. The Doctor opened a box of candy, spilling into his left hand the ten small pieces of taffy. Carefully explaining that the candy was delicious and healthful and well worth more than ten cents, he went on to point out the fabulous gifts available to those many buyers who would find a gift coupon in their boxes. Then the Doctor and the clown brought stacks of boxes of candy down into the audience and began selling them. Although Slim didn't have a dime, most of the kids did, and the young cattle baron completely exhausting his funds, purchased five boxes.

Amos excitedly tore into each of his boxes and yepped with anguish when none of them contained a coupon. Disgustedly he ran to the hired man who had brought him and demanded more money. But the hired hand had none. Sullenly he returned to his spot just below the stage and fumed jealously as a couple of his school mates thrust coupons into the hands of the Doctor's wife and claimed a prize.

Suddenly both salesman ran out of candy, causing the Doctor to jump back on the stage and shout out an announcement: "While Clown and I are gathering up more boxes of candy to bring out there to you, my wife will sing a little song and give the kiddos a little surprise." He ended with an exaggerated smile and wink.

Thereupon, the Doctor's wife took over the stage and began a little song and dance. "Here I have some candy," she sang, "and I'll throw it up to you." Then, dancing lightly to her left, she scattered a handful of taffy candies among the kids standing below that side of the stage, causing excited shrieks amid a mad scramble.

Dancing back to the center, she repeated the performance for the group of kids standing below the stage to her right. Slim's eyes shone with anticipation as she moved again to the center. It's our turn next, us right here in the center, he thought.

It was even better than he thought. The lady drew gasps a she produced a shining fifty-cent piece. Dancing to front and center, she sang, "And here I have half-dollar, and I'll throw it up to you.

And throw it up she did, triggering a frenzied struggle. The coin glanced off the outstretched fingers of one boy, ran like it was alive down the arm of another, eluded several wild grabs; and after bouncing off a couple of legs, plunked on the ground.

Slim Feister, who had been knocked flat on his stomach, saw the coin lying within his grasp. Desperately he reached for it through a pair of legs and let out a victory yell when he felt the coin enter the clutch of his dusty, sweaty right fist. Suddenly though, the owner of the legs through which he had reached sat down on his right shoulder. And he could feel the hand which clutched the coin being roughly raised. Next he felt sharp pain in his right index finger: but he gritted his teeth and held on the half-dollar. But then a sharper, excruciating pain hit that same finger and ran up his hand and into his arm. Unable to bare it, he shrieked with pain and released his grip on the coin. Immediately the weight on his shoulder was removed, and he was able to jump to his feet.

His eyes, filled with pain mixed with anger, stared with disbelief at his bloody index finger. He had known when it happened that somebody was biting his finger. Who was it? He quickly looked for the culprit and was not long in finding him. The leering lips of the young cattle baron still bore a streak of tell tale blood. Thrusting his bloody finger in the face of the obvious thief. Slim angrily accused Amos of biting him and stealing his money. Unaware of the evidence on his mouth, the rich brat coolly replied, "I don't know what you're talking about."   Then, with an arrogant sniff, he tossed his head and hollered, "Hey, Clown, I'll take five more boxes of candy."

Sick with anger, Slim would have automatically claimed and secured his rights as against any other boy, but not the little baron. He found it hard to believe that he would let Amos get away with his dirty deed. But he did. And chest heaving with frustration, his only comfort was drawn from his determined vow to get even some day.

* * * * * * *

As the two stopped their mounts on top of Comanche Hill, Feister ruefully realized that his vow of long ago was as yet unfulfilled. Dundee's wife was not enough, he grimly admitted. The victory would be hollow until Dundee became aware of it.

The baron and his foreman were at a fence, commonly referred to as "the fence" because (aside from small pens and corrals) it was the only fence on the entire one hundred square mile ranch. Running east and west, it separated the ranch into equal sized north and south pastures. They dismounted, and holding them slack reined, allowed their horses to chomp on the grass. Even on top of the rocky hill the grass was lush and green and stood three inches high.

Dundee squinted and slowly rotated in a full circle. "It's never looked better, Feister. Everywhere you look about half of the cows are lying down. It's not even the middle of the morning and those cows are already full."

"Yes, Sir, there's more grass than I've ever seen, We've gotten a rain every time we needed it."

"Feister, you're by far the highest paid foreman west of Fort Worth, and I got you up here today to ask your opinion about something."

Feister's mind instantly went on the alert. His brain was like a bobcat which knows it is being stalked by a man with a gun. One false move and the good life will be over. From long experience, he knew that when Dundee asked for his opinion, he was really seeking an endorsement. The boss already not only knew what he wanted to do, he had also already made up his mind about what he was going to do. It was Feister's self-protective function to accurately guess his boss's secret desire and ultimate course of action and express an opinion identical thereto. In this particular instance, it turned out to be easy.

"How many cows to I have?" Dundee rhetorically asked.

"About 4000 mother cows and about 3800 calves of various ages and sizes."

"I've got a good chance to get some more," Dundee revealed, pausing to unscrew the cap on his canteen and take a swig.

This was all the information Feister needed to protect himself. Dundee had already decided to buy more cattle to put on the lush grass. Feister also knew it was a big mistake. No matter how many more cows Dundee hand in mind, it was too many, The ranch was already over stocked. Oh, at the moment all was well. There was more grass than the cattle could eat, and in the absence of a bad summer drought, the Fall frost would cause the tall grass to "cure out" and make "hay on the ground" to carry the huge herd through the winter. The cattle would make it, but by March they would be lean and poor. And since summer droughts were the rule rather than the exception, the last thing the pastures needed was more mouths to feed. Feister was aware that Dundee knew all these things. But he also knew that Dundee's greed frequently caused him to take big gambles.

'Well, Feister began, "it --uh-- would be nice to have some more cows."

"I can get a thousand cows with calves at their sides," Dundee declared.

Feeling his eyes grow wide, Feister quickly turned his head.

"What's the matter?" Dundee demanded.

"Oh. nothin," Feister lied, "for a second I thought I heard a bobcat."

Dundee continued: "The SOQ, had to throw

in its hand and take bankruptcy. The Referee in bankruptcy is selling all the cattle at a bargain, mother cows with calves for $27.00 a pair, I took out an option on 1000 of 'em. The option runs out next Friday. What do you think?"

"I think it's a good idea, Mr. Dundee."

"Good. That's what I thought too. I'll go into Mesa tomorrow and get a wire off to the Referee. That means you and me and the boys, the whole bunch of us, will need to go up there, so we can cut 'em out and drive 'em back."

"Yes, Sir."

"So be gettin ready. We'll have to be gone at least three weeks.

"Yes, Sir, but I was wonderin---. Do you think we could hold off goin until the Preacher gets here?

Dundee indulged in an infrequent chuckle. "The boys are still restless about the chow, huh?"

"Yes, Sir. As I think you know, I can handle them boys real well, but when I have to put up with bad chow, it about pushes me to my limits."

Dundee smiled. It was good to see his ordinarily cock-sure foreman squirm a little. After all, he didn't like Feister--never had. He endured his foreman for two reasons: One was his hat-in-hand attitude. The other was his competence. Using force, threats, fraud, friendship or flattery, or a combination of two or more of them, Feister could get more out of a bunch of cowboys than any foreman Dundee had ever seen, and he had seen a lot of them.

"I got a letter from the Preacher yesterday,

mailed from Jacksboro the day he was supposed to leave there. According to my calculations, he should be here in two, maybe three more days. We can wait that long."

Feister sighed with relief. "That's really good. Thank you."

It was almost supper time before the two riders made it back to headquarters, As they approached the Dundee mansion, commonly called "Big House", they spotted Bertha Dundee and her eighteen year old daughter, Nora, sitting on the shady second story veranda of the red brick, eleven room house. Nora stood and began waving a handkerchief.

"When she greets me like that, I know she wants something," Dundee growled, "I wonder what it is this time."

Feister shrugged. He had no idea what was going on in little Nora's mind, but he thought he knew the mind of her mother. In the confines of his own mind, he soundlessly shouted, be patient, Bertha. He's goin into Mesa tomorrow. He would have been chagrined to know the truth: At the moment Bertha's mind was empty of passionate yearnings for Slim Feister. She was too busy comparing the two men in her life. She watched them intently, absent mindly tapping her nose with her left index finger, as they dismounted in front of the main house and wrapped their reins around the hitching rail.

At six feet one inch her husband stood two or three inches higher than Feister; and at about two hundred pounds, out weighed his foreman by thirty or forty pounds. Most of the difference in weight was in the form of fat. Dundee's belly overhung his huge silver belt buckle by a good four inches. His blush red face appeared to be swollen, and the puffiness was accented by his long, graying blond side burns. From long practice, his full lips easily curled into a leer or a sneer. A smile required much more of an effort Bertha saw him now with his hat pulled down almost to his gray-blue eyes. But she knew that under the hat, Dundee's blond hair had receded almost to the middle of his crown.

Feister, now rolling a cigarette, was lean and hard. His belly was flat, and his face was tight and thin. His thin lips were usually fixed in a thin, mirthless smile. The areas of his light brown, leathery face surrounding his brown, almost black eyes, were extensively crow-tracked from squinting across pastures in search of cows. His hat was also pulled far down almost to his eye brows; but Bertha knew that its removal would reveal, in sharp contrast to his face, a pearl white forehead, partially bisected by a lock of his thick hair--black but now slightly salted.

Bertha did not love either man. As a matter of fact, she loathed her husband, but she had no thought of giving him up. She liked the position of cattle baroness and all that the title entailed--the big house, the servants, the money, and most of all the aristocratic status. As the wife of a second generation, big land owner, she considered herself to be as aristocratic as any woman in West Texas, probably in the whole state. The Governor as well as other political and financial power brokers were her frequent guests at Big House. And her annual summer lawn party, as well as her regular New Year's party, drew the rich and powerful from all over Northwest Texas.

Of course, there was another good reason why she didn't walk away from her husband. She couldn't. At least in her own mind, she couldn't. He was too rich, too dominating, too almighty. She knew his regal pride would never permit her to leave him, much less would it allow her to run off with another man.

Her eyes softened as she turned her focus to Feister. Sometimes she harbored suspicions that he was using her for some mysterious purpose unrelated to the satisfaction of his physical cravings. However, she was not at all uncomfortable with that possibility. Rather, she used it to cancel the slight guilt she might have experienced because of the goodly measure of deceit she practiced on him. She sincerely enjoyed his affections. That was true, but she used him mainly to prove to herself that she could attract men other than her obnoxious husband. Before Feister came along, she had tried but failed to lure at least a dozen men for the purpose of making that proof. In protection of her own self image, she laid full blame for all of her failures on the great fear which her potential lovers had for Dundee. And in most instances she was at least partially correct. If she had known the conquest would be so easy, she would have practiced her wiles on Feister much sooner. Until it happened, she had not seriously anticipated that the bowing, scraping foreman would have the guts to take her into his arms. She concluded, inaccurately of course, that it was his starry-eyed fascination for her which emboldened him to live so dangerously.

She watched wistfully as Feister stomped on the remains of his cigarette, unwrapped both sets of reins and started leading the horses towards the big barn. Her attention was then claimed by the noises ascending from the first story veranda. They were the heavy clopping of her husband's boots accompanied by the jangling of the big rowels on his spurs. The familiar sound sent a pang of faint nausea to the pit of her stomach. It always did.

Nora, leaving her slower moving mother, ran through her bedroom to the head of the stairs. Beginning her light and rapid decent, she cheerily addressed her father as she always did when she was preparing to ask him for something special. "Daauhdee", she called, pronouncing "daddy" with three syllables and emphasizing each of them. She was tall, blond, blue eyed, big boned but beautiful.

She looks more like my mother every day, Dundee thought.

"Hi, Sweetheart."

She threw her arms around his neck and kissed his cheek. "Hurry and get dressed for dinner," she said, "I'm famished."

Dundee washed up, shaved and changed into a white linen suit. He still felt a little silly about dressing for the evening meal. And he was still uncomfortable about calling it dinner instead of supper. Bertha had brought these customs from her fancy home in St. Louis and had stubbornly insisted on them. In those early days of their marriage, she always got her way in such matters. Since then, although he occasionally growled a private, low key complaint, he had never exerted any effort to effect a change. He realized that such ways of doing put an aristocratic hue on the main house, and he admitted to himself that this served the beneficial purpose of helping to set him and his family apart and above the other people living on the ranch.

Bertha walked into the dining room ahead of the others. Wearing a fresh, semi-formal dress, she could not look better. She could not fairly be called pretty because her face was too round and her nose was too long. However, much compensation was offered by her full, sensual lips and slender, well turned body. Most people described her with the word "cute", and she managed to make herself popular with men by means of a constant flow of flattery.

She still did her wifely duties in bed, but she performed strictly out of duty--mechanically; and she knew that he knew it. She knew too his love for her was as dead as hers for him. She subtly but deliberately pushed him to cheat on her. She would like to have that to hold over him. But if he had cheated, she had no wind of it and therefore disappointedly concluded that he had not. She was correct.

Not all, but some lord and master types are

carefully and snobbishly selective of their women. Dundee was one of those selective snobs. Consequently, Mary Feister, his foreman's wife, was the only woman within striking distance who he would have. And she, not to his surprise since he knew her well, had made it perfectly clear that she would not have him.

Dundee entered the dining room with his cheerfully chattering daughter on his arm. They all took their seats; and after Dundee mumbled his usual prefuctory prayer, they began sipping the soup. It was then that Nora nonchalantly dropped her request on her adoring daddy. "Daauhdee", she began, "I want you to buy me an automobile." Bertha gasped. Dundee's mouth involuntarily spewed soup back into his bowl. "Automobile!" he thundered, "why that's the craziest thing I ever heard of. When is it you're going to St. Louis to start to school, next Monday isn't it?"

"Yes, Sir."

"Well, we might see about an automobile next year, no sooner. Hear me?"
Nora's only response was an over obvious protrusion of her lower lip.

Chapter Six

Not far away, in the foreman's house, Jane Fitzhugh was begging in behalf of the cowboys. "Let's just go over there and cook for them for a few days. 'til the new cook gets here."

"Not on your life," Mary Feister firmly replied. "I'm not about to break my back, much less yours, trying to please that bunch. Not even Amos Dundee has had the nerve to ask me to do that. Besides, even if I did go over and cook for them, I wouldn't allow you to go with me. I'm not going to put you on display before that herd of young bulls every day."

Jane blushed. "Oh, Mama, you shouldn't talk like that. They're nice boys."

"Yes, and I aim to see that they stay that way."

Jane giggled and looked at her mother impishly. "Well, that means I can't leave here without you," she teasingly replied. "I need you to look after me."

"Don't hit me with that," Mary retorted. "Your Aunt Grace is perfectly capable of doing that."

Jane grew serious. "Mama, I promise you, I'm got going unless you come with me."

"Yes you will," Mary firmly declared. "I've said it a hundred times. If you stay here, you'll either wither on the vine or marry one of those young bulls down there, and I couldn't stand it either way."

Jane wrung her hands. "Mama, I don't want to stay. I know there's nothing for me here. But there's nothing for you here either."

"My husband is here," Mary sadly replied.

"But he is mean." Jane hissed. "He hits you. Don't try to deny it. I know he does. And on top of that he commits adultery; and he does it all the way from here to Amarillo." She gasped for breath and continued. "And I'll come right out with another thing: He cheats on you right here on this ranch."

"You don't know any such of a thing," Mary calmly responded. "Can you show me any proof?"

"No. but I know."

"How can you know without proof?"

"I just know, and so do you," Jane accusingly retorted.

Mary closed her eyes and spoke through tight lips. "It doesn't matter. He's my husband. I can't leave him."

Jane put her face on her mother's shoulder. "I know," she mumbled., "that's what you think the Bible teaches. Let's not argue anymore now." Looking up, she smiled. "I really don't have time for it. I've got to go milk that old cow."

Her mother sighed, "Yes, you really do. I

saw Slim heading for the barn more that half hour ago. He'll be here soon for supper.

Jane crammed an old straw hat on her head and grabbed the milk bucket. "If I'm not back by the time you get supper on the table, go ahead without me. I'll get something later.

Jane proceeded to march down to the big barn, pausing at the gate to slip her feet into a pair of Slim Feister's old boots. In the summer, when she mostly went barefoot, she kept them there to protect her feet from the squishy stuff in the barn yard. Slim emerged from the barn and headed in her direction. The sight of him made her face go grim. He was outwardly friendly. "Hi there, little girl."

As they passed, she stiffly returned his greeting by tersely saying, " Slim." That and nothing more.

Feeling the need for greater freedom of movement, she reached down with her left hand and pulled her skirt up high above her knees, more fully revealing two of the reasons why the cowboys' eyes popped when she came into view. There were other physical reasons: She was tall, but she handled her height with grace and confidence. Her body was a bit too slender to be called perfect, but it clearly exuded the message that perfection would shortly follow. Her tanned, pleasingly oval face was studied with a perfect nose, naturally ruby lips and two enormous brown eyes. Curls of her silky black hair fell from under the frayed straw hat and bounced along on her shoulders.

Slim Feister stole one quick look back over

his shoulder. My little step daughter is not so little anymore, he thought.

Old Bess, their milk cow, had already seen her coming and was waiting at the manger. Jane pitch forked some hay into the trough and sat down on the old wooden box which served as a milking stool She had brought a little water in her bucket, and she used it to wash the cow's teats. Satisfied that they were clean enough, she poured the rest of the water on the ground and began, a teat in each hand, causing two small streams of milk to hit the bottom of the bucket with a sharp ping. As she went on, the pinging turned to soft zizzing.

She was strangely content. This place where the mixed odor was of hay and manure, where the cow softly smacked on the hay and regularly swished her tail at the pesky flies, where the zizzing caused the milk to slowly rise in the bucket--this was Jane's sanctum. Nobody., nothing interrupted her here. It was her place to day dream, to sing and talk to herself. It was her place to pray and think things out. Today her thoughts were on her mother.

* * * * * * *

Mary was a twenty year old school teacher in Fort Worth when she was introduced to Sean Fitzhugh. Ten years older than she, he was already a full fledged railroad engineer, the youngest on the Fort Worth and Denver. He was a man who made quick decisions; and the minute he laid eyes on Mary Harrison, he knew he wanted her, now and forever. She was beautiful, and her quiet confidence, almost aloofness, provided a challenge to him. Her education and culture also fascinated and drew him. They made her an exquisite flower, almost but not quite beyond his grasp.

With Mary, it was different. It took several months for her to want him for her husband. His physical appearance was never a problem. He was a big, handsome., black haired Irishman with dancing blue eyes. But she was initially repulsed by his type. He was loud and boisterous, even uncouth at times. And he constantly revealed his not more than third grade education. On the other hand, as might be expected of an opposite, she was attracted by his happy-go-lucky, devil-may-care attitude. Soon, too, she came to know that underneath his boisterous facade, he was a sensitive, gentle man.

Towards the end of their courtship the only stumbling block in the way of their marriage was his Catholicism. She was a Baptist, a strong one, frightened by the thought of marrying a Catholic. And he made it plain that his church was the one and only thing he would not give up for her. Finally though, after repeated and spirited assurances that he would never pressure her to become a Catholic and that she would be perfectly free to raise their children as Baptists, she gave in. She never regretted it. He was a fine, colorful, life-loving man; and he gave her that kind of a marriage.

They moved to Amarillo in 1896 where Sean

took alternate runs to Fort Worth and Denver. Jane, born in 1898, worshiped her father. When he was in town, he managed to have her with him as much as possible. Some of her earliest and fondest memories were of the railroad yards. Big and sprawling, more cattle were shipped from there than any other in the nation during those last years of the nineteenth century. And Jane's father was a big man in those yards. Many railroaders, including himself, held that he was the top engineer on the FW & D. Even before she could identify or understand it, she basked in the warmth of the respect he commanded. She remembered the sight and odor of the coal smoke and cinders, the hiss of the steam and the whistles and bells. She trotted after him as he walked around the engine, sticking the snout of his huge oiling gun into innumerable holes and crevices in the wheels of the iron giant. And the biggest thrill of all came when she sat on his lap in the cab and pulled the whistle cord.

After she started to school, her visits to the rail yards became increasingly less frequent. But Sean's open and obvious ardor for his daughter never abated, He had a habit, beautiful to her even then, which was increasingly precious in her memories. Every day, when he saw her for the first time, whether it was at time of waking or of lying down to sleep or some time in between, he would invariably say, "Hi, Darlin. I'm glad you're here." To this day, the sound of a train's whistle always brought to her mind fond memories of her father, and she took pleasure in knowing that it always would.

Jane was a mixture of the personalities of her parents. From Mary she took softness and sweetness. Like her father, she was outgoing, quick to make decisions and ever ready to grab life by the tail. From both of them she inherited a love for eternal values. But it was from Sean Fitzhugh that she caught the instinctive ability to spot those who were full of those values and those who were not.

Mary quit teaching school when she married Sean. He did not demand that she quit, but she knew he would be embarrassed and insulted if she did not. It was no cause for friction. As a matter of fact, it pleased her very much to be a wife and mother, nothing more or less. Too, they had no financial problems. Sean made top wages, enabling them to live in high style--fine house, fine horse and buggy, good clothes, good food and plenty of it.

But then, one bright August morning when Jane was sixteen., Sean died. Without any warning, this cheerful, cocksure man finished his second cup of breakfast coffee, widened his eyes, emitted a low throat gurgle and slumped over on the table. At 47 he was felled forever by his first heart attack.

If he had been favored by a warning, Sean might have made better financial provisions for his widow and daughter. Maybe. He, after all, was a man for todays, not prone to hang on to yesterday or to dwell at length on tomorrow. He gloried in the present, and that made him fun to live with.

Conversely, it made him no fun to live without. After Mary sold the horse and buggy and paid the funeral expenses, she had $50.53.

Since it was near the end of August, she was able to move out of the big house before another month's rent came due. She thanked the good Lord for her sister, Grace; and thanked him even more for her husband, Eugene. Gene was Sean's fireman and his closest friend. Nevertheless, although his generosity in asking Mary and Jane to move in with him and Grace was not uncommon, his kindness had a quality of insistence and eagerness that made his sister-in-law and niece feel comfortable and wanted.

Jane began her junior year in high school and Mary went looking for a job. She was not surprised to find that all of the teaching positions in the Amarillo schools were filled. She was astonished, however, by the low pay that women commanded as retail and office clerks, the other jobs for which she felt qualified. There were a couple of these jobs available, but she backed away from them. A tooty job like that would never enable her to move out on her own again. She would be forced to depend on Grace and Gene forever. She determined to try something else first. She still had her piano, and she reasoned that with a little luck she could make at least double a clerk's salary by giving piano lessons.

Thinking that she might want to announce the opening of her new piano school in the newspaper, she picked up a copy of the Amarillo Times and turned to the classified section to get ideas about how to word her announcement. Her eyes went immediately to the biggest ad on the page. It read thusly:

"Mr. and Mrs. Amos Dundee of the Dundee Ranch are seeking a tutor for their 16 year old daughter. Their purpose is to see that their daughter is adequately prepared for finishing school in St. Louis next year. The position pays $150.00 per month plus room and board. The position will last for nine months, beginning October lst. Mr. and Mrs. Dundee will receive applicants for this position in their suite at the Hotel Amarillo between the hours of 8 A.M. and 11:30 A.M. on next Wednesday, September 3, 1914."

Mary shrieked with delight. "That's four times as much as a school teacher makes," she shouted. "Grace, look at this."

Grace came trotting into the living room wiping her hands on her apron. "What in the world are you yelling about?"

"Look at this."

Grace read the Dundee ad. "Wednesday. That's tomorrow," she gasped, My goodness, that's a fortune. Reckon there's something the matter with the job?"

"Well, of course there is," Mary replied. "Most teachers would not care for the loneliness that the job probably entails. You know--way out on the ranch, away from your family and friends."

"Yeah, that's bad enough," Grace agreed, "but I wonder if that's all that's the matter with the job. It's passing strange that they haven't gotten a tutor before now."

"Yes" Mary agreed, "I'll admit it sounds almost too good to be true." She paused to throw up her hands and sigh. "Anyway, they probably wouldn't want me to bring Jane with me; and besides that, I wouldn't want to take her. I think it would be a mistake for me to try to tutor my own child. Also, even though those rich people seem to like the idea of a private tutor, I don't. I want Jane to be able to enjoy her classmates and ..."

"Well, now," Grace interrupted, "if its Jane you're worried about, she's perfectly welcome, more than welcome, to stay right here with us and go to school."

"You're a saint," Mary whispered. "But there is another big problem about leaving Jane for nine months."

"I know, I know, you hate the very thought of it."

"I hate it, yes; and I'm not sure it would be the decent, the right thing to do, "It just seems --- She paused to screw up her face and clutch her hands into fists, obviously struggling to find the right words. "It just seems like I would be sacrificing nine months of my life with Jane, sort of burning it up, on a financial alter."

Grace frowned. "I think I catch what you're saying. And you're right. You would be giving up a pretty good piece of your life for some money. You can save almost every penny of your salary and in just nine months be financially secure. As you well know, Gene and I will be glad to have you with us forever. But I know you don't want that---

certainly I wouldn't if I were you. To put it all in a nutshell, you will never again have an opportunity to gain financial independence so quickly."

Mary smiled. "Always the practical one aren't you?"

"Most of the time being practical means being happy," Grace answered.

Mary threw her head back and uproarishly let go of an ironic laugh. "I'm talking like the job has already been offered to me." What if they don't like me? What if they like somebody else better?"

"That won't happen," Grace confidently predicted.

"How can you be so sure?"

Grace smiled, and a far away look came into her eyes. "I can't explain it," she softly answered, "but some things I just know."

That evening mother and daughter carried on a three-hour discussion about the job for which Mary had not even applied. In the end, they tearfully agreed that with a Christmas visit thrown in to mitigate their suffering, they would endure the nine months separation for nine times $150.00.

Early the next morning Mary secured short but glowing letters of recommendation from her pastor and an old friend of Sean's, the president of the Union Bank of Amarillo. She placed these letters in a big envelope containing a now yellowing letter of recommendation given to her by her principal when she resigned from the school in Fort Worth, along with her diplomas and teaching certificate. Thusly armed, she appeared at the Amarillo Hotel at 9:30 A.M. where the desk clerk casually dropped on her the information that she had been preceded by three other applicants.

Entering the lavish parlor of the Presidential Suite, she found herself confronted not only by Amos and Bertha Dundee but by their daughter as well. As she later reported to Jane and Grace, the interview went splendidly from first to last. Inexplicably charged with a surge of quiet confidence, she was articulate and charming, Although her parents, by maintaining a stiff dignity and superior air, managed to conceal their thinking, Nora made scant efforts to hide her's. The minute she saw Mary, she wanted her for her teacher; and, contributing gaily to the conversation, all but came out openly and said so.

Amos, in all of his dignity, still managed to flirt with her. And, it was easy for Mary to see that the fact of his eyes wondering about over her was not lost on his wife. This worried her. Obviously no wife would want to establish in her own household competition for her husband's attentions. However there was in fact, no cause for alarm. From the start Bertha realized that she would be protected, not by her husband, but by a woman whose moral character and religious training would mandate a cold shoulder to the romantic advances of a married man, any married man. Only later, after she had gotten to know Bertha well, did Mary realize that Bertha had astutely discerned that a romance between her husband and Mary would never start, much less bloom.

Mary was relieved to hear that the Dundees had not had trouble with previous tutors. It developed that Nora, who had been in a boarding, school in Denver for the past three years, suddenly decided that rather than returning to Denver for another term, she wanted a tutor to prepare her for Larkingwood, the well recognized finishing school in St. Louis. Somewhat reluctantly, her parents had agreed.

At length, Amos Dundee asked Mary to step out of the room for a few moments to allow him to confer privately with his wife and daughter. She stood in the hall no more than thirty seconds before being summoned back. She had the job.

She found out later from Nora that her competition for the job was almost nil. One of the applicants was a man who in Nora's words, "was rather charming", but Dundee adjudged the man to be a sissy was a gigolo and summarily dismissed him from consideration. The other two were elderly women. After each had departed from the interview room, Nora strenuously voiced her objection: "She may be competent, but she won't be any fun."

It turned out that for Mary Fitzhugh September 30, 1914 turned out to be one of those long, very busy, sad but interesting days that are not soon forgotten. Amid much waving and tears, she departed Amarillo in the early morning on the train. In Clarendon, she transferred to a buckboard and by nightfall she had completed her move to a spacious, beautifully furnished bedroom on the third floor of the Dundee mansion.

The buckboard which got her there was pulled by a pair of the biggest, blackest, finest horses she had ever seen, driven by a man named Slim Feister, who introduced himself as the Foreman of the Dundee Ranch. Along with making himself useful by pointing out various landmarks and places of interest during their trip to the ranch headquarters, Feister was, Mary thoughts ludicrously flirtatious. However she was only mildly disgusted. As a matter of fact, she was as flattered as she was disgusted by this all too eager but not bad looking and reasonably intelligent man who had made a point of letting her know almost at the beginning that he was a single man.

* * * * * * *

Jane was suddenly startled out of her reflections. The cow was scoldingly mooing at her for allowing the milk to overflow the bucket. She was wasting milk that belonged to Bessy's baby. Seeing the warm, white liquid spilling down the sides of the bucket, Jane exclaimed, "Oh. I'm sorry, Bessy, I promise to make it up to Fred tomorrow."

Her promise failed to still Bessy's mooing, however, just as it failed to stop Fred's impatient bahing. Both mother and son persisted in their loud protests until Jane opened the gate which separated them, allowing the calf to greedily began to drain the remaining milk from the bag of his loving, now contented mother.

Smiling, Jane grabbed the heavily laden bucket by its bail and slowly strolled to the well house. There she would pour the milk into another bucket, straining it through a piece of clean cheese cloth. The bucket of milk would then be cooled by immersing it, almost up to its rim, in a vat of cool well water. Not much of the milk would be drunk this hot time of the year. Even in the coolness of the well water only a few hours would pass before it turned blinkey. But the heat of summer would not prevent it from yielding up great golden globs of butter under the patient paddling of the old wooden churn.

Mary glanced out of window. "She's just now heading for the well house. We'll go ahead and eat without her."

"Suits me." Slim gruffly replied. "She ought not to be so slow. I could milk three cows while she's milkin one."

"Probably," Mary agreed, "but you don't have near as much to day dream about."

He started his reply by saying, "Oh, yeah, well...." But she cut off further debate by pushing a plate of fried steak and potatoes, covered with cream gravy, under his nose. She flanked it with a plate full of smoking, hot biscuits. The corners of Slim Feister's mouth involuntarily curled with a grin as he tore into his supper like a hungry hound dog gobbles up a cold biscuit.

"What did you and the big man do today? she asked.

"Decided to bring in a thousand more cows

with calves at their sides," he calmly replied.

"What! You told me not more than three days ago that there were too many cattle on the ranch now."

Mouth crammed with meat and potatoes, Feister nodded and uttered, "Uh huh."

"Then I don't understand. What's all this about?"

Slim swallowed. "It's all about the simple fact that the King wants more cattle. And I ain't about to argue with the King. My old mama and dad were poor, but they didn't raise no fools."

She grimly nodded her understanding. "Where is he going to get the new cattle?"

Slim told her.

"How long will you be gone?"

"Three weeks, maybe a month. We won't leave for a few days though. Dundee promised we could wait until the Preacher gets here."

He's the new cook? she inquired. "Yeah."

"Why do you call him "the Preacher"? "Because he's a preacher. Everybody calls him that. He's a real preacher that's for sure. He'll put the fear of God in you too if you'll let him." Feister put on a crooked little grin. "I don't like all of his Bible pounding., but he's the best ranch cook I ever saw. He puts a smile on the cowhands faces, and the more they smile the harder they work, By the way," Feister continued, "speaking of how long I'm gonna be gone, can I count on her being gone when I get back?"

"Jane?"

He nodded.

"Probably not," she coolly answered. "I want her to leave, but she wants to stay. And she'll probably get her way, at least for the time being."

"I want her out of here," he declared. "She's a trouble maker."

"Now where did you get that notion?" she wanted to know.

"Right after she came at the start of the summer, you got stiff and cold. I call that makin trouble."

Mary closed her eyes and clinched her hands into fists. "I turned stiff and cold about that time. That's true. But it had nothing to do with Jane."

Opening her eyes and looking searchingly into his, she, on impulse, decided to put him to a test. "It had to do with Bertha Dundee."

Feister flushed--out of fury, not embarrassment. "It's a lie," he hissed.

Sensing that she had gained the upper hand on her husband, Mary moved to exploit her advantage. "What's a lie?" she calmly and innocently asked.

"You know what I mean," he growled.

"Is it true?" she pressed.

"No" he thundered. He paused, eyes blazing, "Well, do you believe me," he demanded.

"I don't know," she thoughtfully began, "whether I believe you or not. If you said it was true, I might leave you. Maybe. I don't know for sure. But I know that as long as you deny it, I will never leave you."

She abruptly ended the conversation by

turning and quickly stepping to the back door. "I'm going to get some cool air. I'll take care of the dishes later," she said, without turning back.

Going out onto the small porch, she let go a sad little sigh and settled into a rope bottomed chair to await the setting of the sun. She looked disapprovingly at her hands. They ware red and rough, and there were painful cracks in her knuckles. I've got to put some balm on them, she thought. But the cracks in her hands were petty compared to the crack in her heart. And for that larger crack she had no balm. The larger crack started just before Christmas, about three months after she came to Dundee Rancho

* * * * * * *

Looking back, although she desperately missed Jane, she counted her beginning days at Big House as reasonably happy ones. She was obliged to climb three flights of stairs to her room, but it was spacious and richly furnished with light oak furniture. Besides the huge and rather ponderous beds she had a sofa, table, three chairs, desk and a wardrobe that was twice too big for all of her clothes. The light blue of the heavy drapes matched the color of the several small, thick rugs which were tastefully spread about over the shinning hard wood floor. It was nice. Nice beyond her highest expectations.

At first the Dundee's were nice also. And they treated her almost as an equal. Bertha asked her to take dinner with the family on a regular basis.   She never quite overcame her faint amusement at the nightly sight of people who, deep in the heart of the wind blown plains of Texas, seemed a bit overdressed and over pompous.   Nevertheless, she shortly came to realize that a person who is mostly isolated from the rest of civilization is naturally faced with the threat of a creeping, subtle self-devaluation. And the dignity and self-respect engendered by the formality in the evenings helped to ward off that threat.

Too, her relationship with Nora, with whom she spent six hours a day, though not warm and loving, was acceptable and interesting. The young woman had a hungry, competitive mind which urged her to overcome the inferiority she felt from being what she., with a tone of shame, called a "country girl."

Mary learned, however, that Nora's schooling had hardly been that of the average "country girl". It was, as a matter of fact, about as good as could be had. Through the third grade she and her mother lived in Clarendon during the school terms, and Nora attended a small but very good school there. After that, she attended a well respected boarding school, first in Amarillo and later in Denver. Nora had always excelled in school, but she was not at all confident that she was equipped to compete successfully with the other rich girls in finishing school. And when she arrived in St. Louis next September, she was determined to be on an intellectual par with the best of them. Mary was not surprised to hear that it was Nora, not her parents, who had insisted on a tutor. Though she never got emotionally close to her cool and remote student, Mary found her to be respectful and very teachable.

During those early months, Amos Dundee had bridled his flirtations and treated her with friendly respect, That was a big and somewhat surprising plus. But it was Bertha who furnished the biggest surprise, and it was a delight. For it was this seemingly arrogant and shallow woman who initially inserted an element of real happiness in Mary's life on the ranch, Eagerly reaching for the companionship of a peer, she showered Mary with kindness. Mary was grateful for the expensive, hardly worn dresses which Bertha insisted upon giving to her. And she looked forward to what they called their "little tea times" each morning and each afternoon.

And so they went, those first weeks at Dundee. And with five or six letters from Jane in each week's mail and with a visit with her at Christmas coming ever nearer, Mary smiled a lot. Then, like a blue norther which throws off its disguise of sunshine and soft breezes and strikes without warning, trouble struck.

Chapter Seven

Mary remembered waiting for Jane's train in the shelter of the closed cab of the Dundee's most elegant buggy. The first snow flakes of the season were lazily falling, the sight of which caused her to wiggle deeper under the heavy buggy robe. She was shaking a little, perhaps a bit from the cold, but mostly from excitement. Jane was coming for Christmas--for two whole weeks. Bertha had insisted that she use the best buggy. And Slim Feister had driven her into Clarendon that morning. He had gone to do some shopping, leaving her to look longingly northward along the black twin ribbons of steel for the first puffs of black smoke which would forerun the proud whistle blasts by which the train would announce its arrival.

When Slim told her that he was going to drive her into town, she had entered a mild and modest protests declaring that she hated to pull him off of his important job to perform such a menial task. He acknowledged that he could send one of the cowboys on the mission but that he "needed to tend to some things in town anyway." She believed him, knowing from gossip around the ranch that he used any pretense to take a ride into town. Nevertheless, she noticed that his eyes unabashedly devoured her, and she got mild pleasure from the thought that he wanted to be near her.

Slim, carrying a couple of small parcels, returned to the buggy just as the eagerly awaited black puffs came into view. "Here it comes," Mary shouted. "I'm going to get out on the platform."

Jane was standing in the door smiling and waving as the engine gave up a loud spew of excess steam and the train's porter put the portable steps in place. Tripping down the steps, freshly beautiful, and radiant in a not new but lovely green dress, she ran to her mother with open arms.

She was followed by a grinning young man, tall and handsome, probably four or five years older than she. He was slender, had laughing light blue eyes and a head of reddish blond hair which was distinguished by an unmistakable cow lick. He was dressed in a black suit, white shirt and black string tie. In both hands he clutched a big, white felt hat.

At the end of the hugging and kissing, Jane whirled about and motioned for the young man to join them. He and Slim Feister then became the subject of introductions. The young man was Mike

Vernon, the son of F. O. Vernon, Clarendon's leading lawyer. He was attending law school in Denver and had come home for the holidays. He had quickly introduced himself to Jane when she boarded the train in Amarillo.

"And he was nice enough to ask me to Mesa's Christmas dance," Jane exclaimed, "but I told him I'd have to talk to you and give him my answer later."

Mike turning his charm to its highest glow said, "Aw, please, Mrs. Fitzhugh, let her go with, me. I'm really a nice fellow."

"Well, I'm sure you are, Mr. Vernon, but....."

"I can vouch for that," Slim cut in. "He comes from one of the very best families in Clarendon. And that dance is the biggest and best thing that will happen around here during the holidays. Come on, let her go. And what's just as important," he quickly continued, "why don't you let me take you to the dance?"

Mary was stunned. Before her eyes there loomed the hazy outlines of three smiling faces, persistently, persuasively and expectantly nodding. She frowned and stammered, "I...well..I suppose..yes."

In celebration, Mike lifted his hat high above his head; Jane clapped her hands; and Slim Feister closed the episode by saying, "Good. It's all settled."

It was dark when Feister stopped the buggy in front of Big House, Bertha and Nora walked out on the veranda to greet them. "Hello Jane," Bertha called, "welcome to Dundee."   "Yes, indeed," Nora added.

"Oh thank you," Jane cried. Then she excitedly clasped both of Bertha's hands then Nora's, "I just know I'm going to love it here. It's so very beautiful, and everyone is so very nice."

"Oh, I'm so glad," Bertha replied.

"Yes, I've already been invited to the Mesa Christmas dance and so has mother."

"That's nice alright.," Bertha casually agreed. "And who, pray tell, extended such a quick invitation?"

"Well, there were two invitations," Jane answered, "one for me and a separate one for mother."

"Oh?"

"Yes, Mike Vernon, a young man I met on the train, asked me. And Mr. Feister asked mother. And, of course, we accepted."

Bertha and Nora reacted instantly and in unison. Their eyes bugged. They turned as white as a sheet. They sniffed . They reached down and pulled their skirts up a couple of inches from the floor. They about faced and marched into the house without another word.

Jane, mouth agape, was horrified. "Mother," she gasped, "what happened."

Mary also stood open mouthed. But she was not horrified. She was angry. Instantly she surmised that Nora had set her cap for Mike Vernon; and, in the manner of her upbringing, thought he already belonged to her. However, she did not learn until later that while she had accurately guessed the entire cause of Nora's angry reaction, she had only deduced part of the reason for Bertha's conduct. It was the next morning before she learned the whole truth.

The sun was streaming through a kitchen window onto the mammoth oak table as they finished their breakfast. "It's beautiful out there," Mary declared. "It's cold, but lets bundle up and go for a little walking tour."

Jane readily agreed, and soon they were crunching tracks in the thin blanket of snow which overlaid the trail from Big House, past the well house to the big barn and corrals. Nearing the well house, they stopped to stare at the whipping wheel of the windmill, flashing in the sun. From behind them came a familiar voice, heavily colored with chivalry. "Good morning, ladies. Please let me know if I can be of assistance."

"Oh. Slim, good morning," Mary gaily replied. "And what brings you out so early?"

"I was up at first light. I had to roll the cowboys out and make sure they broke ice on all the tanks and water holes. Cows don't get along too well just lickin snow."

Mary smiled. "I see. Well, I'm just leading Jane on a little tour of the headquarters grounds. Won't you join us?"

"Gladly".

"And, by the way," Mary continued as they walked towards the barn, "I'd like to take you up on your offer of assistance."

"Of course, anything. You name it."

"I need information," she responded. "You no doubt noticed the....uh..shall I call it ... the rather strange way that Bertha and Nora reacted to Jane's little announcement about the Mesa Christmas dance."

"It wasn't just strange, Mother, it was down right ugly," Jane inserted.

"I certainly won't argue with you," Mary replied. Then, looking straight into Slim's eyes, she said, "Call it what you may, can you tell us why they acted like they did?"

He stopped and hooked his thumbs in his belt. "Yeah."

"Will you please tell us," Jane softly pleaded.

He drew a deep breath and let it out. "Yeah, I'll tell you. Why not? That snooty little Nora thinks she already owns that Vernon boy. She and her mother both have the notion that if they want something, everybody else is to back off and let them have it."

"But I didn't know Nora had any claim on Mike Vernon, " Jane protested.

"That doesn't make any difference to high and mighty people like that," "Slim bitterly replied. "They get jealous anyhow. I guess they think if you don't know, you ought to know."

Jane looked at her mother. "I'll have to hand it to you. You guessed that."

Mary shrugged and threw up her hands. "At least we for sure know the straight of it. What a shame."

It didn't come here to cause trouble," Jane said. "I'll send word to Mike Vernon that I can't go to the dance, and We'll let that be known to Nora and her mother."

"No. you will not," Mary sternly replied. "Those two are out of time and out of place. This is not Europe, and they don't have royal blood."

Slim began to roll a cigarette. "Well...." He gave the word a long and tantalizing treatment, causing Jane and Mary to look at him expectantly. "That wouldn't completely put things in order anyhow. You see, I haven't quite told all of the story."

Finishing the cigarette, he deliberately struck a match to it, seeming to enjoy his place at center stage and the suspense he was creating. "It so happens that Bertha has a crush on me."

Exhaling bluish smoke from his nose, he squinted at his wide eyed audience. "It's true. I didn't have anything to do with it," he lied. "I didn't encourage it," he lied again. "But there it is."

"Well, I never!" Mary managed to gasp.

"And for the reasons you just gave to your daughter, you've got to go right on to the dance with me. Right?"

Mary shot Slim with a steely stare. But she let a little defiant smile crinkle the corners of her mouth. And then, tossing her head into a proud tilt, she replied, "Right."

With a tone of afterthought Mary asked, "But what if they come right out and ask us to decline our invitations to the dance? What then?

Slim gave a mirthless chuckle. "You don't understand the ways of royalty. They're too puffed up and proud to ever ask such a thing."

"Anyway," Mary began, in answer to her own question, "We're not going to back down now."

That afternoon Mary responded to a soft rapping at her door. It was Sarah, the Dundee's long time housekeeper. She was big, black and clever. She had always gone out of her way to be nice to Mary. She rolled her big brown eyes and screwed up her face in misery. "I don't know why, Miss Mary, but Miss Bertha she tell me to say to you that it be better if you and Miss Jane not take dinner with them."

"This evening?" Mary inquired.

"This evenin and ever other evenin," "Sarah gravely replied.

"Oh, I see. Well thank you, Sarah."

"I sorry, Miss Mary."

"I know, Sarah. But don't worry yourself. I should have guessed this would happen. And anyway, it's probably for the best."

When Sarah left, Mary broke the news to Jane. "That Sarah," she went on., "is so sweet. And so are the people in the kitchen and all the other hired help." She paused and vented an ironic chuckle. "I would have never imagined that I would say such a thing; but I'd much rather he like the hired help than the Dundees. I guess it's because, well after all, I'm hired help too," she said in a voice strangely mixed with pride and sadness.

Jane's eyes shone with. tears as she hugged her mother. "I'm proud of you." she whispered.

In retrospect, the events of the remainder of the Christmas season always seemed to spin crazily in Mary's mind. All in all it was a happy time. She and Jane read, talked and took long walks and horseback rides. Sarah saw to it that they, as she put it, "ate high on the hog". They exchanged gifts under their own cedar tree which Slim, ever attentive, brought to then from Box Canyon. In addition, Mike Vernon came out twice and took Jane for long buggy rides. At the top of the good things that happened was the Mesa dance. Mother and daughter, each was her generation's unrivaled belle of the ball. Mike Vernon and Slim Feister were at their best that night, seeming to fully grasp the fact that they were the two luckiest suitors in Mesa, if not in all of Texas.

But the holiday swirl had its dark pieces as well. Mary and Jane were not invited to the Dundee's New Year's party.

Mike Vernon came; and Sarah told them later that when he got there, she heard him inquire of Nora as to Jane's whereabouts. Sarah could not make out Nora's answer, but she saw Nora stamp her foot and whirl away from him. "I could tell she shore was mad," Sarah declared. And she went on to relate that the young man promptly crammed his white hat on his head and marched out of the party.

The dark pieces also included the complete aloofness of the Dundee women and the uncomfortable suspicion that they were engaged in sinister plotting. Too, there was that little touch of disappointment which Mary administered to herself. She adamantly refused to add luster to the season by wearing any of the beautiful dresses Berth had given her.

The holidays ended much like they had begun. Slim drove Mary and Jane, this time in the buckboard, to Clarendon where she boarded the train in the smiling company of Mike Vernon. Mary would not see her daughter again until the end of May. By then she would have made the biggest mistake of her life.

Holidays over, Nora reluctantly turned again to her tutor for guidance. The student's natural coolness had turned to a carefully designed coldness. Her respect had turned to an overt, bitter loathing. All of them, Mary and the Dundee family, were trapped. Because she couldn't afford it financially and because of an obligation to her hateful student, Mary refused to resign her position. on the other side, the Dundees could not fire her because they could not, at this late date, hope to find another competent teacher in time to prepare Nora for finishing school.

Of course, Mary had the promise of freedom when summer came, But now, amid the cold, howling winds of winter, that promise seemed to lie far, far away. She missed Sean more than ever. She missed Jane more than ever. It is no wonder then that emotional eyes so hazed over by anger, helplessness and loneliness would see the figure of Slim Feister enveloped in the golden glow of a guardian angel.

Until now, she had never looked upon Slim as a serious suitor. He was no more than a rough, uncouth cowboy with whom she could have some passing fun.

Likewise, Slim had never considered that he had any long range chances with this beautiful, bright and cultured lady. He had thought to merely give her a quick whirl and than let her go. Now, like a fox, Slim sensed his advantage and went all out to exploit it.

Striking swiftly before Mary could throw off her desperation and panic, he made her his wife during the first week of March. And he pulled it off before she found out that two wives had already divorced him; and that under the laws of heaven, he should have been married several other times.

The bride and groom had barely settled down in the foreman's house before Slim's mean came out of hiding, and the scales fell from Mary's eyes. She had ridded herself of a few black months in exchange for an endless succession of gray ones. When it finally came, the truth struck like lightning--swiftly and sharply--but it came too late.

When the month of June rolled around, instead of returning to Amarillo in keeping with the plans made back in September, Mary found herself again meeting Jane's train. This time she came alone, driving an older buckboard which Amos Dundee made available to "the help". "But this time she didn't have come to travel nearly as far, because the railroad had now come into Mesa, only five miles from the ranch. Jane would spend that summer on the ranch before returning to Amarillo for her last year of High School.

In her letters to Jane, Mary had been

careful, or so she thought, to conceal the pain of her marriage . And she was resolved to continue with the secret. There was no good reason to worry her daughter about a situation that could not be changed. While waiting for the train, she was fascinated by the building and bustling that had already gripped Mesa since the railroad arrived just a couple of months ago. A freshly painted sign on the front of one of the partially finished new buildings read: "Ranchers and Merchants Bank". This put her in mind of her financial status. She had sent $20.00 each month to her sister and $5.00 each month to Jane. And she has spent an average of $5.00 per month on herself. Thus, of the $1350.00 which Amos Dundee had deposited in her account in the bank in Clarendon, she had $1092.52 left. Slim did not know about the money, and she congratulated herself for keeping it a secret from him. It was about the only smart thing she had done in the last few months. Shortly after their marriage, Slim had bluntly asked about the money she was "gettin from teachin". Instinctively, as a lioness jumps to protect her cub, Mary had lied. Dundee, she said, was depositing the salary each month in an Amarillo bank in her sister Gracie's account to reimburse Gracie for taking care of Jane. To her great relief, he seemed to believe her and asked no more about it. Although Mary could not help but rue the day she set foot on Dundee Ranch, at least Jane could now enjoy a large measure of financial security. She could even go to college.

Jane stepped off of the train and into her

mother's arms. Immediately the unintentional touch of desperation in Mary's embrace caused her daughter to suspect that all was not well. Clutching Mary's shoulders, Jane pushed her back to arms' length, looked searchingly into her eyes and blurted, "What's wrong, Mama?"

"Why nothing, Darling," Mary lied.

Jane scowled. She was not convinced; and before many days had passed, she would know better.

At summer's end, Jane told her mother that although depressed by Mary's ill disguised melancholy and by the fact that Mike Vernon spent most of the vacation months reading law in a law office in Denver, the summer had been good to her. She had discovered a natural affection for the horses and barnyard animals, and they returned that affection. Moreover, it was not only the beasts which paid attention to her. She had one fun date after another with a string of grinning, lovesick cowboys. Too, Mike came home no less than three times, just to see her. A couple of times Mike had strongly hinted that he was on the verge of trying to secure a commitment from her, but she had deftly held him off. She liked him. She thought maybe she even loved him, but he was trying to move too fast. She was not ready to tie herself down.

* * * * * * *

And now Jane had graduated from High School, summer had come again to Dundee Ranch and so had Jane. As the sun slowly slipped into bed, Mary caught sight of her daughter strolling in from the well house. I've got to get her out of here, she thought, before she gets trapped like I did.

Jane cheerily called out, "I'll need to churn tomorrow,"

"We don't need the butter," Mary replied. "But you can take it down and give it to your adoring cowboys. It'll help them tough it out until their new cook arrives."

Chapter Eight

The Preacher again gave the now familiar two fingered whistle, causing Royal to come back at a gallop. His eyes and the way he held his head seemed to say, "What's wrong?"

And Applegate answered just as if the question had been voiced. "Nothin wrong. I was just wonderin if you been noticin those pheasants over there," he said, pointing to his right.

Royal nodded.

"This is real good pheasant country, and that's about as good a flock as you're gonna ever see. How'd you like to get us a couple for supper?"

Royal nodded but then pointed to his .30-.30 and held up his hands in a gesture of defeat.

"Oh don't worry none about that," the old man replied, drawing his double barreled shotgun from its scabbard. "You can use ol' mule ears, What say?"

Royal's eyes shone with delight. He nodded, grabbed the shotgun, turned his horse to the right and rode away.

"Watch him," the Preacher said to George, "let's see if he does it right."

"He will, George replied.

Given that the evening shadows were beginning to fall, it was a cinch that the fowls were making a bee line for water. George and the Preacher, each to himself, noted with satisfaction that Royal loped his horse in a wide arch around the flock, stopping between them and their water hole--about twenty-five yards to the right of the course they were on. Royal dismounted, and they then lost sight of him in the brush.

"Well, he's done everything right up to now," the Preacher observed. "I just hope he can shoot that ol' mule ears as good as he can shoot that rifle of his."

"He can," George responded.

Applegate smiled. "You sort of like your boy, don't you?" "I do," George replied.

The Preacher looked off into the distance. "So do I. So do I," he murmured.

Just then they heard muffled twin bams from the shotgun. Shortly they saw Royal return to his horse, remount and race back to them holding high two fat pheasants.

"If he could say somethin, he'd say it now," said the Preacher. "Ain't nothin will get a man to talkin like a good hunt."

"Ain't that the truth," George agreed, "but you notice," he sadly added, "he ain't made a sound."

"But I can shore talk," George continued,

"and I want to say that what you did for Royal was somethin special, and I appreciate it."

"What're you talkin about?" the old man asked.

"You know. You and I both know that it's a special thing for a man to loan out his gun; and it's much more special when there's game right there to be hunted and shot."

The old man pulled at his whiskers. "Yeah, you're right," he admitted.

George squinted at him. Well, I don't understand it, but I want you to know that it suits me right down to the ground."

They had a feast that night; and after it was over, Royal, with exaggerated actions, began trying to communicate, He pointed first to Applegate, then to his shotgun. Then, facing Applegate, he held his arms out in front of his chest and gave a little bow from the waist.

"He's sayin...", George began. The Preacher stopped him. "Wait", he said," don't tell me. Let's see if I've gotten the handle on understanding the boy. I say he's thankin me for lettin him use my shotgun."

Royal smiled and nodded.

"Right", exclaimed George. "You're gettin to where you can understand him as good as I can."

"I hope so," the Preacher softly replied. "It would mean a whole lot to me to be able to understand you completely Royal."

Observing that both father and son registered puzzlement and shot him a quizzical look, the old man passed on quickly by holding up his Bible and saying "Bible time".

"Yeah, that's good. Last time you told us that a mess we are in, but you didn't tell us any way out of it."

"I left you in the middle of the mess because I wanted you to have a few hours to think about it before I pointed a way out. As a matter of fact, I pulled a little trick on you."

"How's that?"

"Well, you remember that I read this:

"For all have sinned and come short of the glory of God;"

"That is the 23rd. verse of Chapter 3 of the book of Romans, written by the Apostle Paul. Then you remember I read:

"For the wages of sin is death;"

"Now, that is the first part of the 23rd. verse of Chapter 6 in the same book.

"So...?" George wondered aloud.

"So, the trick is... and by the way, it's a trick done in the name of the Lord."

Good naturedly, George voiced his skepticism. "Huh, We'll have to see about that."

"Fair enough. Anyway, the trick is that I didn't read anything that comes right before or right after those bits of scripture.   And it so happens that in each case the part I read tells you about the trouble you're in, but what comes next tells you how to get out it."

"Huh, you're a preacher alright, but you're also an 'ol reprobate."

The old man laughed. "I guess I had that comin, but now listen. Here's how verse 23 of

Chapter 3 sounds when you add verses 24 and 25 to it:

For all have sinned, and come short of the glory of God; Being justified freely by his grace through the redemption that is in Christ Jesus: Whom God hath set forth to be a propitiation through faith in his blood, to declare his righteousness for the remission of sins that are past, through the forbearance of God."

"And, when you read all of verse 23 of Chapter 6, here's how it goes:

"For the wages of sin is death; but the gift of God is eternal life through Jesus Christ our Lord."

Looking up, the Preacher commented, "So, our ever lovin God gave us Jesus Christ as a way out."

"Yeah, but....", George began.

"Wait, before you ask any questions, I want to put some meat on them bones. Lets look at the 3rd Chapter of John, there it is that Jesus himself teaches us that if you want to get out of the mess and be accepted by God, you have to be born again. And what does that mean? How do you get born again?

Well, Jesus puts it like this. Listen."

"And as Moses lifted up the serpent in the wilderness, even so must the Son of man be lifted up: That whosoever believeth in him should not perish, but have eternal life. For God so loved the world, that he gave his only begotten Son, that whosoever believeth in him should not perish, but have everlasting life. For God sent not his Son into the world to condemn the works; but that the world through him might be saved. He that believeth on him is not condemned: but he that believeth not is condemned already because he hath not believed in the name of the only begotten Son of God."

"But, Preacher, What about........."

The Preacher cut George off, by holding his Bible aloft and saying, "'Now let us pray."

"Now God," he began, "you know I haven't even read all of this Bible, and there's lots of what I have read that I don't understand. For instance, the main thing I don't understand is why you loved me and George and Royal so much that you let your son die for us, I don't understand it, but I believe it. And when I first believed it, you pulled off a little miracle. You made a new man out of me. You saved my soul and made me whole. Now, God, I can't explain all this, even to myself. My son... I mean my friend, George, has some questions. I haven't heard them, but I'm sure I can't answer some of 'em, maybe none of 'em. So. I guess I'm just sort of tryin to cut George off at the pass. I'm askin you to do him and Royal like you did me. You know, just let your Holy Ghost persuade them to have enough faith in John 3:16 to put themselves in the hands of Jesus and see what happens. Amen."

The old man, who had been praying with head bowed and eyes closed, opened his eyes and looked up at the men he had secretly adopted. Then he looked up at the moon and finally asked: "Any questions?"

There followed a thirty-second silence.

Breaking it, George murmured a simple "No."

Giving a response typical of one who is spiritual enough to believe in saying a prayer but human enough to be a bit surprised when it is answered, the old man exclaimed, "Well, I'll be darned."

"No," George repeated, "I may have lots of questions later on, but right now all I can say is that while we have been sittin here, I just turned myself over to Jesus, and I swear to you he got me out of the mess I was in, and he saved me, and I belong to him." That's all I know. I belong to him."

The old Preacher's mouth fell open. "Well, I'll be darned."

"And, I want to be baptized."

"Well I'll be darned."

"Can you handle that?"

"What?"

"Will you baptize me?"

"Oh, sure, of course. First thing in the morning. We'll go over to that water hole where the pheasants went."

George, with all the excitement typical of a new convert, asked, "What about you, Son? You felt it too didn't you?"

Royal, looking grim and puzzled, slowly shook his head and headed towards his bedroll.

The old preacher caught up with him and put an arm around the boy's shoulders. "I don't know what your trouble is, So. I can't figure out why you won't let Jesus save you. But I want you to promise me something. I want you to take this old Bible of mine. It's saved many a soul. And I want you to have it for your very own."

Royal raised his hands and shook his head in protest.

"Don't worry. I want you to have this Bible. I can get another one when we get to Mesa. But in exchange for the old Bible, I want a promise."

Royal nodded.

"I want you to promise me that you'll read and study this Bible and that you'll start by readin the Gospel of John. Will you do that for me?"

Royal clutched the Bible and nodded,

The old man turned away so that the boy would not see the tears in his eyes.

The next morning, George was baptized in the waterhole--a muddy, waist deep natural lake. His happiness was subdued by the fact that Royal did not join him. But he was encouraged when he saw his son riding along with the open Bible resting on his saddle horn.

Seven hours later, the perspiring riders were grateful for the dark, cooling shadow that fell over the grassy plains.

Applegate pointed to the cause of the shade, a slowly boiling blue-green cloud in the Northwest. "We're ridin right into it," he observed, "and it's comin about as fast as a horse can run."

They were awed by the swift thrusts and slashes of the great jagged swords of lightening which gashed the monster cloud and caused it to angrily roar with pain.

"We've barely got time to get ready for it," the Preacher opined.

"Huh," George replied, "what can we do? There's no shelter, no tree, no hole, no canyon. What are we supposed to do, crawl under a clump of buffalo grass?"

Applegate chuckled. "Well, we can't do much more than that. But We've got to get off these animals. That's for sure. There's a strange and scary thing about lightning. It won't hardly ever strike a horse, and it won't hardly ever strike a man; but it really does go after a man on a horse. Don't ask me why. I don't know. But just ask any cowboy out on these plains, and He'll tell you the same thing."

"We'll take your word for it. Would it be a good idea to hobble the horses?"

"Yeah", the Preacher replied, "and get the saddles off of 'em."

After the saddles were on the ground, the Preacher continued: "Every man sees that his tarpaulin is wrapped tight around his bed roll and stowed under his saddle. Now, get your slicker on and put your horse blanket down by your side."

"What's the blanket for?" George inquired.

"If it hails, you can put the blanket over yourself. Here's what to do," he went on, just as the leading edge of the wind kicked up dust in front of them, "turn your back to the wind and get down on your knees. Then sit back on your legs like this. The wind'll be strong, real hard to stand up in. If it hails just a light pea size hail, we probably won't need any help beyond our hats and slickers; but if it gets big and starts popping us real hard, then you'll want to bow down to the ground like an Arab praying and pull your horse blanket over yourself. Got it?"

George and Royal, eyes shining with admiration, nodded and assumed the back-to-wind position which the old man was demonstrating. They had no more than settled own when the storm hit. Almost immediately they were pummeled by chunks of hail half the size of chicken eggs. But just as they wiggled under their horse blankets, the hail turned to pea size and then quickly ceased altogether,

Thankful to be able to throw off their horse blankets and sit erect, the three smiled nervously at each other through the falling lake of water. The lightning cracked and the thunder literally shook the earth under them. Wind whipping their backs, they sat for five minutes, then ten. The wind tamed down, but the rain continued to fall in sheets; and their mild fright now turned to sullen, damp discomfort.

Royal stuck his tongue out and lapped some of the sweet rain. It reminded him of the water at the windmill where he drank from the rusty old tomato can. His eyes turned to the old preacher, and as he watched the water cascading off the brim of his hat, he thought how like that old tomato can was this old preacher. They looked a lot alike--old and rusty and covered with dents. But they were useful, and what came out of them was pure and good.

Twenty minutes after it struck them, the storm passed, and they were able to witness the sunset. They ate cold biscuits and cold beans that night. There was no fire wood, and the cow and buffalo chips were soggy.

After bedding down, Applegate slyly put his hand inside his saddle bag and felt around. Withdrawing his hand, he smiled to himself in the black of the night. The map was dry. He stared at the stars and recalled the story of how the map had come to be. Most of it had been told to him by his Comanche friend, Eagle Feather. Minor details were filled in by the Preacher's knowledge of the geography of the staked plains of Texas and the history of the proud Comanches who once roamed them.

The story began back in 1874.

Chapter Nine

In those early September days of 1874, a Comanche brave who had survived until he was twenty-five years of age would carry several battle scars. He would also be powerful of body, highly skilled with weapons and horses, brave but cunning, filled with hate for white people, and, most of all, very lucky. Eagle Feather was such a warrior. He gracefully slid off his pony so as to more closely examine some of the tracks that had captured the Quanah attention of the small hunting party lead by Chief Quanah Parker. Leaping back onto his pony, he turned to his Chief and said "Comancheros."

"How many?"

"Six. Two with the travois. Four with the ponies."

"How many ponies?"

"About 100."

Quanah nodded. "I agree. What do you think is on the travois?" he asked, pointing to the fresh parallel scars on the ground which had obviously been made by the twin poles of a travois being dragged by a pony.

"Pretty deep ruts". Eagle Feather replied, "could be a wounded man or a white captive. But probably a bunch of buffalo hides."

Again Quanah nodded his agreement and then silently rode his pony in a circle around his hunting party while he pondered his next move. Eagle Feather well knew the things that the Chief was turning over in his mind. His band of Quahanis Comanches had been trading partners with the Comancheros as long as he could remember. As much as the Whites, the Indians despised these lying, cheating, back-stabbing people in whose veins flowed the blood of Mexicans mingled with no telling how many Indian tribes. But powerful economic pressures had traditionally caused the Comanches to close their eyes to their trading partners' disgusting ways. The Comancheros, operating on both sides of the Rio Grande, maintained several home bases in New Mexico where they were safe from all laws, governments and other enemies. These sanctuaries were protected not only by their remoteness and inaccessibility, but by generous bribes to government officials on both sides of the border, as well as--in extreme circumstances-by battle.

These sanctuaries had for many years allowed the Comancheros to maintain the best market for the horses, other property and captives which the Comanches took from the white settlers and their other enemies. In exchange the

Comancheros kept the Indians well supplied with guns, ammunition and blankets. Thus, until recently it would not have entered the blue-eyed, half-breed Chief's mind to pursue the Comancheros and relieve them of their horses and hides. But in the last two months the plains of Texas had been visited by an abrupt and sharp change in circumstances, forcing old friends to become new enemies and old enemies to become new friends.

Three columns of the U. S. Calvary, all under the command of Col. Ranold Mackenzie, had moved out in a savage and relentless campaign against the last of the free Texas Indians, Mackenzie's orders were to "get" the Indians. He was to put them on the reservation at Fort Sill if reasonably possible. If not, he was to bring them under control in such manner and with such methods an he, and he alone, might see fit. These instructions were music to the ears of Ranold Mackenzie, an old Indian fighter, still sore from the everlasting effects of a near fatal wound inflicted by a Comanche arrow. And his persistent, ruthless campaign had already been successful enough to destroy several small bands of Kiowas and Comanches. It had also been successful enough to force the Comanches into an alliance with their ancient enemies, the Kiowas. Moreover, it had been successful enough to cause the always treacherous Comancheros to accept bribes and U. S. Calvary protection in exchange for information concerning the whereabouts and plans of the Kiowas and Comanches.

Quanah Parker pondered all these things. Too, although he was sure that the ponies which were herded by the Comancheros were not Comanche, they definitely were Indian ponies, meaning that they had been stolen from his new friends, the Kiowas. In the end though, it was the deep tracks of the twin travois poles which caused the Chief to snarl with anger and wave his small band of warriors in pursuit of the Comancheros. He deduced that loaded the travoli was loaded with buffalo hides, purchased from the hated White buffalo hunters who left countless corpses of the huge animals to rot and waste. Each corpse pointed to a sad ending for the Comanches: either starvation or reservation. The very thought of the Comancheros taking a profit from the slaughter heated Quanah's brain. If anyone should have the hides, it was the Indians.

The Comanches were three full days' ride from their main camp in the Palo Duro Canyon when they caught up with the Comancheros. They slipped up on their unsuspecting former allies on a moonless night, rendered inky black by high clouds which obscured the stars. Eagle Feather, without remorse carried out his assignment to noiselessly cut to death one of the new enemies. Five other Comanche warriors similarly and simultaneously dispatched the other five Comancheros to the unhappy hunting grounds. Afterwards, the large herd of ponies having remained still and quiet during the swift change in ownership, required no special attention. This being the case, the bone weary Chief decided that the new owners would get some sleep before turning back towards the Palo Duro.

In the early morning light, Quanah told Eagle Feather to inventory the load of buffalo hides on travois. There was a gasp of surprise after he lifted and laid to one side a single buffalo hide. The remainder of the weight and bulk on the travois came from a crude chest, rectangular in shape, about two and one-half feet long, two feet wide and one foot deep. Made of rough cedar, it obviously had been crafted by a White settler. Without waiting for a command from his Chief, Eagle Feather excitedly raised the heavy lid and peered inside. Shrieking with delight, he immediately plunged his hands into the chest and brought forth two hands full of gold coins which he allowed to trickle like water down his wrists and forearms and to fall back into the box.

The Indiana soon discovered that the box contained many coins, both gold and silver, mostly gold, along with several items of jewelry. Eagle Feather was not sure, but his experience in looting from Whites told him that at least some of the bracelets, rings and beads were very valuable.

"Where did they get it?" Chief Quanah wondered aloud.

His followers shrugged their shoulders. Then Eagle Feather said "Stole it."

Quanah nodded his agreement. "Yes. They got the chest from the Kiowas, just like they got the horses. We know the ponies are Kiowa, and we know the Kiowa did not trade the ponies to the Comancheros because the Kiowas are as short of ponies as we are. Besides that, we know that the Comancheros have thrown in with Mackenzie and that Mackenzie even has a couple of soldiers riding with them. That means that the Comancheros would not have traded anything to the Kiowas.

He paused to rub his chin before announcing his final conclusion. "This chest contains a collection of stuff that the Kiowas stole over many years, and the Comancheros stole it from them. "Anyway", he finished, "it belongs to us now.".

Heading back to Palo Duro Canyon, Eagle Feather drew the honor of riding beside the pony which pulled the travois. He wondered why the Comancheros had trusted "the gold" as the Comanche band had dubbed the contents of the chest, with so few guards. Why had they not kept it with their main force which, after all, was under Mackenzie's protection? Mackenzie, he thought, that's the answer. They had somehow managed to steal the chest and ascertained its contents without the knowledge of Mackenzie or any of his men. And, knowing that Mackenzie would probably take possession of the gold as soon as he heard about it, they kept it disguised, just as had the Kiowas, as a bale of buffalo hides and casually sent it along with the small party charged with the responsibility of herding the stolen ponies to the New Mexico sanctuary.

Carefully herding a hundred precious ponies was slow work. It was five full days before they came to the rim of the Palo Duro. Eagle Feather looked down into the deep, green gash in the staked plains. He had seen it many times, but he was always startled by the sudden interruption in the seemingly endless miles of rolling grass and sage brush. The sheer rock walls at the rim gradually gave way to grassy slopes which ended at the canyon floor. The slopes and the floor were generously dotted with squat, evergreen cedars. The little creek, which over the eons had patiently dug the vast ditch was still meandering along the middle of the canyon floor. Tepees were thick for three miles up and down the creek, and hundreds of ponies grazed on the slopes. This was the main camp of the Quahanis Comanches.

As they made their slow descent from the rim by way of a narrow slant in one of the rocky walls, Eagle Feather paused to marvel at the near impregnability of this Comanche fortress. He had voiced questions back there when Quanah had ordered the Quahadis, men, women and children to move into the canyon. He had argued that the canyon robbed the Comanches of their greatest asset in battle, their mobility on horseback. Too, and even more importantly if Mackenzie found then and swiftly moved his calvary to the rim, the Indiana would be trapped in this huge hole in the ground.

At the council, Chief Quanah had patiently heard his best warrior's objections and had overruled them. He pointed out that with the soldiers coming at them from three directions, they didn't have very many options for a main camping ground. He also observed that Mackenzie would be lucky to find them; and if he did, he would not have enough soldiers to cover the entire rim of the canyon; and that as long as Mackenzie fought from the rim, they could survive by hiding and sniping by day and making hit and run raids by night. He reasoned too that if Mackenzie came in through one of the far away open ends of the canyon, the Indiana would escape through the other end or over the rim. And, if the white Col. was stupid enough to divide his force and come in through both of the opens ends, Quanah's warriors could easily defeat either section of the divided force. He concluded by firmly predicting that the only way Mackenzie could defeat them was to somehow slip up on them and manage to secretly accomplish by a long and slow dribble, the movement of a large body of troops to the canyon floor. This, he confidently predicted, Mackenzie could not do.

As usual, Quanah was right, Eagle Feather thought as his Chief was leading his hunting party and their herd of captured ponies in a slow, single-file descent. If Mackenzie whipped the Comanches in the Palo Duro, his troopers would also be to make such a descent. Eagle Feather smiled.

However, the smile left his face as he lead the pony pulling the travois down the rocky slant He thought more than once that he would be forced to use other means to get the gold to the bottom of the canyon. Despite the slow pace, the travois bounced hard and twisted crazily. Twice it tilted to the left so far and so abruptly as to tear the right pole from its mooring on the pony. Repairs were quickly effected however; and the chest securely tied to the cross-poles, was never dumped.

Eagle Feather smiled again when he reached the bottom, not only because he had gotten the gold safely to its new home, but also because he was greeted by the smiling black eyes of Purple Flower. Like a young doe, she tripped lightly and gracefully through the grass, ostensibly gathering fire wood. Actually, without coming any closer than 25 feet and without uttering a sound, she discretely welcomed him home with the light in her eyes and the pucker in her lips.

He was not alone in judging this eighteen year old maiden to be the most beautiful of all the Comanche women. And she is mine, he thought. But his thoughts were wistful, and he was shortly jolted out of them by stark evidence of the chilling reality that she was the wife of another man. As he boldly approached her, he saw a purplish ring around her left eye and a like colored puffy spot on her right cheek. It was clear that her husband had beaten her again. The fact that Eagle Feather's roots were in a culture where squaws were chattels and were frequently, and many times off handedly, knocked about by their husbands, did not mitigate his horror and anger. Instinctively throwing discretion to the wind, he hold out a sympathetic hand, inviting her with his eyes to clasp it. She, not so foolish as he, ignored his outreach, but flashed to him a quick smile before darting away.

She was the youngest of Hail Face's four wives. Polegomy was, of course, perfectly acceptable in Comanche society. The practice was limited somewhat by the well entrenched opinion that the amount of bickering and feuding within a family was directly proportionate to the number of wives. Mainly, however, the practice was limited by economic factors. The father of a bride could command a payment of at least five ponies for almost any daughter. And a daughter like Purple Flower would bring many more. As a matter of fact, Hail Face had paid fifteen ponies for Purple Flower. And with the near starvation times that the Comanches had endured for the last three years, he and Chief Quanah were probably the only two braves who could have afforded to pay fifteen ponies for a wife.

Hail Face was a has been medicine man. Five years ago Chief Quanah had stripped him of his credentials and knocked him from his lofty position because his medicine was no good. He was old and wrinkled now, too old to fight but too young to die and still rich in ponies and blankets from his days as a medicine man. Sour and disgruntled, he spent his days with the women and children and amused himself by beating his four wives.

Eagle Feather and Purple Flower had been lovers for over a year, but they had been careful to cover their tracks. The tribal laws concerning adultery were not to be taken lightly. The aggrieved husband represented both himself and the tribal society in exacting punishment for adultery. Eagle Feather rolled over in his mind the probable consequences if he and Purple Flower were caught in an embrace. As to his young wife,

Hail Face would cut off the end of her nose and quite possibly notch her ears and cut her hair to the scalp. Maybe he would keep her in his camp, maybe not. As to Eagle Feather, Hail Face would undoubtedly exact the maximum damages of ten ponies. If Eagle Feather refused to come to terms, it would be up the Hail Face and his friends or paid representatives to whip Eagle Feather into submission.

Reaching his own tepee, Eagle Feather released the tired pony from the travios and sent him off the graze. Then he moved the cedar chest into his tepee. Quanah had told him that he was to protect it with his life. He was tired but could not rest. Purple Flower's bruised face kept passing before his mind's eye. Finally he hit upon a plan to save his lover, and it was only then that he passed into a deep sleep.

In keeping with his plan, Eagle Feather went directly to Hail Face's camp the next morning. And, with dogs barking and women and children buzzing and pointing with surprise and excitement, he boldly walked up to Purple Flower, kissed her on the mouth and took her by the hands. Still holding one of her hands, he gently pushed her behind him as he approached her husband, sitting by the camp fire.

Looking steadily into Hail Face's scowling, pox marked face, he began stating his case with a simple confession. "Your wife, Purple Flower, and I are lovers. We have committed adultery."

The old man's eyes bugged out with anger and astonishment as he gained his feet. Swiftly he reached for his wife, but Eagle Feather defeated him by simply taking a couple of steps backwards-- pushing Purple Flower with him.

"You will pay ten ponies," the old medicine man angrily announced.

"That I will do".

"And, you will deliver them today."

"That I will," Eagle Feather agreed.

"And, you will hand my wife back to me so that I can punish her.

"No."

"Yes," Hail Face insisted. "You will give me ten ponies. I will keep my wife, and I will punish her as I see fit." He paused to put a crooked smile on his face. "This is the law of the Comanches."

"I will pay the ten ponies. But you will not mutilate your wife, and I will keep her."

Hail Face was furious. "That is against our tribal laws," he roared.

Looking around, Eagle Feather saw that the unusual confrontation had drawn a huge crowd, including Chief Parker. He was a bit unnerved, but due to careful planning he was able to want continue the debate in icy calm tones. "It is also a part of the law that if the guilty brave will not come to terms with the husband, then the husband or his friends or some paid warrior can beat him into submission or kill him."

Hail Face's only response was a furious glare.

"And so", Eagle Feather concluded, "I will take Purple Flower to my tepee, and I will wait for you or your friends or your paid warrior to come to me."

And with that, he turned and started away, gently pulling Purple Flower after him. It was at this point that Quanah Parker intervened with a stern announcement: "If this matter has not been settled before the sun goes down, there will be a council.

Taking Purple Flower with him, Eagle Flower moved in a daze to his own tepee. What did Quanah mean when he said, "If this matter is not settled." What does settled mean to the Chief? He was fearful that the clever Chief had seen to the end of his plan. As he played that plan out in his mind, he saw no friends coming to Hail Face's aid. As far as he know, the old man had no friends. Also, since he, Eagle Feather, was probably the strongest, best warrior left in the tribe, it was unlikely that Hail Face would be able to hire a warrior to help him. And even if such a warrior were to appear, Eagle Feather was confident of his ability to defeat him. Thus, as played out in his mind, the plan was a perfect one. He would satisfy the tribal laws and still have Purple Flower for his own. But had he overlooked something? He wondered.

About an hour before Quanah's deadline, a messenger came from Hail Face. "You do not have to pay the ponies, but you must send Purple Flower back," the messenger said.

"Tell him I said No," Eagle Feather replied.

When the messenger turned to got Eagle Feather allowed a grim smile to flick the corners of his mouth. The offer revealed the old man's weakness. As he had predicated, nobody appeared on behalf of the aggrieved husband. And after the sun dipped out of sights he allowed himself a short sigh of relief. However, there still hovered in his guts a bit of anxiety, vague but gnawing.

Even now the tribe was moving to the center council area. Eagle Feather took Purple Flower's hand. They must go and play out the last scene in their little drama which the whole tribe had been following with fascination. It was easily the most exciting thing that had happened in many moons. Quanah had announced that there would be a "council". The word was a misnomer. Now, "council" simple meant that the tribe would come together to hear instructions from the Chief. Six months ago, with the tribe on the verge of extinction, the Chief had seized emergency powers. The two surviving members of the seven-man council which formerly ruled the tribe would be present at the meetings, but they would not be consulted. Quanah Parker would dictate the proceedings and results of the council. Thus, the holding of a "council" was nothing more than the now dictator paying lip service to an old custom.

The Chief motioned for Eagle Feather and Purple Flower to stand before him. The warriors crowded around them, leaving the women and children on the outside of the circle. The Chief signaled for silence. His face was stern, his lips tight, it was clear to all that he did not want to do whatever it was that he was going to do.

Quanah spoke in a loud, clear voice. It was easy for those at the rear to hear. "On this day our usual law on adultery has not worked justice," he observed. "For the good of the tribe, for the good of our children, I will not allow this adulterous woman to go unpunished. Likewise, I will not allow a young warrior to force an old warrior to give up a wife in exchange for ponies, that and nothing more. Therefore," he continued, gazing directly at the adulterous couple, "I will impose upon you an ancient rule of the Comanches. We have not used it recently, but our fathers used it often. Both of you are here and now banished from this tribe forever. You will leave this camp at daybreak and never return. You will take two blankets and two ponies. Nothing more," And, with that, the Chief turned and walked away.

Purple Flower gasped and started to wail and cry. Eagle Feather was thunder-struck. He was addled as if he had been struck between the eyes with a tomahawk. When his head cleared, he was angry. Banishment was the most embarrassing, the most cruel of all punishments. In many cases, especially now with game being so scarce, it meant slow death. Eyes wild, Eagle Feather turned in a full circle shouting over and over, "It is not fair."

But his words fell on deaf ears. The others, following the example of their Chief, were already heading back to their tepees. Whatever their individual convictions might be, they were in no mood to question Quanah's decision. It was too firm, too final.

"But I never heard of banishment for adultery," Eagle Feather angrily screamed.

There was no response. And the two lovers were left alone in the council circle. After a few moments of silence, they walked slowly to Eagle Feather's tepee. When they entered it, Eagle Feather said, "Our lives will probably now be short, but they will be full and good."

She smiled and nodded.

A couple of hours later Eagle Feather went out and caught his best two ponies, placed rope halters on them and tied them to a cedar tree just outside his tepees. At first light, he and his beloved would be able to quickly depart.

Chapter Ten

On that same morning, just at the crack of dawn, Col. Ronald Mackenzie arrived at the rim of the Palo Duro. He had ridden all night, leading a column of some 550 mounted soldiers. When he peered into the great canyon, he grunted with satisfaction. His now allies, the Comancheros, had not misled him. Here was the main camp of the Comanches which he had so eagerly sought.

Quickly and quietly the old Indian fighter gave his orders. He pointed out that it would be necessary for each man to descend into the canyon in single file, leading his horse. The thirty-five scouts were to lead the way; and, upon completing their formation on the canyon floor, were to immediately attack. The men of "A" Company would go next, and when the company was formed, would promptly cut the Indians off from their horses and stampede the herd. The other companies would follow in alphabetical order and would join the attack just as soon as their formations were complete.

The Comanches were completely surprised. Quanah Parker had gone to sleep knowing that the main body of U. S. Calvary was camped near Tule Canyon, a long day's march away. Inexplicably, the experienced Chief had made no special preparations against the possibility of an overnight forced march. Some of the sleeping warriors were roused by sounds of the soldiers and their horses slipping down the canyon wall. However, yawning and blury eyed, they took no action until the whole camp was awakened by the sharp reports from the scout's carbines and pistols.

Uncharacteristically, the Indian camp was momentarily thrown into a state of confusion and panic amid the dive for weapons, running, screaming and whizzing of bullits. It was only a matter of a few minutes before Quanah was able to form a line of rifleman along the creek and to order a contingent of twenty-five warriors to run to the grazing horses and herd them behind the Comanche line. But he was too late. The men of Company "A" had already stampeded and taken charge of the 1400 ponies. Thus it was that the Quahadis Band of Comanches, perhaps the most skilled horsemen that the world has ever seen, was deprived of its greatest asset in battles.

Quanah Parker's disciplined line held while the women and children escaped, scaling the canyon walls. Then, covering for each other, the warriors withdrew, scrambling up and out of the canyon , almost miraculously leaving behind only four dead. However, they also left behind their tepees, their hides, their stores of food and ammunition, clothing and supplies. And most damaging of all, they had lost forever all of their precious horses without any reasonable prospects of replacing any of them.

The above assessment of the Comanche losses is not precisely accurate, however, because as the last of Quanah's warriors were escaping, two Comanche ponies were making a long assent out of the Palo Duro at its narrow northwest end. One was being ridden by Purple Flower. The other, pulling a travois, and ridden by Eagle Feather. Although he had intended to be gone at break of day, Eagle Feather, like most of his follow tribesmen, was awakened by the shots from the troopers' guns.

Automatically, he took hold of his rifle and ran towards his Chiefs tepee. Then, suddenly struck by the chilling recollection of his banishment, he stopped and retreated into a cedar thicket to observe and get his bearings. He saw the Chief form his line along the stream and saw the soldiers stampede the Indians' horses. Quickly perceiving that the Indians were in for a horrible defeat he ran back to his own tepee where Purple Flower was anxiously waiting.

"We must get out of here," he gasped, "right now. Roll up the blankets and get some corn and meat."

Quickly he untied his two ponies and lead them to the front of the tepee. There, using a rawhide rope which he pulled under the pony's neck, he lashed the blankets and deer skin pouch containing the food to the back of one of the ponies so that the bundle was positioned in front of the rider. In response to his motions, Purple Flower mounted that pony and started to move away.

As Eagle Feather was about to jump astride the other pony, his eyes fell upon the empty travois. Calling for Purple Flower to wait, he briefly paused and reviewed the battle scene again. Then with a shrug of his shoulders, he went inside the tepee brought out the cedar chest and placed it down on travois. After quickly hitching the poles of the to his pony, he jumped on the pony and let out a loud, contemptuous whoop as he nagged the pony into a gallop. Unaware of the contents of the chest, Purple Flower had a question mark on her face. But she obediently, and with a sudden rush of relief and joy, followed her lover.

By the time the sun was straight overhead, the Comanche lovers were up and away from the canyon, heading southeast through the tall grass.

"I'm very thirsty," Purple Flower announced.

Eagle Feather scowled and inwardly scolded himself for neglecting to bring any water. Looking around, he tried to remember the location of a close source of water where neither Indians nor soldiers were likely to be found. His mind stopped on a little spring located about 15 miles to the southeast. It was a place where Comanche hunting parties liked to camp. But with their horses gone, there would be no danger from hunting parties. And he doubted that the soldiers even knew the location of the spring.

Reluctantly he explained to Purple Flower that it would be best for them to hide and rest themselves and their ponies in a nearby scrub oak thicket. At nightfall they would head for the spring. He knew it was a long time to go without water, he told her; but they could make it.

Soon they were lying in the shade of the thicket with their heads resting on their rolled up blankets. Tenderly he fingered the shining braids of her jet black hair and looked into her liquid black eyes. "Don't be afraid," he softly pleaded. "We are safe here."

She smiled and emitted a low mirthless chuckle. "As safe as we ever again will be," she opined.

His face clouded and he sat upright. "That is true. We will never really be safe again. I'm sorry, I thought I was so smart, but the possibility of banishment never crossed my mind." She clutched his right arm with both hands and pulled herself into a kneeling position. Then, placing her nose against his, she emphatically spoke: "No. Do not be sorry. I'm not safe, but I am happy."

Sitting back on the calves of her legs, she took his hands in hers. "You should be happy too," she continued, "both of us have traded safety for love and freedom. Is that not a good trade?"

Without answering, he returned to the horizonal position, gently pulling her with him. She trembled a little as they lay in silence. At length he whispered, "I am happy too, very happy." Her trembling ceased, and he turned his gaze on her face just in time to see her close her eyes with a faint smile on her lips. In a moment she fell into a deep sleep. He soon followed.

For September 28th it was a warm day on the staked plains, but at sunset a chill north wind blow into the nest of the banished lovers causing them to shiver awake. They traveled all night, taking infrequent short stops to rest the ponies. It was obvious, that Eagle Feather's mount, weighted by the heavily laden travois, had grown dangerously weary, causing Eagle Feather to walk the last three or four miles of their journey.

In the first pink streaks of dawn they were rewarded by the sight of a stream of water cascading down the side of an outcropping of rocks. The spring seemed completely foreign to its surroundings. But Eagle Feather and Purple Flower had neither the time nor the inclination to contemplate the strangeness of the water's location. They were too busy drinking it and playfully splashing it into each others faces.

After watering the ponies and staking them out to graze, they rested in the shade of an ancient hackberry tree the only tree in sight. they ended their 24 hour fast, greedily consuming all of their meager supply of corn and buffalo jerky.

"That's all we have," she sighed. "I'm sorry but that was all of the food there was in the tepee."

"I know," he replied. "I must kill an animal. We must have food. "Also," he went on, holding up the now empty deer skin pouch, "we need a hide to make another water sack. This one will hold water but not enough. It is not wise for us to move from this place without a way to carry more water. And it is not wise for us to stay here for very long. The country is too open. Sooner or later the soldiers will find us."

"You are a great hunter," she proudly answered. "It will not be difficult for you."

"In normal times it would be easy," he gravely responded. "But game is scarce. I'll be lucky to find a rabbit." He paused and rubbed his chin. "I'll need your help."

"But I know nothing about hunting." she protested.

"I'll show you what to do. We will need both horses, and I need to take the travois off of mine. As a matter of fact, we need to hide that cedar chest and come back for it some day, maybe after a moon, maybe after several moons. We will never get off of these plains alive if we try to take it with us now. It is too heavy."

She shrugged. "Suits me. But why do we need to hide the chest? What is in it?"

He slapped his forehead in amazement. "You mean I have not told you what is in that chest?"

"That's right," she murmured.

"It's full of gold and silver and finger rings and beads," he excitedly shouted. "Look," he invited, lifting open the lid of the chest.

She stared with disbelief as she fingered a string of pearls. "Can I have these?"

"Of course," he replied.

Black eyes shining, she put the string of pearls around her neck and giggled with pleasure.

Reclosing the box, he wondered aloud, "Where can we hide this thing?"

In answer to his question, he walked to a large flat rock which was slightly longer and wider than the top of the chest. He dug enough earth from under one edge of it so as to allow him to take hold of it with both hands. He was delighted to discover that the rock was thin and light enough for him to lift and turn over. On the spot were the rock had rested, using his tomahawk and hunting knife as well as a sharp flat rock which served very adequately as a shovel, he and Purple Flower began to dig. In about an hour they had excavated a hole in the rocky soil big enough to accommodate the chest. They lowered the chest into the hole, covered it with dirt and then replaced the large, flat rock in its original position. Lastly, they carefully scattered the excess dirt and small rocks so as to leave the scene in almost the same condition as they had found it.

Purple Flower was mystified by Eagle Feather's next actions. He stood on the large flat rock and marched diagonally to the east side of the spot where the water carme gushing out of the rocks, counting his paces out loud. He frowned and shook his head. Then he turned and marched in the direction of the flow of the water until he was at a point perpendicular to the flat rock. Turning to his left, he then marched to the flat rock.

He explained: "We will remember always that the chest is buried under a flat rock and that you can find the rock by marching twelve paces, along the line of the flow of the water from the mouth of the spring and then turning left and marching straight for 7 more paces. Twelve and seven. Will you remember?"

"Twelve and seven," she echoed. "I will remember, Twelve and seven."

* * * * * * * *

At about the time the Indian lovers began digging, Lt. Ben Fitzgerald held up his right hand and hollered, "Halt" He was two miles north of the spring.

Dismounting, he continued, "Ten minutes break, Sergeant. Give the order."

Fitzgerald looked over his command and shook his head. He had twenty-three in his motley crew--nine who were seriously sick or wounded, one doctor and thirteen whose enlistments were almost ended and who were refusing to "reup". They were on their way, hauling the wounded in two wagons, to Fort Richardson, about 200 miles to the southeast.

After the battle in the Palo Duro, Col. Mackenzie and his troopers had returned to Tule Canyon, herding 1400 Comanche ponies before them. Upon their arrival at Tule, Mackenzie ordered that all of the Indian ponies would be forthwith destroyed. And they were. They were shot and left to rot, eventually leaving a vast expanse of bleached white bones. The Col. then broke his command into seven detachments. Six of these were sent out in different directions to seek and capture or destroy the horseless Comanches who now wandered in small bands over the vast grassy plains, vainly seeking the buffalo which had almost completely vanished from the earth.

The seventh detachment was what Mackenzie called the "sick detail", and it was given unto Lt. Fitzgerald, Mackenzie's least favorite officer, to lead them to the home base at Fort Richardson. Fitzgerald's job was lonely and loathsome. The able bodied in the detail were misfits and to a man they were sullen, undisciplined army haters.

Somewhat of an exception was Captain Collins, the doctor. He was not a pure misfit, because he loved the army. He was, however, arrogant and sullen in his attitude towards Fitzgerald and downright abusive to the enlisted men. The doctor managed, as Fitzgerald put it, "to stay not plumb drunk but just comfortably drunk" most of the time. But notwithstanding his vast consumption of alcohol, his skill and dedication as a surgeon had never been questioned. Nobody liked him, but he did his job well. So well that although his services were needed by the sick and wounded men, Mackenzie would not have allowed the doctor to return to the Fort had he not been convinced that the dehorsed Comanches now posed scant threat to his command.

"Alright, Sergeant," Fitzgerald yelled, "lets get 'em movin".

* * * * * * *

Eagle Feather and Purple Flower had been so completely engrossed burying the treasure and making plans for its recovery that they did not see Lt. Fitzgerald until he was only 200 yards away. Purpose Flower pointed and shrieked "Soldiers". Without another word, they ran to their ponies, untied them and started riding away. They were too late. Lt. Fitzgerald and his small detachment of misfits were already upon them. They had not covered more than fifty yards before the soldiers began discharging their carbines. One of the bullets struck Purple Flower at the base of her skull, knocking her off her pony and killing her instantly. Eagle Feather immediately pulled up his pony, jumped to the ground, ran to his lover and gathered her into his arms. In a matter of a few seconds he was in the middle of a tight, milling circle of mounted troopers. One of them yelled, "Want us to shoot him, sir?"

"No," Fitzgerald shouted, "don't shoot. Our orders are to capture 'em instead of killin 'em if we can do it safely." With surprise and wonder, he paused to contemplate this scene of a Comanche brave wailing with grief over the loss of a squaw. It had never crossed his mind that an Indian warrior could harbor such emotions, much less that he would display them. "This one sure don't look like much of a threat," he opined aloud. "We'll take him to the Fort, and the powers that be can send him on to the reservation at Fort Sill."

Later, when Sgt. Bean tapped him on the shoulder and beckoned for him to follow, Eagle Feather immediately obeyed without the slightest offer of resistance. Two minutes later his whole demeanor changed. He was peacefully standing beside the mounted Sgt. when Lt. Fitzgerald gave the command to move out. When Eagle Feather realized that they were leaving the body of his lover to rot or be consumed by buzzards and wolves, he shrieked with anguish and anger as he ran to her body. Kneeling, he hugged her close and with eyes blazing seemed to dare the soldiers to do anything about it. At Fitzgerald's order, they accepted the dare. Three of them broke his hold on Purple Flower and pulled him, kicking and wailing, back to the side of the Sgt.'s horse. There, the noose of a rope was put around his neck, with the other end being tied to the Sgt.'s saddle.

"What's eatin him?" The Lt. wanted to know.

Dr. Collins answered the question. "I've been out here long enough to know that's troubling him. He wants to bury his squaw up high and cover her with grass and bushes so that the wolves and buzzards won't get her. That's the Comanche way."

Fitzgerald spat on the ground. "Well, I saved his life, but I ain't got time for him to go through some pagan burial ceremony."

"Yes, I see your point," the doctor replied. "But before we pull out, I'm wondering if you will let me have charge of the Indian. I could sure use him to carry wood and water and help me with the wounded."

"You really think you can tame him enough to get some work out of him?"

The doctor's eyes turned hard. "I think I know how."

"Alright, he's yours."

Sgt. Bean gratefully surrendered the rope to Collins who tied the and of it to his own saddle. And for the rest of that day the proud Comanche warrior, with a noose around his neck, walked and trotted behind the doctor's big black horse. During most of the next twenty days, Eagle Feather was allowed to walk along without the noose around his neck, and sometimes he was allowed to ride on one of the wagons. Dr. Collins set out to break the Indian much as he would undertake to break a stubborn, wild mustang. Collins punished with the noose and by withholding food and water. He rewarded with extra water and food freedom from the noose and rides on a wagon. And long before they reached Fort Richardson, Collins enjoyed complete success. The spirit of the lonely, grieving, once proud warrior was completely broken. He went about like a freshly whipped dog, with scared eyes and bowed head, instantly executing the doctor's commands without a murmur. The doctor had himself a slave.

Many times after supper the doctor amused himself by conversing with Eagle Feather. Putting his scant knowledge of Comanche with Eagle Feather's scant knowledge of English, and generously supplementing with hand signs and pictures drawn in the dirt, they communicated surprisingly well. Collins learned much about the Comanche life and customs. He also, as a sort of bonus, found out that Eagle Feather had been banished from his tribe and that if he were to be delivered into the company of his fellow Comanches on the reservation at Fort Sill, he would most certainly be killed.

Shortly after arriving at Fort Richardson, Collins went to the Fort's Commander. Placing before him the fact of Eagle Feather's banishment and his plight upon delivery to Fort Sill, Collins asked that Eagle Feather be spared and volunteered to hire him as a servant and "look after him."

The careful Commander granted the doctor's request only after receiving Eagle Feather's "hang dog" assurance that the arrangement was satisfactory to him. Slavery had been abolished in this nation for almost ten years, but Eagle Feather didn't know it; and the doctor conveniently and contemptuously ignored it.

Being careful to refer to the Indian as his servant rather than his slave, Collins established Eagle Feather in a small, one-room "servant's quarters" behind his own quarters. And in exchange for being treated much like a mule, Eagle Feather worked from morning until night, seven days a week, cooking, chopping wood, washing clothes, cleaning house, milking the cow, taking care of the horses and driving the doctor to and fro in his fine buggy.

When Collins retired from the army in 1884, he moved into the town of Jacksboro where he practiced medicine and continued his slavery arrangement with Eagle Feather. Year after year, there was little change in the Indian's numb, dull-eyed existence. Then 65 years old, Eagle Feather, horribly bent and wrinkled, had the appearance of one much more ancient.

Preacher Applegate, who preached the doctor's funeral, took note of Eagle Feather and wondered what would become of him. Upon inquiry, he quickly ascertained that the Indian had thrown up his hands and stoically concluded that he too would soon die. He had nowhere to go, nothing to do, nobody to take care of him. Barely retaining the instinct to live, he was too numb to be very frightened.

Characteristically the Preacher befriended him, restored his spirit and in a very real way brought the old Indian back to life. Applegate not only saw to Eagle Feather's physical needs, he gave him loving companionship and dignity. Eagle Feather all but worshiped the Preacher; and, correctly perceiving that he was in his last days, told Applegate the story of Purple Flower and the buried treasure. Applegate went over the location of the cedar chest several times with the old warrior; and, with his own knowledge of the territory involved, was able to draw the map which he carried in his saddle bag.

The map was important to the old Preacher. In his own mind it constituted a kind of muniment of title to the treasure. And now that he had determined by his own yet secret devices to acquire heirs, the map became even more precious.

Chapter Eleven

Early on the morning after the rain storm, Applegate and his companions rode into Mesa. For many years the sleepy little trading center had consisted of nothing more than a general store, a saloon and a small school house which doubled as a church. But when the railroad came in April of last year, the place went boom. Already there were six more store buildings and an equal number of half-tents, all carrying on a brisk retail business of one kind or another.

With a few exceptions, the mostly male townspeople were living in the dozens of tents which were pitched along both sides of the only street in town. The place was a huge pot, boiling with men and horses, buggies and wagons. The air was filled with the raw, robust sounds that men make when they are rushing to build a town-- hammering and sawing, yelling and laughing.

"Don't look like the Mesa I've always known," the Preacher commented, "looks like a bunch of ants gettin ready for winter."

After the three travelers had traversed the whole of the town, from the train depot on the south to the livery stable on the north, they back tracked to the new barber shop and hitched their horses.

The barber greeted them eagerly. "Come in, Gents. What'll it be?"

"How much do you charge?" Applegate wanted to know.

"Two bits for a hair cut, two bits for a shave and a dollar for the whole thing."

"What's the whole thing?"

"Haircut, shave, bath and clothes washed."

"That's awful high," George broke in, "but at least we don't need the whole thing. We bathed and washed our clothes in Turkey Creek not more than four days ago. Me and my boy will take a shave and haircut though."

"Just a haircut for me," said the Preacher.

As the freshly shorn men came out of the barber shop, George pointed to a board nailed above the door of a wooden structure covered with a gently flapping canvas roof. The board bore crude black letters spelling "CAFE". "Lets go in there and get some grub," he suggested.

"I ain't goin in there," the Preacher snorted. "They're doin highway robbery without a gun. I can tell you that right now--without the trouble of goin in."

"What do you mean?"

"They'll be chargin boom town prices. That's what; just like the barber. And I'll bet I can out cook whoever is doin the cookin in there."

"Well, it won't hurt to find out for sure," George argued, ducking into the cafe.

He returned with a red face. "They want fifty cents for a plate of ham and eggs," he fumed. "I'm not about to pay that."

Applegate laughed. "Well, I......".

His sentence was interrupted by the shrill whistle of a train. Puffing into town, it so charged the air with excitement that at least half of the populace dropped what they were doing and flocked to the depot to watch it unload. Among other things, the train disgorged about two dozen lean and hungry looking men, each clutching an old suitcase or a paste board box bound with rope. They immediately began mingling with the crowd, asking about work.

The old Preacher flashed a knowing smile. At least you won't have near this much competition for a job at the ranch."

"Can we make it on to the ranch today?" George asked.

"Yeah, but it would be late and we'd be awful tired. Why don't we rest up a little and bed down early under some cottonwood trees that I know about just north of town. Then we can get there tomorrow, all bright eyed and bushy tailed."

The Renfros went along with the Preacher's suggestion, and the rising sun found them clopping along the narrow road running due north from Mesa.

"We're now about two miles from Mesa," the Preacher noted. "We're riding through Dundee's south pasture and right now We're riding right along the west line of the Armstrong Section--your land."

The Renfros reined in their horses and enjoyed a long, fond look at their land.

Applegate smiled and pointed. "See that little hill out there. You can mark it by the lonesome hackberry tree. It's right close to the middle of your north line. It's hard to believe but on the west side of it there's an ever flowing spring."

"How much water does it put out?"

"Oh, I don't remember real well, but I'd say eight or ten times the flow of an ordinary windmill. It flows on down into that little lake which you can barely see from here. George feasted his eyes on the hundreds of acres of high grass which gently sloped away from the hill. "That ought to be more than plenty of water for us."

"Yeah," the Preacher agreed, that's just one of the good reasons why you should be real careful about moving on that land. Dundee carries a big stick around here, and it ain't likely that He'll give up that water without a great big fight."

George and Royal looked at each other. Their eyes glitted at the challenge. "We'll see. We'll see, "George grimly responded.

Without warning, Royal suddenly flicked the reins against the rump of his horse and headed towards the hill. Applegate quickly whistled, causing the boy to look back. Applegate emphatically motioned for him to stop and return. With a big show of reluctance, Royal wheeled his horse around and came trotting back.

"What's the matter? George demanded. "He just wants to see the spring. So do I."

The Preacher had authority in his voice. "It's not a good idea. Somebody might see you. And believe you me word of us paying special attention to the spring would get back to Dundee. And sure as the world he would want to know why. Besides that, we don't have time right now. We need to get on to the ranch and get settled in."

"OK," George unhappily muttered, "I guess you know best."

Two miles further they came to the big corner post standing at the west end of the fence which split the Dundee Ranch in half. Looking along the fence, they say a lone rider racing towards them at a gallop.

"Hey," the rider shouted, "that's you ain't it, Preacher."

"Yes," the Preacher shouted back, "and who might you be?"

Coming closer, the rider dismounted an jerked off his hat. "This here is Happy Boswell. You remember me, don't you, Preacher?"

"Oh, sure do, Happy."

Applegate was telling the truth. Nobody who had ever known Happy Boswell had ever forgottin him. Standing before them, his tight fitting jeans tucked into knee-high, black boots, served to draw the boundaries of the remarkably huge space between his short, bowed legs. Now fifty, his thinning orange hair was flecked with gray. Red rimmed, watery blue eyes were set in a face which was eternally blistering and peeling.

Completing his memorable appearance where the corners of his mouth, always heavily marked with dark brown ozings from his ever present "chow" of tobacco.

However, it was not Happy's physical markings which most caused him to be remembered. It was his attitude, a turn of mind which long ago had given him his nickname. He went out of his way to find silver linings, to point out rainbows.

"How've you been Happy?"

"Jest right down marvelous, uh, well except, well, let me put it like this: the chuck is gonna get even better now that you're here."

After meeting and greeting the Renfros, Happy swung back into his saddle. "Here it is Saturday noon. I should already be back at the house gettin washed up to go to town. I'll run this horse back to the barn and spread the good news about you bein here. See you after while."

Happy turned his horse to leave, then turned back to face the Preacher. "I forgot to tell you. You're in for a little excitement right out of the chute. We're goin off on a chuck wagon trip to get some new cows. Supposed to take about three weeks to get 'em rounded up and herded home."

"Where we goin?"

"Up to the SOQ," Happy replied. "Gettin a thousand mothers with calves at their sides."

"My, my, Mr. Dundee must be real low on cattle."

"Nope," Happy emphatically replied. "Not low at all. As a matter of fact, he probably has too many now."

"Well, then, why more?"

"Search me. I'm sure it's all gonna work out fine and dandy. I just haven't got it all figured out yet."

Happy smiled and then waved and rode off in a run.

Applegate chuckled. "Now there's a man whose mother must have swallowed a blue bird right before he was born."

A short while later, George pointed into the distance and omitted a low whistle to express his awe. "Man, look at that."

He was pointing at the Dundee mansion. "Is that Dundee's house?"

"You guessed it. Everybody calls it the "Big House."

Looking alternately from his wide eyed secret heirs to the big house on the hill, Applegate's back bone was visited by a thousand tiny pen pricks, and his arm pits were suddenly hot and wet. He was taken aback by the dark, foreboding question which flashed across his mind. Was he leading his family into the very jaws of a hell on this earth? He wondered, but he kept his doubts to himself; and he never swerved from his original resolve. They were being drawn, he thought. God meant for them to go to Dundee. And they would go. For better or worse they would go.

The so called main gate to the Dundee Ranch was massive stone arch. Across the top, written in black wrought iron were the letters spelling the single word: "DUNDEE". The gate was a so called one because it stood alone, miles from any wall or fence. You could freely pass on either side of it. Nevertheless, it was impressive, forming the entrance to the quarter mile of road which led from the main north and south road up the front of Big House.

The three newcomers were pleased to note that Happy Boswell had spread the news of their arrival. They were greeted at the gate by all of the cowboys. At times they were like overgrown children, and this was one of those times. Gently spurring their horses, they whooped and hollered as they escorted new cook and his companions to the front of the mansion.

Smiling with pleasure, the Preacher hollered, "I feel like visiting royalty."

"Hey, we'd never treat royalty like this," Happy yelled, "just good cooks."

When they stopped in front of Big House, the laughing and yelling gave way to a quietness, broken only by the squeaking and cracking of leather as the men, with a touch of nervousness, shifted around in their saddles. Flanked by his wife and daughter, Amos Dundee stood on his veranda. With arms folded he stood like a king awaiting the respectful approach of his subjects. And that is exactly what the newcomers did. They dismounted and walked to the steps of the veranda. As they did so, Feister, Mary and Jane, who had been approaching in response to the cowboys' yelling, stopped and stood beside the cowboys.

The Preacher pulled off his hat. "Afternoon, Mr. Dundee, Mrs. Dundee, Miss Dundee."

"Afternoon, Applegate," Dundee stiffly replied. "Welcome back to Dundee."

"Thank you, Sir. Pointing to George, the Preacher continued, "Now, I'd like to make known to you my friend, George Renfro, and....."

Nora, who was devouring Royal with her eyes, couldn't wait for the Preacher to finish. "And who are you?" she saucily inquired through puckered lips.

"Why this young fella is......," the Preacher began.

"Now, Preacher, Nora sternly interrupted, "I want to hear it from him. And who are you?" she purred, looking straight at Royal.

"I'm sorry, Miss, but....", the Preacher began.

Nora peevishly began to protest: "Preacher.........".

"Daughter, let the Preacher speak," Dundee commanded.

"The fact is that this young man is not able at the moment to speak for himself. He has been struck dumb. We have high hopes that his affliction is not a permanent one, but at least for now, he can't talk."

Nora flushed and curled her upper lip in disgust. "You mean he's a dummy?"

Applegate ignored the question while shooting little Nora with a hard stare. "Anyway, he's a fine boy, and his name is Royal Renfro.

And, by the way Mr. Dundee, I'd like to talk to you about jobs for George and Royal before the day is done. George is a carpenter."

"Alright, come to my office in a couple of hours."

"Yes, Sir."

"And bring them with you."

"Yes, Sir."

Applegate took his leave filled with a wad of disgust, but only half of it came from snooty little Nora. The other half was generated by her mother. The old man knew lust when he saw it, and he saw it in Bertha's eyes when she looked at George. He shook his head. It occurred to him that things were getting a little more complicated than he had anticipated.

As a matter of fact, the brew was already more bubbly that even he realized. Not knowing that Slim Feister had up a case with Bertha, he had no reason to suspect that in Feister's mind the plain passion in Bertha's gaze at George served to mark him as a competitor for her affections. So the Preacher was surprised when Feister later privately accosted him and growled, "Why did you bring those other two with you? They don't look like cowboys to me. They look more like farmers."

"Well, they're not cowboys," Applegate admitted. "Even so, I'm surprised you wouldn't want all the help you could get."

"I just want good help. Didn't you hear me tell the boss that George is a carpenter?"

"We don't need no carpenter."

Applegate frowned his disbelief. "You

could've talked all day without sayin that. It's easy for anybody to see that a big outfit like this always needs a good carpenter."

"We've been gettin along just fine without one," Feister retorted as he turned and walked away.

It was more than an hour before the appointed time for the Preacher's meeting with Dundee, but he was convinced that Feister would try to beat him to the boss and block George out of a job. Running to the bunkhouse, he stuck his head in and yelled to the Renfros, "Quick, boys, come with me."

"What's up?" asked George as he and Royal trailed after the fast stepping old man.

"We're goin to see Dundee."

"But We're more than an hour early."

"Yeah," Applegate agreed as he glanced back and saw Feister come out of the foreman's house. "We're early, but not a minute too soon."

"What are you talking about?"

"I'll explain later," the Preacher promised.

If the Preacher had taken the time he would have probably guessed that he had already gotten help from within the walls of Big House which rendered unnecessary his breathless approach. Bertha had already exacted her husband's promise to hire "the carpenter". She had impressed upon Dundee her pressing need for a new kitchen cabinet, more shelves in several closets and, as she put it, "I just don't know what all else."

Dundee scowled as the Preacher and his companions entered his office. "You're early," he growled. Glancing at the giant grandfather clock setting against he wall on his left, the Preacher said, "My goodness, it does appear that We're a little early. Sorry, Sir."

"Well, might as well come on in," Dundee grunted.

The Renfros' mouths fell open with undisguised awe. Their experience in offices, having been limited to those in the County Court House of Van Zant County, Texas, did not prepare them for this. Dundee was sitting in a large leather covered judge's chair behind a massive mahogany desk. His backdrop was a life sized portrait of a man with arms folded, looking into the distance. The other walls were decorated with oil paintings of various scenes on the ranch. Also serving as a reminder that the office was a ranch, several steer hide rugs were scattered over the glossy oak floor. Each of the six overstuffed leather chairs was flanked on one side by an elegant mahogany ash tray and on the other by a brightly shining copper spittoon.

Dundee gestured for them to take a chair; and they did so, gingerly, almost reverently.

The Preacher pointed at the portrait. "That's your father, right?"

"Yes."

"The man who started all this, right?"

Dundee stiffened and then took a quick puff on his enormous black cigar. "Yes," he slowly replied, but I'm the one who is making it bigger."

"Yes, Sir. Indeed. Well, uh, I just wanted you to get to know my friends here and let me recommend them to you. As I said, George here is a carpenter."

Dundee interrupted. Looking at Royal, he asked, "And what are you, boy?"

Royal opened his mouth, but nothing came out.

"Oh, I forgot, you can't talk."

"Yeah," Applegate went on, "he can't talk, but he's bright."

"He doesn't look like a cowboy."

"He's not, but he can learn, and he already has an outfit." Applegate rushed on. "And while he's learning he can be a carpenter's helper and also be my helper."

Dundee gave his consent by saying, "The boy'll get half wages."

"That's fine," George responded. "We appreciate it."

The Preacher got to his feet. "It's all settled then. Thank you, Mr. Dundee. You won't be sorry. George'll stay here, but I'll take Royal with me on the chuck wagon in the morning. I'll make him into a pretty good cook before we get back."

Dundee flushed. It struck him that this preacher was getting a little too uppity, saying who would go and who would stay.

"Sit back down, Preacher," the Baron curtly commanded.

The hair on the back of Applegate's neck stood on end, and he opened his mouth to declare that he didn't want to work for Dundee after all. But then, like many a parent who swallows pride for the benefit of his children, he soundlessly sat back down.

"George will stay here. You got that much right, Preacher. My wife has already lined up several projects for him, including a new kitchen cabinet. And the boy will stay here too and help his Daddy."

"But...." the Preacher started. But Dundee's icy stare stilled the embryo protest. Then to make the abortion sure, the boss added, "And that's the way it will be."

The Preacher's nostrils were pinched above a white upper lip, but he managed a cheerful little smile. "Of course, Mr. Dundee, whatever you say. Whatever you say."

As they strolled back to the bunkhouse, George said, "I'm not sure We're doin the right thing. It wasn't so much what he did or what he said. It was the way he said it and the way he did it that got under my skin. Got under you skin too didn't it?"

"I gotta admit that, the Preacher replied, "but we won't have to mess with him for long, Son. Not for long."

Meanwhile, in the foreman's house, Jane seized upon the recent scene at the veranda to remind her mother of Slim's infidelity. "Looks like your husband is going to have a little competition," she endured. "Of course, since Nora is leaving for St. Louis tomorrow, Bertha will probably be wild enough to take on both of them."

"I'm not going to claim I don't know what you're talking about," Mary retorted. "But I'll remind you that everything you saw came from

Bertha. Slim did nothing. Anyway," she rushed on, "enough of that. Lets talk about you."

"Why me?"

Mary smiled knowingly. That boy can't talk with his tongue, but there's nothing wrong with his eyes. And when he turns them towards you, they say, 'I want you'."

"Oh, for Pete's sake."

Mary laughed. "You noticed it too." she accused. "You stayed in a continuous blush."

"Really? Did it show that much?"

"Yes, Dear, it showed."

"Well," Jane replied, "you don't seem to be upset. As a matter of fact, you seem to be enjoying the idea that Royal and I might be drawn to each other. Why so? What makes him any different from these cowboys who you think are not good enough for your darling daughter? After all, he's just a farmer boy, and he can't even talk."

Mary, serious now, thoughtfully pondered her answer. "I can't give you a logical answer, 'I just have a feeling in my bones'. I have a feeling that he is something very special." Her voice fell to a whisper. "Strange, but it's much like the feeling I have about your Daddy."

Jane closed her eyes and took a deep breath. "Yeah, I agree," she dreamily murmured. But before the mother and daughter could continue their conversation on romance, they heard the familiar clopping of Slim Feister's boots on the entry porch.

Jane gave a resigned shrug. "Oh, well," it's time for me to go milking anyway."

Grabbing the bucket by its bail, she brushed past her step-father without a word.

In a bunkhouse not far away, the Preacher was looking out the window of his private room. The shadows were finally falling on the long June day. It was a good time for him to meditate. And he was thankful he could be alone for awhile. His cook's room afforded him a privacy unknown to the cowboys whose bunks were side by side in one big rom. The cook was obliged to get up at least an hour before everybody else, and he was also obliged to sleep an hour earlier. In recognition of these facts, the cook was given a small room at one end of the bunkhouse. It was separated form the big room by a partition and a door that could be bolted from the inside. It also had a private outside entrance.

Applegate's meditations were troubled. He was feeling a responsibility that he had never known before. During all those years on the Texas Plains he had experienced a general responsibility for all the lost souls who needed to hear the gospel. But he had never before had any family responsibilities. It's different, he thought, as he rubbed his left arm. Being a family man had brought new joys, but they were accompanied by strange new worries. He wondered if the unfamiliar tingling in his left arm was in some way connected to his new found stress.

It was Bertha who troubled the old man. He had known for many years that she was a selfish, haughty woman; but he never dreamed that she might cause him any personal misery.

This afternoon, though, he realized in a flash that she could cause him pain because she was clearly enamored with his son. The woman was dangerous, and she could foul up every dream that he had for his son and grandson. Suddenly he grinned. I'll just stop her before she can get untracked, he thought.

Unbolting the door, he caught George's eye and signaled him to come on back.

"Hey, this is a nice room you got here."

"Yeah, that's one advantage they give to the cook. Sit down, George."

George sat in one of the cane bottomed chairs. "What's up?"

"First, I notice Royal has started writing notes. He never did that on the trail. How come?"

"Yeah, I don't know. I could never get him to write, but when he got here, he started writing notes to the cowboys. I take it as a good sign.

"Oh, yeah, I like it too. It'll help me communicate with him. I'm gonna get to the bottom of his trouble if it takes the rest of my life. I wish I didn't have to go and be away from him for three weeks. Speaking of that and gettin down to the main reason I called you in here, I just wanted to offer you a little advice. I wanted to warn you about some things."

"I'm listenin."

"Well," Applegate rambled on, "the truth is I just wanted to warn you about one thing. Now I'm not near as smart as I'd like to be, especially now that I have..uh, anyway I'm not near as learned as I'd like to be. About all I ever read is the Bible, but then of course..."

George cut in. "Seems like you're havin a hard time gettin down to it. It must be somethin pretty bad."

The Preacher cocked his head to his right and squinted his left eye at George. "Did you see how that woman made eyes at you?"

"What are you talkin about?" George innocently inquired.

"You know what I'm talkin about."

George's answer was a little hot. "No I don't," he insisted.

The Preacher was skeptical until it suddenly dawned on him that this unworldly East Texas farmer, who was still grieving for his lost wife, was telling the truth. He was probably the only one facing Bertha who missed her point. "I'm talkin about Bertha Dundee."

"Oh, yes, very handsome woman."

The Preacher moaned. "Well, that little observation doesn't help matters," he dryly muttered.

Aware now of the Preacher's suspicions, George protested: "But she wasn't paying me any special attention--not that I noticed. Besides that, what if she did, it means nothing to me. She is married, and I not interested in any woman. After all my wife has only been dead for a couple of months."

"You had a good marriage didn't you?"

"The very best."

"That makes for a dangerous situation," the Preacher opined. "Widowers that come from good marriages are the most likely to fall into a bad woman's trap. I've seem it over an over."

"Come on, Preacher, I'm a grown man, 43 years old. You don't have to worry about me."

"You still worry about Royal don't you?" the old man countered. "And you'll worry about him when he is 43 won't you?"

"Sure, but he is my son. That makes a difference."

"Yeah, yeah it sure does. Anyhow, I've got that Bertha sized up as a dark cloud with lots of thunder and lightning which produces floods of tears.

The old man began to walk the floor and preach. "I tell you she is no Mary. She is no Ruth. She is no Marian. I'll tell you who she is. She is Eve. She is Potiphifer's wife. She is Jezebel. She is...."

"Hold on, Preacher. You're gettin way yonder too upset. I don't know a lot about any of those women. But I think I get your point. You think if I fool with Mrs. Dundee, I'm gonna get burned."

"Well, yes; but that's not my main concern. The big problem is not you fooling with her but her fooling with you. You're liable to get burned either way. In other words, if you let her fool with you, you'll get burned; and if you don't let her fool with you, she will still burn you. Joseph got burned that way you know."

"No, I don't know much about Joseph. But I can handle myself. Quit worrin."

"OK, but stay as far away from that woman

as you can. Hear me?"

George smiled and put his right hand on the old man's shoulder. "Thanks, Dad. Now get on that bunk and get some sleep. I want a good breakfast."

When George shut the door, the old man laid back on his bunk and closed his eyes. Suddenly he bolted upright. "What did he call me?" he whispered aloud. Then he fell back again, plopped his head on his pillow and went to sleep with a smile on his face.

Chapter Twelve

Amos Dundee and his foreman joined the cowboys for breakfast before hitting the trail. Glancing at the upcoming meal, the big boss gave out a rare smile. "Man, that looks good. This gonna be one trail drive that I'm gonna enjoy."

The meal was even better than it looked. Applegate had strutted his stuff, putting out broiled T-bone steaks, sourdough biscuits, thick milk gravy and stewed peaches. Of course, there was plenty of strong coffee to wash it down. For a climactic closing, the Preacher instructed them to split one more biscuit. Then he passed among them and generously ladled on each biscuit a thick syrupy concoction which he called "a Little Heaven". It was nothing but sugar and eggs mixed with some condensed milk and brought to a rolling boil. Nevertheless, the cowboys thought it was aptly named, and they swung into their saddles with full stomachs and light hearts.

Applegate had hitched his team to the chuck wagon before he routed the cowboys out of bed. So now, working quickly, he loaded his gear onto the wagon and was ready to pull out with the others. The big boss led the way, and the chuck wagon brought up the rear.

Royal pulled a little note pad from his shirt pocket and wrote a note to his father: "I wish we were going."

"Yeah, me too. But We'll make the best of it. We've got to get on up to Big House now and see what Mrs. Dundee wants us to do."

Royal shot a knowing glance at his father and wrote another note: "Think I know what she wants you to do."

George blushed. "You sound like the Preacher."

Note: "Oh, he saw it too?"

"Yeah, he saw it," George dryly replied. "I think there are some imaginations running wild around here. When we meet with her, I'll bet you change your mind. Come on. Let's go."

Royal shook his head and pointed to the barn.

"You need to see about our horses?"

Royal nodded.

"You're right, but come on up as soon as possible."

It's down right silly, George thought as he walked to Big House. That rich lady would be as likely to take a shine to a dirt farmer like me as she would to a fence post. And as for me, he continued, I'm certainly not interested in any woman, much less my neighbor's wife. Anyway, his mind raced on, if I wanted to get mixed up in a mess like that I'd choose that sad-eyed woman, Mary, the foreman's wife. Feeling a pang of guilt because of the direction his musings were taking, he shook his head and was relieved when his mental wanderings were chased away by the sounds of his heavy brogans on the steps of the veranda.

Earlier that morning a rented hack from the livery stable in Mesa had picked up Nora and all her baggage for the trip to St. Louis. With her daughter out of the way, Bertha Dundee had been waiting for George. Obscured by the screen door, she had watched him from the time he left the bunk house. She pushed open the door. "Do come in, George."

Entering, George pulled off his hat and muttered, "Thank you, mam, I've come to see about those closet shelves. If you have time, I just hoped you'd tell me what you want."

Smiling and puckering her lips, she extended her left hand and lightly gripped his right arm. "Oh," she provocatively whispered, "do you really want me to tell you what I want from you?"

It was not a very subtle question, but Bertha was in a hurry, and she had concluded that this physically attractive man was, after all, a clod hoper who would not understand subtleties. Somewhat betrayed by the red roses which shot into his cheeks, George's reply managed to manfully ignore the question's plain implication. "Yes, mam. Shelves can be all sizes, and I just want to make 'em like you want 'em."

Bertha disengaged her hand from his arm

but let her eyes continue to smile at him. Her instincts quickly taught her that this farmer was not stupid and that he would be much harder to get than she had imagined. "Of course," she replied, giving him a limp wristed wave, "I want to describe the shelves for you, but I just can't do it before I have my coffee. Come on back to the kitchen. We'll have some coffee, and I'll tell you all about it."

The invitation scared George. Where is Royal? he fumed to himself. He's taking too long with those horses. His frustration was thankfully ended by the soft rap on the front door facing. "Ah, it's you, Royal," he said with ill disguised relief," come on in."

Royal's arrival triggered Bertha into assuming the role of the naughty mistress, crisply giving detailed instructions about the shelves. She also added that she needed a new kitchen cabinet and new quarters for the house servants. "There will be plenty for you to do around her," she promised.

Later, out of her presence, Royal took pad and pencil in hand and wrote: "She's mighty stinking uppity."

"Yeah," George agreed, "but I found out that she has another side that's worse than uppity."

Royal shot his father a look of amusement. It made George uncomfortable. "Now don't start punching me. I need all the help I can get." He soberly added, "You just stay right by my warm side. Hear me?"

Royal wiped the grin off his face and gave

his father a sympathetic nod as he wiped the perspiration from his forehead. They were working under the shade of a hackberry tree in front of the building called "The Stop". It was a large barn-like structure which, until about eight years ago, had been called "Big Barn" because it was the largest barn on the ranch. When the present Big Barn" was finished, all of the blacksmith and carpenter equipment had been moved to the old barn, causing it to take on its current name.

When the Renfros had entered The Shop earlier that day, their eyes were first drawn to the center of interest, a blacksmith's anvil and forge with its accompanying bellows. Royal was captivated. He had always liked blacksmith shops. The whole inside reeked with the odor of the soot which dinged the unpainted boards, the results of scores of forge fores, stoked hot enough to put an orange glow onto a horseshoe. The looks and odor of soot can be repulsive, but in a blacksmith shop they are natural and altogether pleasant.

The Shop also housed all types of blacksmith's and carpenter's tools, along with work tables, benches and saw horses. There were several rolls of barbed wire, several kegs of nails and a large stack of cedar posts in the back. And, oddly, there were small piles of worn, discarded horseshoes here and there, near the wall on both sides. Pointing to one of the stacks of old shoes, George shook his head. "Guess nobody has figured out what to do with them."

Looking up, they saw the source of their

lumber.   The rafters bulged with boards of all dimensions, along with dozens of buckets of paint--some white, some red--no other color.

The Renfros like the looks and smell of the place, but it was a sweat box on this hot summer day.   That's the reason they had moved their operations out under the hackberry tree.

Jane would look back on her accident that evening, wondering if the accident was pure or had been encouraged by some subconscious desire. Regardless of the cause, she was forever grateful that it happened.   She was in full view for the Renfros, heading to the well house, carrying a full bucket of fresh, warm milk.   Suddenly she turned an ankle and fell so awkwardly as to turn the bucket over and give herself a milk bath.   She uttered a series of sounds---first of surprise, then of pain, and finally of embarrassment.

Both Renfros bolted to the rescue; but after a few steps, George stopped and turned back. Grinning, it struck him that it would be better for his son to handle this rescue all by himself. Rushing up to her, Royal fell to his knees and whipped out his note pad.

"Are you hurt?" he quickly scribbled.

"I don't think so," she replied. "I seemed to have turned my ankle, but it's not hurting very much."

Relieved, he sat back on his heels and grinned.

"Well I never," she holtly began, "it is not funny."

He wrote: "You look funny---like a wet

kitten." He held up the note with one hand and seized one of her's with his other, so as to help her to her feet.

She jerked her hand away and heatedly inquired, "How would you like it if someone made fun of you because you can't talk, and what if....."

She cut herself of and looked up with anguished eyes. "Please forgive me," she whispered hoarsely. "I'm sorry I said that."

He smiled and wrote; "I'm the one who needs to be forgiven."

She gave him a grateful look. "Friends?"

He nodded and extended his hand. This time she took it and allowed him to pull her to a standing position. She winced. "Ouch, it still hurts."

He wrote: "Can you walk?"

He held the note for her to read, but before she could make a reply, he impulsively swept her up onto his arms and started carrying her towards the foreman's house. Without any show of embarrassment, she put an arm around his neck. You're going to get milk all over yourself," she murmured.

He smiled and nodded.

"I never said I couldn't walk."

He continued to smile and nod.

His arms were warm and strong under her shoulders and knees. a tingle rippled through her body as she possessively but gently ruffled the hair on the back of his neck. "Why won't you talk?" she whispered.

"Ah..." he began, but was unable to go

further.

"You started to say something," she exclaimed.

She wiggled out of his arms and grabbed him by the shoulders, "Go on, say it."

He hung his head,

Quickly she put a hand under his chin and tilted his head up. "It's OK. It's fine. "I'm sorry I pushed you. But sometime will you tell me why you can't talk? Gasping, she added, "Oh, you can write it out."

He nodded his promise.

Plainly pleased, she suddenly ran back, retrieved her empty bucket and ran home. He watched her all the way, taking note that she did it all without the slightest hint of a limp.

She was bright eyed and breathing hard when she burst in upon her mother. Seeing the empty bucket, Mary said, "I thought you had gone to milk."

"I did, but I fell and spilled it. See I got it on my dress." Excitedly she went on, "Can we have them to supper?"

"Have who for supper?"

"Mr. Renfro and his son."

"Oh, no," Mary responded. "I don't think that would be quite proper with Slim gone and all. Maybe when Slim gets back we can have them for supper sometime."

"But please, Mother, I don't want to wait three weeks."

"What is all this about?" Mary demanded, "I know the boy is attractive. I've already said as much, but you're acting downright silly."

Jane blushed but was not deterred from giving her mother a breathless, detailed account of her recent encounter with Royal. "So," she pertly ended, "if waiting to be with him again today is silly, just call me silly."

Mary laughed and hugged her daughter. "You are silly. But it's a good kind of silly."

Jane clapped her hands. "When can we have them for supper?"

"No," Mary firmly replied, "but you can ask the boy."

A frown slowly pushed the smile from Jane's face. "That won't do."

"Why not?"

"Because he won't come without his father."

"Oh, I'll bet he will."

"No," Jane argued, "he won't want to leave his dad all alone, to eat by himself in that empty old bunkhouse. I just know he won't."

"I'm sorry, honey."

But Jane was not to be denied. "Look, Mother, there is nothing improper about asking that man and his son to come to supper. They've been working hard all day. There're all alone. They probably don't even know how to cook. It's just the neighborly thing to do."

Mary closed her eyes and paused before answering. She admitted to herself that even in her husband's absence, welcoming the Renfros to Dundee by having them for supper was, in and of itself, nothing more than a neighborly gesture. In a flash she probed the inner recesses of her mind and discovered that if a supper invitation to George Renfro would be improper, it was strictly because she didn't trust herself. That's absolutely absurd, she shouted to herself. Popping her eyes open, she firmly announced: "Alright, you may ask both of them."

Jane hugged Mary, bolted out of the door and ran to the hackberry tree just as the Renfros were preparing to quit work for the day.

Making no effort to stifle her excitement. Jane extended the invitation: "Mother wants you to come to supper at our house."

Royal smiled and went for his note pad. "Sounds good to me," he wrote.

Meanwhile, George's face fell, and he felt his body grow warm as he very deliberately placed the hammers and saws back in the tool chest. "I, well, I don't know," he stammered a he stalled for time. This is about the craziest day of my life, he growled to himself. There are only two woman on this great big ranch, and I'm afraid of both of 'em. Bertha Dundee I'm scared of because of what she's thinkin, and Mary Feister I'm scared of because of what I'm thinkin.

"Tell your mother that I really appreciate the invitation, but I'm awfully tired, and I think I'll just get right on to bed. Tell her maybe some other time. "So," he continued, looking at Royal, "you go on by yourself."

Plain disappointment swept over Royal's face. He wrote: "No, I'll not go."

"Oh, yeah, you go ahead."

Royal shook his head adamantly.

George looked back and forth from Royal to Jane. The glow had gone out of their eyes. George didn't want his son to be sad. For that matter, he didn't want this girl to be sad either. He sensed that she was good enough for his son. It wasn't just that she was pretty. He liked the strength in her face, the tone of her voice, the way she tilted her head and flexed her shoulders.

"Oh, well," he blurted, "I guess I'm not all that tired. Tell your mother thanks and that We'll be there. What time?"

Jane clapped her hands. "Wonderful. In about an hour."

Mary greeted two guests whose overalls were clean as were their blue shirts--wrinkled and unironed, but fresh. Their faces had the after-glow of a recent shave. Their hair caused her to suppress a giggle. Both heads of dark, too-long hair were plastered down with something that gave them an unnatural sheen. Probably hog lard, she thought. They smelled vaguely of Bay Rum. "Do come in," she said.

Jane also came to greet them. She was struck by the dark, goods looks of the father and son. She noted their resemblances and also the startling contrast between Royal's dark blue eyes and George's dark brown ones.

"Well, don't you two look nice," she gushed. "Come on to the table. Everything is ready."

"It was the second good meal the Renfros enjoyed on their first day at Dundee. They had second helpings of green beans, mashed potatoes, pork sausage and biscuits with thick milk gravy.

Desert was hot biscuits with butter and strong, dark honey.

The table conversation was stiff but light. They talked about the food, Bertha's shelves and Jane's accident. George called Mary "Mrs. Feister" and she addressed him as "Mr. Renfro. Both of them liked what they saw of the other--the way Mary threw her beautiful head back when she laughed, the way George's eyes softened when he looked at his son. But both of them kept a tight rein on their emotions, immediately dispatching each indiscrete thought as it reared its head. And both of them, almost as if by prior agreement, carefully guided their outward relationship to one of cool friendliness.

After the dishes were done, Jane grabbed an extra lantern and lighted it. "I want to take Royal out to the barn and show him the new calf."

Both parents, now confident that their friendship was so securely plutonic that they could trust themselves to be left unchaperoned, answered in unison: "Fine, go ahead."

The trail to the barn was bathed in moonlight. Royal took the lantern from Jane; and, holding it by its bail with his right hand, nonchalantly clasped her right hand in his left. His nonchalance was outward only. His face was hot and he had a strange tingling in his arm pits.

Jane's effort to be nonchalant were decidedly less intense. Bringing both her hands into play, she stroked his long, slender, sun-tanned fingers. "You have strong, pretty hands," she said.

The East Texas farm boy was a bit startled

by her use of the word "Pretty". He had never before heard it used to describe a man. He was at once pleased and vaguely uncomfortable. He decided to change the subject. Resting the lantern on the ground, he took out his pad and started writing, but he had not finished the first word when the pencil lead broke.

"Oh, my goodness," Jane wailed. "But look, don't take up time sharpening that pencil. Just use sign language."

He nodded and began. He pointed to her.

"Me?"

He shook his head.

"Jane?"

He nodded. Then he lightly touched her lips with his right index finger. Withdrawing it, he began to quickly open and close the four fingers of his right hand against the thumb.

"Jane talk?"

He nodded; then, in military fashion executed an about face.

"Jane talk back?"

He shook his head, and did another about face.

"Jane talk about face?"

He smiled and pointed to her face while shaking his head.

"That's not it?"

He nodded

"Jane talk about...." she tentatively began.

He nodded enthusiastically, pointing emphatically to Jane.

"Jane talk about Jane?"

He nodded and gave a victory sign by clasping his hands together and holding them high.

She laughed. "I think I'll let you sharpen your pencil next time. But sure, I'll tell you about myself if you'll promise that some time soon you will write a long letter to me, telling me all about you.

He nodded his agreement.

It came to pass that their visit to the barn turned into an hour long sojourn during which Jane recited her life and family history, not neglecting her mother's obvious unhappiness in her marriage with Slim Feister and her own suspicions as to Feister's infidelities, especially with Bertha Dundee.

While his son was listening, George was talking. He and Mary were sitting in rope bottomed chairs on the entry porch, taking advantage of the cool breeze with which every summer's evening fanned the hot face of the Texas plains. Mary had started his flow of words when she said, "When did Royal stop talking? Tell me about it."

He began with a thumb nail sketch of their life in Van Zant County. Then, he told about the robbery, the murder of Kate, and about how Royal strangely froze and refused to shoot at the murderers. We went on to pin point that occurrence as the time when Royal stopped talking. He carefully omitted any reference to Uncle Joseph and the land, as well a their real reason for coming to West Texas.

"Was he sorry that he couldn't shoot or didn't shoot?" she asked.

"I don't know," George replied. "I know he was horrified by Kate's death. That's all I know for sure. I've never asked him about whether he is sorry or glad that he didn't shot at the killers."

"Maybe you should."

"Maybe," was his tight lipped reply. "Maybe some day I will ask him, but I think I'm gonna give his brain a little more time to heal before I start picking at it. He's a smart boy, and I keep thinkin He'll come out of it by himself,"

"I think you are very wise," she whispered.

"That's the first time anybody ever told me I was wise. I kind of like it."

They exchanged that comfortable smile of a male and female who are intimate but not too intimate.

Chapter Thirteen

The Preacher squinted at the lowing, listless herd. They were hungry and thirsty, he thought. It had taken two days to round up the Dundee purchase--1000 cows with calves at their sides. They had been herded into the SOQ holding pasture which consisted on only 640 acres. There was not a blade of grass left for them to eat. They had already eaten every clump down to the bare, brown ground. And a cow had to be desperate with thirst before she would go to the one small windmill tank and plunge into the never ending, ugly contest for water.

Applegate addressed Feister: "You need to get them cows to a bigger pasture. They're sufferin somethin terrible."

Feister shot him a hard look. "We're startin home tomorrow."

"Huh," the Preacher came back, "they won't get much help on the way home. The grass is already turning tan. We need rain real bad."

"You ain't tellin me anything I don't already

know," Feister testily replied. "What do you expect me to do about it?"

"Did you tell the Boss he was makin a mistake buying all those extra cows?" Applegate asked.

"You got a habit of stickin your nose in other people's business, don't you?"

"Maybe so," the Preacher calmly replied.

Feister's only response was to swing into his saddle and ride away.

Later, at the end of supper, as he was ladling "a Little Heaven" on Feister's biscuit, Applegate asked, "Where's the big Boss?"

"Oh, I forgot to tell you he wouldn't be here for supper. He's up at SOQ headquarters havin supper with the bankruptcy referee and some other big shots from Amarillo. He's gonna fork over his check for these cattle."

"It's too late then," the Preacher sadly said. "I had about gotten up the guts to ask him if he didn't think he was making a mistake."

"Wouldn't have done any good," Feister replied. "Besides that, look out there. There's a cloud comin up. We're not in a drought after all."

The Preacher squinted at the dark rolling cloud. "It's mean. But it's small and there's not much water in it, just a lot of thunder and lightning."

Feister jumped to his feet and yelled, "Happy, you and Newt and Ben come here." As the three of them drew close to him Feister said, "You boys notice how them cows are gatherin in the southeast corner. That cloud's comin hard out of the northwest. That means they're gonna wad up against the fences in the southeast corner. If lightning strikes that fence, and it's likely to, We're gonna have a big bunch of barbecued beef. So, the three of you get down there pronto and herd 'em away from the fences and keep 'em away until this storm has passed."

All three cowboys blanched, and Happy Boswell started what was obviously a protest: "But, Slim....".

Applegate, eyes wide with fright, interrupted him. "Slim, that's too dangerous. You know how lightning likes to crack down on cowboys on horseback."

"That's an old wives tale."

"No it's not and you know it," the Preacher angrily retorted."

"I know this. I know takin care of them cows is what We're paid to do," Slim argued.

"It ain't worth the risk. You're telllin these men to put a big risk on their lives in behalf of a few dumb animals."

"Are you saying that the lightning probably won't strike the fence?" Feister asked.

"I didn't come close to saying that," the Preacher answered.

"I don't try to tell you how to cook do I?"

"No."

"Alright then. You men get in the saddle. Right now. That thing is fixin to hit."

The three cowboys grimly turned and marched towards their mounts.

Feister's eyes flashed with hate. "And now,

Mr. Know-it-all, I'll show you that I'm willin to back my own play." Swinging into his own saddle, he put his horse into a gallop after the three cowboys.

The other cowboys unsaddled their horses and gathered under the shelter of the twin wagon sheet tent which the Preacher had erected as a chuck tent. They saw Feister and the others ride into the herd along the two fences that came together at the southeast corner. And they observed as the cowboys successfully moved the herd back a good hundred feet from the fence.

"Well, they got the first part of it done," the Preacher commented. "I didn't think they could do it before the wind hit."

He had no more than delivered those words when the storm struck. It did not hit slowly or in increments. It seemed to instantly pound down with all of its dark fury. The wind came low and hard, blowing so much rain under the wagon sheets that Applegate and his companions were soon soaking wet. Their view of Feister and his helpers was greatly obscured by the rain and darkness. But intermittent streaks of cracking lightning illuminated the scene of a nervously milling herd and four men on horseback frantically moving to and fro waving their hats over their heads. Each streak of lightning was followed by a clap of thunder which shook the chuck wagon and rattled the Preacher's pots and pans.

Suddenly they saw what Feister had feared. A bolt of lightning struck the fence, momentarily causing strings of light to play along the wires.

Feister, on the scene, congratulated himself. He had saved numerous cows, and not a man had been hurt.

His self-congratulations were premature. The wad of wild eyed cattle was like a mound of black powder waiting for a spark. And the lights flashing along the wires furnished that spark. The herd exploded with unmitigated terror and rushed headlong toward, into and beyond the southeast corner fences.

The stampede over the muddy, slicky ground was a great, inexorable tide, sweeping all before it, trampling under hoof many of its own members. The fence posts, standing at ten foot intervals, were torn out of the ground. And the four strands of wire, still nailed to the crazily tumbling and swinging posts, cut, tripped and felled many of the horrified cattle before much of it was broken into small segments and carried away on the backs of the animals or simply trampled into the mud.

The cowboys whose mission was to protect the herd were utterly powerless. They and their half-crazed horses were battered and swept helplessly along by the tide. Their only hope was that they could stay on their horses and that the horses could somehow manage to stay on their feet. Feister, Newt and Ben were lucky. Their mounts suffered many cuts on their legs as they stumbled over the broken wires and posts, but miraculously, they kept their hooves under them. Within a couple of hundred feet beyond the fence, these horses were brought back under control by their riders.

For reasons known only to his maker, Happy Boswell was not allowed such a miraculous escape. The raging torrent bashed his horse into the strong, double-thick corner post, breaking it off at the ground and causing the stunned horse's front legs to buckle. Then, led by hooking horns, the bellowing tide gave the horse's rear a mighty push, sending him into a somersault. The old cowboy's instinctive and successful effort to extricate his feet from the stirrups so as to prevent the horse from falling on him was probably a mistake. Likely it would have been better if he had been instantly crushed under the horse than to have been battered, pitched about, gored and finally trampled into the mud by dozens and dozens of sharp, heavy hooves.

Ironically, if the nervous mob of cattle had paused for just a few seconds after the lightning hit the fence, they probably would not have gone into a total frenzy. It so happened that just as they began their mad rush, the storm passed, just as abruptly as it had struck. The broad flashes of lightning in the storm's tail allowed Applegate and the cowboys standing near him to have a clear view of the disaster. By the time it was over, they were running, as fast as they could in their high heeled boots, through the mud towards the site of the carnage which they hoped against hope would be confined to beasts.

The ground on both sides of where the fence had been was strewn with dead and dying cows and calves. The air was filled with anguished moos and baas. The old Preacher was not insensitive to the plight of the suffering beasts, but at the moment the main thrust of his investigation was to find out what had happened to the humans. He got part of his answer when he saw Feister, Newt and Ben riding towards him. The rest of the answer came when he spotted a muddy, bloody heap several yards beyond the fence corner. Happy was face down, with a small patch of his orange and gray hair sticking up, oddly undefiled by the mud.

When Applegate feverishly pulled on the flesh-torn, mud-covered shoulders, Happy's face came out of the soft ground with a sickening slurp.

Feister dismounted. "Is he...."

"Yeah," the Preacher answered sadly, "he is dead--very, very dead."

The cowboys waited until daylight the next morning before they took Happy's body to the windmill tank where they reverently washed him and clothed him in a clean shirt and overalls. They also cleaned the mud off his boots and replaced them on his feet. They were loading the body into the chuck wagon when Amos Dundee rode up, fresh from an inspection of the disaster site.

"What are you men doing?" he demanded to know.

"We're puttin Happy's body in the wagon so we can take him back and bury him," Newt replied.

"I can't allow that. We'll have to be here at least three more days getting this mess cleaned up. In this heat we can't begin to leave his body out of the ground that long."

Newt, having appointed himself spokesman, pulled his hat off in a slow of deference. "But, Mr. Dundee, Sir, we sort of thought we could make a quick trip back to your ranch and bury Happy and then get on back up here and finish up."

"That would take at least four, maybe five days," Dundee snapped. No telling where those cows would be by then. After this mess, I can't afford it."

Newt slammed his hat to the ground. "Well, I never in my borned days heard of such a mean thing. Boys, I for one quit."

Several "me too's" rang out before the Preacher held up both arms. "Wait a minute," he shouted, "let me be heard on this matter."

"Men," he began, "my reasons are a whole lot different from Mr. Dundee's, but I also think it would be better for us to bury Happy right here. Now let me tell you why. I've known Happy a long time, about 30 years. He was old for an active cowboy, right smart older than any of the rest of you. When he was 20 he turned up that the Triple X with nothing but the clothes on his back. The bunch at the Triple X started callin him 'Happy'. The name fit. And the name stuck. Very few discouraging words ever passed his lips.

Nobody ever knew where he came from or who his folks were or why he turned up at the Triple X. He never volunteered any of that information; and, of course, nobody ever asked him. For the next 35 years he wandered back and forth across these wide prairies, workin for first one ranch and then the other--the Triple X's, the XIT's, the SOQ's the Matadors, the Spurs, the Dundee--and he's worked for most of them more than twice.

There are a few others like him out here-- tough, wandering cowboys who have helped tame this wild county and make it not only what it is but what it is gonna be. He never owned any land, yet in a way he had a claim on all of it. Free and independent, like a coyote he wandered over all of it, and made all of it his home. And like that coyote, he belonged nowhere in particular but everywhere in general. It is no more appropriate to buy him on the Dundee Ranch than any other spot on the Panhandle and Plains of Texas."

The old man paused and took stock of his audience. From long experience, he knew he had them in the palm of his hand. He continued in a quiet, somewhat hoarse voice. Therefore, men, I put it to you that we should bury Happy right out there where he fell. It is fitting that he should be buried on the spot where he died. It is also fitting for him to finally own a piece of this country and that it would be the place where he lost his life."

Observing that several of the sad eyed cowboys were slowly nodding, the Preacher extended his right arm and pointed to the site of Happy's death. "We'll bury him out there on that prairie, and then We'll put our ropes around a big bunch of those dead animals and let our horses drag 'em over on top of Happy's grave. In a few months there will be a big mound of sun-bleached bones out there. And that mound will mark

Happy's grave and stand as a monument, a monument not only to him, but to all those lonesome cowhands who roam and make their marks all over this land. Those bones will be there for your children and grandchildren to see. And if you are a mind to, you can tell them how the bones came to be there and what they stand for."

When the Preacher finished, there was not a dry eye in the crowd. They didn't discuss; they didn't debate; they didn't vote. The question of where Happy would be buried was settled. Without a word, the cowboys and their preacher entered into a compact and began to act upon it.

They borrowed picks and shovels from the SOQ and dug Happy's grave. It was deep-deeper than most of them stood tall, so deep that he would never share his part of the land with any carnivorous animal. Before they lowered him into the ground, the Preacher recalled with satisfaction that Happy became a Christian at one of his camp meetings years ago. And he declared that while it was true that Happy had finally found a permanent home on this earth, "his real home was up yonder where he would freely roam forever all over God's pastures."

The cowboys pulled the carcasses of a dozen cows to the grave site and then pitched the carcasses of a dozen calves on top of them. When they were finished, Feister dispatched Ben back to Dundee with the message about the storm and its consequences.

The Dundee crew stayed on the SOQ for four extra days, burying Happy, rounding up the herd and repairing the fences. Dundee lost thirty cows and fifty calves. Some were killed outright, others were mercifully dispatched with a bullet from a rifle. Hundreds of other cows and calves were bruised and gashed, but they survived. The carcasses of the dead were left to rot and stink and to become prime pickings for the coyotes and buzzards which seemed to gather from all over West Texas.

But the bones endured.

*　*　*　*　*　*　*

The rambunctious, killer cloud had quickly dumped an inch of rain on an area no more than a square mile. To a major West Texas a drought, slowly gathering strength for a mighty onslaught, that rain was but a minor nuisance. The trail back to Dundee was hot and dusty; and the melancholy lowing of the cattle exactly parallel the mood of the men. Man and beast alike seemed to be filled with dark foreboding.

The Preacher's brooding was enhanced by his lonesomeness for his family. And, most unsettling of all, he was regularly visited by that now familiar, but still unfriendly, numbness which crept down his left arm into his fingers.

Chapter Fourteen

The sands of Goose Creek, dry most of the time, meandered north to south through the West half of the Dundee Ranch. Along its banks, near the cottonwood trees, the grass was still lush and green. Royal and Jane left their horses in that grass, confident that they would not wander far.

Impulsively, Jane pulled off her boots and socks and wiggled her toes in the sand. "That feels cool and good, but it's gonna feel even better. Come on, pull your shoes off and I'll show you."

While he was taking off his brogans, she busily scooped out a deep hole in the sand. She pointed into the hold. "Look."

He looked and saw that water had seeped up into the hole, half filling it.

"Try it," she invited.

He stuck his right foot in the hole, pulled it out and then gave his other foot a cool bath. By that time she had finished another tiny well and was alternating her own feet in and out of the water.

"How do you like this for a good way to spend a Sunday afternoon?" she gaily inquired.

He smiled and nodded. Then he grabbed her hand and led her to the base of a cottonwood tree where he sat down and pulled her down to his side.

She closed her eyes and let her head fall back against the truck of the tree. "I've known you exactly two weeks and one day," she dreamily commented. "Well, really just two weeks because I just saw you that first day, didn't meet you or anything."

He wrote a note: "Been two real good weeks."

She lazily scratched her back against the tree bark. "Yeah, sure has. By the way, you haven't written that long letter to me about Royal."

He wrote: "Sorry. Been too tired."

"I know. It's OK. You'll get around to it pretty soon. Anyway, I need to tell you that you don't have to cover that awful part about your mother's murder and all that.

He gave her a quizzical look.

"You see," she explained, "your father told my mother all about that part of your life, and she told me. So I know when you quit talking, but I still don't know why, except that it has something to do with your mother's murder. Are you going to tell me why?"

He shrugged his shoulders and turned his hands palms up.

"You mean you don't know?"

He wrote: "That's right."

"OK, I won't press you any further on that. But I will press you on something else. Your father also told my mother that you read the Bible a lot, but you're not a Christian. Is that right?"

He nodded.

"Why?"

"Are you?" he wrote.

She chuckled. "That's a fair question. Yes, I am. My father was Catholic and I liked going to church with him, but he gave in to my Methodist mother on that score, so I turned out to be a Methodist."

She persisted. "Now, are you going to tell me why you are not a Christian?"

He jumped to his feet.

"Now don't get upset," she begged.

His smile cut off her alarm. He cocked his right arm at the elbow and held his hand up, palm out. She knew by now that he was saying "Stop-- hold on."

He walked swiftly to his horse and took from his saddle bags the old Bible which the Preacher had given to him. He looked a the index and then turned to the twelfth chapter of Romans. He sat back down beside Jane and pointed to verses 17-19 of Romans, Chapter 12.

She read the verses slowly and completely. She shrugged. "So, we are not to go around trying to get even with people who hurt us. We're not supposed to get revenge on mean people. God will take care of getting revenge. That's his business. Isn't that what it says?"

He nodded. Then taking the Bible from her,

he turned again to the index and pointed to the word "revenge". She looked at the index and then back at him with bafflement written all over her face.

He wrote a note: "It says that same thing in at least five or six other places in the Bible."

"So?"

He threw up his hand with frustration. Then, after turning to another place in the index, he leafed through until he settled on the Twelfth Chapter of Mark. He pointed to the 25-26 verses. She read them.."OK, it ways we are to forgive those who do evil to us. So?"

Royal emphatically pointed again to verse 26. "Yeah," she responded, "and if we don't forgive other people, God won't forgive us for sinning against him. I'm not sure that I've ever read it before in Mark, but I know that the same thing is in the Lord's Prayer and probably several other places."

He nodded.

"Well," she went on, "he forgives us if and when we forgive others. It's that simple."

His eyes grew wide with astonishment.

"Oh, you don't think it's so simple?"

He nodded.

"Yes, you do think it's simple or yes, you don't think it's simple?"

He wrote: "It is not simple."

"Maybe not," she admitted. "I wish I hadn't bought up the subject. I really don't know enough about the Bible to argue with you, much less help you. I've always just sort of relied on John 3:16

and not gotten too nervous about the rest of it. You know, 'For God so loved the world that he gave his only begotten son....'"

Royal had raised his hand, giving the stop sign.

"OK, you know that one."

He nodded.

"Have you talked to the Preacher. I mean have you gone over this with the Preacher."

He shook his head.

"Why?"

He wrote: "Don't want to squabble."

"Have you prayed?"

He shook his head.

"Why? Don't want to squabble with God," she teased.

He gave her a good natured smile. But after a pensive pause, he wrote: "That's right. I don't want to squabble with God. I'm already in enough trouble."

She smiled and frowned at he same time as she grabbed his hand. "Enough. I don't want to squabble with you either." She closed her eyes. "Let's just hold hands and listen to the breeze in the cottonwood leaves."

He closed his eyes too, and gave her hand a little squeeze. But not a minute had gone by before he hungered to look at her again. He opened his eyes and was startled. She had done the same thing.

That night Royal started writing his promised letter. Not far away, Mary Feister, as mothers are wont to do, decided to pump her daughter. "You're getting pretty thick with Royal aren't you?"

"Yes," Jane's answer was quick and filled with delight.

"What about Mike Vernon?"

"He's in Denver," was Jane's evasive reply.

"That's not fair answer," Mary came back. "How many times last year did he interrupt his studies and go all the way to Amarillo to see you?"

"Four," Jane proudly answered.

"And he promised to come to see you this summer?"

"That's right."

"Well, then," Mary bore on, "what about him?"

"I still say, he's in Denver."

"That won't be forever, and you know it," Mary impatiently argued.

Jane's eyes took on a far-away look. "I know. And I guess the best way I can answer your question is to say I love him."

"You love Mike?"

"Yes."

Mary gasped. "Then don't toy with Royal. You'll hurt him and hurt yourself in the bargain."

"I love Royal," Jane replied.

"But you said you loved Mike," Mary shot back, showing her frustration.

"I do."

"But you can't love two boys at the same time," Mary declared.

"I do," Jane evenly answered.

"Well, I never!"

"Don't worry, Mother, I'm not driven to a choice. After all, even though Mike has hinted, neither of them has asked me to marry him." She giggled. "Thunder, Royal hasn't even kissed me yet."

That broke off the conversation, but later, after Mary had crawled into bed, Jane stuck her head into the dark bedroom and whispered, "I'll tell you something else, though. "Even though I love both of them, I only want to become a part of one of them."

Her mother made an educated guess: "And that's Royal."

Jane sighed. "That's right."

Mary struck a match to the coal oil lamp beside her bed and turned up the wick. "I can't go to sleep on that. You said you hadn't been put to a choice, but it looks like you have already made one."

"Yeah," Jane thoughtfully admitted as she sat down on the bed beside her mother, "looks that way."

"What if Royal doesn't ask you to marry him?"

"He will," Jane confidently replied, "and very soon I think."

"But what about college. You know I want you to go, and you know I have the money saved for it."

"I don't want to go to college. Not now."

"Why? I went. I loved it."

Jane drew a deep breath and slowly exhaled. "I know I would probably like college too, but I just don't have time."

"Oh, come on, I was through college and teaching school before I even met your father."

"I know, but I just don't have that much time. I'm a girl, but I'm itching, I guess it's better to say I'm burning to be a woman. I'm ready right now to start doing all the things that only a woman can do."

"But the boy is not a Christian," Mary argued.

"He will be."

"What makes you think so?"

"Because I'm praying about it, and I think he is too."

The answer stunned Mary. She didn't care to argue with it. So she swallowed hard and took another tact. "He can't even talk," she blurted.

"He'll start talking again," Jane predicted.

"How do you know that?"

Jane pensively rubbed her chin. "I just know."

"The truth is you know no such of a thing," Mary retorted.

"I do know," Jane firmly insisted, "anyhow it makes no difference. I fell in love with him when he couldn't talk, and I'll love him even if he never talks again. And besides that, I got the idea that you thought Royal was something special."

Mary had tears in her eyes. "I did and I do. There's something about that boy that absolutely charms me. But this all happening so suddenly. You haven't known Royal but two weeks."

Jane smiled and stroked her mother's hair,

shimmering in the flickering light. "Try not to worry. How long did it take Daddy to know he loved you?"

"Well, it took me several months to........"

Jane gently but firmly cut her short. "That is not what I asked. I said: 'How long did it take him.....'."

Mary sighed. "He always said it happened the first second he saw me."

Jane made her point: "Well, you have always said that I was a lot like Daddy."

"Yes," Mary admitted, "and that's not bad."

"Anyway," Jane assured her, "it won't happen tomorrow or next week or next month."

"But soon?"

Mary had to wait a moment for Jane's answer. "Yes, soon." Then, turning so that she could look deeply into her mother's moist eyes, she added, "Please don't ask me why because I don't know why, but I'm very sure that Royal and I should get together quickly."

Awaiting a response, Jane stood and looked down at her mother. Mary turned the lamp wick down again, plunging the room into darkness. Falling back again against her pillow, she resignedly said, "Alright, that's one 'why' I won't ask."

Jane bent down and kissed her mother's cheek before silently moving out of the room.

Mary did not get to sleep for a long time. Her mind swirled with battle between disappointment and empathy, an empathy disturbingly colored with guilt. If she would let go and let herself, she could fall for George Renfro just as her daughter had fallen for his son. But, she would not let go. That much was settled.

* * * * * * *

The next morning George pointed to a stack of large cedar corner posts at the back of the shop. "We'll saw six of these in half and use 'em to make a foundation for the servants' house. That means we'll have to dig an even dozen holes."

Royal nodded.

George went on: "The diggin won't be fun, but it'll be good to work outside again and get away from that woman. I thought we never would get those cabinets built. She nearly drove me batty, always changing her mind."

Royal penciled a note: "Always rubbing up against you too."

"Yeah, that too," George growled. "I've said, 'No' to that woman every way I know to say it without just comin out in the open with it. She just keeps flirtin around in such a way that if I come out with a flat, open 'No', she would swear she didn't know what I was talking about. By the way, speakin of females, you're gettin sweet on that Jane aren't you?"

Royal nodded his affirmation.

"She's a fine girl. I feel it in my bones. But you don't want to rush things."

Royal wrote: "Why not?"

"Because, Son, she's your first girl friend."

Royal wrote: "So?"

"So you don't know anything about girls."

Royal wrote: "Who does?"

George chuckled and threw up his hands. "You've got me there," he admitted, "but still you don't want to rush into a marriage."

"Why?" Royal wrote.

Irritated, George tore his hat off and slammed it against the stack of posts. "Because you're not ready for marriage."

"Who is?" Royal wrote.

George blurted out his answer. "One who is older than you and has a steady job and who knows where he's goin. That's who."

Royal stared at his father for awhile before writing: "Was that you before you married Mamma?"

George's neck turned tomato red. He pulled his hat back off his head and growled. "Go get those saw horses and bring 'em back here."

For two hours father and son worked in a silence broken only be the sounds of sawing. To prevent it from rolling they lashed each end of a cedar post to a saw horse with a length of rope. Then, using the long, two-man cross-cut saw, they swiftly cut each post in half.

Finally George said, "Have you told this girl that you love her?"

Royal shook his head.

"Have you kissed her?"

Royal blushed and shook his head again.

George sighed with relief. "Well, you're not very far down the road yet are you?"

Royal nodded.

You say yes. Do you mean you are not very far down the road?"

Royal shook his head.

George threw up his hands again. "I give up. Come on, lets go get dinner. We can warm up those dried black-eyed peas and have some cold corn bread and buttermilk to go with 'em."

A smile fell over Royal's face. He knew his father would not push him anymore about Jane, at least not for a day to two.

Chapter Fifteen

It was the middle of September and George proudly announced to his son that they now had the servants' quarters "in the dry." "all we got to do now is stick some paper on the inside walls so wind won't come through the cracks so bad."

Building the little house had almost been fun. Most days he and the Preacher shared Royal. Royal cooked in the mornings and carpentered in the afternoons. Sometimes though, at least one day each week, they would turn him over to Newt who promised to make a cowboy out of him.

Bertha still flirted with George; but, with the return of the outfit from the SOQ, her ardor had cooled to a more respectable temperature. Her advances were less frequent and far more subtle. Thankful, George at first credited the change to the return of her husband. And he still thought that Dundee's watchful eyes were a factor. However, it soon became clear that the main reason for the change consisted of her biweekly visits from Slim Feister.

Every time Amos Dundee left the ranch headquarters for any length of time, which was about twice a week, Feister would turn up at the back door of Big House, hat in hand. He would be let into the house and would stay fifteen, maybe twenty minutes.

"Why don't he just announce what he's doin and go in the front door?" George asked the Preacher. "Oh, might as well. Everybody but her husband knows what he's doin; and sometimes I wonder if her husband don't know."

"Oh, he don't know," the Preacher replied. "If he did, he'd kill Feister, or at least he'd try."

George's eyes narrowed. "It's almost like Feister wants somebody to tell Dundee."

"Sure," the Preacher agreed. "He's runnin a terrible big chance, and he's bound to know it."

"What about Mary," Applegate continued, "Do you think she knows?"

"She's bound do," George answered. "Royal tells me that Jane says that her mother knows what's goin on but just won't admit it."

"I haven't known Mary very long," the old man began, "but I would guess that to be true. Also, it doesn't surprise me that she stays with him."

"The real wonder of it is that nobody has told Dundee," said George. "Wonder why."

"Why don't you tell him?" the Preacher answered.

"Well, I guess because I don't think it is any of my business."

"I guess that's my reason too and everybody

else's," the Preacher replied.   "But," he thoughtfully added, "sometimes I get all mixed up about what is and what is not my business. You know some things a man does are everybody's business."

"But this ain't one of those things, huh?"

"Well, up to now it seems that way, but I don't know how long it'll last."

Amos Dundee had not seen a drop of rain fall on his ranch since he acquired the SOQ herd. The grass was brown and scarce, and all of the waterholes had dried up. The cattle were relegated to walking long distances to share the three working windmills. Throughout the month of August, the big boss had remained optimistic, saying repeatedly that it always rained during the first week of September. But with that week having come and gone, he quit riding the range or asking any questions about the cattle. He seemed to block the awful drought out of his mind.

Toward the end of August, one morning, George had casually and innocently inquired of Feister as to why Dundee didn't buy some hay or grain sorghum bundles to help carry the cattle through the drought.

"There ain't none," Feister had crisply replied, "and even if there was, he'd have to pay a fortune for it."

George had then observed that it might be a good idea for the ranch to plant four or fine hundred acres in grain sorghum every year so there would be some feed to carry the cattle through the bad times.

When Feister had curtly responded that it wouldn't have done any good because "sorghum won't grow anymore than grass when it don't rain," George had respectfully reminded him that it rained some years; and when it did, the grain and stalks could be stored in the barns for insurance against the next drought.

Feister had put an abrupt end to the conversation by curling his upper lip and scornfully saying, "You're a farmer, but this ain't no farm."

Over all, the Preacher had seldom been happier. He drew ever closer to his adopted family and day-dreamed about the not too distant time when they would move to the Armstrong land and share the Indian treasure. Too, his cooking was appreciated, and he appreciated being appreciated. He also found happiness in the success of his preaching. He preached every Sunday morning, gathering his flock in the mess hall. Everybody on the place attended, the cowboys, the Feisters and even the Dundees. He blistered them with hell fire, but he also told jokes and stories. His audience liked him and that helped them like what he said. And, forming the crown on his success, two cowboys "came to Christ."

The old Preacher's single disappointment was Royal. He anguished over his failure to put his finger on the reason for his grandson's muteness or his consistent rejection of the gospel. He wanted to approach the boy on both counts but had not seen a suitable opening. The old man acknowledged to himself that he had never before been confronted with a matter quite so delicate.

As for Jane and Royal, they had started kissing in early August and had been kissing a lot ever since. With the first kiss, Jane had written a letter to Mike Vernon, letting him down as easy as she knew how. It was only fair, she thought, I'm going to marry Royal. Now, almost four weeks later, she was still confident that she would marry Royal some day, but she had become increasingly surprised and frustrated by the fact that he had not asked her to be his wife.

She wanted to blame his failure to pop the question on his inability to speak. But she ruefully admitted that he seemed to be able to ask every other question under the sun, either by signs or the written word. She became more and more convinced that his reluctance was rooted in a desperate desire to conquer his muteness before he asked her to marry him. Also, the perception grew on her that his muteness was somehow connected to his rejection of Christianity. She couldn't explain it, but that was her definite feeling. She thought of taking her suspicions to George, but instead, decided that the Preacher would be the more appropriate person.

Her chance came sooner than she expected. She had finished milking and was in the well house, pouring warm milk through a cheesecloth into a large crock jar. She shivered. The mid-September sun had already gone down. She mildly scolded herself, thinking that she should have put on a jacket and brought a lantern. It was too dark for her to see the tiny particles of dust and manure that were caught in the cheesecloth, but she knew they were there.

Suddenly the little house was aglow in the light of a lantern swinging from its bail in the hand of William T. Applegate. Jane was glad to see him. "Hi, Mr. Applegate, come on in. I was just finishing up."

"Now, honey, you just call me Preacher. Everybody else does."

"OK, thanks. I will."

"I came to see if I could get a couple of pounds of butter for breakfast. I'm all out."

"Oh, sure, I've got five or six extras down there in the bucket. I'll get a couple for you."

Making her word good, she unhooked the end of a rope from a nail on the wall and began pulling it through a pulley mounted on a cross beam about four feet above the mouth of the well. Soon a big wooden bucket emerged at the top of the well. She pulled it out and placed it on the circular table surrounding the well opening. Reaching into the bucket, she produced one, then two blocks of butter wrapped in cheesecloth.

"Can you talk a minute?" she inquired, as she returned the bucket, feeding out the rope until she heard the bottom of the bucket slap the top of the water.

"Why sure. I would be glad to talk to you anyway.   But I'm especially glad to talk to somebody who my grandson thinks so much of."

Jane looked surprised. "Is he really you're grandson?"

"Not exactly. But...well just let me put it

this way: for all intents and purposes he is."

Jane was still puzzled, but she decided not to press that particular matter. "I want to talk to you about why Royal can't talk and about why he's not a Christian."

"I'd like that, but I'll warn you in advance. I don't have any answers. Here, "he went on as he pulled off his jacket and draped it over her shoulders," get under this. I have on a heavy shirt, and I'm hot natured anyhow."

"Thanks," she said, pulling the faded blue jacket around her arms. "I have the notion that the reason he can't talk and the reason he won't become a Christian have something to do with each other."

"That's an interesting theory. What have you got to go on?"

"I have a lot to go on as far as him not being a Christian is concerned. He told me about that. But, as far as how that fits in with the fact that he can't talk, I don't have anything to go on but pure intuition."

The Preacher chuckled. "That's not a bad thing to rely on. I learned a long time ago not to scorn a woman's intuition, especially if it has to do with somebody she loves. But back to the facts, what did he say about why he's not a Christian?"

"He showed me right in the Bible what's bothering him," Jane replied. "I wish we had a Bible so I could show you. But I can get by without one. I don't know any of the parts that trouble him by heart, but I can give you the gist of them."

"I can run get my Bible," the Preacher

offered.

"Oh, no, it's not necessary. The first thing that bothers him is the part where God tells us not to seek revenge on our enemies--on those that hurt us; and that he'll take care of getting all the revenge that's to be gotten."

"Vengeance is mine, not yours, sayth the Lord, that sort of thing?"

"That's it," Jane replied. It's in the Bible several times, and Royal knows 'em all."

"Is that all?" the Preacher asked.

"Oh, no," she replied. "There's another thing--the part where God tells us that he will forgive us only if we forgive other people. And, as Royal pointed out, that's in there in several different places too."

The Preacher frowned. "It doesn't exactly say that," he argued.

"I won't try to argue with a preacher about the Bible, but that is what the words that Royal pointed out say to me. And I'll just ask you to look at the index in your Bible under 'forgive'. It's in the book of Mark someplace. And also it's in the Lord's Prayer and several other places."

The Preacher nodded gravely. "Alright, I understand what you're sayin. Now, what else?"

"Nothing," she replied.

The old man pulled on his chin whiskers and began thinking out loud. "So, it seems that Royal resents it because God tells him not to seek revenge, and he doesn't think he wants a God like that. It also seems that somebody has done something bad to him, and he doesn't think he can ever forgive that particular person. So, he's got it all doped out that since Royal can't forgive somebody for sinning against Royal, God won't forgive Royal for sinning against God."

"I think you've got it down exactly right," she replied. "How to cope with it, I don't know. I tried, but I didn't get anywhere. That's the reason I brought the whole thing to you and sort of threw it over on your shoulders."

"That's what a preacher is for," he gently answered. "This gives me a startin place and that's a whole lot more that I had before I came after this butter."

Applegate walked Jane home, and then he took his time, slowly trudging towards the bunkhouse. Finally, he stopped, turned off the lantern and stood looking at the millions of stars blinking their friendly lights down on him. He whispered, "Help me, Lord. Help me figure this out." Having an afterthought, he added: "And if you don't see fit to let me figure out all of it, I'd appreciate it if you'd let Royal figure out the rest."

He frowned and shook his head. I'm not even sure I'm makin good sense, he thought. Anyway the good Lord always knows what I'm driving at even when I don't say it very well.

It was just then that the old Preacher witnessed the sparkling glory of a falling star. Spewing a million sparks from its tail, it was a splendorous display, rightly claimed by the whole universe. Yet, like every other falling star, this was an awesomely private and personal thing; that is to say, every person who saw it had the feeling that it belonged to him and him alone. The Preacher smiled. He didn't believe in omens and didn't trust people who did. Yet he could not deny the all-is-well warmth which went surging through his old bones.

When he got back to the bunkhouse, he sought out George. "Would you mind to come to dinner and supper a little early tomorrow."

"I guess I don't mind. What's up?"

"I need to go into Mesa for a load of groceries. I have to leave right after breakfast, and I can't get back until after supper. I'll get up a little early and cook enough stuff for both meals, but I need you to put a little fire under it and get it all warmed up for the boys. Also, and remember this: you'll need to ration them dried peaches, one ladle full to a man. If you don't, some of 'em will go kinda crazy and eat too many, make themselves sick."

"I can do it," George responded, "but why not let Royal do it?"

"I want him to go with me. There'll be some heavy liftin and my old back ain't what it used to be."

Raising his eyebrows, George shot the old man the hard questioning stare of a doubter.

"And besides that," the old man went on, "I need to talk to that boy."

"OK, he's all yours. I'll protect your backside."

Chapter Sixteen

Looking sternly at his grandson, the old preacher said, "We ain't ever gonna get to town if you don't quit blowin on that coffee. You need to get on down to the barn and hitch 'ol Blackie and Red to that new wagon."

Royal took a gulp of the scalding liquid. His eyes bugged as he slammed the tin cup down on the table. And with mouth wide open, he made a big scene of painfully blowing breath over his blistered tongue. Looking accusingly at the Preacher, he then stomped out and down the trail towards the barn.

"And bring your rifle," Applegate shouted after him, "We might see a deer."

One hour later, Blackie and Red, feeling extra frisky, had pulled them a couple of miles towards Mesa. They communicated very little, being content to lose themselves in private thoughts amid the soft din of the clopping hooves, the rattle of iron hooped wheels and the sundry creak and groans of the heavy wagon. The sun shone on a sea of short grass, browned first by thirst and then by light frost. A strong east wind was buffing the left side of the wagon's canvas cover. Finally, the Preacher found his tongue. Taking a deep breath, he said, "Son, I need to talk to you. First, I'll not try to hide the fact that Jane and I have been talkin about you."

Royal was immediately roused out of his musings. He put a "tell me more" look on his face.

"Ha, that got your attention didn't it. Well, you see, it's like this......" suddenly the old man pulled the horses to a stop. There was alarm in his voice. "Look at that," he shouted, looking to his left and pointing into the distance.

What they saw was a wall of thick, white smoke, running north to south about two miles long. "It's about two miles off and movin this way," the Preacher hoarsely observed, "we've got to stop it or it's gonna be about the biggest prairie fire that's ever been seen around here."

Oddly, the excitement and fear in the old man's voice was now replaced by a calm confidence. "Is there a lariat rope back there?"

Royal looked back under the canvas. Pulling his head out, he nodded.

"One?" Applegate asked.

Royal nodded.

"I was afraid of that. We need two. But we'll get by somehow. Now the first thing for you to do is shoot one of those big cows over there."

He pointed to a gathering of a half dozen cows about 100 yards in front of them.

Royal responded with a face full of puzzlement and disbelief.

"Just do it. Right now. Get your rifle. Just do it. I'll explain later."

Reluctantly, Royal whipped the stock of this rifle to his shoulder and quickly squeezed the trigger. They saw a cow slump to her knees and roll over on her side.

"Now, Royal," the Preacher calmly began, "we don't have much time. I will run out there and start skinning that cow. While I'm doin that, you unhitch the team. We're gonna ride the horses. Hear me now," he went on emphatically,"cut off the two long reins about two feet from each horse's head...Leave enough so we can guide the horses. Then tie the long reins together. That'll make a leather strap about as long as the lariat rope. Then bring the reins and the rope and lead the horses over to where I am. You got all that?"

Royal nodded, but the old man didn't see it. He was already trotting towards the dead cow. When he arrived at the carcass, he unsheathed his long hunting knife and with the quick, deft strokes of a true expert began relieving the late cow of her hide. He had almost finished when Royal came running up with the horses.

Applegate looked approvingly at the bit of harness which had been left on the horses and at the long belt of leather formed by the long reins. Swiftly he stretched the bloody hide and then tied one end of the lariat rope to the right side of the hide and one end of the leather belt to the left side.

"I've seen this work, but never on a fire this big. Here's what we do. You take the other end of the rope and get on Red. I'll take the rein and get on Blackie. We'll drag the hide between us and ride up to the north end of the fire. Now let's get goin and I'll explain the rest on the way."

After they managed to urge the wagon horses into a lope, the Preacher yelled, "When we get there, you ride over into the burned off part. I'll stay on this side, the unburned side. Got it?"

Royal nodded.

"Then we'll ride slow, south along the line of fire, and we'll pull the hide along over the fire. That ought to snuff it out."

Sounds dumb, Royal thought. Nevertheless, he carried out the Preacher's instructions and was surprised and pleased to see the flames dying under the hide as it was slowly pulled over the thin line of fire. The horses were moving along about 40 feet apart with the hide in the middle. Royal soon realized that he had the better side of the operation. The bellowing white smoke enveloped the Preacher, and from time to time Royal heard him gasping and wheezing. Twice Royal stopped, intending to hold up the operation until he could change sides with the old man. But each time, the Preacher stubbornly and impatiently insisted on jerking the hide along without a pause.

At long last, just after the lone surviving orange finger of flame was suffocated, Royal saw the Preacher emerge from the cloud of smoke.

Wheeling Red to the right, he triumphantly moved to join the old man and was thunder struck to see him suddenly go limp and fall, as lifeless as a sack of potatoes, heavily to the ground.

Jumping off of his horse, Royal fell to his knees beside the Preacher who was sprawled out on his back. Royal stared wildly at the old man's ashen face. His eyes were closed. His snow white beard outlined his blue--almost purple--lips. Suddenly it dawned on Royal that the Preacher might not be breathing. He looked for the rise and fall of the chest. Seeing none, he thrust a near over the old fellow's nose and strained his hearing. He detected nothing but the soft rustle of brown grass in the wind.

Royal was cool and deliberate. The smashing effects of his mother's death and the immediate aftermath thereof were not all bad. They had slipped steel into his backbone that would never melt away. After turning Applegate over on his stomach, Royal turned the old man's head to the right and rested the left side of his face on his left hand, palm against the ground. Royal then stuck his fingers between the blue lips and pried apart the clenched teeth. Sitting astride the old man, he began to push heavily with both hands, directly below the shoulder blades. He could hear air blowing out of the lifeless mouth. Abruptly he released the downward pressure and heard the quick suck as air was pulled through the old man's mouth and into his lungs. He repeated the motion---push down, quick release. Rythumatically, he did it over and over--about twenty times--pausing before each new push to see if the Preacher's lungs would pull air without help. Finally he was rewarded by the sound of a shallow gasp followed by another, followed by a great deal of gasping, sputtering and coughing. After a full minute of such noises, the old man cleared his throat, took a deep breath and tartly inquired, "What are doin on my back, Son?"

Royal sprawled on his back, weak with relief. He pulled out his pad and pencil and wrote a quick note: "You took in too much smoke and quit breathing. I'll explain more later. Lie still. I'll go and get the wagon."

Applegate offered no resistance. He felt no pain, but he was very, very weak. The ground was hard and a bit chilly, but he didn't want to move--not a toe, not a finger--nothing. He had the odd thought that it would be nice to sort of melt into the earth on which he lay.

Royal, working quickly, effected temporary repairs to the harness, hitched the horses back to the wagon and drove to the old man's side. He took hold of both the Preacher's hands and started pulling him to his feet.

"Aw just let me stay here and rest," the Preacher begged. "You can go on and get the groceries and pick me up on the way back."

Royal shook his head, and wrote another note: "No. You need to see a doctor. Now don't give me any trouble, Grandpaw."

When the old man saw the word "Grandpaw", a smile spread over his face, and he managed to get to his feet with a little help.

Staggering to the back of the wagon, he crawled under the canvas and gratefully stretched out on his back.

Racing to Mesa, Royal stopped twice, once to put the Preacher's head on a wad of pinto bean sacks which had been left in the wagon, and once to give his patient a drink of water. The old man was having coughing attacks--deep and hacking; and he was spitting up a lot of bloody foam. Royal was scared, and by the time he drove into Mesa, Red and Blackie were in a heavy lather. Pulling up in front of the barber shop, he ran in and penciled a note: "Where is the doctor?"

"Right up the stairs." the barber replied.

"Is he here?" Royal wrote.

"I think so."

Royal pointed out to the wagon and excitedly motioned for the men in the shop, three in all, to follow him.

It took all four of them to get the Preacher up the stairs and laid out on a black leather davenport in the doctor's office. Mesa's doctor, Dr. D. K. Spencer, immediately began to examine the Preacher.   He made extensive use of his stethoscope; and--it seemed to Royal--spent an uncommonly long time thumping here and there on the Preachers upper body. Twice during the examination, the Preacher had a coughing spell and spit up blood.

"What happened?" the doctor asked.

"Well, I don't know exactly..." the Preacher gurgled.

"Now, don't you try to talk, my friend. Not

just now.   Can anybody else tell me what happened?"

Royal pointed to himself and proceeded to write a brief note, giving the doctor the bare outline of the Preacher's battle with the fire and smoke and his own action in getting the Preacher to breathe again.

After reading the note, the doctor rubbed his chin for a few seconds before declaring that he thought his patient had contracted a form of pneumonia. He went on to opin that the old man needed to stay in the hospital for a few days. At that, the Preacher opened his eyes and gurgled a strong protest in a very weak voice: "I'm not stayin in any hospital."

Swiftly the doctor grabbed Royal's left wrist in his big boney right hand and pulled him down a hall and into a large room containing six bunk size beds. Closing the door, the doctor whirled around and confronted Royal with a hard stare. "Are you related to the old man?"

Royal shook his head, but then held up one finger in a wait-a-minute signal. On his pad he wrote: "I know him real well, and he sort of treats me like I was his grandson."

"OK," the doctor responded, "that's good enough. I was hoping for some kind of a family relationship, because somebody has got to talk some sense into the old rascal, otherwise we're gonna lose him. We may lose him anyhow, but if he won't stay here with me for a few days, we just was well give up."

"That bad?" Royal wrote.

"Yeah. You see not only has he picked up this wild pneumonia, he's also got a very bad ticker."

Royal's face registered puzzlement.

"Ticker. His heart. He's got a bad heart. It's liable to quit on him anytime."

Royal nodded his understanding and wrote: "I'll see what I can do."

When they got back to the Preacher, he was sound asleep. The barber and his companions were still waiting, nervously whispering in a corner of the room.

Royal wrote, "Doctor, let's just get these men to help us move him onto one of those hospital beds. I'll figure out some way to keep him here after he wakes up."

The doctor grunted his approval and gave the necessary instructions. Soon the old man was lying on a hospital bunk, undressed down to his underwear, still sleeping. He coughed and spit a couple of times but never seemed to wake up.

Royal wrote: "Thanks, men," and held the note up for all to see.

"You're as welcome as the flowers in May," the barber replied. "Why shore," said the other two.

After the barber and his friends took their leave, Royal wrote: "What now?"

"You stay here with him. I've got to go and fix up some medicine for him and make arrangements with Mrs. McCardy to make a pot of chicken soup. It'll take me awhile."

During the doctor's absence, Royal wrote

two notes, one to his father: "Dear Dad, we were in prairie fire. Preacher got too much smoke an got sick. He is in hospital in Mesa. I'll be back tomorrow. I don't have any money so you will need to pay the man who brings this note. Royal."

The other note was the barber: "Can you get somebody to ride out to the Dundee Ranch and deliver this note to my Dad, George Renfro? I don't have any money, but my Dad will pay him."

When the doctor returned, Royal went down to the barber shop and showed the notes to the barber.

"Oh, shore, I know a young fella that'll be glad to do that little chore. He'll get the note out there by supper time."

Hunger pangs sent Royal to the wagon where he dived into the lunch the Preacher had packed for them. It was mid-afternoon, and the cold steak and biscuits, beans and dried peaches tasted awfully good. Next he drove the team to the livery stable an made arrangements for Red and Blackie to spend the night there.

Later after he had spooned a bowl of chicken soup through the Preacher's lips, he sat on a bunk next to the Preacher and read a magazine for a couple of hours. It was long past dark now, and he felt washed out and sleepy. He was grateful that the Preacher was the only patient in the hospital and for the doctor's invitation to spend the night at the Preacher's side. He knew it was before 10:00 p.m. because the single drop cord electric bulb was still shining brightly, and the Dr. had forewarned him that Mesa Electric Company did not furnish "juice" after ten. Moving to insure against total darkness throughout the night, he lite a coal oil lamp, pulled the cord on the electric light and dozed off.

Several hours later, he never knew exactly how many, Royal heard his name being called.

"Royal, Royal, is that you, Son?"

Royal stuck his head close to the old man's eyes and nodded.

"Good. Turn that light up, will you. I want to talk to you." The old man was talking in a raspy whisper.

Royal obediently turned the lamp up as high as it would go.

"That's better. Well, I see you and the Doc got me into the hospital after all. I must be pretty bad off."

Royal shook his head vigorously and started writing a note.

"Never mind the note. You're just gonna tell me that I'm just gonna have to rest awhile and that I'm gonna be alright. Right?"

Royal grinned and nodded.

The old man flashed a weak, knowing smile. "That's what people always tell a sick person."

He paused and gulped air into his lungs, giving Royal time to quickly scribble: "Don't talk, you can talk tomorrow."

"Huh, like I've been preaching for forty years--tomorrow may never come." He paused again for breath. "I'm gonna get this said tonight, right now."

Stopping after every couple of sentences to

laboriously catch his breath and now and again to cough, the old Preacher painfully delivered his speech:

"I told you I'd been talkin to Jane. She said you told her why you keep on turnin Jesus down. Now I planned to talk long and hard about your problems. But under these circumstances, I'll be brief. First, you got to understand that revenge and justice are two different things. God may want all vengence for himself, but he wants people to seek and do justice. Got that?"

Royal nodded.

"Next you got to understand that God has never said that you have to forgive all those who have wronged you before he will save you. He never did say you had to stand before him with all your sins forgiven before he could save you from those sins. Will you think about that?"

Royal nodded.

"Now, after you are saved, if you ever are, the question of whether God will forgive you if you don't forgive others can be handled at that time with the help of the Holy Ghost. Well, I'm gettin awful tired. I'll wind up by sayin that if people could ever forgive like God they'd be as good as God. And if they were as good as God, they wouldn't need God."

The old man closed his eyes, and Royal moved to turn down the lamp.

"Wait a minute, the raspy voice commanded. "I forgot something." Keeping his eyes closed, the Preacher went on, "If I go to meet the Lord, I want you to look in my saddle bags.

You'll find a piece of oil cloth that's been folded a couple of times. Inside the oil cloth you'll find a map to the treasure. The treasure will be yours and George's. He's my son and your my grandson. You know what I mean?"

Royal nodded, held his right index finger up to his lips and turned the lamp down low. The Preacher, though coughing frequently, slept the rest of the night. Royal did not.

Later Royal would refer to that night as his night to wrestle with an angel. He had no intention of engaging in such a contest when he closed his eyes, locked his fingers behind his head and fell back on the hospital cot. But almost immediately his eyes popped open to the eerie scene on the ceiling. The flickering flame of the lamp caused ghostly shadows to play tag with dim ripples of light.

He had the strange but comfortable feeling that he had somehow been lifted onto a level of consciousness that he had never before known. Putting his feet to the floor, he thought, I need a Bible; and he remembered seeing one in the doctor's office.

Grabbing the lamp, he walked into the office and found the Bible. Turning the lamp up, he sat on the davenport and opened the book to John 3:16. He read it and continued through several more verses.

His life seemed to zoom through his mind, leaving big sparks behind for him to contemplate-- the teachings against violence and revenge which he recalled at his mother's knee, his mother's murder, the Preacher's teachings, his Bible readings, Jane's notion that you could get to God with nothing more than John 3:16. He sighed when his mind stopped on the last still glowing spark--his intense hatred for the men who killed his mother. He had not forgiven them. He felt incapable of forgiving them. As a matter of fact, he defiantly thought, I don't even want to forgive them. He slammed the Bible closed and stood to his feet. Then a strange weakness hit his knees, causing him to sit back down on the davenport.

For several minutes he thoughtfully rubbed the well-worn, black cover on the Bible. Finally his swirling brain began to throw off conclusions. It says right here, he thought, that God did not send Jesus to judge us but to save us. That would mean that Jesus doesn't want to judge me for me hate; he wants to save me from it. So, if I believe in him, he will save me, just as I am, hate and all.

Then it was that Royal Renfro, though still mystified by some seeming conflicts between God's love and God's demands, believed in Jesus and experienced that mystical, not completely describable new birth which Jesus recommended to Nicodeamos.

Jumping to his feet, he took up the lamp and stepped quickly to the door of the hospital ward. His excited intention was to shout out to the Preacher, I'm a Christian!" But he sobered and stopped at the door. I can't even talk, he ruefully thought. He turned back to the davenport, and his thoughts turned to his muteness. Always before he had harbored the instinctive notion that to seek the key to his muteness would be to aggravate the pain of it. Inexplicably, that notion had been swept from his mind, and he began a quiet, but excited search for the key.

For the first time since it happened, he allowed his mind to go back and concentrate on the events that transpired immediately before and after his muteness had set in. He remembered that as he was about to squeeze the trigger, his mind seemed to hear his mother's voice, clear and strong, saying, "Son, don't ever hurt anybody; don't ever do revenge." That had been one of his gentle mother's favorite admonitions. And it was that imagined voice that had caused his finger to freeze and which had allowed her killers to escape. He now also recalled the huge load of guilt which immediately fell on him when he let the killers go free. Simultaneously he was abruptly filled with searing, numbing hate--hate for the killers, hate for himself, and hate for God who had seemed to claim the exclusive right to deal with the killers. And it was in the grip of this overwhelming, three-pronged hate, until now unrecognized, that his muteness had struck.

The Preacher had said, "justice", and Royal saw now that God would not have been displeased if he had brought the killers to justice. He suddenly realized that his hate for God and for himself and even for the killers had evaporated from his life. On the other hand, he was not sure he had forgiven the killers. He thought that he had not. But he also felt that he could successfully deal with that later. At the moment, he was happily confident that he had torn away the underpinnings of his muteness.

He thought carefully about what he wanted his first spoken words to be. He decided on "Grandpaw, I am a Christian." Excitedly he walked back the Preacher's bedside and opened his mouth. His tongue moved, but his voice box refused to perform. The words simply refused to come out. Crestfallen, but still serenely confident that he could soon break his silence, he fell on his bunk and into a peaceful sleep.

Royal was awakened by a shaft of sunshine which shot thought the hospital's curtainless windows. He squinted and bolted upright, gripped by the fear of not knowing where he was. He was calmed by the familiar voice of William T. Applegate. "You're in the hospital with me."

The Preacher was sitting up, slowly stirring a steaming bowl of corn meal mush. "This ain't much of a breakfast, but I'm so hungry it looks good."

Royal wrote: I'm glad you are better."

Thereupon, Applegate went into a spasm of coughing and spitting, after which, in a thin but defiant voice he declared, "Yeah, I'm better."

Royal wrote his good news: "Grandpaw, I'm a Christian."

The old man's eyes bugged, and he dropped his spoon on the bed. "Last night?" he gasped.

Royal nodded.

The Preacher smiled and laid his head back on his pillow. "You know, when I woke up this morning, I thanked God for letting me live a while longer. I guess I never thought I'd be more grateful for anything than just being alive. But I am."

The old man's eyes wailed with tears as he reached out and took possession of Royal's notebook. He tore out the page containing Royal's announcement and briefly pressed it to his lips. "I'd rather have this than life itself," he whispered.

Royal beamed and allowed himself to soak in the glory of the moment. Then, facing the realities of Applegate's new lease on life, he picked up the spoon, filled it with mush and held it to the Preacher's lips. But the old man gently pushed the spoon away. "Thanks, but I can feed myself; but before I do, I want to say a couple of things to you as you start your Christian life. You've got a big conscience, the biggest I ever saw. That's good as long as you don't let it get bigger than your gumption. You can well afford to let your love get bigger than your mind, but never your conscience. You understand?"

Royal wrote, "I'm not sure."

"I'm not either," the old man growled. "but think about it. OK?"

Not waiting for a response, Applegate raced on. "Well, enough of that. Hopefully you'll have to hear me preach a lot, so I'll spare you any more right now. What you need to do now is go and get yourself baptized. I'm sure there's more than one preacher here in Mesa who will be glad to put you under."

Royal shook his head vigorously and penciled, "I won't let anybody baptize me but you."

The old Preacher was obviously pleased. "I think God wants new Christians to be baptized as soon as its practical; and in this case, I've got the definite notion that he thinks it'll be practical only as soon as I'm able to do it."

Royal wrote: "Now, will you eat your mush?"

Accepting the spoon from Royal, the old man began to devour the cold mush with noisy relish.

Chapter Seventeen

George Renfro took the steps two at a time. Sticking his head into the hospital room, he said, "Time for you to quit lazin round. I saw the doctor in the barber shop, and he said I could take you home today--said he'd be up in a little while to give you one last talkin to."

"Bout time. Do you realize I've been here two solid weeks."

George chuckled. "You're not the only one who has suffered. Royal found out pretty quick that a good cook's helper is not necessarily a good cook. He's improvin right along; but if the cowboys didn't like him, they would have sent him packin by now."

"Aw they just like to bellyache, but I'm sorry the boy's had to take so much of it. What else has been goin on?"

"Not much except that the cows keep gettin thinner and worse lookin all the time. Every day they have to drift further and graze harder for less and less grass. All the rain fed water holes are nothin but mud holes with a thin skim of water in the middle."

"That makes for a dangerous situation," the Preacher put in.

"Yeah, some of those thirsty old cows got to walking out so far in the mud that they bogged down and couldn't get back. The boys managed to lasso most of 'em and get the horses to pull 'em out. But even so, we lost four cows, and Feister finally ordered that temporary fences be thrown up around all the holes."

"How are the wells and springs holding out?" Applegate asked.

"Fair, runnin about three quarters of normal. But they're few and far between. The cows are havin to walk an awful long ways to water. It's a shame. They ought to have a lot more windmills, and those dirt tanks ought to have been dredged."

"Well," the Preacher responded, "I guess there's not much me or you can do about that. Back to Royal. He told you he's a Christian I guess."

"Oh, sure. He was right giddy."

"And Jane? Did he tell Jane?"

"As a matter of fact, he told Jane and me at the same time. He wrote one note for both of us. You know," he went on, "lookin back on it, Jane acted a little odd-like. At first, after she looked at the note, she laughed and hugged and kissed Royal. But then, when she turned away--I could see it but Royal couldn't--her face fell, and she had this sad look in her eyes."

"I'm not surprised," the Preacher replied. "You see, Jane had the idea--and about sold me on it--that Royal's muteness and his mad-on at God were somehow connected. And she had talked herself into thinkin that if he would become a Christian, he would be able to talk again. It just didn't happen that way, and she's naturally a little upset."

George threw up his hands. "I'm glad you told me. I never thought about the two things bein related."

The Preacher put on a sad smile. "I still think they are, but....Anyhow, be that as it may, before the doctor gets here, I want to talk to you about somethin else--somethin special."

"OK, what's on your mind?"

"You're father and mother are dead aren't they. Didn't you tell me that one time?"

George nodded. "That's right."

"Of course, I'm sorry, but it seems to me that leaves it open for me to legally adopt you as my son, and that would make Royal my legal grandson."

"You mean to go to a lawyer and get some papers drawn up?"

"Sure."

"Aw, as long as it suits us, why go into all that legal stuff?"

"Won't cost much. At least I don't think it will. And that's the way I want it--all legal. You got any objections? Had you rather not be my legal son?"

"Oh, Great Day, No. Don't get testy. I like

bein your son, and if you want to get some papers fixed up, so be it."

"Good," the Preacher replied. Then, seeing the doctor darken the door, he said, "Come on in doctor and tell me the damages. I'll have to give you a check on the bank in Jacksboro, but it'll be good."

"That's fine," the doctor replied, holding out a sheet of paper. And here's your bill."

George rashly grabbed the bill away from Applegate. "Hey, what's goin on," the old man demanded.

"I grabbed it because I'm gonna pay it. Well, not me exactly, but me and a bunch of others. Me and Royal and all the cowboys sort of took up a collection, and it looks like we took in a little over enough to pay this bill."

"No, you can't do that," Applegate protested. "I won't allow it."

George quickly responded by handing the doctor the exact amount of cash to cover the bill. "You ain't got anything to say about it. The bill is paid. Anyhow, if it'll make you feel better, the boys said you'd probably throw a fit and try not to take the money; and they told me to tell you that you had it commin because they had never paid you anything for all your preachin."

Plainly pleased, the old Preacher smiled. "Well, God, bless 'em. God bless 'em everyone."

"Yeah, God bless 'em," the doctor echoed as he fingered the money. This stuff fells good to me. I don't get paid half the time. And when I do, a lot of it comes in pigs and chickens and hominy--stuff like that."

"By the way, Doc," said the Preacher, "I need another type of professional services. Is there a lawyer in town?"

"No. One is supposed to be on the way, but right now the closest thing to a lawyer we have is the Honorable Julius J. Van Cleve."

"Who's he?"

"He's the Justice of the Peace. He's not a lawyer, but he practices law a lot. He is reasonably honest abut it though. What I mean is--he'll look you right in the eye and claim to be a lawyer, but he will quickly follow it up by putting you on notice that he does not have a license."

"Does he know what he's doin?"

"Aw, I guess so," the doctor replied. "At least as far as he goes, he probably does more good than harm. He writes up deeds and wills and bills of sale--things like that. Anyhow, if you can't wait to get over to Clarendon, he is all we have."

A few minutes later, as they walked towards the Justice of the Peace's office, George inquired, "Why can't we wait until we can get into Clarendon and for sure get this done right?"

"Oh, come on there's nothin to this legal stuff. All of 'em just copy out of one book or another. I'll bet this J.P. can do just as good as anybody. Anyway, I can't wait to go to Clarendon. I need to get this done today. I got my good reasons."

When they walked into the office and closed the door, a deep bass voice came rolling through the doorway leading to a back room. "If you're here to pay a fightin fine, just put your name on a piece of paper and leave two dollars. I can't get out there right now."

"We're not here to pay a fine," George hollered. "We're here to get some legal work done."

"Fine. Just make yourselves comfortable. I'll hurry up--be there in a couple of minutes."

True to his word, Julius J. Van Cleve appeared, looking fresh shaven and reeking of bay rum. The too-long sleeves of his dingy white shirt were held back with gaudy red garters ringing his upper arms. His shinny black pants were held up by clack suspenders which matched his bow tie. He set himself off with a hard, black derby hat. He was shewing on an unlit cigar.

"Welcome, Gents," he boomed, "please forgive my tardiness. I was up most of the night dealing with drunks and fighters. With the courthouse being over at Clarendon and all the other judges being over there to, it's up to me to try to bring law and order to Mesa. Believe me, right now it ain't easy. Well, what can I do for you?"

"I want to adopt George, this man right here," Applegate declared.

Van Cleve frowned. "First time I ever heard of one grown man wanting to adopt another one."

"Well you've heard of it now. Can you do it?" Applegate asked.

"If anybody can, I can. I'm a lawyer. Now listen though, I don't have a license to practice law, and I'm not claiming that I do. You understand that?"

"Oh, yeah."

"But, I've had tons of experience."

"Alright," the Preacher responded.

"Alright," the J.P. repeated. "Does that mean that you want me to go ahead and represent you on this adoption business?"

Applegate was beginning to be a little leery. He decided he'd better sound the J.P. out about his fee. "What'll it cost?"

Van Cleve pursed his lips, narrowed his eyes and allowed himself about ten seconds to size up the economic status of his potential clients. "It'll be five dollars," he announced.

"That'll be alright," Applegate replied. "Now, tell me what you're gonna do."

Thereupon, Van Cleve took in hand one of the three books on his desk, the one entitled: "LEGAL FORMS". He licked his fingers, turned to the index, then back to page 180, at the top of which, in black capital letters, were the words: "Deed of Adoption". After glancing over pages 180 and 181, Van Cleve announced, "Well, this calls for the parents of the child, the one who is being adopted, to give their consent."

"My parents are dead," said George.

"Well, since they're dead, I'll just leave them out of it. Yeah, I can skin this cat. Just give me about thirty minutes. All I need is your names."

After writing down the names, the J.P. pushed the derby to the back of his head, inserted a sheet of paper into his Oliver typewriter and begin to peck away. He was forced to stop and think several times as he adopted the printed form to his rather unusual situation; but well before thirty minutes had elapsed, he produced a one page, single spaced document, entitled, "DEED OF ADOPTION".

"This is a good deed of adoption," Van Cleve confidently declared. I left out the part about the parents and/or guardian. But, to make up for it, I added this: "George Renfro, the one who is being adopted, is over the age of twenty-one years, is of sound mind and freely agrees to this adoption'. Also, instead of the parents, I fixed a place for you to sign at the bottom, Renfro. And, of course, there's a place for Applegate to sign."

The Preacher took a pen out of a holder on the desk. "OK, let's get on with it."

"Don't you want to read it?" Van Cleve asked.

"Oh, I guess so. Let's read it, George."

After a pause, the old man inquired, "All done?"

George said, "Yeah".

"is it OK? the J.P. asked.

His clients nodded.

"OK sign right above where your name is typewritten."

They did, first George and then the Preacher.

"Alright, now, do each of you acknowledge that you executed this instrument for the purposes and consideration therein expressed?"

"I do," they said.

The J.P. signed his name at the very bottom

of the page, right above the line reading, "Julius J. Van Cleve, Justice of the Peace and Ex Officio Notary Public, Miller County, Texas." He then impressed a seal on the bottom left side and said, "That'll be five dollars."

After Applegate paid the fee, Van Cleve gave his final instructions. "Now when you get a chance, go into Clarendon and get this document recorded in the County Clerk's Office. Got that?"

"Got it," the Preacher replied.

* * * * * * *

The next day was Sunday.

The strong windmill-whirling breeze came cold that morning. But the Preacher and his grandson did not seem to mind. The main windmill tank was directly behind them. It was circular, twelve feet in diameter, with wooden sidewalls which stood four feet high. Similarly dressed for the occasion, their upper bodies were covered only by the tops of their long underwear. At the bottom, the underwear was covered by blue canvas trousers. Boots had been left in the bunk house in favor of dingy white woolen socks. Hatless, facing East, they had a slight case of sungrins. Before them, warmly dressed, stood the entire compliment of the Dundee Ranch.

The old Preacher cleared his throat. "First, please allow me a few personal words. I thank you from the bottom of my heart for paying my medical bills. I..." At this point his voice choked. Regaining his composure after a moment, he continued: "I guess you can tell that I've come to an age in life where I cry a lot. I used to be ashamed of crying, but now--well, I may still be a little bit ashamed, but I do it anyhow."

Reaching into his back pocket, the Preacher brought forth a folded sheet of paper. "I consider that what I'm about to do will be the crown on my ministry. I've been preaching out here in this West Texas wind for 40 years. And sometimes I think that most of my words have been caught in the winds and blown away without ever influencing anybody. But once in a while some of my words have defeated the wind and fallen into a person's heart." Laying a hand on Royal's shoulder, the Preacher choked again.

After coughing, he continued: "I feel all warm and good. The Lord has filled my cup til it runs over. When the Lord allowed me to lead to Christ the young man who twice saved my life, you would think that was more than enough of a reward for an old preacher. But the Lord went even further than that. You see, that young man is my grandson."

With that, Applegate dramatically unfolded the paper in his hand, held it out first for Royal and then the whole gathering to see. "Royal didn't know about this. It just happened yesterday. This is an official document of adoption in which I adopted George Renfro as my son. Royal, that makes you my grandson."

Royal smiled through his tears as he hugged his grandfather's shaking shoulders.

Suddenly the Preacher was completely

composed. He walked forward and handed the deed to George. Returning to the tank, he said, "Let's move over there to the steps, Royal, and get ready."

As they approached the steps near which the pipe was gushing clear, cold water into the tank, the Preacher paused, stuck his right hand into the stream of water for a moment and turned back to his audience. "One time Jesus asked a woman of Samaria for a drink of well water, water about like this. Later in the same conversation, he observed that anybody who drank of the well water would get thirsty again. 'But,' he said to the woman, 'if you ask me, I'll give to you living water, and if you drink it, it will change you and your spirit will never get thirsty again."

The Preacher put his foot on the step. Help me, Son," he said.

Responding, Royal placed his hands on the side of the tank and gently vaulted into the water. He put up his hands to his still weak grandfather and supported him as he too made his way into the water. The older man then led his grandson to the middle of the tank and signaled for the audience to move closer.

With his eyes closed, the Preacher paused for a long moment, a moment during which the only sounds were the whirring of the windmill, driven by the wind that nobody could see, along with a soft creaking of the sucker rod and a barely-heard gush of life giving water.

"Royal, my grandson, do you come to this water for baptism because you have already drunk of the living water that comes only from Jesus Christ?"

Royal nodded.

"That being the case, I now baptize you, my grandson, in the name of the Father, the Son and the Holy Ghost."

Swiftly but gently the Preacher bent Royal backwards until the water lapped over his face. Royal came up sputtering; and, almost lost in the sputtering, he also said some words. Nobody, not even the Preacher, could understand what he said. But they knew he said something. Royal and the old man stood looking at each other, eyes wide with wonderment. The faces of the witnesses were struck with awe too. Hushed and waiting, they questioned their own ears.

Finally the Preacher pleaded, "Say it again, Son. Say it again."

Shading his eyes with this right hand, Royal caught the eyes first of Jane and then his father. Then, his eyes swept upward, past the sun, into the cloudless blue; and he softly but clearly intoned, "Thank you, God."

Chapter Eighteen

When evening fell on the day Royal was baptized, the Dundee Ranch furnished the sites for four simultaneous conversations, each separate and apart from the others. Each conversation, though involving only two people, subtly influenced and made prophecy about the lives of all eight of the participants.

* * * * * * *

In the cook's room, the cook addressed his son: "George, sit down and keep me company for a spell. Did Royal tell you about where to find my treasure map?"

"Yeah, he told me."

"Well, what he didn't tell you is that the treasure is located on the Armstrong tract, your land."

George raised his voice, "What? he said with disbelief. "No, he never told me that."

The old man chuckled. "Don't get all unsettled. He didn't tell you that because I didn't tell him--didn't have time. Now, let me tell you the whole story of that map. I'll tell Royal about it later, or you can, which ever one of us gets to it first.

The Preacher then unfolded the story of Eagle Feather and the Comanche treasure.

"Right after I got the map," Applegate continued, "I decided to go out to the Dundee Ranch and see what I thought I could do to take possession of the treasure. Knowing Amos Dundee, I knew I needed to scout out the territory, take my time and plan carefully. So, the offer to come out here and cook for the ranch was an absolute God-send."

"Well, I guess so," George dryly allowed.

"Then, when you told me where your land was located, I knew right away that the Comanche gold was buried on your land."

"Then you realized that you had to worry about me and Royal as well as Mr. Dundee."

"Right," the Preacher admitted. "But then as time went on, just a few days as a matter of fact, I was so drawn to you and Royal I wanted to throw in with you and make you my family. That's the reason I talked you into comin out here to work on the Dundee."

George laughed. "Well," he began in a voice dripping with pleasure, "it looks like my old daddy is a conniving old rascal."

"Yeah, I'll have to admit that's about the size of it. But it's all worked out so far, and now that we're all together in this thing, I think we need to make our move."

"What do you mean?"

"I think we ought to move on the land and see what Amos Dundee will try to do about it."

"What's the hurry, George wanted to know. "I thought you were the one who was so sure that Dundee would be hard to deal with."

"I was, and I don't take any of that back. I don't know what all he'll do or try to do. He can be mean. That I know. But we might as well get on with it--find out where we stand."

"We haven't saved up enough money yet, "George argued. "We can't buy enough cows. Besides that, it'll be hard to get started as long as this drought holds on."

"We'll get plenty of money from the treasure," Applegate exclaimed. "And that spring right there close to where it's buried will never run dry."

"Maybe," George replied, "but we don't even know for sure that the treasure is there. And if it's there, we don't know what it amounts to."

"Oh, no question about that. Eagle Feather settled that, he said the box was full of gold and silver and jewels."

"Yeah, and that Indian may have been the biggest liar the Comanches ever produced. And even if he told the truth as best he could, we have to remember that his memory could have faded through the years. He could have been an old man dreaming dreams. That box, if it's there, may contain nothin more than a few silver coins and a bunch of glass beads."

"But.." "Applegate started to protest.

George cut him off. I don't want to move on that land and thumb my nose at Amos Dundee and then get caught short and be forced to starve out. I say we follow our original plan. And if there is a real treasure there, it'll be a big bonus."

"Aw shoot," the Preacher replied plainly showing his disappointment. "But I'll admit that after I almost went to live in my heavenly mansion the other day, I may be a little too anxious to speed up my life. I'm getting scared I won't get to do all of the living I have in mind to do."

"Just hang on a little longer. This is the biggest thing that will ever happen to us, and we sure don't want to mess it up."

The Preacher's voice was tired. "OK, I guess you're right. Anyway, it's time to go to bed."

* * * * * * *

Clutching a cup of coffee, Amos Dundee sank into the overstuffing of a blue velvet chair in the parlor of Big House.

"You shouldn't be drinking that coffee," Bertha scolded, "it'll keep you awake."

"Can't sleep anyhow," he snapped.

"I know. I know you're worried."

"I'm not worried about anything," he lied.

"I know better," she smartly rejoined. "I hear you walking the floor almost every night."

He gave her a dark scowl. "So?"

"So, I know you are worried. And for the life of me I...."

"You what?" he demanded.

"Well, maybe it's not the proper business of a wife to say this, but I'm wondering if it would be a good idea to sell some of those starving cows."

"Right now I couldn't get half what I paid for them," he argued.

"But if you don't sell them you won't get anything. They're starving to death by the dozens."

"They're hungry, but they're not going to starve to death. But you were right about one thing. It's not any of your business."

She threw up her hands. "I was just trying to help," she blurted. "Slim is always telling me that....". She stopped and blushed. "Oh, forget it," she said off handedly and started swishing out of the parlor.

"Wait just one minute," he curtly commended.

She defiantly whirled about.

"How come it is that you see Slim Feister so often that he is...what did you say? yeah, 'always telling' you something?"

She coolly lied: "I didn't say that. I said 'he told me'. I ran into him one time a couple of days ago, and he just commented that it looked like a bunch of the cows might starve to death."

Dundee fixed his wife in a cold hard stare. "It's none of Slim Feister's business either." Then through clinched teeth, he added, "I'll tell you something else. I didn't like the way you and Slim looked at each other this morning at the baptizing."

"Now you are being perfectly silly. I won't stop to even argue with you about such a ridiculous thing." Sensing that she had attained an advantage in the duel of words, she made an exaggeratedly haughty exit.

Amos sat staring into the fireplace. Finally he drained his cup. He made a face when he swallowed. The coffee was cold, very cold.

Upstairs, Bertha slipped into bed and fixed her eyes on the ceiling. I don't think he knows anything, she thought, but he's getting too close for comfort. She resolved to locate Slim the next day and tell him to back off for a while.

* * * * * * * *

In the foreman's house, Mary struck a match to the lamp. "There. Now we can read for awhile."

"Might as well," Feister answered, reaching for a magazine."

"Wasn't it thrilling the way Royal recaptured his voice?" she said.

"Thought you wanted to read," he growled

"I do. I just though I'd mention it."

"What?"

"About Royal being able to talk again; but never mind."

"He was just puttin on," Feister snorted. "I thought that all along."

"That's outrageous. How could you say that about that fine boy."

"It's easy," he sneered, "I don't like him."

"Well, of all things," she exclaimed. "It looks like he and Jane are going to get married some day. What do you have against him?"

"It's his daddy. I don't like his daddy, and he goes with his daddy as far as I'm concerned. Whatever his daddy does rubs off on him."

"Any why in the world don't you like George Renfro?"

Slim wrinkled his forehead and searched her eyes with his. "For openers he's a farmer and a trouble maker."

"Oh for Pete's sake, Slim, farmers are not necessarily trouble makers, and you know it."

"This one is. He talks about farmin some of the land and diggin tanks--that sort of thing."

"Has he mentioned things like that to Amos Dundee?" she wondered aloud.

"Not that I know of, but he's liable to. I think he'd like to make me look bad."

"Then why don't you make some of those suggestions to Dundee yourself? And by the way, why don't you suggest that he sell some of those starving cattle?"

Feister got to his feet and slammed his fist on the kitchen table. "In the first place, I ain't no farmer, and I won't have any part in turning this outfit into a farm. In the second place, I got where I am by keepin my mouth shut at the right times, and this is one of those right times. And the third place, you don't know what you're talkin about.

You're a woman who is way out of line. And another thing...." He paused to get his breath.

Color shot into Mary's cheeks, and her eyes flashed fire. Her native intuition, honed sharp by anger, suddenly revealed to her the other thing that was on Slim's mind. And, without thinking, she launched a preemptive strike. "Just one minute, Slim, speaking of someone being 'way out of line', I didn't intend to say anything about it, but now I will. It was downright embarrassing the way you and Bertha looked at each other during the baptism service."

Slim's face went white then, save for a line along the entire width of his upper lip, went red. "Are you accusing me of chasin after Bertha Dundee?"

"If the boot fits..., I saw what I saw," she evenly rejoined.

"Alright," he said through clinched teeth, "I'm just gonna say it once. If you ever mention anything again about me and Bertha, I'm gonna give you a whippin you'll never forget. You hear me?"

Mary stood silent.

"And I'll tell you what else is on my mind-- what I was gonna say before you started in on that junk about me and Bertha. I couldn't have been lookin much at Bertha because I was lookin so much at you lookin at George Renfro like a dying cow, and him lookin back the same way. And that's another good reason why I don't like him."

Successfully winning a hard fight to control herself, Mary managed to calmly say, "That is completely absurd."

Feister snorted. "Huh, the funny thing is that you probably think you're tellin the truth."

She grabbed a coat. I'm going to take a walk in the moonlight," she murmered.

"Stay gone as long as you want to," he snapped.

* * * * * * * *

Standing in the hay loft of the big barn, Royal and Jane gently broke a lengthy clinch. "Oowee," she happily sighed, "let's sit on the hay and look out at the moon."

His response was to sit down suddenly and pull her down on top of him. "Hey," she gleefully whispered, "you're kinda frisky tonight."

She rested her head on his shoulder and said, "Say it again."

"What?"

She playfully slapped his leg. "You know what."

"I love you," he whispered.

She closed her eyes and smiled. I guess the main reason I wanted you to be able to talk was to hear that."

She opened her eyes, reached up and lightly touched his lips with her index finger. "Do you have anything else to say?"

"Naw, guess not. Oh yeah, there is something I want to tell you."

Charged with excitement, she jerked her head from his shoulder. "Tell me quick," she begged.

Proudly he announced, "Well, my dad and I own some land."

Her face fell. "Oh, well that's nice."

"Yeah, but by the way, you'll have to keep that a secret. Don't even tell your mother, OK?"

"OK, but why so secret. Where is this land-- back in Van Zant County?"

Moving to hushed tones, he replied, "No, it's right here; right on this ranch."

"That's crazy."

"Sounds like it, I know. But we own 640 acres of land which is right in the middle of Dundee's south pasture."

She gasped. "No wonder it's a secret. What makes you think you own some of Mr. Dundee's ranch?"

"It's a long story. I'll tell you some other time. But right now, take my word for it, we own a section of land on this ranch."

"What do you intend to do about it," she asked.

"As soon as we've save up some money, maybe in about a year, we'll move on our land."

She frowned. "Then you'll quit working here."

"Sure. Say, you don't seem very pleased about it. I thought you'd be glad. It'll give me a chance to same day make you proud of me."

"But I'm already proud of you," she argued. "And I think it's nice, the land. It's just that it seems like everything is going sort of be turned upside down for a long, long time. There's no house on your land, whereever it is, and..."

"Well," he cut in, "things may move faster than you think. My new grandpaw also has the map to a treasure. So we may have lots of money. You'll sure have to keep that a secret too."

"Aren't you full of surprises," she exclaimed. "Where is this treasure?"

"I don't know."

"What kind of a treasure is it, a gold mine or what?" She giggled. "Don't tell me it's a gold mine on the Dundee Ranch."

"It was Royal's turn to frown. "I don't know. I'm sure he'll tell me, but he hasn't had time yet. He just told me about the map when he was in the hospital."

"Oh, Royal," she signed, openly displaying her despair.

"It'll be OK," he soothed, "I'll find out all about it."

She gave him a little smile. "I know. It's OK. I don't suppose you have any other surprises for me."

"Can't think of any. Looks like that would be enough for one night."

She put her head back on his shoulder and tried to think things out. He won't ask me now, she thought, or anytime soon. He wants to move on that land and find the treasure and I don't know what all before he wants to get married. Her shoulders involuntarily shuddered.

He was astonished. "Are you crying?"

"Just a little," she softly sobbed.

"But why?" he wondered.

"Oh, I'm just so happy."
She raised her head enough to look past his head and up into the heavens. Don't get too upset, God, she thought, after all I'm crying partly because I'm happy.

Chapter Nineteen

Nora Dundee, arriving home for Christmas, stepped off the train clinging to the arm of Mike Vernon. Attracting every eye on the platform, she was, in a word, fetching. A two piece blue woolen suit clung tightly to the contours of her tall, slender body. The skirt narrowed gracefully from hips to ankles, limiting her black, high-heel shod feet to half steps. Her neck was enclosed by the dainty lace-top funnel of the white blouse which rose under the coat from her waist. Her short blonde curls were crowned with a huge blue hat adorned with white ostrich feathers. The outfit, purchased in one of the most fashionable salons in St. Louis, was fit for the homecoming of the daughter of a cattle baron.

"Wow!" she exclaimed, looking around in the bright sunshine, "Mesa has grown. And it looks so good." Pausing to turn her smiling eyes on Mike, she purred, "And you look good too, Mike Vernon."

"You're the one who looks good," he

countered. He said it soberly, like one assessing the value of a work of art.

"I feel so lucky to have run into you. I can hardly wait for the Christmas dance," she gushed.

"Me too. In comparison, I'm afraid things are going to be a little dull until then. I'll admit though, I'm excited about meeting Dad and looking for office space here in Mesa."

"Oh, I think it would be so grand if you moved down here and established a law practice. Mesa needs a lawyer, and I need you close to me.

"Yeah, that would be nice. Hey, there's my Dad now. Hi, Dad."

The elder Vernon extended his hand. Hi, Son."

"Dad, you remember Nora Dundee."

"Indeed I do, good to see you too, young lady, " he said, squeezing the fingers of Nora' right hand. "By the way, there's a young fellow from the ranch looking for you. I was talking to him when the train came in. There he is."

Lawyer Vernon was pointing to Royal Renfro who was standing near the Dundee Ranch's best buggy. He waved and started towards them.

"Good gosh," she spudered angrily, "that's the dumb boy. Why would they send him?"

"You mean he's stupid?" Mike softly inquired.

"Well, I guess so. He can't talk, can't say a word.

Welcome home, darling Nora," she said in a mocking, contemptuous tone. "This makes me so mad I could spit."

"Well, he certainly is a handsome young man," the elder Vernon observed. "And I distinctly heard..."

Royal interrupted: "Hello, Miss Dundee, "I'm Royal Renfro from the ranch. Your mother sent me with the buggy to take you home."

Nora's eyes widened, and her mouth fell open.

In her silence, Royal extended his right hand to Mr. Vernon and said, "Sir, I'm Royal Renfro."

"Pleased to meet you. I'm Robert Vernon, and this is my son, Mike."

Royal and Mike shook hands and carefully took the measure of each other. Each liked what he saw.

Nora gave an embarrassed little giggle. "I must admit I'm a little bit taken aback. Just as you were walking towards us, I told Mike and his father that you were dumb." She flushed. "I mean I told them you couldn't talk."

"I'm sorry you're embarrassed," he soothingly replied. "Please don't be. After all, the last time you saw me I couldn't talk. I just regained my voice a couple of months ago."

"Oh good," she exclaimed. "Then I don't feel so..." She laughed. "So dumb."

Royal rewarded her little speech with his most engaging smile which seemed to trigger her to move from Mike's side and to take Royal's right arm in both of her hands. Smiling radiantly she said, "They're unloading my things now. I'll go with you and point them out."

Pulling gently on Royal, she cocked her head at Mike. "Bye, Mike, Mr. Vernon. Give my love to Mrs. Vernon."

After Royal and Nora moved away, Mike observed with an amusement, only slightly tinged with sorrow, that he might not have a date to the Mesa Christmas dance after all.

Royal had hardly started the horses towards the ranch before Nora purred, "I notice you've been calling me Mam and Miss Dundee. Now, my friends call me Nora. And you are one of my friends, aren't you?"

"Oh sure, Nora," he replied.

And so began a long, animated conversation in which she told him about school and St. Louis, and he told her about the prairie fire and about how he regained his voice.

As the horses pulled up to the Big House veranda, she possessively placed her left hand on his right one. "We have really gotten to know each other, haven't we. I don't know when I've enjoyed a ride so much."

He grinned. "Yeah, me too."

* * * * * * *

Jane's big, brown eyes raged with pure jealousy. "Well," she fumed, now that you can talk, you're good enough for the princess herself. She didn't waste any time that's for sure and certain. She hasn't been home a full day, and she's already asked you to come to dinner at her house."

"Aw, come on, Jane," he begged, "she didn't

ask me. The big boss himself asked me."

"Huh, it doesn't take a genius to figure out who's behind it."

"All I know is that the boss himself asked me. Now, I ask you fair and square: what was I suppose to say? Maybe something like: Sorry Mr. Dundee, but I have another engagement?"

She put a reluctant smile on her face. "No, I guess not. But you'd better behave yourself."

Later, discussing the dinner invitation with her mother, Jane returned to her jealous fears. "What if he falls for her? Why not? She's beautiful. She's rich. She's..."

"Not you," her mother finished, "and Royal is crazy about you."

Then, in a striking example of love triumphing over jealousy, Jane exclaimed, "Oh, mother, I don't want him to embarrass himself. What if he doesn't know which fork to use, how to eat soup--all of that."

"You know," Mary replied, "that might be a problem at that. Maybe you ought to go find him and find out if he knows all those things."

"Mother, I couldn't ask him that. But you could. Will you?"

"OK, I'll do it. I love that boy, and I'd rather embarrass him that to have him be embarrassed at Big House."

Finding Royal stirring a pot of beans, Mary said, "I hear you are going to have dinner at Big House tonight."

"Yeah. Jane's mad too, but I can't help it."

"She'll get over it. But, look, Royal, I have

something to ask you, and I hope you'll realize that the question comes from a person who admires you very much. OK?"

"Why sure, Mrs. Feister, ask anything you want to."

"Well, do you know which fork to use?"

The frown crossing Royal's face conveyed his befuddlement.

"Tonight," Mary explained, "they'll have two forks, probably three spoons and maybe more than one knife at your place at the table. There will be a big plate and probably two smaller ones. There will be at least two glasses and a cup and saucer."

By this time Royal's puzzlement had turned to astonishment. "What do they need all that for?"

Mary laughed. "I was afraid of that. Now listen, and I'll put you though a dry run on the whole dinner."

She did, and he listened. And that evening he moved through the meal with all the smooth correctness of a finishing school graduate. He also managed, at first to entertain, then to capture, the Dundee family with his excited flow of words and complete candor.

Afterwards, Nora pulled him out on the veranda for a look at the moon. "Have you heard about the Christmas dance?" she asked.

"Oh, sure."

Brushing against him, she tilted her head and gave him a saucy smile. "Well...?" she whispered.

He swallowed hard. "Well, I --uh-- hope I get to see you there. I hope I get to dance with you."

Her face fell. "Are you taking that Jane to the dance?"

"Yes."

Quickly regaining her composure, she gaily went on, "Well, I just wondered if you were going. I'll try to save you one dance. Of course, I have a date with Mike Vernon."

Meanwhile, Jane was taking her time straining the milk. She was softly sobbing, and she wanted to regain control of herself before going home. Her mother would think she was silly for crying.

A voice cut into her musings. "Hey, you got any extra butter?" the Preacher asked. Say, now how did you get all that water in your eyes?"

"Oh, I'm just feeling a little sorry for myself," she admitted. I can't be with Royal tonight. He went up to the Big House to have dinner with Princess Dundee."

The Preacher chuckled. "Yeah, I know. That's the real reason I came out here to see you. I figured you might be a little upset."

"Preacher, I'm scared. What if he falls for her. She's everything any boy could want."

"Not Royal," the old man declared, "he's too smart. You're the one he wants."

"I hope he knows that."

"Look, Jane, even if he were to get a crush on that girl, he'll get over it. He'll always come back to you."

Her eyes were dry now. "We don't have time for such as that. We need to get on with it, get married."

"You're in kind of a hurry, aren't you? Has he asked you yet?"

"No, but.."

"Oh, he will," the Preacher assured her. I didn't mean to imply to the contrary. He will. But why are you in such an infernal hurry?"

She shivered and pulled her jacket together around her shoulders. "I don't know. I can't explain it. I just have this deep down feeling that we need to move fast."

"I know how you feel," he replied, "at least in a way I do. I want to get on with it too. Ever since I nearly croaked out a couple of months ago I've been in a hurry."

"A hurry to what?"

"Maybe I'd better not tell..."

"To get your treasure?"

"Royal told you," he guessed.

"Yes, but don't worry. He swore me to secrecy. I won't tell anybody."

"Good," he responded. "Yes, I'm anxious to move on the land and get the treasure. Did he tell you the treasure is on the land he and his daddy own?"

"No."

"Well, he just hadn't had time. I just told him about it today."

"That land," she began, "that's another worrisome thing. If they move on that land, there's no telling when Royal will be ready to marry."

The old preacher closed his eyes and rubbed

his temples for a few moments before responding. "Young lady, I know you'll worry and I'll not try to keep you from it. As a matter of fact, knowing you will worry keeps me from worrying about you and Royal. You see I too have insights which you call deep down feelings, and they tell me that you will do or say whatever it takes, not only to get Royal to marry you, but to do it quickly."

"You must think I'm awfully forward and conniving."

"Not all the time," he thoughtfully replied. But you will be bold and yes, conniving, when you need to be." Then extending his right hand and lightly touching her shinning black hair, he went on: "What's more, those are valuable and admirable characteristics for a perfectly lovely young woman who knows what she wants and who wants the very best."

* * * * * * *

George Renfro was smiling and shaking his head in disbelief. "I've been hearing about the Mesa Christmas Dance for three or four months, but I never caught on that it was this big."

"Biggest gathering between Fort Worth and Amarillo," the Preacher declared. "Wish I could get this many people to hear me preach sometime."

"Where in the world did they find such a big tent?" George wondered.

"I'm not sure," Applegate replied. "This annual dance started about ten years ago, and they've used the same tent from the start. I wasn't around for the first couple of dances, but they told me that the tent came from a bankrupt circus. And all these coal stoves, they say came from the same place. Every year a bunch from around here take the tent down after the dance and stack the board flooring. Then come the next Christmas, they put it all back up again."

"Who is 'they'?"

"Oh, they have an association that does all that. You know, an association with members and a president and secretary and all that."

"Where do all these people come from?"

"From all over," the Preacher answered. "Of course, it started small, but they tell me the crowd gets bigger and bigger every year--partly because Mesa keeps growin and partly because the dance keeps gettin more and more famous. People come from all the ranches around here and from Clarendon and even from Amarillo. They even had a write up about it in the Denver Post one time, or so they say."

George pointed. "There's Mary Feister standing all by herself. Let's go over and keep her company."

"No, you go on by yourself," the Preacher replied. "I'm thirsty. I'm gonna get some punch. But you be careful."

"What do you mean by that?" George demanded.

His answer was an ambiguous shrug of the shoulders and a quick scuffle of boots towards the punch bowl.

"Evenin Mary."

"Oh, Hi, George."

"You look awfully..."

She quickly interrupted, "Big crowd, huh."

"I -uh-wonder," he stammered, "do you think it would be alright for us to dance--just one dance?"

Mary could feel her cheeks burning and her body tingling. She was furious with herself. This is not a big thing, she said to herself. Then she heard herself coolly and stiffly whisper, "I would judge it to be perfectly proper for good friends to dance with each other once a year."

George didn't wast any time. He grabbed her; and holding her almost at arm's length, surprised her by gracefully gliding then into the rhythm of a slow waltz.

It was a long time that night before Slim Feister paid his wife any attention. In the interim, he spent a lot of time outdoors, taking long pulls on a bottle of whiskey. And his time indoors was spent in dancing and jesting with those who the Preacher called 'them wicked, painted saloon girls'.

It was during this interim that George's 'just one' turned into three more well-spaced dances, all slow waltzes. And that original arm's length had slowly dwindled to nothing.

In the meantime, Mike Vernon gave Jane's ego a muchly needed boost. Holding her close, he whispered, "You know I'm still crazy about you."

Without missing a beat, she gently pushed him away a couple of inches. "Oh, Mike, that's music to my ears right now," she said, shooting an angry glance at Royal who was dancing with Nora. "But you know how it is. I won't mislead you."

"Yea, I know. That's one of your charms."

"Speaking of charms," Jane replied, "the bubbling, blonde princess has plenty. Why don't you sweep her off of her feet and wipe out my competition?"

He chuckled. "She's no competition for you."

"Oh, no," she heatedly retorted, "just look over there. They've danced four dances, and they get closer together everytime. And his silly grin gets sillier all the time."

"She's trying hard," Mike admitted. And you can't blame Royal. She's beautiful and fetching and -uh- rich."

"Well, you're not making me feel any better," she complained.

"Never despair. If she catches him, she's just throw him back. She..."

"Say, now that really makes me mad. You think Royal's not good enough for her."

"On the contrary, I think she's not good enough for him. Otherwise she would have the good sense not to throw him back. Anyway," he went on, "She'll never have the chance to throw him back because she'll never hook him in the first place."

"What makes you say that?"

"You," he whispered softly but emphatically. Sure, he may get a temporary crush on her. I'm not saying he won't, but in the end he won't trade you for her."

"That's reassuring in one way, but in another it's not."

"I don't understand," said Mike.

"That he will eventually choose me--that's comforting, but the problem is I don't have time for him to fool around. Since you don't think he and Nora will get together in the end, why don't you just move in right now and claim Nora?"

He laughed as he led her off the dance floor. "You don't mind manipulating a little do you?"

"I don't see how it's going to hurt anybody," she replied, "as you say, 'in the end'."

Mike paused to look up at the ceiling for a moment. "I hope you won't think I'm too arrogant." He paused again. "Anyway, I'll go on and say it: "I can get Nora in the end. That is, I can get her unless she happens to run into some prince charming in St. Louis. The truth is that I'm about the only one around here with the right age, education, power and money to suit her regal tastes. I can get her most any old time, but..."

"Well then..." Jane eagerly began.

"But," he cut in, "there are two things that keep the present from being one of those old times. First, I haven't made up my mind that I want her. I don't consider her to be a really good second choice. Second, I'll have to catch her between crushes. That means I can't move in while she's got a crush on Royal."

"Just look at him now:" Jane furiously exclaimed. "He looks like the cat who just lapped up all the cream."

Royal was inclining his ear to Nora's full red

lips. She whispered, "You'll be my partner at the Dundee New Year's Party, won't you?"

"Of course," he whispered back. He immediately realized he had made a dumb response. But he somehow didn't care. His logic had been smitten by the perfume in her blonde curls, the dreamy beat of the waltz and the warmth of her gently twitching body.

It was about this time that if finally soaked in on a whiskey soused Slim Feister that his wife had been paying a lot of attention to George Renfro. Seeing them dancing, he staggered to the side of his boss and pointed an accusing finger. "See that, Mr. Dundee. What would you do if your wife danced like that with another man?"

"My wife has been doin it all night," Dundee dryly answered. "You're drunk, Slim. You ought to go out and get in the wagon."

Intoxicated out of his customary kid-glove handling of his boss, Slim persisted. "I ain't too drunk, MR. Dundee, to notice that my wife is dancin too close to that clod hopper."

"You'd better get on out of here, Slim."

"And, I'll tell you somethin else," Slim's thick tongue went on, "that farmer don't talk too nice about you neither."

That aroused Dundee's interest. "What's he been sayin?"

"It's just that he don't like the way you run your ranch," Slim replied. "He says you ought to bust out a bunch of ground and farm it in grain sorghum so you'd have some feed for dry spells. Oh, he's a smartaleck all right. He says you ought to dig a bunch more windmill wells and dredge out the tanks."

"Does he know how to grow grain sorghum?" Dundee asked.

"Maybe," Slim replied, "I guess so. He's a farmer. I'll run him off the ranch if you give the word. You want me to run him off for sayin those things?"

Dundee gritted his teeth hard enough to make his jaw bones stick out. "No", he snapped as he turned and walked away.

Bleary eyed, Slim waded out onto the dance floor and moved close to Bertha and her partner. "I'm cuttin in," he thickly announced. "You told me to back off, but I ain't gonna stay backed off forever."

"Go away, Slim," Bertha hoarsely whispered. "Leave me alone. You're a drunk."

Bertha's partner happened to be A. T. "Big Boy" Wheelis, the foreman of the H.I.I.., who towered some six inches over Slim. Without any warning, he swiftly placed his huge hands under Slim's arm pits and lifted him so as to cancel the difference in their heights. Looking sternly into Slim's blood-shot eyes, he said "You heard the lady, go away."

Slim's nostrils pinched. He was not too drunk to get angry. On the other hand he was not drunk enough to throw all caution to the winds. He managed a sick grin. "OK, Big Boy. I was just tryin to have a little fun."

Next, still in a half stupor, Slim approached his wife and George. "Get away from my wife," he snarled.

"Slim, get out of here. You're drunk," Mary pleaded.

Planting himself between Mary and her husband, George said, "I don't want any trouble, Slim."

"Why shore. I bet you don't want no trouble. You dumb sod buster, you wouldn't know what to do with a little trouble, would you?"

With that, Slim made a miserably slow attempt to land a round house right fist to George's jaw. George caught Slim's right wrist and spun him around. Giving the wrist a quick jerk upwards along Slim's backbone, George whispered, "Slim, do you want me to break your arm or do you want to walk away from me?"

Slim glanced about. The music continued, and the other couples were still dancing. "I'll get you, Renfro," he hissed.

"What'll it be, Slim?"

"OK, OK, let me go."

George released the wrist, and Slim painfully pulled it around to his stomach. Then, with head down, like a whipped dog, he managed to dodge dancers as he stepped, half-blindly, to the door.

"Good night, George," Mary sadly said. "I'm sorry, But I've got to go after him. He may need me."

Totally bewildered, George protested, "For Pete's sake, Mary, don't go to him now."

"He's my husband," she firmly replied. And she left George gravely shaking his head.

* * * * * * *

At 2:00 a.m. the moon shone down on a ghostly sight. The slowly plodding horses, strung out single file for about a mile, were heading back to Dundee Ranch. Most of the riders had wrapped the reins around their saddle horns and were dozing in the confidence that their horses knew the way home. Those that traveled from the dance in separate buggies--the Dundees, the Feisters and Mike Vernon and Nora--had whipped up their horses and gone on ahead.

Royal and Jane brought up the rear. Jane's horse followed close behind Royal's. A couple of times she started to urge her mount along side his but thought better of it. He definitely was sullen, had been ever since they left the dance. She was puzzled. After all, she thought, I'm the one who is mad, who has the right to be swelled up.

Finally she could endure the silence no longer. "Want to talk?"

"What about?" he muttered without turning his head.

"Well, we might talk about Princess Nora."

He turned in his saddle. "Or, Prince Mike Vernon," he snapped back.

Both of them saw the light at the same time. They laughed the laughter of relief. He explained, "I was so busy being jealous, it didn't dawn on me that I could have been making you jealous too."

"I know. Me too," she replied.

"Hey, look there's the fence, " he said, pointing to the wire fence along the north line of the Dundee south pasture. "Let's stop for a minute."

They dismounted and walked to the corner post by the side of the road. "Our land is right out there. The west side of it runs south along the road, and the north line runs to the east along this fence."

"And where is the treasure located?"

"I don't know exactly. You know that. But the Preacher says its out there, and I believe the Preacher."

As they gazed on the moon washed land of his hopes and dreams, a message came to Jane. It came oozing from the marrow of her bones. It told her that this was the time to look down her future. She commenced with an affirmation. "I love you with all my heart."

He put an arm around her shoulders and drew her close. "I love you too, with all me heart. You know that don't you?"

"Yes. And when you dream about moving on that land out there, do you include me in the dream?"

"Sure," he replied, "I mean--some day..."

She became very intense. "I don't mean some day. I mean am I in you dream from the very start? I mean will I be with you when you and your father first move on that land?"

"Oh, Jane, there's no place to live...I mean..."

"I don't care," she said. Then, plunging ahead without hesitating, she asked, "Are you going to marry me?"

"Well of course."

"You have never asked me."

Quickly he met the challenge. "I'm asking you right now."

"The answer is Yes," she whispered before engaging his lips with her's.

Pulling her lips from his, she asked, "When?"

"When what?"

"When will me be married?"

He threw up his hands and swallowed hard. "Hey, give me a chance to get my breath. As soon as we can, I guess but I don't know when that'll be. We don't have anything--not even a place to live."

Aren't you in a hurry to marry me?"

"Well, sure... but we can wait awhile--have to."

"I'm in an awful big hurry to marry you," she declared. "And I don't see why we have to wait. I don't want to wait."

"It's not like I was asking you to wait for several years or anything like that," he protested, "What's gotten into you? Why are you in such an all fired big hurry?"

She looked up at the dark cloud that had momentarily eclipsed the moon. There was wonder in her hushed tone: "I don't know. I really don't know."

"We'd better go on home," he said, "the Preacher will be gettin me up at the usual time to help with breakfast."

As they remounted, she said, "Promise me one thing."

"What's that?"

"That we will marry before you and your dad move on that land out there."

"But...," he commenced.

"I'll live in a tent. I'll live in a dugout. I'll live in a cave. Promise?"

He threw up his hands again. "What am I gonna do with you? OK. I promise."

"I love you," she softly responded.

As they resumed their journey, he snapped his fingers. "I did a kind of dumb thing tonight."

"What was that?"

"I agreed to be Nora's partner at the Dundee New Year's party."

She gasped and shouted, "You did what?"

"Now don't get all riled up. She asked me," he lamely began, "and she's the boss's daughter and all, and...?

Jane pulled her horse to a halt. "So?" she loudly demanded.

"Oh, settle down. I'll get out of it."

"Promise?"

"Promise," he grimly replied.

Then he smiled at her and threw her a kiss. As they rode in silence, she kept anticipating that the song in her heart would be subdued by a pang of guilt. It never came. The Preacher had been right. She had done what she had to do.

Chapter Twenty

George Renfro was engaged in a bit a black smithing on that last day of the year when Amos Dundee first addressed him on the subject of farming. George and gotten himself into some regular horseshoing chores quite by accident. Last November when his horse had thrown a shoe, he had fired up the forge and taken care of the problem. He could shoe a horse as good as anybody and saw no need to wait for the itinerate blacksmith to make his semi annual call on the ranch. Ever since, first one and then another of the cowboys had prevailed upon him to take care of their horses' hooves. He didn't mind, especially during the winter months when carpentry was slow.

As Dundee approached, George had the iron tongs in his left hand and was holding an orange glowing horseshoe against the anvil as he repeatedly pounded it with a sledge hammer. At length he held the shoe up and carefully eyed it. Satisfied, he plunged it into a tub of water, causing a sharp sizzle, followed by a wisp of steam. It was only then that he became aware of his boss's presence.

"Mornin, Mr. Dundee."

"Mornin, George. Looks like you've sort of become the blacksmith around here."

"Guess so," George acknowledged, "just tryin to help the boys."

"Feister tell you to do it?"

"Naw Sir, I just kinda got into it on my own."

"I see. Speaking of Feister, he tells me that you have some big ideas about how some of this ranch should be put into cultivation. Is that right?"

"Yes, Sir," George quietly affirmed.

"What do you have in mind?"

George's eyes glowed, and he rubbed his hands together. "Well, I'd start easy-like with about 640 acres. There's a narrow strip of flat land running along both sides of Goose creek. I'd put in about 320 acres on each side of the creek."

"When would you plant it?"

"First of June or you can go on into July, depends on the rain. Of course, we need for it to rain before we even try to break the ground."

"What would you need in the way of men and equipment?"

"I've thought about that," George replied. "I'd say six riding plows and six four-horse teams of horses, or maybe mules. And, of course, about six plow hands."

"Where would you get the plow hands."

"Mesa," George replied. "Town's full of East Texas boys lookin for a job."

Dundee scowled as he bit the end off of a fresh cigar. "And you think we could grow lots of grain sorghum, do you?"

"You bet. If it rains that new ground will put out a big lot of feed."

"What about the tanks, dredging out the tanks? Feister says you mentioned that too."

"Yes, Sir."

"Know how to use a fresno?"

"Sure do," George confidently replied.

"Think you could teach some of the others how to handle one?"

"Don't see why not."

Dundee paused to strike a match and hold the flame to his cigar.

"Also I think there should be more windmills," George volunteered.

"I didn't ask about windmills," Dundee peevishly snapped. Then, in a clear show of power, the big boss drew on the cigar and blew smoke out--not directly at George--but in such a deliberately careless manner that much of it drifted into his face. "Think you could oversee a farming operation if I told you to."

"Yes," George confidently replied through tight lips.

Dundee's eyes narrowed. George's failure to follow his last "yes" with a "Sir" had not been lost on him. "We'll see," he grunted. And with a toss of his regal head, he turned and walked away.

Later that same day Dundee was accosted by his enraged daughter. "Daddy, I want you to fire them right this minute."

"Fire who?"

"Royal Renfro and his daddy."

"What in the world brought this on?" Dundee demanded.

"Royal broke a date with me. He said he would be my partner for the party tonight, and now he says he can't."

"Why don't you get Mike Vernon for your partner? Didn't he ask you?"

"Yes, he most certainly did. And I was planing to go with him; but when Royal asked me, well, I told Mike I was sorry but I couldn't go with him."

"So you broke a date with Mike, and Royal broke a date with you. Is that about the size of it?"

"Yes," you can put it that way. But the fact remains that I have been utterly humiliated, Daddy; and I demand that you do something about it."

Dundee did not take his daughter's request lightly. She was spoiled, but she was his and that gave her the right to be spoiled. And under almost any other circumstances he would have not hesitated to appease her wrath. However, at this particular moment, his mind's eye was full of pictures of the dozens of dead cows that littered his pastures. It was going to get worse, and he did not intend to ever have another such disastrous winter. In short, he needed George Renfro, and he knew it. He could not afford to lose his ranch over his daughter's pride.

"Look, Honey, for business reasons it would be very disadvantageous for me to release the Renfros at this time."

"But, Daddy...."

"Now wait, Honey. I know best about business. Now, look here, Mike Vernon is coming to the party isn't he?"

"Well, yes. But he may be bringing some other girl," Nora replied.

"So, can't you latch onto him and beat out the other girl, if there is one?"

She frowned. "Well, sure, but..."

"Couldn't you take care of your problem that way for the sake of your old Daddy who just might give you an automobile when you finish school."

She quickly trumped her pout with a big smile. "Oh, alright," she yelled, throwing her arms around her daddy's neck.

* * * * * * *

The New Year's Eve parties were Bertha Dundee's bits of heaven on earth; and the adamantly refuses to make allowances for the drought. In fact, because of the fireworks display, she spent more money then ever before.

Mike Vernon came to the party by himself. After Nora threw him over, he started to get a date, but it occurred to him that if Nora successfully claimed Royal as her partner for the night, he could probably successfully claim Jane for his. He fully realized that partners for the party had only a remote chance to translate into partners for life. Nevertheless, the party, he thought, would be his last chance to get Jane, and he didn't intend to loose it. In any event, he reasoned that the worst that could befall him by showing up without a date was to end up with Nora. And, of course, that is exactly what happened.

When Nora possessively took his arm, Mike commented, "I don't see Jane or Royal."

"Well, of course not," she replied, "you know very well that the hired hands are not invited to this party."

Mike's eyes hardened. Two years ago a similar remark had caused him to cram his white hat on his head and stomp away from the party. Now his anger was tempered by caution. He soberly took note of the smiling, beautiful Nora and of the finery which surrounded her. Perhaps this was the best he was going to have. It was second best, but it wasn't too bad, and it was an option he resolved not to summarily discard.

The fireworks display began promptly on the stroke of midnight. It was a spectacle which could not be withheld from the hired help, and all of them had stayed up to enjoy it. Royal and Jane were sitting in the hay loft, legs dangling out of the door. "That was beautiful", she exclaimed after the last rocket had blown sparks across the sky. Would you like to do that some day?"

"Do what?"

"Put on a big fireworks display, make enough money to do that," she answered.

"Is that what you'd like for me to do?"

"Oh, I don't know," she began, "I just wondered how you felt about--oh you know--trying to get rich and all that."

"Being rich would be fine with me, but it doesn't play a very big part in my day dreams. Mainly I want you. But also" he thoughtfully continued, "I want to have a place of my own, some land and a house. I want to be my own boss." He paused and kissed her on the nose. "I guess though, when I come right down to it, I want to do whatever will make you and Dad and the Preacher proud of me."

"Don't worry about that," she quickly assured him, 'we'll always be proud of you."

He smiled. "Yeah, I guess that's right, and I guess that's easy." He wrinkled his forehead. "Come to think of it I left out the hard part."

"What's that?" she whispered.

"In the end what I want is to be proud of myself."

She nestled her head on his shoulder and dreamily whispered, "That sounds like my Royal?"

"Hey," he said, playfully pulling her ear, "what about you? What do you want? Do you want to be rich, fireworks-rich?"

She laughed. "Of course."

"You don't sound very convincing."

"It's no wonder," she softly replied, "because it suddenly came to me that what I want most is to have your baby. Nothing else matters very much."

Royal jerked his head back and yelled, "What!"

"Shh," she whispered, "hold it down. You'll wake the horses."

"What do you mean--baby?"

"Baby," she repeated. "It came to me that I want your baby more than anything. And it came to me that I want it very soon. And that...." She paused, looked up at the stars and continued as if her words were being slowly revealed to her form an outside source. "That is the reason why I'm in such a hurry to get married."

* * * * * * *

Amos Dundee lost almost 900 cows and almost 1000 calves that winter of 1915, almost as many as he had purchased from the SOQ. Because the carcasses were well scattered, it looked like even more had perished. A cowboy could ride over most parts of the vast ranch without ever being out of sight of at least one animal which had finally turned its back to the wind and laid down on the barren ground, never to get up again.

In spots the stench was almost unbearable. The dead were too numerous to bury or burn and too many for the coyotes and buzzards to clean away. In a few weeks the foul odor of rotting flesh would fade away, but if would be months before the carcasses would be reduced to hides and bones. And many more months would pass before the hides disappeared into the dust and wind, leaving only the ghostly white bones as permanent reminders of that horrible time.

It could have been worse. Mercifully it finally rained on March 10th and again on the 11th and 12, three inches in all. The thirsty earth swallowed most of the water, leaving little to run off into the tanks. But the drought was broken. Coincidentally, the weather turned unseasonably warm, causing the spring grasses to vie with the winter grasses for the right to grow. And grow they did--all of them--painting the rolling pastures with what the Preacher called "resurrection green".

The rain-softened ground also turned Amos Dundee's thoughts again to farming. He approached his banker in Amarillo with some reluctance. He had not quite rid his mind of the notion that turning to farming for help put the brand of weakness on a cattleman. He was pleasantly surprised. The steel-eyed banker had no such misguided notions about successful beef production. He congratulates Dundee for his ideas, foresight and leadership. He declared that Dundee was about to set an example that would lead Northwest Texas to heights of stability in beef production which otherwise could never be reached. In the end, he cheerfully gave Dundee a blank check loan to finance his farming operation.

With his financial support in place, Dundee returned to the ranch just long enough to check on things and to pick up George Renfro. Then, with George at his side, traveling as swiftly as possible by train and fast buggy from Mesa to Clarendon to Amarillo and back, he managed in one day less than a week to acquire and put en route to the ranch all of the things George said he would need. These included men, wagons, plows, horses, harness, feed and seed, as well as tents equipped with stoves, cots and bedding.

Two men stayed close together except at meal times and at night. Dundee stayed in the finest room in the finest hotel available in each of the three cities. Each evening he would hand some money to George, always with the words, "Here's enough to cover your room and breakfast." George would then find a room which could be had for his allowance. Then, for each dinner and supper, Dundee would go his separate way but would give George money for each particular meal. Never did he dole out any money in advance. George was both angered and amused at the petty extremes to which the cattle baron went to guard his exalted position.

Since Mesa had depended on tents and half tents during the height of its boom, there was a quick and convenient supply of cheap but good used tents, stoves and cots. George made the erection of the tents, the new homes of his helpers, his first priority. In three days he and Royal had hauled to the ranch and set up three large tents, two which would accommodate four men each and one for cooking and eating.

Nearby they put up six more large tents to serve as temporary sheds for the plow horses. "It's not much," George observed, "but we don't have time to build a barn right now."

On the afternoon of all three days they were

visited by a lone rider who would slowly ride up close, within fifty feet of the tent site. Never again, but on the first occasion both Renfros called out a greeting, to which the rider pointedly refused to respond. Never breaking silence, Feister would stop and stare long enough to roll a cigarette, smoke it and carelessly flip away the very short butt. Then he would abruptly turn his horse about and gallop away.

* * * * * * **

Chapter Twenty-One

On the evening of the third day after the plowing started, Royal stuck his head inside of one of the tents. Its four inhabitants were lying on their cots trading yarns in the light of the lantern. In his most friendly voice, Royal said, "Jack, could I talk with you outside for a minute?"

He was addressing Jack Crawford, a bearded, black eyed man in his late twenties. Crawford slurred his reply. "Wha bout?"

"Just a little private business between you and me."

Curiosity aroused, Crawford got to his feet and unsteadily followed Royal a few paces away from the tent. "Wha ja want?" he inquired.

"You're half drunk," Royal accused. He was talking to a man who was no taller but some forty pounds of fat heavier than he.

"So what?" was the thick tongued inquiry.

"And I saw you take a drink when you were plowing this afternoon."

Crawford leered. "So?"

"So my Dad said that if any of you had to drink, it would be only on Saturday afternoons and night when you go into Mesa. No drinkin out here. Drinkin don't fit in with hard work and livin so close together."

"Yeah, that's what yur Daddy said, little boy; but I need my drink, so I took the matter to a man that's higher than him. And he said I could drink if I wanted to--said anybody what rode a plow all day ought to be allowed to drink when he wanted to." Crawford had started talking loudly, and by the time he had finished, he was fairly yelling.

"And who was it who said that?" Royal quietly asked.

By this time all the other plow hands had gathered around them.

"Mr. Feister, the foreman," Crawford answered.

"Well, Mr. Feister just got you into trouble. He's not runnin the farm part."

Crawford glanced around at his fellow workers. "By the way, you ain't running this show either, little boy; and I don't appreciate you stickin your nose in my business. I think maybe I'll just teach you a little lesson in manners."

With no more warning that, he suddenly bashed Royal's nose with his right fist. He hit the wrong nose. Royal, much leaner and quicker as well as more sober and more filled with righteous wrath, swiftly socked Crawford senseless with a couple of punches to the stomach and head, and finally one to the jaw.

While the plowhands were buzzing, Royal calmly fetched a bucket of water and poured it on Crawford's head. The beaten man sat erect, wiping the water from his eyes.

"Can you hear me now?" Royal asked.

Crawford sat silent.

Royal grabbed his hair and pulled his chin up. "I said, can you hear me?"

"Yeah, I hear ya."

"Then hear this. Pack up and git."

"You ain't the boss. You ain't got no authority to tell me to git."

"That's right," Royal slowly admitted. "I ain't got the authority to tell you to git, so you don't have to git."

A smirk spread over Crawford's face as Royal turned and stepped away. Suddenly he whirled around and pointed his right index finger at Crawford. "But I'll tell you something else, if you don't git, I'm gonna whip you every day you stay."

That brought a laugh from the crowd. "Hey, why don't you stay, Jack", one of them yelled, "That'd be a lot of fun for the rest of us."

The cat calls on top of his bruises were more than Crawford could take. He marched into the tent and stuffed his extra clothes into a flour sack. Handing a note to one of the other men, he said, "Tell Renfro to have my money for the three days sent to this address in Mesa."

"You ain't gonna lite out tonight are you?"

"Yep."

"On foot?"

Crawford took a long pull from his whiskey bottle. Pounding the cork back in, he said, "Yep. I've had enough of this place."

Royal went directly and told George about the fight. "I was mad," Royal admitted. "I hope I didn't mess up too bad."

"You did great. I'm proud of you."

"Whew, that's a load off my mind."

"The other men saw it all and heard it all?" George wanted to know.

"Yeah, I'm afraid so."

George rubbed his chin. "That's good. That's real good."

"Why's that?"

"Respect, Son. They'll respect you. And respect can take you a long ways down the road."

* * * * * * *

Twenty-four hours later, the Preacher said, "There's light in the well house. That means Jane is there. I'm going over and get some butter."

"I'll go with you," George replied.

The door of the well house was wide open, and although they were still fifty feet away, they got a clear view of Royal and Jane locked in a passionate embrace."

"Oh my," the Preacher whispered, "would you look at that."

"Quit looking," George hissed, it's not right to spy on them."

"Well, you're lookin," the old man shot

back.

"Yeah, well lets both retreat and come back some other time for the butter."

Walking back, the Preacher allowed as how "that young couple needs to go on and get married."

"Yeah," George agreed, "but they can't do it yet. They don't have anythin, not even a place to live."

"Well, if you'd let us go on and move..." the Preacher commenced.

George cut him short by suddenly snapping his fingers and saying, "That fight."

"What fight?"

"The fight Royal had last night. It made me start thinkin. I think I might be able to figure out a way for those kids to get married."

"How's that?"

"Don't push me," George replied. "I don't have it all thought out yet."

"Well if you ain't the mysterious one."

"Just give me a day or two," George insisted.

The old man gave up. "OK, OK," he replied, "let's go to bed."

By the middle of the next morning when he rapped on the door of the boss's office, George had settled on his strategy.

"Who is it? Dundee growled.

"George Renfro."

There was a pause.

"Alright, come in."

When George walked in, Dundee had his

head down and with pencil in hand was ostensibly placing a check mark alongside of some of the items on some sort of a list.

Hat in hand, George respectfully stood before the cattle Barron for three or four minutes. At length, Dundee dropped the pencil and looked up. Then, after cramming an unlighted, half consumed cigar in the corner of his mouth, he said, "I don't recall sending for you, Renfro."

George was pleasant but crisp and confident. "You didn't, but I have never been told that I was not to approach you until you sent for me. Am I to understand that I should leave now?"

In Dundee's mind, George's response was uppity. And three months ago he would have put him down by merely snarling "yes". But all those dead animals scattered over his rolling plains had trimmed his arrogance. Even the second generation rich are sometimes forced to swallow some of their pride. He couldn't afford to make this farmer mad enough to quit.

"No," Dundee replied. Then he quickly salvaged some of his pride by adding, "But what you have on your mind better be important."

"It is," George coolly replied.

Waving George to take a seat, Dundee said, "Alright, let's hear it."

"I have several things to request in connection with the farming operations. First, I think I ought to get paid more than ordinary top hand wages. I think I ought to get ten dollars more a month."

George stopped and listened for Dundee's

reaction.

"Well?" Dundee asked.

Now it was George's turn to exercise a little temper control. Through tight lips, he managed to evenly reply, "Well, I wonder how you feel about giving me a raise."

Dundee lite his half-smoked cigar. You said you had several things to request. Suppose you list all of 'em. Then I'll let you know what's on my mind."

George looked straight into the boss's eyes. His anger had cooled. His own eyes glowed with faint amusement. It was downright funny what the boss had to do to keep himself convinced that he was bigger than anybody else.

"Fair enough," George said. "Here's the rest of the list. I want to build a three-room farm foreman's house, about the size of the cattle foreman's house. I want you to make my son assistant farm foreman and raise his wages to top hand's pay."

A new though struck George, causing him to hold up for a moment. In a flash he proved that being a poor East Texas farmer did not disqualify him from being a keen student of human nature. It came to him that if he got all he wanted, he would be compelled to ask for more than he wanted. He must, he thought, throw out something for Dundee to turn down.

"Is that all," Dundee demanded.

"No, not all. I want you to start paying Jane half wages for milking the cows and taking care of the butter making. Up to now she had received nothing but her room and board."

"Is that all?"

"No, I want you to give the Preacher a nice raise."

Dundee slammed his fist down on the desk. "No," he bellowed. I will not. He's already makin more than any cook has ever made."

"Oh," George soothingly rejoined, "I didn't realize that. What about the other things?"

Dundee eyed him suspiciously. "What if I don't give those things?"

George had not anticipated that question. He had intended to get by on a vague, unspoken threat to quit. Now that he was put on the spot, he gave himself a little time to think and in the end determined neither to bow to the ground nor to articulate a threat.

"It's your ranch," was his ambiguous answer.

Again, like a recurring nightmare, pictures of dead and dying cattle played acress Dundee's mind. He swallowed hard and scowled. "Alright," he said, "you can have all of it but the Preacher's raise. But I'll tell you right now, you have run out of your right to any favors for a long time. Understand me?
"

"Yes, Mr. Dundee, and I thank you very much."

As he walked away, George stopped and started to go back. But he didn't dare. He had intended to ask for some of the old furniture stored in the basement of Big House, enough to start housekeeping in the new farm foreman's house. That request had been left behind by a mind racing to outwit the boss. Although he wanted to kick himself, he was still so happy he wanted to throw his hat in the air and holler. After all, they could somehow scrape up some furniture.

And so it came to pass that George Renfro laid low the mountains, filled the valleys and made a smooth road for Royal and Jane to travel. They would occupy the new house. They planned their wedding for the second Sunday in June.

Chapter Twenty-Two

Last September and October the deer and antelope, sensing the scarcity of fodder for the winter, had wandered far south of the Dundee Ranch. Most of them had drifted back now, romping in the April sunshine while they waited for does to go into the thickets and bring forth their spring fawns.

The robins, mocking birds, blue jays and meadow larks had also returned; and, along with the sparrows which had never left, filled the air with song. The moist brown earth turned up by the plows lent a rich look and fragrance heretofore unknown. And the early wild flowers splashed the green pastures with reds, purple, whites and yellows. It was a time of renewal, a time of hope, a time of beauty.

But this time for rejoicing was lost on Slim Feister. Not since Bertha had directed him to back off had she beckoned him forward again. He had grown listless during the desolation of the winter;

and when the rains came, all of the excitement and attention centered on George Renfro. He was, Slim thought, losing his grip on Dundee Ranch, on Bertha, on Mary--even on the cowboys who resented his dark and sullen ways.

Since the Christmas dance, he and Mary had ceased to communicate. They didn't even argue anymore. She prepared his meals and kept his clothes clean. She had left his bed for a cot, an extra one from the bunkhouse. For over two months he had drunk himself to sleep almost every night. And what was more, he uncharacteristically had started drinking on the job, a fact that did not escape the attention of Amos Dundee. If, in the midst of his dark gloom, Slim felt despised and rejected, he had good reason: he was.

The second time Dundee found Slim drinking on the job, he summoned him to the office at Big House. After he had been chastised, warned and threatened, Feister had the good sense to ask for a week off to, as he put it, "sort of gather myself together." And Dundee had the good sense to grant the request.

When he boarded the train in Mesa, Feister was sober and feeling almost of good cheer. He would go to Amarillo, play and rest for a week and come home refreshed, ready for a new start. Had the plan not included whiskey and women, it would have been a good one.

As fate would have it, his seven day program of rejuvenation was interrupted forever on his fourth night in Amarillo. He was rudely blown into the next world directly from the bed of another man's wife. The irate husband, taking full advantage of the so called "unwritten law" dispatched both lovers, each with a well placed, heavy load of buckshot from no farther away than the foot of the bed.

The Sheriff in Amarillo wired the news to the Sheriff in Clarendon who wired the Constable in Mesa who took the message by horseback to the Dundee Ranch. Amos Dundee was sensitive enough to get the Preacher to break the news to Mary. The Preacher was considerate enough to make sure that Jane was at Mary's side when he broke the news. As the events transpired, these precautions for Mary's well being were appropriate but not for the usual reasons.

The Preacher, convinced that shielding Mary now from the truth would serve to worsen and prolong the agony, spilled out all of the details he knew. These details, scarce and bare as they were, sufficed to supply a clear snapshot of the wages of adultery as decreed by the "unwritten law". Jane knew her mother despised Feister, and the Preacher had reasonable suspicions that she did not love or respect her late husband. Yet both of them were a bit taken aback by her reaction. She was obviously not shocked, only mildly surprised. Dry eyed, the only emotion she evidenced was embarrassment. She immediately began to fluster about, opening dresser drawers and tossing clothes on the bed, dragging a suitcase from under the bed and muttering disjointedly about needing to get up to Amarillo.

"I'll go too," Jane declared. "And I know

Royal will want to go."

"Mary, will you bring him back here to bury? asked the Preacher.

"No," she instantly answered.

"Well, then I'm goin to Amarillo also," the Preacher responded.

Interrupting her packing, Mary closed her eyes and bowed her head for a moment. Then, with a flinty stare, she uttered a short, final "No."

"No," she repeated, "I know you want to help, and I love you for it, but I must, I will do this all by myself."

"But, mother," Jane protested, "You can't....."

"I mean it, Jane. I will be terribly upset if you go. I can endure this a lot better alone."

The Preacher turned to go. "I'm not gonna argue with you, Mary. You know your own soul better than I do. I'm just here to help if you need me."

"Oh, Preacher," Mary said, as she ran and put her arms around his shoulders, "I didn't mean to sound ungrateful."

"You didn't," he assured her, "sometimes people just function better without help."

She broke her embrace and gave him a grateful smile. "You're nice." She shook her head with disbelief. "Yes, you're nice even though you must think I'm awfully calloused and sinful for not crying about my husband's death. And I guess I am. But I'll tell you something else," she went on through clinched teeth, "I don't feel the least bit guilty about it. Am I so very wrong and sinful,

Preacher?"

The Preacher pulled on his chin whiskers for moment before he came out with his answer. "I've got the feeling that if God thought you should feel guilty, you would."

Royal and Jane went with Mary to Mesa and put her on the train. After that, without notifying her sister and brother-in-law, she slipped into Amarillo and did what she had to do. She claimed the body, purchased a cemetery lot and arranged for the burial. She rejected the mortician's offer to secure a preacher to "say a few words." She did not actually attend the burial, preferring to witness it from the other side of the cemetery, some fifty yards away. After the grave diggers had covered the coffin and departed, Mary walked over to the grave. There, she took a Bible from her bag, opened it to the Twenty-Third Psalm: and, in a clear voice, read only the first two lines: "The Lord is my Shepherd. I shall not want."

Head bowed, she started walking out of cemetery. She was serene. She had gotten herself into the Feister mess all be herself, and it was fitting that she should get out of it without bothering anybody else. Nevertheless, she was now visited with such overwhelming lonesomeness as to cause her shoulders to shudder. It was only then that she looked up and saw Jane and Royal who had caught the next train from Mesa. Smiling and shaking her head, she ran and grabbed them-- an arm around each of their necks. Then and only then did she cry, not tears of sorrow but of gratitude and relief.

"Mother," Jane began, "we've got to go and see Aunt Grace and Uncle Eugene. They'll be hurt if we don't."

"Oh, I know. I intended to see them after the burial."

When Grace saw Royal stop the rented rig in front of her house, she ran to greet them with tears in her eyes. She hugged Mary and Jane, then exclaimed, "And this must be Royal. I'm go glad to know you, but I'm sorry we have to meet under such sad conditions."

"I'm glad to know you too," Royal replied. Ms. Feister and Jane say a lot of nice things about you."

"I knew I was gonna like you," she replied. "Well," she went on, "I've been looking for you. Of course, I read about Slim in the paper and all. When will you have the funeral?"

Mary quietly explained what she had done and why.

"So it's all over, "Grace responded in a tone of disbelief mixed with disappointment. "Honey, I know you did what you thought was best, but we were here for you, and we're here for you now."

Mary sadly nodded. "I know. And I know that I made a mistake. In trying to shield you and Jane, and..." She paused to look fondly at Royal, "Royal, I managed to hurt you, all of you. It's taught me that sometimes the best way to help those you love is to let them help you."

Grace changed the mood. "Good!" she exclaimed. "The first thing you can do to help me is to stay for supper and spend the night with us. You can't get a train back until tomorrow anyway."

"Sounds great," said Mary, "I was hoping you would ask."

"And the next thing you can do to help me is for you and Jane to move right back to this house just as soon as possible."

Mary curled her lips into a sad smile. "I'm afraid we'll have to take you up on that. It won't be for long. Jane will move back to the ranch in June after she and Royal are married. And I'll get a job and get a place of my own, surely in a few weeks."

"Honey, you can stay here the rest of your life," Grace replied.

* * * * * * *

The next day the Preacher met their train in Mesa and drove them back to the ranch. George wanted to come, but he didn't dare. He was afraid that when he looked into Mary's eyes he would say something that would embarrass him or her or both of them. He determined to stay away from her for a few days but to let her know he was thinking of her by sending a short, plain sympathy note. Shortly after he met the train, the Preacher delivered the envelope containing George's note. "This is from George, and he wanted me to be sure to tell you that he'll be talking to you in a few days."

Mary read the note quickly and without comment. She was relieved that he had decided to send a note. Her misgivings about an early personal encounter were a match for his.

Over in Big House, the reaction to Slim Feister's death resembled a game of cat and mouse. Amos Dundee watched his wife like a hawk when she heard the news of Slim's Death. And for several days there after she looked for unusual behavior on her part. He saw absolutely nothing that would confirm his vague suspicions. Someday somebody might tip him off. But not Bertha. She would go to her grave without giving him any hint that but for the grace of God it would have been him who availed himself of the unwritten law.

It was on the third morning after Mary returned from Amarillo that the Preacher knocked on her door. She was sitting in a cane bottomed chair beside a stack of clothes.

"Come on in, Preacher. Why are you giving me the pleasure of a visit this time of the day?"

"Just thought I'd see how you're gettin along," Applegate replied. "What are you doing?"

"Packing," she answered, gesturing to a large trunk and a couple of suitcases. "Jane and I will be leaving in a couple of days."

"Uh huh, I guessed that. That's the real reason I came. You don't have to be in a hurry to move."

She threw him a questioning look.

"You see," he went on, "there is no reason for you to move at all."

"I'm afraid you don't understand, Preacher, it's a long story that I won't go into now. But suffice it to say that Bertha Dundee hates my guts and has no love for Jane. She is not about to let me stay on in this house, not even until a new foreman is hired."

"But Bertha Dundee won't have a say in the matter," the Preacher countered. "This is the foreman's house, and I'm the foreman."

Her mouth fell open. Then she began to laugh the soft laughter of relief. "I can't believe it. Why? I wouldn't have guessed that you would even want the job."

"I didn't want it, or at least I didn't think I did. What happened was that Dundee called me up to his office early this morning and out of the blue offered me the job. Of course, I was surprised, but after thinkin about it for a few minutes, I took him up."

"Well, I never!" said Mary. "Who's going to cook?"

"Oh, he had that figured out too. The other day in Mesa he ran onto Pete Scoggins, an old friend of mine from XIT days. He was lookin for a cook's job. He's a real good cook too. I know."

She shook her head in disbelief. "You'll be a great foreman. The boys all respect you, but I still can't believe you took the job."

"Well, my first reaction was to turn it down; but after all, I figured I owed Dundee a certain amount of loyalty. And on top of that, I got to thinkin about you and Jane and George and Royal and about this house, and it suddenly came to me that I very muchly wanted to be foreman.

"Well, I never," she repeated.

"Now, you and Jane can keep right on livin

here.   Of course, when Jane and Royal are married, they can move into the new house. But you can keep right on livin here just as long as I'm foreman, either by yourself or with George."

Mary blushed and gasped with a great show of indignation.

The Preacher was unruffled. "Well," he calmly continued, "I mean if you and George get married, he'll move in with you."

She replied with amazement. "Preacher, how could you talk of such a thing."

"Why, George is a nice man," he innocently replied.

"You know very well what I mean." she sternly retorted. "Of all people--I can't believe that you, a preacher, would mention such a thing so soon after my husband's death."

The Preacher remained calm. "The Bible says that God is not for the dead but for the living. May I sit and talk with you for a little while?"

She forced her answer through tight lips. "I suppose so."

"First let's talk about your late husband. From all I know and hear, he never did but one good thing in his life, to-wit, he married you; but he didn't even have the good sense to recognize that. Slim was the kind of man that we don't like. We love his kind as best we can with God's help, but we don't like 'em. And when they're gone God doesn't expect us to cry."

"We've got to respect the dead," she argued.

"You didn't respect him when he was living. Why respect his corpse? Look, I don't have time for you to interrupt your life with a bunch of unnecessary guilt and mourning."

"What do you mean you don't have time?" she incredulously demanded. "Why don't you have time? And besides that, what difference does it make whether you have time or not?"

"I need to get my son settled," he answered. "It's that simple. Look, you are a parent. You want to get Jane settled and happy as soon as possible don't you?"

"You know I do."

"Same with me, except that I'm much older than you, and I might die any minute. Also there's another big thing about all this and that is that life is too short to waste any of it, and takin time to mourn over Slim Feister is a pure waste."

"I'll have to admit that," she said. "But getting married again real quick, that's another thing entirely. I would not feel right, an it wouldn't look right."

"Huh, if I'm any judge, you won't be getting married again too quick if you married again today. I'm sayin that the soul went out of you marriage to Feister months and months ago. And I'll bet your body went out of it almost that long ago."

"I won't deny that," she calmly replied, "but what would people think?"

"Worryin about that is another waste of time," he shot back.

"This whole conversation is ridiculous," she abruptly exclaimed. "What makes you think George and I would want to get married anyway--

at anytime?"

"Funny you waited until now to ask that question," he dryly remarked. Please don't try to play little games with me. I know both of you like the back of my hand. I've seen you look at each other."

She blushed again. "Is it really that obvious?"

"Probably not to everybody," he soothed, "but to me it is."

"I'm embarrassed."

"Don't be. We don't have time for that either."

"You and Jane. You're both in such a hurry. Why?"

The Preacher got up and walked to the window and stared out of it for a moment. "I'm not sure. I just know we need to get on with it. And that brings up a little problem."

"Now what," she asked.

"Under the circumstances we can't expect George to make the first move. He'll think that you'll think it's too soon, that you would be offended. That means you'll have to make the first move towards gettin you and George into a quick marriage."

She held her head in her hands. "I can't believe all this."

"You'll have to make the first move," he repeated. "Will you do it?"

She sighed and smiled. Then, shrugging her shoulders, she quietly said, "Maybe."

The Preacher opened the door to take his

leave. "Good. Remember: never do a good thing tomorrow that can be done today."

"It that in the Bible too?" She teasingly asked.

"If it's not, it ought to be" he cheerfully replied.

* * * * * *

It was almost supper time. The shop door was open, so he saw her coming. Quickly he dropped the hot horseshoe and ripped off his gloves. Then, like a little boy in a hurry to get to the supper table, he wiped his hands and face on a clean towel and arranged his hair with his fingers. By the time she reached the anvil, he was ready.

Without apology, their eyes met in a fond embrace. "Welcome, Mary."

"George," she quietly began in her best school teacherish tone, "recently I read in McCALLS Magazine some statistics which say that you and I have only about one-third of our lives left to live."

This sentence was spoken only after several hours of thought, and she had intended it to be an excuse for her forwardness in opening a discussion which she hoped might eventually lead to a meaningful, romantic relationship. Dizzied by his utter infatuation, George read a lot more into her statement. He heard an invitation to share the last one-third of her life with him. Impulsively and without the slightest fear of rejection, he grabbed her shoulders and kissed her full in the mouth.

She pulled her lips from his and stared at him bug-eyed. Then she threw her arms around his neck and kissed him--kissed him for a long time. Breaking the kiss, she whispered, "I love you, George."

"I love you too," he replied. "How about a double wedding?"

She pushed back from him. "With Jane and Royal in June?"

"Sure. Why not?"

"That would be lovely. Of course, it will have to suit them. And Jane will get to make all the plans. After all, we don't want to butt in and start trying to change things."

"Of course not," he agreed, "We'll just tag along. I'm sure they'll like the idea."

"Oh, I think so too. Do you know what Jane's planning?"

"No, I haven't heard anything about it," he replied.

"She's planning an outdoor wedding. She wants to have it on a little hill beside a spring. She says it's the most beautiful spot on the ranch and is located about half way between Mesa and the main gate. Do you know where it is?"

George smiled. "Yeah, I know. It's on the Armstrong sections."

"The what?"

He glowed with pleasure. "Come," he replied, "let's take a walk before supper, and I'll tell you all about it."

Chapter Twenty-Three

In a voice filled with wonder, the Preacher began the wedding ceremony by exclaiming, "Look at that spring."

He was addressing the crowd that had gathered for the double wedding. Grace and Eugene were the only guests from outside the ranch. All of the ranch residents were there except Bertha and Nora. Earlier, when Amos Dundee appeared alone, he mumbled something about his wife and daughter not feeling very well.

They were standing on the Armstrong land at the base of the hill from which the spring gushed. They had come together in the evening shadows of that cloudless day in late June. The green of lush grass was sprinkled with the deep red of late Indian Blankets. Far below, a dozen cows with calves at their sides were contentedly grazing. Immediately above and to their left, four blue birds fluttered and chirped as they bathed in the splashes of the spring.

For the first time in over five years the Preacher was attired in what he called his Preacher suit. He had to dig it out of the bottom of his duffle bag. It was all wool, black and a bit glossy from long service. The glossy black of the suit was matched by his boots as well as the long string tie which adorned the collar of his boiled white shirt. His beard was trimmed, and his heavy head of gray hair was well combed. He had made sure that he would be appropriately dressed and groomed for one of the highlights of his life.

The brides were stunningly beautiful in their wedding dresses. Mary had fashioned them on her trusty treadle sewing machine which she had thoughtfully had Grace to ship to her almost a year ago. Jane's dress was of white crepe. The bodice was tight with simulated pearl buttons down the front. The abundant gathered skirt fell to her ankles. Her shoes were white as was her straw hat with veil. Mary's dress was made from the same pattern but was blue. She wore black shoes and a blue straw hat without veil.

The clean shaven grooms stood hatless and handsome in their new blue denim trousers and white shirts. Their wide black ties fell half way to their belt buckles. They were shod in brand new black cow-hide boots, the first boots that either of them had ever owned.

"Yes, look at the spring," the Preacher repeated, "and listen to it." He pointed to the sparkling stream which came bursting from the side of the rocky hill. It came shimmering with sunlight, gushing, gurgling and splashing, casting flecks of foam on the rocks and making the mists which alternately captured and quickly released the tiny, fleeting rainbows. It plunged, then raced, finally slowing as it spread out and gave itself to the thirsty plants and animals below.

"How can we liken this spring to a good marriage?" he rhetorically asked. "Both are pure and sweet, never dull, ever sparkling and shrouded with bright colors. A good marriage is not without pains, but like the froth on the rocks, it is mostly left behind in the rush to give refreshment, fulfillment and new life."

Turning his eyes from the spring, Applegate looked again into the faces of those he was going to join in marriage. "Your marriages will be good," he prophesied. "I know they will because you, each of you, will let God go with you."

The Preacher broke out in a broad smile. "Thank you," he said, with his eyes and voice encircling the entire crowd. Now it's time for the little black book." Reaching into an inside coat pocket he brought forth a well worn, black book. Holding it up, he explained, "This is my 'Episcopalian Book'. I've been marrin people with it for forty years. It ties a real tight knot."

The Preacher dropped his folksy ways for a few minutes and proceeded with all the dignity, formality and solemnity of a fully frocked priest in a stained glass cathedral. Rigidly following the directions in the little black book, he explained, admonished, recited scripture, prayed and demanded vows from the participants. After pronouncing them man and wife, he ended by reciting the Lord's Prayer. And that was a thrill. With his eyes open and fixed on the horizon, speaking as though the words were being slowly revealed to him from on high, he drew from that most familiar of all prayers fresh strength of spirit for himself and all those within the sound of his voice.

(The Dundee family was not represented at the big party after the ceremony. Amos listened to the music and singing from his upstairs veranda. Bertha and Nora preferred to swelter behind closed doors and windows, trying to shut out the sounds of celebration.)

* * * * * * *

Mary and George held hands and smiled down on the grain which was almost ripe for harvest. The tall green stalks, crowned by heavy heads of orange maize, seemed to speak not only of material abundance but also of serenity and quiet confidence in the future. The hot August winds had prevented the individual grains from being all they could have been. Nevertheless, they were good; and in total were big enough to fill the Dundee barns with ample insurance against the next drought.

"I wish it could last forever," she whispered.
"What?" George asked.
"This summer, this time of happiness for Jane and Royal, for you and me."

He kissed her lightly on the cheek. "There'll be happiness in the fall and even in winter."

"I know," she wistfully agreed, "but I have walked in sunshine this summer and I will hold tight to the memories of it."

"Hey, you love birds," the Preacher called, "I hate to disturb you, but I've got an important matter on my mind."

Mary laughed. "You could never disturb us, Preacher. What is this important matter?"

"Well, I just think we've all been workin too hard, and before the grain harvest starts, we ought to have a little family picnic."

"Sounds good," George replied. "When and where?"

"Tomorrow afternoon. After I get through preaching, we'll pack a lunch and go over to the spring on the Armstrong Section. I've already talked to Royal and Jane, and they're rearing to go."

"Well, OK," Mary responded, "but why go so far. Couldn't we just ride down to the cottonwoods on the creek?"

George nudged her arm and whispered, "It's OK."

She emitted a little gasp followed by a knowing smile. "Oh, of course, I know why it'll be good to go over to the spring."

"Thanks," the Preacher replied. "That's one of the good things about gettin old folks usually try to humor you." He fell silent, watching the evening shadows spread over the hundreds of green stalks, barely nodding their burnt orange heads.

"It's been a good summer," Mary murmured.

The old man drew a deep breath and let it out. "It's been a good life," he softly responded.

* * * * * ** *

They enjoyed the picnic supper in the shade of the lonesome hackberry tree. Royal yawned. "It's been a perfect day," he contentedly commented. "The wind hasn't even been blowing hard, just enough to turn the windmills."

"Yeah," the Preacher agreed, "and when you get as old as I am you begin to get a little insight into what God meant when He said a day was like a thousand years to him and a thousand years like a day. This day has been as good as a thousand years to me."

Jane waited a minute, then changed the subject. "Why and how did this old tree get here," she wondered aloud. "It's the only tree anywhere around here."

"It's hard to figure out the mind of God," Applegate answered. "All I know is that he sometimes comforts the earth by putting shade where it's really not supposed to be. And sometimes he does the same with water."

"Yeah," Royal interrupted; and gazing fondly at his grandad, he added, "and sometimes he does the same thing with a person."

Royal's meaning was not lost on the old man. He kissed his grandson with his eyes and then hoarsely changed the subject. "George, are you plannin to fence off a part of that low land for grain sorghum?"

"You bet."

"Think you can get the water spread over it?"

"Sure," George replied. "It'll take a lot of diggin but me and Royal can handle that. I figure we can irrigate 160, maybe 200 acres. Part of it will be in wheat for winter grazing."

"You think you can make as good a grain crop as you made for Dundee this year?"

"Of course. Now, we won't have near as many acres planted, but we ought to make two, maybe three times more per acre."

"That's good," the old man commented. "This is good land, and I'm glad to be sittin on it. I'm luckier than old Moses. He just got to look on the promised land, never to go on it. Of course, I haven't possessed the land; but the four of you soon will, and that will be possession for me too."

"But you'll help possess it," Royal protested.

The Preacher smiled. "In a sort of a way. Right down there about fifty feet below this tree, I want you to bury me."

"Oh, Preacher..." Mary began.

The old man waved her off and interrupted, "Oh, I'm not tellin you to bury me tomorrow or anytime soon, but just be sure to plant me somewhere close around here. When you do, I'll possess the land; or it'll possess me. I don't exactly know which, but at least me and this land will always be together."

The old man sprang to his feet and stepped lively to the east side of the spot in the rocks where the water gushed forth. Turning, he walked along the flow of the stream, counting out twelve paces. Turning abruptly to his left, he marched another seven steps and stopped on a big, flat rock. "Just don't try to bury me under this rock," he gleefully hollered.

* * * * * * *

William T. Applegate died that night. He died in the cook's quarters, all alone. Well, not really alone. They found him with his hands clutching his Bible, opened to the 23rd Psalm.

* * * * * * *

Thirty-six hours after he selected his gravesite, the Preacher was back there in his coffin. Everybody on Dundee Ranch was there.

Royal put his hand on the coffin and cleared his throat. It was his first public speech. "The family has asked me to say a few words over my grandad," he nervously announced.

Opening the Bible the Preacher gave him, he said, "When Jesus started his ministry, he stood up in the synagogue and read the words about himself which had been written by the prophet Isaiah several hundred years before:

'The Spirit of the Lord is upon me, because he hath anointed me to preach the gospel to the poor; he hath sent me to heal the brokenhearted, to preach deliverance to the captives, and recovering of sight to the blind, to set a liberty them that are bruised.'

As far as I am personally concerned," Royal continued, "the Preacher was a lot like Jesus. He preached the gospel to me. I was spiritually blind, but now I can see. I was physically dumb, but I can speak. He made it so that I could see the face of God. The Bible tells us that Moses, even when he received the Ten Commandments, never saw the face of God. I guess I'm luckier than Moses because in my grandad I saw the face of God. I know he made most of you, as well as many, many others, see the face of God too. And, well...." Royal stopped and glanced at George, "Well, I guess I'll stop. After you say that a person made you see the face of God, there's really nothing else to say."

George then stepped up and joined Royal. "Alright boys, let's put him down." That was the signal for he and Royal, joined by four of the cowboys, to grab the ropes attached to the coffin and lower it into the grave.

George took hold of a shovel and began to sing, "When the roll is called up yonder, I'll be there." All of them joined in and continued to sing as the shovel was passed from George to Royal and then to each of the cowboys as they filed by. Each threw a shovel full of dirt into the grave. This went on until George, after taking the shovel for perhaps the tenth time, gently plopped the back of the shovel on top of the mound. When that plop was heard, the low mournful singing ceased as if on command. Tears were streaming down the faces of men who had not cried since they left their mothers' knees.

Royal broke the silence. With an air of finality, he brought the funeral service to a simple close by saying: "His memory will last as long as that hackberry tree.. Thank you, God."

Chapter Twenty-Four

It was not the first time George had been compelled to squirm in an overstuffed leather chair while the Baron pompously wrote words and figures on a tablet in the middle of the great mahogany desk. At long last, Dundee laid down his pencil, lifted his balding head and allowed a benevolent smile to flicker the corners of his mouth. "I have good new for you, Renfro. I have selected you to be the new foreman of Dundee Ranch, not just the farming part, the whole thing. You will start right now. Any questions?"

Dundee scowled with surprise as George, without saying a word, stood and walked over to the west window. With hands clasped behind his back, he stared out of the window for a full two minutes before turning and walking back to the desk. Still standing, he quietly said, "Mr. Dundee, I thank you, but I can't take the job."

Although Dundee's surprise was heavy, it was outweighed by his anger. After all the job offer was also a royal demand. "Why?" he bellowed.

"I just don't think it would be fair to you. You see..."

Dundee cut in. "Don't worry about that. I appreciate your humility, but I'm a good judge of men. I'm not gonna get hurt."

"Thank you, Mr. Dundee; but the truth is that I don't expect to stay on the ranch very much longer; and I'm afraid it wouldn't be fair for me to take the foreman's job knowing that I'll be moving on pretty soon."

"Moving where?"

George took a moment to ponder his answer. Dundee frowned as his unruffled employee lifted his eyes and seemed to study the large portrait of the founder of the Dundee Ranch. George's first reaction was to push Dundee off with a vague, general answer and keep secret his claim to the Armstrong Section. But intuitively he quickly but thoughtfully decided to wave the red flag in the big bull's face and check his reaction.

"I claim," George began, "in fact I have a deed to what's called the Armstrong Section. It's a piece of homestead land where that spring is-- where we had the weddings, where we buried the Preacher."

Dundee's eyes glitted with hate. "I am fully aware of which land you're talking about," he snorted. "You mean you're gonna try to move on that land and claim it?"

"Yes, Sir," George firmly replied.

"Over my dead body you will," Dundee yelled. "That land is my land. It's a part of this ranch. We've been using it all these years. I know all about those sorry Armstrongs. They were a bunch of worthless nesters who starved out. Whatever deed you may have its not worth the paper it's written on. You bought a pig and a poke, Plowboy. Somebody made a fool out of you."

"Maybe," George replied. "I guess we'll just have to see."

Dundee slammed his fist down on the desk. "We'll see alright. I'll have the Sheriff standing by, and if you try to move on that land, he'll be ready to throw you off--put you in jail if necessary. And speaking of the Sheriff, you and your boy and your wives have until sundown tomorrow to get off this ranch; and if you're not off, I'll have the Sheriff to throw you off. You hear me? Now get out of here."

When George reached the door, Dundee called, "Renfro." George stopped and put his hand on the door knob but did not turn around. "Renfro," Dundee repeated, "you are disloyal and ungrateful, and I'll not ever forget it."

Choosing not to reply, George marched down to the foreman's house, opened the back door and threw his hat into the kitchen at Mary's feet. Mary giggled. "Now, what naughty thing have you done that causes you to throw your hat through the door first?"

George was sober faced. "I'm afraid it's no joke. I've just gotten us into a big mess." He went on to recite, almost word for word, his recent conversation with Dundee, winding up with the comment: "Truth to tell, I guess I am a little disloyal and ungrateful."

Mary exploded. "That's preposterous. You don't owe him a thing. You have worked like a mule for every cent he's ever paid you. He's got his nerve. Who saved his bacon by teaching him how to save his cattle when the next drought comes? You did. That's who. Why he's the one who is....."

George, now laughing with relief, stopped her. "Hey, I'm convinced. You've made a believer out of me. Now we've got to round up Royal and Jane and tell them what we're up against."

When Royal and Jane heard the news, they hugged each other with glee. "That's music to our ears," Jane cried out. "We were saying last night that we wished we would go ahead and move. Heck, we can live off of wild game if we have to."

"A sad smile crossed George's face. With a sigh he said, "We really needed to save some more money."

"Remember, George," Mary put in, "I still have most of the money I made from tutoring Nora."

"Yeah, but I don't want to use your money."

"Don't be silly," she retorted, "what's mine is yours."

"Oh, I don't know...."

"And what's mine is also Jane's and Royal's," Mary added.

George threw up his hands. "You got me there," he admitted.

"Besides that," said Royal, "we're gonna be rich from the Preacher's treasure."

"Huh," George grunted, "I've never had much faith in that Indian treasure."

"I have" Jane declared. "If faith will make it happen, we're gonna be on easy street."

"We'll see," George replied. "In the meantime we've got to pack up and get out of here."

"Well, at least it's not a long move," Royal observed.

"About that," George thoughtfully began, "I think we best not go directly to our land. In view of what Dundee said about our deed being worthless, I think we need to be a little cautious. After all, the only things we know are what Uncle Joseph told us. Our deed from him hasn't even been recorded at the courthouse."

"Why don't we go to Mike Vernon," Jane suggested. "He's got his law office open in Mesa, and he'll be able to tell us how we stand."

"Good idea," said George. "Tell you what, Royal, you take our deed and get to Clarendon to the courthouse and put it on the record. Then come back to Mesa and meet us. In the meantime, we'll set up a camp just outside Mesa." He stopped long enough to chuckle. "We need to get used to camping out anyway." "Then," he continued, "when you come in from Clarendon, we'll all go to Mike Vernon and find out about our legal rights.

* * * * * * *

Lawyer Mike Vernon, appropriately dressed in seersucker suit, white shirt and black string tie, grinned at the nervously twitching Renfro family. "You're by far the biggest crowd I've ever had in my office," he announced, "If there had been anymore they would have had to stand up."

"It is good of you to see us on such short notice," said Jane.

Mike laughed. "Well, I promised myself I wouldn't start out practicing law with a lot of pretense, so I'll just admit that it was easy to work you in. I don't have but two other clients. Anyhow, what can I do for you."

"Show him the deed, Royal," said George.

Glancing at the outside cover of the deed, Mike remarked, "I see you just got it put on record yesterday." After carefully reading the document, he looked up and a with a quizzical frown. "Isn't this that piece of land on the Dundee Ranch were that big spring is?"

"That's it," Royal acknowledged.

"Son-of-a-gun, that's the best piece of ground in Miller County."

George stated the problem: "The trouble is that Amos Dundee says that land belongs to him and says if we try to move on it, he will have the Sheriff throw us off."

"Indeed," Mike replied, "Well now I would hope the Cattle King wouldn't have it so easy. However, he's a fierce competitor. I've seen him crossed before, and he doesn't take kindly to it." He paused to draw a legal pad in front of him and take pencil in hand. "Tell you what, Mr. Renfro, why don't you tell me how you got this deed and everything you know about the land, and I'll take a few notes as you go along."

George answered by telling the story of his

Uncle Joseph and the story the uncle had told him about how the Armstrong brothers had homesteaded the land.

Mike got up and walked over to a land map of Miller County hanging on one of the walls. He placed his finger on a spot and said, "This new map shows that section to be made up from four separate 160 acre patents from the State of Texas. So far, so good; but I'll need to go to Clarendon and do a lot more checking at the courthouse."

"When can you go?" Mary asked.

"Oh, I'll catch the afternoon train and try to be back morning after next. No, that will be Sunday. So, I'll be back on Monday Morning."

"We really appreciate it," said Royal.

Mike sat back down behind his desk. "Don't leave yet. I need to talk to you a little more and give you some warnings. I've first got to go and check out your paper title. But even if it is OK, we still have a big, big problem. And I just as well throw it out to you right now. You say that Dundee claims the land, says he's been using it all these years--right?"

"That's right," George replied.

"He runs cattle on that land now doesn't he?"

"No doubt about that," George acknowledged.

"And, he probably has been running cattle there for many years and probably can prove that he's been claiming the land for a long time."

"What are you gettin at? Royal asked.

"Limitations," said Mike.

"What's that?"

"It's what we lawyers call the law of limitations, more properly the statutes of limitations. Under those laws, a person can take over a claim a piece of land for so long of a time that he becomes the owner of it.

Anger and fright crept into Royal's voice, "How long of a time?"

"Well, here in Texas sometimes it can be for three years, sometimes for five, sometimes ten and sometimes it takes twenty-five years. However, unless Mr. Dundee has some sort of deed on the record, his only chance would be under the ten year statute."

"Do you think he has a chance, a good chance," Jane asked.

Mike's face was grim. "Yes, a very good chance. However, that land is not fenced is it?"

"No, just on one side," said George.

"That's good, because he can't claim but 160 acres under the ten year statute, so you would have the remaining 480 acres."

"But which 160 acres could he get?" asked Royal.

Mike frowned. "Now, that's another problem. I don't know for sure, but my off-hand opinion is that he could designate whichever 160 acres he wants the most."

"Oh, well," George said gloomily, "we just as well give up. He'll take the part were the spring is, and we can't make a living on the rest of it. We've got to have that water."

Mary got to her feet. "Alright, now," she

said, "let us not hang black crepe until the time comes."

"That's the spirit," said Mike. "Let me go to Clarendon and check the records,a nd I'll also read some law and talk to my father. He's been in this law business a long time, and he may be able to come up with a simple solution."

Sick at heart, the Renfros trudged back to their camp beside Goose Creek, just north of Mesa. "We'll just have to pray a lot," Royal glumly offered.

"Yeah," George agreed, "and while we're praying, we'd better pray that the Indian treasure is really big."

Royal snapped his fingers. "Say, we forgot to tell Mike about the treasure."

"I didn't forget," George snapped.

"If Dundee gets the land where the treasure is, does he get the treasure?" Royal wondered.

George again snapped out his answer, "No."

"Well, how did you find out what the law is on that?"

A hard glit came into George's eyes. "I don't know what the law is, but I know what's right," George firmly retorted. "And I know that if we get that treasure in the dark of night, it'll be ours."

"If it's not the law, it might not be right," Royal argued.

Mary joined George: "But that treasure belonged to the Preacher, and he gave it to us. That makes it right for us to have it."

The Apostle Paul says we are to follow the law," Royal came back.

George looked at his son with hard brown eyes. "Paul ain't ever been without a job, livin in a tent in a place where blue northers are fixin to start blowin in."

Jane quickly poured oil on the troubled waters. "Let's just pray and wait for Mike," she quietly suggested.

Later, George threw another dead limb on the fire, sending up a shower of popping cedar sparks. "Lawyer Vernon didn't leave us with much hope," he glumly muttered.

Mary put an arm around his waist and laid her head on his arm. "Oh, Honey," she sighed, "you know what they say: 'where there's life there's hope."

"Maybe," Royal joined in, "but I learned something else when I went so long without being able to talk: Even when there's no hope, you've got to just keep on going."

* * * * * * *

And so it was that on Monday morning the Renfros were much more persevering than hopeful when they watched Mike Vernon step off of the train. But their barely glowing embers of hope were instantly fanned to flames by the big smile on his face.

He was still smiling when they filed into his office and took their seats. "Let me tell you about it," he began, "it's almost too good to be true. When I got home Friday night, I talked to Dad, and the more we talked, the sicker I got. We couldn't figure out any way under the sun for you to beat Dundee on his limitations claim on 160 acres of that section, and Dad was positive that he could go to court and get the part that the spring is on. Anyhow, like a good little soldier, I went to the County Clerk's office Saturday morning and checked out the title. And it turns out that your paper title is as good as gold. And I thought to myself: What a shame for them to lose such a good title to limitations.   Then I found an instrument recorded in the chain of title which was the last document which was filed before your deed was recorded just the other day."   Mike stopped long enough to wave a clinched fist high in the air. "And guess what it was? A lease, a ten year, paid-up lease under which the Armstrongs leased the whole section to Dundee." He paused again, folding his arms and looking like the cat which ate the bird."

"Come on, Mike," Royal urged, "tell us. That must be good, but we don't have any idea as to why."

"Well," Mike triumphantly answered, "limitations does not run when the claimant is occupying the land under, a lease. That lease was dated on January 1, 1900, meaning that Dundee held the land under the lease until 1910. It's only been five years since the lease ran out, and five years is five years less than ten years, so you win."

Mike was surprised. Instead of shouts of glee and backslapping, he beheld a silent scene. The smiles on his clients' faces plainly told him that they were happy, but their mouths and eyes were closed, and their heads were bowed.

332

Chapter Twenty-Five

Standing near the spring, Royal noticed the lone rider when he was still a full mile away. He thought it peculiar that a rider would be coming from the direction of Mesa so early in the morning. The sight filled him with dark foreboding. He tried to make himself feel better by reasoning that the horseman was probably on his way to the Dundee Ranch, looking for a job. But his mind remained ill at ease. Things had been going too well, he thought, it's about time for something to go wrong.

He was forced to smile as his mind ranged back over the past six weeks. By nightfall on September 15, 1915, the day Mike Vernon gave them the good legal news, they had pitched their tents on their promised land. Bright and early the next morning they went after the treasure. Since the Preacher, on the day before he died, as much as told them where to dig, they didn't really think they needed his map. However, it seemed sort of irreverent not to use it since the Preacher had so painstakingly made it and guarded it with his very life. And so it was that they gathered together with a great deal of unspoken solemnity and formality for the opening of the pouch containing the map. George carefully withdrew and unfolded the map. Then he held it up for all to see.

The map led them to the flat rock on which the Preacher had stood when he told them where to bury him. They found, as had Eagle Feather some forty-two years before, that the big flat rock was thin and rather easy to move. Their shovel, being a far better tool than Eagle Feather and Purple Flower had used, soon struck the top of the chest. The rawhide hinges had rotted away, and the iron latch broke and partially crumbled when George pried off the top. But the thick cedar boards were surprisingly firm. They gasped with delight when the sun struck the contents of the chest. George quickly ran his hands through the contents and let some of the gold coins flow like water down his wrists.

"We're rich," Mary said with a hint of awe and disbelief.

"Yeah," said George. It sure looks like we're rich. How rich I don't know because I don't have any idea about the value of all those jewels and beads. But there's enough gold here for us to start this ranch."

Shortly afterwards, George and Mary took a trip to Amarillo where they ascertained that aside from a couple of gold rings set with small diamonds and one strand of real pearls, the other beads and jewelry were "Indian trade beads", with very little value. Nevertheless, within the next month they were able to bring on their land a fine Hereford bull, together with forty-five cows with large calves. They also brought a good supply of coal, two more horses, a wagon, barbed wire and cedar posts for fencing, and lumber for pens and for the fronts of their "dug out" houses. Moreover, there was money left over for other things including a plow, grain sorghum and wheat seeds, as well as lumber for barns.

"Thank goodness," George said to Mary. "You'll be able to spend your money for furniture and nice things. When we get through, we'll be broke, but we'll be so well started, it won't matter."

The two sets of newly weds maintained separate sleeping quarters, a tent for each couple, while they were constructing their more substantial "dug outs". It took most of a week to make each "dug out", one either side of the spring, about fifty feet from the water. They tunneled back into the hill and shored up the ceiling with lumber. The front doorway was only slightly larger than a man's body, but after a short, narrow tunnel, the cave expanded into a large 12 ft. by 12 ft. room. They planted a cedar post on each side of the door opening and hung a heavy wooden door to keep the blue northers at bay. Night or day, they needed their coal oil lanterns, but the caves were warm in winter and cool in summer. To make each home into a two room affair, they pitched a tent directly in from of the dug out. Each tent was made cozy with a small "two-hole" coal burning stove.

The cattle presented a problem. Although they had the wire and posts to fence their land, it would be several weeks before they could build a good four-wire fence on the three unfenced sides. The grass was lush on the Armstrong section, giving the cattle no reasonable cause to stray over onto the Dundee. However, cattle are not reasonable animals and are sometimes prone to roam just for the sheer pleasure of roaming. Knowing that Amos Dundee would immediately appropriate any cow which wandered onto his ranch, the Renfros took the precaution of enclosing 100 acres with a single wire fence before they bought their cattle. The fence, having only one post every thirty feet, was flimsy, but it served the purpose.

Royal ended his reflections when he saw the rider turn off the road and head towards him. By the time he arrived, Royal had been joined with George. They recognized the visitor. He was the Deputy Sheriff. He pulled his horse to a stop and inquired, "Is one of you Renfro?"

"Both of us are," George replied.

The Deputy pulled an envelope from his vest pocket and looked at the writing on it. "This is for George Renfro."

"That's me," George said.

"Mr. Amos Dundee was in Mesa yesterday evening and told me to deliver this to you this morning," the Deputy said, as he handed the envelope to George.

"You run whatever errands Dundee tells you to?" Royal crossly inquired.

The Deputy came out with a thin grin. "Pretty much I do," he admitted. "He and my boss, the Sheriff, are pretty close." With that he turned his horse towards the road and spurred him away.

By that time the Renfro men had been joined by their wives. "What brings him out here?" Jane asked.

"I guess the answer is in here," George replied as he broke open the envelope and withdrew a folded paper. He unfolded it and handed it to Royal. "We just as well all hear it all at once. Read it out loud."

"Well," Royal commenced, "we start out with the letterhead of TOMPKINS, HURST and TATE, Attorneys at Law, 900 Polk Street, Amarillo, Texas. It is dated day before yesterday, and it says: 'Mr. George Renfro; Sir: This is to inform you that this law firm represents Mr. Amos Dundee in regard to a dispute with you concerning the land on the Dundee Ranch commonly called the Armstrong Section, same being the section which you and your family are now occupying and claiming. This is to advise you that without acknowledging any right you have claimed in regard to said section, Mr. Dundee will completely fence off the Armstrong Section from the other part of the Dundee Ranch, including the public road. When the fencing is completed, you will have no ingress or egress to or from the Armstrong land. In other words, you will be fenced in with no way to remove yourselves, your cattle or your other possessions. Be further advised that Mr. Dundee will begin this fencing project immediately and expects to finish it before ten days have elapsed. However, you are herewith placed on notice that Mr. Dundee will not complete the fence that runs along the road until ten days from the time the Sheriff or his Deputy delivers this letter to you. Therefore, you are granted the legally reasonable time of ten days within which to vacate the land in question.' Then", Royal continued, "it's signed at the bottom, 'Very truly yours, R.V.T. Tompkins for the firm', and there you have it", Royal ended.

"That's crazy," was George's indignate response. "That's just some more of Dundee's big shot bluffing. First he claims we have no right to the land. Now he's as much as sayin that we have a right to it, but he can fence us off from it."

"Let's go to see Mike Vernon," said Royal.

"George," said Mary, "why don't you and Royal go to Mike and let Jane and I stay here to watch over things?"

"OK, let's go, Royal."

* * * * * * *

The scowl on Mike Vernon's face grew deeper and deeper as he read the threatening letter. When he finished, he looked up with fire in his eyes. "I can't believe that is the law. I learned in law school that when you bought a piece of land, you are entitled to ingress and egress. Somebody has to give you a way to get to and from your land, otherwise you could buy something that you simply cannot use."

"That makes good sense," Royal remarked.

"Yeah, but there are a few exceptions where the law doesn't make good sense," Mike replied. "And what bothers me is that old Judge Tompkins and his partners are very good lawyers. They are hard nosed and about half mean, but they're not the kind to go around making threats that they can't back up. To tell you the truth, I'm afraid they may know something I don't."

"Well, what do you need to do to find out?" Royal asked.

Mike gestured towards the ten or twelve volumes of books on his book shelf. "I can't get my answer form the little bunch of books. I need to run up to Clarendon and use my father's library. Also, I need to talk to my father."

"When can you go?" asked Royal.

"On the afternoon train. I'll be back tomorrow or next day probably the next day. Tell you what, just let me ride out to your place when I get back. I want to see what you're doing out there anyhow."

"OK," Royal replied, "We'll look for you when we see you commin."

The next day a Dundee fencing crew began building a fence along the south side of the Armstrong Section. They began at a pile of buffalo bones marking the southwest corner of the section and began digging post holes in a line moving due east.

On the afternoon of the following day Mike Vernon hitched his big, black horse to his buggy and headed for the big spring and a meeting with his clients. His heart was heavy, but he harbored one last bit of hope which must be tested by a physical inspection of the premises. When he reached the southwest corner of the Armstrong Section, he observed the pile of buffalo bones where the fencing crew had commenced. Moving north on the road, he also noticed a similar pile of buffalo bones at what he presumed to be a quarter-section corner and another such pile at what undoubtedly was the northwest corner of the Armstrong Section as located by the surveyor when it was homesteaded.

Royal yelled, "Here comes Mike."

"Does he have a smile on his face," asked Jane.

"Can't tell...naw, he's not smiling."

Mike stepped out of his buggy and gratefully accepted a gourd dipper filled with cold spring water. "Thanks, Mrs. Renfro."

Royal was impatient. "Come on, Mike, lay it on us. I can tell it's not good."

"You're right," Mike sadly responded. "I hoped, after I inspected on the ground that I might have some good news but I don't. Without going through all the legal mumbo jumbo, it comes down to this: Dundee has a right to fence you in."

"Well, George began, "I'm not necessarily interested in all the legal details, but I'd appreciate havin such a crazy law as that explained to me."

"OK," said Mike, "let me put it like this: If Dundee had sold you this land, he would have been legally burdened with the obligation to give you access to the public road. In other words, he would have the duty to furnish you with an easement across his land so as to allow you ingress and egress to the public road. But the facts are that Dundee has never owned this land, and he didn't sell it to you or to the Armstrongs. The Armstrongs homesteaded the land and got good title to it from the State of Texas. Therefore, Dundee owes you nothing."

"What about the State of Texas?" George asked.

"Good question. The State, in a manner of speaking, promised the land to the Armstrongs and to you, their successors in title; but the State never promised to give you or the Armstrongs an easement across somebody else's land."

"Well, then the State gave the Armstrongs, and us, a piece of land that we can't use," Royal angrily remarked. "That's just plain not fair."

"I agree," Mike replied, "but fair is not always law. My father and I looked into this matter very carefully, and we can't figure out any way to help you. Of course, you are perfectly free to go to another lawyer."

"Naw," George replied, "we have confidence in you."

"What was the good news you thought you might have before you made your inspection this morning?" Royal asked.

"If," Mike began, "that public road which runs north and south along your west line were over on you land, or if it just ran flush with your west line, then you'd be OK because Dundee would not have a right to build a fence on the road. But the trouble is that the road, even though it is now considered to be and is maintained as a County road, is really a public road by right of prescription."

"What does that mean?" asked Jane.

"Well, in brief, it means that the general public used the road for so many years that it finally belonged to them. It's a sort of a public road by limitations. And the significance of that is that the public only has a right to the existing road bed."

"Mike, I'm a little confused," Jane complained.

"I can see why. Look, let me put it this way: The road is only about one foot from your west line. That means that the strip between your land and the road belongs to the Dundee Ranch, and Dundee had a perfect right to build a fence on his ranch."

"So," Royal concluded, "even now we're trespassing on the Dundee Ranch when we go from here to the road."

Mike laughed. "Not if you step over that little strip. Of course, I trespassed with my buggy wheels a little while ago. But I'm not in any danger. There is no criminal trespass law in Texas."

George's face showed his astonishment. "You mean I can go and just squat on somebody else's land."

"Not exactly," Mike began, "the owner can use reasonable force to evict you or he can go to court and get an eviction order. However, neither he nor anybody else can have you prosecuted for trespassing. In other words, you can't be made to pay a fine or go to jail; and the Sheriff can't get mixed up in it without a court order."

Royal chuckled. "I think I'm beginning to see a little bit of hope."

"Well, tell me about it," Mary begged, looking at Mike.

"It's like this," said the lawyer, "you will be able to legally crawl through or go over the fence; and you will be able to easily step over Dundee's strip onto the public road."

"So," George reasoned aloud, "if he builds the usual four wire fence, we'll be able to go between the wires and hand things back and forth, through and over the wires without ever touching his land."

"But what if he builds the fence to where we can't get through it and so high we can't get over it?" Mary asked.

"Oh," Mike replied, "he could make it extremely hard on you by building a high fence with many closely spaced wires, but it would cost him a fortune, and you could probably always build ladders and get over it. However, the best reason why he probably won't build such a costly fence is that he doesn't need to."

Royal nodded glumly. "Yeah, I see that. There's no way we can get cattle or horses or wagons through or over a four-wire fence."

"That's it," said Mike . "And it's a criminal offense to cut the wires, felony as a matter of fact. In short, Mr. Dundee is screwing down on you, and I don't know how to stop him."

When darkness fell that evening, it was matched by the mood of the family Renfro gathered in front of the stove in the parents' tent.

"He will not steal my land," George grimly declared.

"How do you intend to stop him?" Jane asked in a sad, low voice.

Without hesitation, George replied, "Cut the wires."

Royal took issue with that. "Oh, no. You can go to the penitentiary for that."

"Not if you don't get caught."

"You'd get caught," Royal countered. "And even if you didn't Dundee would accuse you of it, and that's all it would take to get you convicted in this County."

"I'll take my chances," George sullenly replied.

"Besides that," Royal went on, "it would not be right."

"It might not be legal," George hotly retorted, "but it would be right. It would make things fair wouldn't it?"

Royal did not respond.

"Well, Son, so you want to just give up?"

"No, but I don't want any wire cutting."

"Then what do you suggest?"

"I don't have any suggestions."

"Well, then...."

"But I want you to promise me that there will be no wire cutting."

"No," George emphatically answered.

"Then promise me you'll put it off as long as possible and not ever do it until you give me a chance to talk you out of it."

"George rubbed his chin. "You're serious aren't you?"

"Yes, I am."

From the looks on the woman's faces, George could see that he was out numbered. "Alright, I promise."

"I can't understand a man like Dundee," Mary exclaimed. "How could he be so mean. Why does God let a man like him live?"

"I for one sure don't know," Royal replied, "but I'm sure God doesn't want him to be evil." He paused long enough to fix his blue eyes on his father's brown ones. "What's more, I'm certain God does not want us to let Dundee push us into being evil too."

George flushed. "Alright, Son, how much more do you think you've got to say to make your point?"

"Hush, both of you," said Mary.

"OK, I'm sorry, Dad," Royal quickly began, "but I want to put in one more thought. I think I know what the Preacher would say for us to do. I think he would say for us to hang on and let God give us a way out."

George let his breath out with a low whistle. "Alright, I'll go along with that, but if God can't figure out how to do it, I will."

"Now, that's enough," Mary firmly declared.

"I know, Honey. I'll quit arguing. Now we need to get to bed and get some rest. We're gonna be busy the next few days hauling coal and lumber."

"Yeah," said Royal, "and we need to get a milk cow and a couple of plows and three or four more horses, and I don't know what all."

"It's going to be exciting," said Jane, "and think of all the labor and money we're going to save."

"What are you talkin about," Royal wanted to know.

"Well, Mr. Dundee is fencing our land for us."

Royal grinned sheepishly and gave his beautiful wife a playful whack on her backside. "I walked right into that, didn't I?"

Chapter Twenty-Six

At noon on the eleventh day after the deputy sheriff delivered the notice, the fencing crew stretched the wires and nailed them to the corner post at the northwest corner of the Armstrong Section. The enclosure was completed. Ironically, the reasonable time within which to vacate which the Dundee lawyers had so carefully granted was utilized in the opposite fashion. The Renfros, in 10 days of feverish, ant-like in gathering, had either eliminated or substantially lessened their need for anything beyond the enclosure.

The fence never stopped gnawing in the backs of their minds, but they were busy and happy. Before the next September rolled around, they had plowed and cross-fenced their cultivated land, harvested a bumper crop of irrigated grain sorghum, built three small barns and watched their cows wean their big calves and drop a new crop of babies.

Most important of all, on August 12, Jane

gave birth to William T. Applegate Renfro. Royal had raced into Mesa and fetched the doctor in plenty of time. Both the mother and her son were healthy and happy. Royal leaned towards calling his son "Preacher", but Jane would have none of that. They called the boy William T., but it usually sounded like "Wim T." Soon they left off any effort to overcome their slurring; and so the boy came to be called Wim T.

* * * * * * *

"We can plant the wheat tomorrow," Royal opined.

George nodded. "I think you're right, and it ought to be good winter grazing. The problem is there'll be too many head trying to eat it. We need to sell most of those big calves along with all three of those cows that didn't drop new calves. Besides that, we need a sale to raise money for houses, and we need a windmill on the east side, and ....."

"I know, I know," Royal grimly replied. "You know, ever since Wim T. was born that fence has been more and more on my mind."

A knowing grin widened George's mouth. "Havin a son will do things like that to a man," he impishly replied.

Ignoring the reply, Royal went on: "I've been thinkin that I might just go and talk to Mr. Dundee."

George sneered. "See that 'ol bull out there. Talkin to Dundee would be as worthless as talkin to the bull."

"Probably," Royal conceded.

"Jane, Mary, come here," George shouted. "You know what this crazy son of mine is thinkin about doin? Goin to talk with Dundee about the fence. That's what."

"Royal," cried Mary, "it won't do any good, and he might hurt you."

Royal turned to his wife, who was holding Wim T., "What do you think?"

"I don't think it'll do any good," Jane answered, "but if you want to go, I want you to go."

"I don't think I can stand it," George wailed. "You'll have to walk, and there you will go: walkin up to Mr. Almighty with your hat in your hand, bowin and scapin and beggin."

Fire came into Royal's eyes and his nostrils pinched. "I'm not gonna do any of those things-- except walk. I can't help but walk."

"You would ride if you cut some wires," George caustically suggested.

Mary instantly scolded him by the way she called his name, "George!"

George held his forearm over his face. "Sorry, just forget I said it."

"When do you plan to go?" Jane asked.

"I didn't really have any specific plans before we started discussing the subject, but..." He halted long enough to look up at the noonday sun. "I'll have plenty of time to go today. So, I think I'll go right now."

George's face still carried a look of consternation as he watched his son slip through the top two wires of the fence and start walking north.   There was pain in his voice when he croaked, "He's bound to know he can't win."

"Somewhere, a long time ago," Mary responded, "I read that nobody is quite so noble as on who endeavors to scale a height, knowing that he will surely fail."

"Huh," George growled, "then he's about the noblest one who ever came out of the chute."

"That just may be true," Jane serenely stated, as she allowed Wim T. to take a nipple.

* * * * * * *

Like father, like son.   Now it was Royal's turn to stare at the portrait of Amos Dundee's father as he waited for the cattle baron to grant him an audience.

Dundee smirked as he chewed on his cigar an pretended to deal with some figures on a ledger. He took his time.   He reasoned that the boy had come to beg for terms, probably to be allowed to move off of the ranch and take their cattle and other belongings with them.   I'll let them do that, he thought, but I'll tell him they'll have to get off in three days.   No, I'll send word that I'll let the fence down for three days if they want to move.

Having thusly formulated his answer, he now sought to elicit the question.   Looking up with a haughty curl on his upper lip, he deliberately loaded his voice with impatience.   "What do you want, Boy?"

Anger pricked the back of Royal's neck, but he refuses to be deterred.   Striking Dundee with one of his blue-eyed, righteous stares, Royal calmly asked, "Mr. Dundee, do you think you are treating us fairly?"

The eyes, the voice, the question combined to jolt Dundee, causing him to delay his response. He had expected a beggar. Instead, he was confronted by a self-appointed moral judge, who disconcertingly gave the appearance of acting without any trace of audacity. At length, however, anger overcame shock. "Fair," he bellowed, "you ignorant plow boy, what do you mean by coming in here and talking to me about what's fair?"

Royal tried to politely break in. "I just don't think it's...."

"That's right," Dundee yelled, "you don't think and neither does your dumb daddy. You've got your nerve making me out to be unfair when you and your bunch are squatting on my land, claiming some sort of nester's right."

Outwardly Royal was unruffled. "It looks like I approached you the wrong way," he dryly remarked. "Let me try this, he evenly continued, "I now have a little son, and...."

"I heard about it. What's that got to do with anything?"

"Well, it seems to me that when you have a baby, it has to do with just about everything. As for me, it makes me want to have a piece of land where Wim. T., that's his name, can sink his roots."

"People like you don't..." Dundee began.

"And I was wondering" Royal went on, "if maybe there is some way we could settle with you.

Maybe we could give you our this year's calf crop. We've got forty-five big weaned calves. I think I can get my dad to go along if..."

"No," Dundee thundered. "Not for forty-five calves or forty-five thousand calves. Do you hear me?"

"I hear you," Royal coolly replied.

"Now you hear the rest of what I have to say, Boy. You and your daddy have a place. You are good workers, and you have a kind of native intelligence that made you good hands here on the ranch. People like you are good work hands. That is all. That's your place. You're not fit to own land."

Royal stood to leave.

"One other thing," Dundee continued, "Talking about fair. I'm gonna make you the fairest proposition you'll ever hear. If you or your daddy come and ask me in a nice way within the next twenty-four hours, I'll lower the fence and give you three days to move, lock, stock and barrel, off my land. You got that?"

Royal, still standing, replied only with his eyes. Their slashing blue rays caused Dundee to blink and struggle, almost involuntarily, to his feet as he silently watched Royal slowly turn and then march smartly out of the room.

George saw his son coming. He had seen the boy in trudge step before, and he knew the news was not good. "Comin in with you tail between your legs?"

Royal stopped and put his hands on his hips. "No" was his defiant reply. "That man is not ever gonna make me behave like a whipped dog."

George started to reply but thought better of it. He knew his son had more to say, and decided to let him say it in his own good time.

Royal had fully intended to report his whole conversation with Dundee, including the parts where the big man had disparaged and demeaned the Renfros and their ilk. However, as he looked into the bitterness shooting from his father's eyes, he decided not to relate all that, at least not now. Instead, he dropped his hands from his hips, let a little grin crinkle the corners of his mouth and said, "I'm ready to help. You just say the word."

George didn't ask for or need any further explanation. "Some dark and stormy night," he muttered.

* * * * * * *

Two weeks later, just at dusky dark, a fast moving, dark cloud descended upon the Renfros from the north, bringing 50 mile an hour gusts and torrents of chill, October rain, mixed with small hail balls. The lightning played and the thunder boomed.

"Is this the night?" Royal quietly asked.

"Looks like it," George replied. Turning to Mary and Jane, George said," Me and Royal are gonna have to saddle up and go see that the cows don't get too spooked."

Mary gave a little gasp. "The lightning..." She stopped to swallow. "Do you have to go?"

"We do," George softly but firmly replied.

Jane said nothing, but her wide eyes, following Royal's every move, told of her fright.

"We'll be OK," Royal promised as he bent down and planted a kiss on his son's forehead.

Their yellow slickers and big, black felt hats held them in good stead. Nevertheless, the pelting racket of the windblown hail and rain made intelligent conversation impossible until they were inside the barn. Even there, as they saddled their horses, the clatter on the sheet iron roof made it necessary for them to shout.

George gave instructions. "I'll go on down to the middle of the south side and cut the wires, the top three." Then I'll come on back and help you. We'll push the whole herd through the opening."

"Why just the top three?"

"Tryin to make it look like the cows did it," George answered. "Maybe it'll look like the storm caused the cows to stampede against the fence and break the top wires."

"It's worth a chance," Royal hollered back.

The storm still raged, but the hail stopped as they clinched tight their saddles. George went on outlining his plans. "In the morning we'll cut out the calves that need to be sold, and Mary and I will herd them to Mesa. You and Jane can get the rest of 'em back into our pasture." He stopped and looked out the barn door at an especially long, two-pronged streak of lightning . "We could get killed out there."

"Yeah."

"You willing to risk dieing for this piece of

land?" George yelled the question.

Royal mounted his horse before shouting his answer. "That's not all there is to it. It's not just land. It's my son's future."

It was too dark for Royal to see the understanding smile which spread over his dad's face, but he knew it was there.

They had urged their horses only a couple of hundred yards to the south before they spotted their whole herd, emitting frightened moos and baas, gathered in a tight knot, around which the bellowing bull was nervously circling. Suddenly a sizzling bolt of lightning struck the ground about one hundred feet east of the herd and was followed by a clap if thunder which literally shook the earth. The frenzied bull lowered his head and charged. He happened to be headed south. Instantly he was followed by the thundering hooves of the whole panic stricken herd.

Helpless to do anything to stem the mad torrent of cattle, Royal and George spurred their horses and followed in horror stricken wonder. The intermittent flashes from the heavens allowed them broken, ghostly scenes of the bull's heedless collision with a post along about the middle of the south fence. The post snapped off the ground, and the whole fence seemed to be carried away. The closely following cows and calves thundered after the bull, seemingly without any hindrance from the fence. The morning light later revealed that the wires were broken near the post where the bull made his exit, and two other posts, one on either side of the broken one, were leaning down almost to the ground. The bull had blasted a good hole, and the herd miraculously suffered only a few minor cuts and scratches.

Almost as soon as the stampede through the fence was completed, the storm angrily rumbled away. Dazed, George and Royal pulled their mounts to a halt and sat silently gazing. Royal's voice was filled with awe. "God did it for us. He fixed it so we wouldn't do anything wrong."

"Maybe", George replied. "Even so, we'd be kinda dumb to think God is gonna stampede the cattle every time we need to take some of 'em to market."

Royal shook his head. "I think you're wrong. I think he sent us the message that he will take care of us."

Again George said, "Maybe," but this time he didn't elaborate. He saw no good reason to push the debate any further.

Amos Dundee did not discover the damage to his fence for thirty-six hours. In a rage he summoned the Sheriff who investigated for a whole day before announcing to the skeptical Cattle King that the Renfros did not cut the wires. Seemingly numbed with rage, Dundee took another three days to get the fence repaired. In the more than five-day interval, the furiously working Renfros managed to procure and move onto their land all of the animals, equipment and supplies they would need for several months.

Chapter Twenty-Seven

It was the 3rd day of January, 1917. Hammers in hand, the Renfro men stood in front of their new barn, watching the man. He rode to the northwest corner of their property where the dismounted and tied his horse. Taking the saddle bags in hand, he ducked through the fence and began to slowly approach them.

They had just put the finishing touches on the big barn. There was not enough lumber left for one house, much less two. "We just didn't have time to bring in enough," Royal lamented, "but we can make out in the caves a while longer."

"No. doubt about that," George replied, "but we'd better get the livestock moved into this barn before our wives beat 'em to it."

Royal gestured towards the approaching stranger. "Wonder what he wants. Who in the world is he anyway?"

"Never saw him before," George answered. "Looks kind of slick though."

The grinning, waving stranger was dressed in a gray suit, over which he wore a black overcoat, open in front. He wore black patent leather shoes, topped with gray spats. His head was crowned with a black derby. Undoubtedly the clothes had been expensive when they were purchased, but obviously that had been a long time ago. Coming close, the hand he extended for shaking was noticeably white and smooth, the hand of one who does not do hard labor with that particular member of his body. The wrinkles in his pallid face joined the abundance of gray in big, once all black, sideburns to give him the look of a man in his middle fifties.

"Well, Gents," he started out, "I already know your names. Mine is James R. Worthington. I hail from St. Louis."

"What can we do for you?" George wondered aloud.

Worthington smirked and narrowed the slits of his black eyes. Patting one of the saddle bags, he replied, "Mr friend, I'm confident that we can do a little business together."

"You sellin insurance?" George asked impatiently.

Worthington chuckled. "Well, now that you mention it, I am sort of, but not exactly."

"Well, I think you better, not sort of, but exactly get on off this place," George said. "We don't need any insurance."

"Please, Sir," Worthington smoothly

answered, "hear me out. I'm really not peddling insurance in the ordinary sense of the word. But if you will give me a few moments to make my presentation, you will perceive why I think the word 'insurance' is not an inappropriate name for the commodity in my saddle bag which can, I assure you, insure a happy future for you and your family."

Royal, more curious than George, was afraid his dad was going to run the stranger off before he would reveal his wares. "We can give you a few minutes," he said. Catching George's hard glance, he quickly continued, "Just a few minutes though. You'll have to be quick."

Worthington smiled. "Could we just move into the barn--out of this wind?"

Inside, Worthington said, "This is much better. Now, if you gents will kindly sit with me on this floor, I will bring forth my commodity."

Worthington pulled from his saddle bags numerous photos, letters, newspaper clippings and sworn affidavits. One by one, he presented the documents and pictures with an explanatory narrative. When he had finished, the Renfros had been, as Worthington put it, "notified of the well documented, mortal sin of Amos Dundee."

Worthington's presentation told the story of how the young Amos Dundee, on a drinking spree in St. Louis, had gone a whoring. A few weeks later his favorite whore confronted him in a saloon and announced that she was going to have his baby. In an embarrassed rage, he savagely beat the woman senseless. Even though the woman was of ill repute, her apparently mortal injuries caused the Marshal to arrest Dundee. And it was only by the spreading around of a great deal of money that the young baron extricated himself from jail, got the charges dropped and left St. Louis, never to return.

The major recipient of the hush money was the whore who survived his vicious beating. She never again practiced her profession, choosing to move to Kansas City and lead a quiet, respectable life. She had no visable means of support, but she and her son never lacked for any material need. She explained to friends that her deceased father had left her comfortably fixed. She was dead now, but her son was grown and working in a bank in St. Louis.

That the woman's son was Dundee's child was abundantly clear from the photos. Nobody else could have been his father. However there was more, much more documentation to prove Worthington's story.

"Looks like you've got Mr. Dundee nailed to the cross," George opined. "But why are you showin all this stuff to us?"

Worthington began to carefully replace his documentary proof into the saddle bags. "Well," he answered in a half whisper, "the thought struck my mind that you gents might be interested in purchasing these items."

"Why's that," Royal asked.

Worthington threw out a sneering half-laugh. "Don't try to tell me that you wouldn't know how to use these papers if you had 'em. You see I've been hanging around Mesa for most part of a week, and I know what Dundee did to you and what he's still doing to you. I doesn't take the mind of a genius to figure out what you could do to him if you had these papers. In short, my friends, these documents could tear down a lot of fences."

"Why don't you sell the papers to Dundee?" Royal inquired.

"Tell you the truth that's just exactly what I intended to do when I went to the trouble and no little expense to gather all this evidence., And that's what I intended to do when I stepped off the train in Mesa last week. As a matter of fact, I still might do just that."

"You can sure talk a lot without answering a question," George remarked.

"That's true," Worthington good naturedly replied, "but you want to know why I approached you instead of going directly to Dundee; and I'm just trying to tell you."

"OK, get on with it."

"Well, I took time in Mesa to check very carefully on Mr. Dundee. I wanted to find out how best to approach him with my--shall I say 'merchandise'--how embarrassed he might be if his dark secret was revealed and about how much money the merchandise might be worth."

"And, you decided that Dundee wouldn't play your game," Royal concluded.

"No, that's not it. At least that's not it exactly. I figure that Dundee will buy me out alright--probably pay a lot more than you gents could possibly raise. Nevertheless, I also figure that I'll never convince him that I haven't duplicated the documents and that I won't come back again. Now, to keep from making the story any longer, let me say it like this: I figure that if Dundee buys my merchandise, he will never let me get back home alive. He's mean enough, smart enough and rich enough to see to it that my poor bullet riddled body will be found under mysterious circumstances somewhere between here and St. Louis. Know what I mean?"

The Renfros grimly nodded.

"So?" George asked.

"So, I sort of thought maybe you Gents might be willing to cover my expenses and maybe a little more. In which case, I'd just steal away home and look for a more profitable venture."

"How much did you have in mind?" George asked.

"Five hundred dollars."

"Two fifty," George counter offered.

"That won't cover my expenses."

"Two fifty," George insisted.

Royal started to protest. "But Dad..."

Reading his son's mind, George tersely interrupted. "Just insurance, Son. We don't necessarily have to use it."

"Three fifty," said Worthington.

"No," George replied.

"OK, two fifty it is."

"I'll be back shortly," said George as he left the barn. When he returned, Worthington sourly exchanged the substance of his blackmail scheme for two hundred fifty dollars; and, without a word or a wave goodbye, ambled back to the fence, remounted his horse and rode away.

Neither father nor son spoke until Worthington had disappeared from sight. "It would be blackmail," Royal blurted.

"This is insurance," George countered. "Maybe we'll never be forced to use it."

"We've got to let the Lord provide," Royal argued.

"Maybe the Lord provided insurance."

Royal hooted. "Huh, in a pig's eye."

"Alright, what do you want to do, burn it up?"

Royal looked up and saw Jane, carrying Wim T., come out of their tent and start down the trail to the barn. "No," he admitted.

Chapter Twenty-Eight

The Renfro family wiggled through the wires and walked into Mesa twice each week, on Saturday afternoon for shopping and visiting, and on Sunday morning for church and visiting. Between the visiting, the Amarillo Daily News the Saturday Evening Post they were about as well informed about the War as anybody else in the country. However, even though Royal, who turned twenty-one in May, registered for the draft on June 1st., the Renfros were numbered among the few detached spectators of the war. Restricted as they were by Dundee's fence, not even the rising price of beef had any influence on their lives.

But then, on Saturday 3, 1917, the long arm of the great war reached into the Panhandle of Texas and placed a cold, bony hand on the shoulder of Royal Renfro.

Royal came out of the post office waving his draft notice. "This is bound to be a mistake," he confidently stated.

"What is it?" Jane asked.

"This," he replied, shoving the draft notice under her nose.

Jane turned white. "Is this a joke? You've got a baby, and you're a farmer. They're not supposed to take you."

"Let me see," said George, gently taking the notice from Jane. "You'll have to appeal this. We'll go talk to the Draft Board Monday morning. They just don't know the facts. They won't make you go. Everything will be OK.

* * * * * * *

On their way to the Draft Board meeting, the Renfro men ran into Mike Vernon. After an exchange of greetings and an explanation for the Renfros' unusual presence in town on a Monday morning, Royal looked up the street and saw Amos Dundee entering the Draft Board office. "Wonder what Dundee is goin in there for."

"He's the head of it," Mike replied.

Royal was thunderstruck. "What!" he yelled.

"That's right."

`George's face also registered his surprise and frustration. "Why was his name not on the draft notice?"

"Oh, those notices are sent out by the Secretary, Bill Fowler. But rest assured, Dundee runs the show. The rest of 'em are obligated to him up to their chins."

It followed that Royal presented his protest

to the Board with a dry mouth and a sick heart. Knowing now that an exemption or long term deferment would be out of the question, he limited himself to a plea for a six months deferment so that he could help his dad get the sorghum in the barn and so his baby would at least be weaned.

When Royal finished, Dundee stated that the Renfro family had no right to be farming that land in the first place. As to the baby, he opined that Royal should be right proud to go over there and defend his baby from those Germans.

The other four members of the Board, sitting stone-faced, voted unanimously to reject the deferment.

"And so," Royal later concluded, after relating to teary eyed Jane and Mary his adventures before the Draft Board, "I'm to report to Amarillo three days from now."

"Aren't they supposed to give longer notice that before they send you off? Mary asked.

"Probably," Royal replied, "but that's all I get."

As the women softly sobbed, George stood and clasped his hands behind his back. "It's not all over yet," he grimly declared. "We still have our insurance."

Mary stopped sobbing. "What are you talking about?"

"We have certain documents which will not only keep Royal from goin to the army but will also pull down Amos Dundee's fence." Then, in response to the women's wide eyes and open mouths, George quickly went on to tell them about the visit from Worthington and the purchase of his documents. "Now you can see why we are in a good position to force Mr. Dundee to do justice."

Mary's response was strikingly different from Jane's. Mary clapped her hands and exclaimed, "Marvelous." Jane remained silent as she quizzed Royal with her sad brown eyes.

Royal stood and emitted a sound which was started as a groan of despair but which immediately changed into a sigh of resignation. "Dad, do you remember what the Preacher said about worms in hell?"

George frowned. "Yeah," he replied.

Jane spoke up. "I don't remember his saying anything about worms in hell."

Royal explained. "He said it when Dad and I were on the trail with him, before we got to Dundee Ranch, before we ever saw either of you."

"What did he say?"

"Well, I can't say it by heart, but there's a place in the Bible where it says that people in hell will be eaten on by worms and that those worms will never die. After the Preacher had read that one night, Dad asked him what the worms had done to cause God to make them live in hell. The Preacher's answer was that the worms deserved hell because by nourishing themselves on the people who had been condemned to hell, they were, for a fact, making a living off of the sins of those people. He went on to say that people who take advantage of the sins of others are no better than the worms of hell."

George opened his mouth as if to respond.

"I know, I know," said Royal, "it sounds a little strange, maybe even a little silly, but it somehow makes a lot of sense to me." With that, Royal gently plucked Wim T. from Jane's arms and said, "Will you all come and go with me and Wim. T. down to the barn?"

When they had assembled in the barn, Royal asked, "Where is the stuff you bought from Worthington?"

"You know as well as I do," George answered, "wrapped in that old slicker up there on the rafters."

"Here," said Royal, passing Wim T. over to Jane. Then he scrambled up some rungs which they had nailed to the side of post, found the yellow slicker wrapped bundle and brought it down to the ground. "Now," he said, "I'd like for all of you to follow me out to the big rock, the one under which we found the treasure."

George held his peace but cut his eyes suspiciously. Mary and Jane, almost in unison said, "But why?"

"I'll explain when we get to the rock, Here, I'll carry Wim T." And so, with his son under one arm and the yellow bundle under the other, Royal led the way to the rock.

"He got directly to the point. "What I want us to do is put all these papers and pictures on this rock and burn them."

"Hey, not so fast, Son. If you don't want to use those documents right now to keep you from going to war, I'll honor your decision. But to destroy them and cut us off from our only sure hope of surviving on this piece of ground, well that's too much. How about if I promise not to use these papers while you're off to war; and then, when you come back, I promise I won't use 'em without your consent. How about that?"

"I'd like for you to promise not to cut the fence while I'm gone."

"Sure, alright I'll promise that. But what about the papers?"

"I think," Royal softly commenced, "that these papers cry out for more than a promise."

"Huh," George broke in, "you don't trust me. Not only that, you don't even trust yourself."

"Maybe that's part of it," Royal acknowledged. "I've read where war does strange things to people."

"So," George responded, "if the war changes our lives, you won't be the same--none of us will be the same--when you come back. So, why don't we let our future selves make the future decisions?"

"You make a good point, Dad, but I have this deep feeling against putting off on my future self what I ought to do right now. And I know this: I don't want to go off to war with the weight of these papers on my back. I want us to sacrifice them to God on the alter of this rock, right now.

George glanced at Jane and Mary. Their eyes were glistening; their heads were nodding.

Without another word, George took the yellow bundle from Royal, unwrapped it and carefully placed the documents on the alter. Then, striking a match, he set fire to the stack in three places.

"Let's hold hands," Jane suggested, "And they did, forming a circle around the little fire.

When the smoldering remains gave up their last whisp of smoke, George sighed, "I'm not sorry we did it, but now what are we gonna do?"

Royal looked up at a whispy white cloud. "You remember what Isaac asked his father Abraham as they were climbing up to the place were Abraham was going to offer a sacrifice? He asked, 'Father, what are you going to use for a sacrifice?' And you remember what Abraham answered. He said, 'The Lord will provide."

Royal bent his head and kissed his son on the forehead. "The Lord will provide," he repeated.

Chapter Twenty-Nine

Dr. Spencer and George stood at the entrance to the Renfro barn watching a taffy colored nanny goat licking her twin kids. "I appreciate you comin out, Doc."

"Glad to," the doctor replied. "I wanted to see how it was all working out."

"Well, it's been ten days since we started givin Wim T. that goat milk, and since then he hasn't had one lick of trouble. You sure knew what you were doin, Doc."

The doctor chuckled with pleasure. "Well, I don't deserve too much credit. It was easy to see that Wim T. was allergic to cows' milk. And usually when that's the case, the baby can handle goat's milk without any trouble." He frowned before going on. "It's a crying shame though that you and Mary had to lift the nanny goat over the fence."

"It's wasn't such a big problem," George replied. "She's not very heavy."

"Yeah, but it's the principle of the thing."

"How well I know," George glumly agreed. Then he brightly related that after they had successfully transported the goat and her twin kids over the fence, they had half seriously entertained the idea of raising sheep or goats instead of cattle. "Probably wouldn't work. Dundee would probably just build his fence a little higher. Anyhow, it's something to think about."

The doctor changed the subject. "What do you hear from Royal?

"Oh, we've been gettin a letter nearly every day. He's fine--passed the physical examination with flyin colors in Amarillo, and then they shipped him directly to San Antonio. He's been at Camp Travis for the past four months, learnin how to drill and all that stuff." George paused to proudly grin. "He's already won a medal, too."

"Say, now, what for?"

"Marksmanship. That target practice is about the only thing he likes. He shore don't like the food. He's pretty plain about that."

"I imagine he's mostly just homesick," the doctor suggested.

"No doubt about that."

* * * * * * * *

It was customary now for one or more of the Renfros to walk into Mesa on Wednesday as well as on the weekends in order to pick up letters from Royal and mail their letters to him. Almost invariably Royal wrote one letter addressed to Jane and another addressed to all of them--"Mr.

and Mrs. George Renfro, Mrs. Royal Renfro and William T. Renfro."

On the Wednesday after the doctor's visit, they received two letters from Royal, both addressed to all of them. The first one was to the tenor of most of his others--giving the details of his daily activities, or something that had reminded him of home and expressing his love. The second was a bit different:

"Dear Jane and Wim T., Dad and Mary,

It is June 11, 1918, and we're for sure heading for France tomorrow. They say we will get on a train in San Antonio and go somewhere in New York or New Jersey. Then we will get on a boat and go over to Europe, maybe straight to France, or maybe to England first. So, if you don't hear from me on a regular basis for the next few weeks, you'll understand why.

I'm with a tough bunch of boys, and we're well trained. We're ready to fight, and I think we'll give a good account of ourselves. I guess all of us, for one reason or another, dread to go over there. Nobody admits it, but it's easy to see that we're all at least a little bit afraid of getting killed. There is a lot of talk about it, but most everybody says there's nothing that can be done about it. When your number is up, it's up, whether you are here at home or in the trenches in France.

Anyhow, I don't worry much about that, and I don't want you to. I'm certain that God means for me to come back home. The main dread I have is being away from all of you for so long. There is talk that the war may go on for two or three more years. Of course, I don't think it will last anything like that long. Once a big bunch of us get to France, we'll get it over with in a few months, maybe weeks.

The other big dread I have is that I might show a yellow streak, but I feel pretty sure that God won't let me get into anything like that.

Well, they are turning out the lights. That's probably good because I've probable already said too much. Give Wim T. a kiss for me and tell him I'm glad he's doing well on the goat's milk.

Love to all,

Royal

P.S. Please keep writing letters. However don't mail then until I get to France and send you my new address. They say they won't forward mail, or if they do, it takes forever. But keep writing. It will be nice to get a big bunch of letters at one time."

Ten days later they received a brief note, saying that all was well but that he couldn't tell them his location. It would be over a month before they heard from Royal again. His next letter, written in La Harve, France on July 5, 1918 arrived in Mesa on August 1st. In the meantime, the Renfro family, like most every other family in the Western world, was obliged to deal with the killer influenza epidemic of 1917-1918.

The flu waited until July to start moving its sharp scythe through the Panhandle of Texas. But when it started, it moved swiftly and with a special vengeance. Eighty per cent of the population of Miller County was stricken in the first three days of that month.

Doctor Spencer's face took on a yellow cast in the light of the flickering lamp. "She's got it," he sadly muttered, as he released Jane's wrist.

Jane opened her blood-shot eyes and through cracked, fever parched lips, whispered, "Got what?"

"The flu," my dear. Now take these two pills and rest easy. Everything is going to be alright."

He motioned for George and Mary to follow him out of the room. "She's in a bad way," the doctor explained. This is a killer flu. She'll need care around the clock. You'll need to keep her fever down with cool, wet cloths. Wipe her face, hands and legs at least once every hour. Let her have clear soup and water, lots of water--nothing else. With that kind of care, she has a good chance. Without it, she'll never make it."

"We'll take care of her," Mary assured the doctor.

"I know you will. She's lucky to have both of you to wait on her. Most of my patients don't have anybody." He shook his head sadly. "This is the worst thing I've ever seen. People are dying like flies, and there is nothing I can do about it. The well people are so afraid of catching it, they won't nurse anybody outside of their family; and I can't blame them. To make matters worse, there is not telling how many houses contain at least one dead body. People are even afraid to bury the dead."

"My stars," Mary gasped. "I had no idea it was that bad."

The doctor sighed. "Believe me, it is; and, like death, this flu is no respecter of persons. It hits the high and the low, the rich and the poor. They're all alike. The Dundee Ranch is a prime example. All but two of the cowboys have been laid low, along with the entire Dundee family-- Amos, Bertha and Nora."

"Who is taking care of them?" Mary inquired.

"Nobody is looking after the Dundees. The two cowboys who are still on their feet have all they can do, and more, just trying to keep their friends alive. And the Dundee's maid and all the kitchen help left them shortly before the flu broke out. Seems that Bertha got into one of her stinking moods one day and ran the whole bunch off the place. I'm sure she's sorry now, but that's the way it goes."

Mary was perplexed. "Well, if there is nobody there to help them keep cool and see to them, what's going to happen to them?"

The doctor shook his dead again. I've done all I know to do. I've left instructions as to how they can help each other. But..." his voice tailed off before continuing, "but they are so weak and sick, it will be a miracle if any of them survive. The truth is they don't have any really good friends; and even if they did, the friends would probably be tied up with their own families."

After the doctor left, Mary asked, "What are you going to do?"

"About what?"

"You know."

"Yeah," he acknowledged.

"So?"

He hedged. "You need me here."

"That's very true, but I can make it for a few days, unless I come down with it. So, it's up to you."

"I don't want to go," he muttered.

"But you will," she firmly predicted.

His frustration came out in a long groan, at the end of which he voiced his typical affirmation: "Yeah".

* * * * * * *

Amos Dundee's voice came in a weak, hoarse whisper. "What are you doing here?" he demanded.

I've come to help," George matter of factly replied.

Dundee closed his eyes and fell back on his pillow. "I didn't send for you."

Ignoring the stubborn yet weak protest, George inquired, "Where are your wife and daughter?"

"Both in Bertha's room, down the hall."

When he opened the door to Bertha's room, George was forced to gulp and hold his breath. The odor from Amos had been offensive, but this one was doubly bad--stifling, sickening, a rare combination of vomit and various human excretions. Amazingly his nose and stomach, in a matter of few moments, came to terms with the stench sufficiently enough to allow him to tip toe into the room and look upon the ashen faces of the Dundee women. Their eyes were closed, and both of them were moaning and asking for water. There were two water pitchers and two glasses in the room, all dry. George grabbed the pitchers, and after stopping off in Dundee's room to secure a third pitcher, went immediately to the cistern pump on the back porch and filled them with cool, clear water. After his three patients had gratefully drunk, George spent the rest of the day cleaning their bodies and beds.

That evening he patiently spooned between three sets of lips the liquid from a stew he had prepared from onions, potatoes, canned tomatoes and a chunk of salt pork. By midnight when he finally, for the first time, dozed briefly in a chair in the hall, he had established a routine of bathing and ministering to his patients every hour, night and day. In his spare time he would cook, haul water and snooze in his chair. And, once each day, he would race home to check on Mary, Jane and Wim T. Thankfully, Jane began to show strong signs of recovery on the second day.

On the fourth day of George's nursing, Nora and her father broke out in a sweat, almost at the same time, each soaking the bed clothes. After that, both of them rapidly rallied. Their fever broke, and they began to talk rationally and to call for solid food. Bertha was not so lucky. She continued to moan and rave, and no amount of bathing with cool water seemed to control her fever. She deliriously refused water and soup, and on the sixth day after George began his mission of mercy, she convulsively died in his arms.

Stunned, his eyes fixed upon her icy death stare for several moments. His thoughts were on his own feelings towards her. When he had first bathed the hauty woman who had tried so stubbornly and so vainly to seduce him, he had experienced repulsion oddly mixed with triumph and shame. These initial emotions had quickly melted into sheer pity. It also occurred to him that his attitude towards Amos had gone from hate, to resentment, to pity, even as the look in Dundee's eyes had moved from resentment to appreciation and back to resentment. It was only as to Nora, he thought, that his feelings had remained constant. He had pitied her from the beginning. Also at this time he came to the interesting, conscious realization that he had personified the flu into an evil being, one who was trying to jerk his patients away from him, one who he was fighting and trying desperately to outlast, one who has just gained a victory over him. At he end of his musings, he closed Bertha's eye lids over her last stare. Suddenly he felt drained of all emotions save a dull sense of duty.

He lifted Bertha from her bed and turned to face Nora. It was the first time in his life that he had been too bone weary to experience ordinary human sorrow. Strangely, he realized a bit of shame for his lack of remorse, but he excused himself with the fact that he was too tired to be sorry. "I've got to bury her," he croaked.

"Can't you wait a day or two until I am able to be up and around?" Nora asked.

George shook his head and left Nora quietly sobbing. When he carried his lifeless burden into Dundee's room, the baron was sitting up in bed and had just filled his glass from the pitcher. His eyes went wide and he dropped the glass, spilling water on his bed.

George dully muttered, "I've got to bury her."

Dundee eyed him resentfully and dumbly nodded.

George carried the wax-faced, emaciated body of the once proud and sensuous mistress of Dundee Ranch to the garden. There he slowly and with great effort dug a shallow grave and laid her to rest. His mind was not too worn out to sicken at the sight of the first couple of shovelfuls of dirt that hit her face, but he was quickly comforted by the thought that if either Amos or Nora survived, he or she could arrange for a more fitting funeral and burial at a later date. If neither of them lived, it wouldn't matter much anyway.

When he finished the burial, he immediately collapsed on his stomach, with the right side of his face in the dirt, his mouth pressed against a clod. He slept without moving for two hours. He arose as refreshed as if he had slept for a whole night in his own bed.

On the fourth day after Bertha expired, George ascertained that his two remaining patients had sufficiently recovered to care for themselves. He was glad because he was not at all sure he could minister to them any longer. Suddenly feeling like he had been struck in the back of his head with a sledge hammer, he called Amos and Nora into the hall where he addressed them. "I've fixed a big pot of soup. Now I'm going and I won't be back."

Dundee gave him a loathing look, nothing more.

Nora spoke impulsively. "Well, we just want you to know that...." her sentence was cut off by a cold hard look from her father.

Bleary eyed, George took his leave and made his way home in a half stagger. When he collapsed through the door of his dug out, Mary knew immediately that she had another flu victim on her hands.

* * * * * * * *

When Mary's sweat soaked patient opened his eyes and looked at her inquiringly, he was astonished to learn that he had been delirious for three days. He shook his head in disbelief and tried to tell Mary about his crazy dream, the one where the cattle kept climbing the barbed wire fence, up and up, finally out of sight. But he was too weak to pull all the words together.

"Don't try to talk anymore now. You can tell me all about your dream later."

George fell back with a tight little smile on his pale face. Mary is still well, he thought. Jane is OK, and he could hear Wim T. laughing. The Renfros had whipped the flu. Then the smile left his face. At least the Renfros on this side of the Atlantic Ocean had whipped it. He wondered if

Royal had been so lucky.

Chapter Thirty

"Dear Jane and Wim T., Dad and Mary,

It is July 5, 1918, and her I am in France. I've been here for a couple of days, but this is the first time I've had a chance to write. I'm in a city called La Harve. You write to me at this address: Pvt. Royal Renfro, Company C, 359th Infantry, 90th Division, AEF La Harve, France.

I thought we would never get off of the boat. Because of several submarine scares, we zigged and zagged a lot and lost a lot of time. We put in first in England, at South Hampton, and stayed there for two whole days (never getting off the boat) before coming on over here.

Even if things had gone well, the boat trip would have been bad. We were packed on board like sardines, four men assigned to a single hammock, so that each of us could sleep six hours per day. Of course, with all the noise and seasickness I never got to sleep six hours at one time. On top of everything else, nearly everybody on the boat caught the flu. I watched them bury over fifty boys at sea.

Fortunately, I never came down with the flu. My closest buddy, Sam, is from Abilene. He is bothered with malaria and so had brought along a big supply of quinine. He gave me a bottle of it and advised me to take a nip every few hours, said it would ward off the flu. I followed his advise and kept a little quanine in my stomach all during the worst of it. I'll never know, of course, whether it was the quinine that did it or not. All I know is that Sam and I did not get the flu. They say the flu has hit all over the world. I hope it hasn't hit any of you.

We had no more than landed here when we were told that we would be put through several weeks of training before we go up to the front. This was a big surprise. We think we are already ready. Anyway, it looks like we will have some more of Camp Travis right here in France. I have got to pull K.P. tomorrow. (That means I have to help kitchen.) I'll guarantee that I could make the food better if they would let me, but I'm sure they won't.

Well, I'll close now. It's late, and they'll be after me for K.P. at four in the morning.

Love to all,

Royal."

* * * * * * *

During the next several weeks the family received many letters from Royal, three or four per week. In his August 12th letter he picked up on the news from home about the flu:

"I'm glad and thankful to God that all of you lived over the flu. I can imagine how bad it must have been. Dad, I'm proud of you for taking care of the Dundees. Sorry you lost Bertha. I'm sorry too that big Amos didn't see fit to give you a single word of thanks. However, like the Preacher once said, "You can expect your kindness to come back and slap you in the face sometimes, but that mustn't keep you from being kind.""

His other letters, except for the one written on August 16, 1918, were pot boilers. The letter of August 16th read in part as follows:

"Before I close, I want to tell you about running into the men who killed my mother. It turns out that I had been in training with them and on the boat with them all the way from New York, but for some reason I had never seen them up close. That may seem hard to believe, but you have to remember that although they're in the 90th Division, they're not in my battalion. I'm in the 359th Infantry, but they're in the 357th from Oklahoma.

Earlier today I was in the town of Nancy on pass. I was walking along the street with Sam, my buddy from Abilene, when all of a sudden I saw them. I recognized them immediately. They were weaving along, plainly drunk, coming to meet us. When they got real close, they both got a scared look on their faces. One of the pointed at me and asked the other if they didn't know me from somewhere. One of them then asked me where I was from; and when I said 'Texas', I'll swear their eyes nearly popped out of their heads. Then he asked me what part of Texas, and I said, "Northwest--Panhandle part'. When I said that, they looked real relieved, said they didn't know me after all and walked on down the street.

Please don't be alarmed. I'm not going to try to get even with those men. I left all that up to God a long time ago. I'm not going to sit here and tell you that I love them like God and William T. Applegate would like for me to love them. Maybe some day I can go that far, but right now I mainly feel pity for them. On top of being sorry for them, I feel just a little bit of a sort of love for them by reason of the fact that they are in the uniform of their country and will be fighting in the trenches pretty soon.

I guess if you wait long enough, God will give you a reason to love almost anybody at least a little bit. I want Wim T. to know that. I'll tell him myself some day, but just in case something happens and I'm not able to tell him, you do it. Please, when he is old enough to understand, tell him that his Dad once said that if you wait long enough, God will give you a reason to love almost anybody.

By the way, Dad, in my mind I'm handling Amos Dundee the same way. I think that some day God will give me a reason to love him, maybe just a little bit.

Love to all,
Royal"

Chapter Thirty-One

Until now the high point in the life of James Hancock had been his participation in the charge up San Juan Hill. Even before that day was done the gore of it had been partially obscured by the glory of it. In later years that spilled blood was not forgotten, far from it. Nevertheless, amid the boisterous, yet sentimental, reunions of the Rough riders and the ascension of their leader to the White House, almost all anguish over the ultimate sacrifice of their comrades was lost in the memories of their nobility and the righteousness of their cause.

In the almost twenty years since his return from Cuba, Hancock had been a successful husband, father of four daughters, civic leader, churchman and banker--Vice-President and finally President of Austin Security Bank. All though those active and productive years his recollections of those Rough riders' glory days grew ever fonder; and it was those memories which inspired him to find the time to work his way from Private to Captain in the Texas National Guard. Those same sentiments had also caused him to volunteer for service in France. And now, at 44 he surely was one of the oldest company commanders in the American Expeditionary Force. He was glad for the generous scattering of gray in his black hair. That allowed him to establish himself as a father figure and to be chummy with his men, all without loss of military respect.

These days in France the soft rain fell without ceasing. As Hancock walked through it towards the enlisted men's barracks, he was well aware that he night was too young for him to find very many in his company who had returned from the adventures of their twenty-four hour passes. However, rather relishing his father image, he reasoned that it was those who had not gone on the town or those who had come back early who probably stood in the greatest need of a cheerful word from their company commander.

Noiselessly entering the barracks, he noted with satisfaction the orderly by-the-book arrangement of beds and equipment. This reflects the shape of this company, he thought. After six weeks of extra training by French and English instructors, they are ready. They will fight and fight well. At first he thought the barracks was completely empty of men. Then on his right, towards the end of the long room, he heard a faint sigh and the soft scuffing of shoes on the earthen floor. Silently drawing closer to the noise, he saw his favorite soldier. If he ever had a son, Royal Renfro was like the man he would like for that son to be.

"Good evening, Private Renfro."

Royal gasped and jumped to his feet.

"At ease. It's OK. I'm sorry I scared you."

"That's alright, Sir. I was just writing a letter home."

"Fine. Did you go into town?"

"Yes, Sir."

"Back a little early, huh?"

"Yes, Sir."

It was then that Hancock observed the unmistakable "just saw a ghost" look in Royal's eyes. Fascinated, he took a seat on Royal's bunk and said, "Well, why don't I sit down with you and hear all about what you did in town. How about that?"

"That would be fine," Royal replied as he joined his company commander on the bunk.

"I'm guessing that something unusual happened to you in town."

"Yes, Sir. I saw the men who killed my mother," Royal blurted.

Hancock grimised. "What did you say?"

Royal's stare went far away, and he answered in a dull monotone. "I saw the two men who killed my mother many years ago."

"Tell me about it."

"It was still daylight," Royal began, "but it was dark and misting heavy. I was walking along the street with Sam, my buddy, when all of a sudden I saw 'em. They were a half block away, and they were shaved and had haircuts and had on army uniforms; but I knew who they were just like that," he said, snapping his fingers. They had their caps on the backs of their heads and were walkin sort of unsteady like. They were comin our way, and when they got almost to us, one of 'em got this awful scared look in his eyes. He stopped and pointed right straight at me. Then he asked his brother, "Don't we know him from somewhere?"

His brother sort of shook his head and blinked his eyes and seemed to sober up right there on the spot. Then he stepped up to my chest. I swear his face was as white as a sheet, and he looked like he had just seen a ghost. He asked me, "Where you from?"

I said, "Texas." He swallowed real hard and took on the look of a scared rabbit. Then he asked me what part of Texas I was from. I said 'Northwest--Panhandle part'. And when I said that, he looked real relieved and sort of grinned. Then he said, "We don't know him, little brother, let's get on with our good time."

"Why were they so afraid of you?" The captain inquired. "What's the story?"

That was all the invitation Royal needed. In a rush of words, he recounted the story of his mother's death and his reaction to it. It was getting late, and most of the men had returned to the barracks before he finished.

"So now you have forgiven these men?" Hancock asked.

"Well, I think, with God's help, I've done

about as well as a man can do. I'm not sayin I love those fellas, not like God loves them; but at least I've given up all thoughts of tryin to get even. And I hope they make good soldiers, and I hope they don't get hurt when we go up to the front. That's about as well as I can tell you about my feelings."

"Could you tell what outfit they are in?"

"Yes, Sir. They wore the patches of the Oklahoma National Guard."

"Good," Hancock grunted. "You'll probably never see them again."

Royal nodded. "Funny, we never thought they might go to Oklahoma. We always assumed they were in New Mexico."

It was the next night before Royal was able to complete his letter home, telling about his meeting with his mother's killers.

* * * * * * * *

It was September 14, 1918. They had been on the front, near St. Mihiel for forty-eight hours. "C" Company had lost eight men, four dead, four seriously wounded.

"Captain, Sir, I have some replacements for you," the Sgt. announced.

"How many?" Hancock asked.

"Two."

"Only two. I need eight."

"These are all they sent, Sir. They broke up a couple of companies of the Oklahoma 357th and spread 'em around, but his is all they had for you."

"Alright, Sergeant," Hancock replied,

returning the sergeant's salute. "It's not your fault. You can go on back now."

Turning to the replacements, he said, "What are your names?"

"Hawks, Sir. I'm Les and he's Pete."

"You are both named Hawks?"

"Yes, Sir., We're brothers."

Uh Oh, Hancock thought, and he quickly averted his face to hide his surprise. Recovering quickly, he remembered that Royal was in Third Squad of First Platoon. The two platoons of his Company "C" were spread out, single file, along the forward trench, with First Platoon on Hancock's right and Second Platoon on his left. The third squad in Second Platoon had been his hardest hit squad, suffering three casualties. These circumstances allowed him to put some 100 feet between Royal and the brothers from Oklahoma. They probably won't see each other until after we are relieved, he reasoned. I'll wait until then to decide whether I'll keep the brothers in my company.

Hancock addressed his First Sergeant. "Sergeant Mullins, these men go to 2nd Platoon. Lead them down to Lt. Addy and tell him I said they are assigned to his third squad."

"Yes, Sir."

"And you two new men," Hancock threw in as an afterthought, "we're glad to have you. You don't have much time to get ready. We go over the top at dawn--about thirty minutes from now."

* * * * * * *

Captain Hancock eyed his watch and waited for the series of flares, four at five second intervals, which would be the signal for him and all the other company commanders to blow their whistles and lead their men over the top. I've already done this twice, he thought. I don't really want anymore chances for fame and glory. It's bad enough out there wading through the mud and rain with machine guns chattering and mortar shells bursting, and men screaming; but blowing a whistle and leading out--well, that's about more than I can take.

Nevertheless, when the fourth signal flare burst in the gray sky, Hancock dutifully blew his whistle and climbed out of the trench. Raising his pistol aloft, he cried out the words which were popular with company commanders up and down the American lines: "Come on men, you don't want to live forever do you?"

Royal heard the whistle and his captain's shout. And after he scrambeld out of the trench and started towards the tangle of barbed wire in the misty distance, he unconciously began to drift to the left, towards his leader. Not surprisingly several of the others, including the brothers from Oklahoma, also began an unrealized drift towards Hancock's encouraging cries.

Suddenly a strange and erie silence fell over the battlefield, a quietness broken only by the noises of heavy breathing and the steady slurping of muddy shoes. Royal noted with great relief that the American mortars had done their job. Their shells had put big holes in the barbed wire tangle.

But just as he crawled through one of the holes in the German fence, his ears were deafened by the bursting of enemy mortar shells followed by the presistent chattering of a machine gun. He saw two of his companions jump or fall into a shell hole only ten feet or so to his left. The hole looked good to him. Correctly gauging the intervals of the machine gun's sweeping fire over his head, he made a desperate and successful lunge for the shell hole. Falling headlong into the relative safety of the depression, he was shocked to discover that he shared the hole with his mother's murderers.

Horrified, Royal quickly noted that the muddy trousers of both men were soaked in crimson blood. Their helmets were off. They were white-faced and breathing hard. The one called Pete managed to gasp, "You've got to help us. We're hurt real bad."

"Nobody can help you until somebody stops that machine gun," Royal shouted.

Royal turned on his back and began to concentrate again on timing the intervals between the whissing of bullets over his head. Suddenly his eyes popped at the sight of a German hand gernade, a potatoe masher, lazily descending on him. As if it were a baseball, he let go of his rifle, threw up his hands, caught it and slung it up and out, as hard as he could, towards the machine gun's chatter. He heard the explosion, followed by screams. And he noted that the chatter had ceased.

"You took it out," Pete incredulously observed. "Now you can help us."

"I'll try," Royal grunted as he looked over the top of the hole. "Oh my gosh," he exclaimed. "It looks like the whole German army is comin' at us."

Royal heard his captain shout: It's a counterattack. Pull back men. Pull back."

"You got to get us out of here, man," Pete pleaded.

"I can't handle both of you."

"You can pull me out and come back or get somebody else to come back for him," Pete argued.

Royal glanced again over the top. "No way I can do that, but I'll do what I can," he promised.

Crawling out of the hole, he half ran, half crawled to the German machine gun nest. Miraculously the gun was still intact, with a belt of ammunition in perfect place. I've never shot one of these things, he thought; but I guess you just pull the trigger. And pull the trigger he did, spraying bullets at the advancing, now passing Germans. During the next 90 seconds (it seemed much, much longer to him) he was able to cut down dozens of Germans and to keep them away from his shell hole. Presently though, he had his second encounter of the day with a potatoe masher. This one he never saw.

At first it hurt, but then he felt numb all over. His head swam and he passed briefly into a painless coma. Only a few seconds passed before his eye lids fluttered open. He saw the ancient hackberry tree, then the spring. Next he saw them holding hands around the flat rock--his dad, Jane, Mary, the Preacher, and Wim T. (Strangely, Wim

T. was all grown up, had gray hair.) And Royal was there too, holding hands with Jane on one side and Amos Dundee on the other. Although it would be a couple of more seconds before he understood what he saw, Royal smiled.

* * * * * **

Captain Hancock witnessed much of what Royal did, but it was only after the counterattack had been finally repulsed and he had found the bodies of the brothers from Oklahoma that he fully realized what his favorite soldier had done.

Chapter Thirty-One

As it turned out, the Renfro family received three more letters from Royal, but all of them came after the Mesa telegraph operator rode out with a telegram for Jane. It was from the War Department. Royal had been killed in France near a place called St. Mihiel on September 14, 1918.

Jane screamed in anguish. Then, sobbing out of control and pushing her mother away, she grabbed Wim T. out of his bed and ran out to the big hackberry tree. There she knelt and cried herself dry. George and Mary held each other close, wetting each other with their tears, each trying unsuccessfully to hold down the complusive shutters of the other.

Later George walked to the hackberry tree; and without a word, lifted both Jane and his grandbaby in his arms and carried them to Jane's bed. He left the totally exahusted mother there but took the now sleeping Wim T. back into his arms and walked to the treasure rock. He stopped on the rock, facing the sun which was about to go down. "It's not fair, Wim T.," he muttered. "What happened to your grandmother and your daddy was not fair."

Tears welled in his eyes as he rambled on, thinking out loud. "But then, on the other hand, I guess it was not fair for me to have a wife like Kate; and it was not fair for her to have a son like Royal; and it was not fair for me to have a son like him, and it was not fair for me to have a grandson like you." He stopped talking long enough to witness the sun take leave of his part of the world for a while. "I guess," he went on, "when you come to think about it nothin in life is fair, but maybe the good not-fairs sort of balance the bad not-fairs." Then he looked with delight on his grandson and kissed him. "In fact," he concluded, "the good ones weigh up a lot heavier."

George moved to step off of the rock, but he abruptly stopped and caught his breath. "I just thought of somethin that sure enough is fair, Wim T. It's just plumb fair that the worms in hell won't ever eat on your daddy."

* * * * * * * *

Three weeks later the tears flowed again when Jane received a letter from Royal's captain. Much like those citations which the military officers read in a loud voice immediately prior to bestowing a medal, the letter spoke of Royal's unwavering valor and devotion to duty, of his loyalty to his country and his fellow soldiers, and of his supreme sacrifice in trying ot save two of his buddies.

"It turned out," the letter went on, "that the two soldiers he tried to save were from Oklahoma, and Royal had previously identified them to me as the brothers who killed his mother."

The letter continued, saying that Royal had been recommended to postumously receive the Congression Medal of Honor. At the end, he said, "I knew your husband personally, and I want you to know that I have never known another man quite as good as he, nor have I seen another man die quite so nobly as he."

* * * * * * *

Royal's flag-draped coffin arrived at the depot in Mesa on December 15, 1918. They had the funeral the next day.

Towards the end of the service, George thought the pastor had done about as well as anybody could have done under the circumstances. After all, not even the family members who had been privileged to glance into the depts of his soul could quite do justice to Royal with words. The pastor praised Royal as a good Christian, husband, son and father in the usual way that preachers talk about good men at their funerals.

He also read aloud Captain Hancock's letter to Jane and read part of Royal's letter of June 22nd, the part where he asked them to tell Wim T. that his father once said that if you wait long enough, God will give you a reason to love almost anybody.

Looking up after his closing prayer, the pastor was surprised to see Amos Dundee standing at the rear of the building. Realizing that many of the men of Mesa would jump at the chance to demonstrate their sympathy for the fallen hero and his family; and being convinced too, that this was not a proper time for confrontations or battles of any kind, the pastor repeated some admonitions that had already been privately given to the pallbearers.

"In closing, allow me to assure you that Royal would want us to obey the law. Therefore, I will remind the congregation of a matter that has already been brought to the attention of the funeral director and the pall bearers. When the funeral coach nears the gravesite there will be a fence separating the road from the place of burial; and, as most of you know, there is no gate in that fence. Also, as most of you know, it is against the law for us to cut the wires. Therefore, it will be necessary for the six pall bearers to lift the coffin over the fence and for the six honorary pall bearers to crawl through the wires and receive it on the other side. The rest of us will then crawl through the fence and proceed to the gravesite near the big spring."

All the way from the church George kept asking God to remove his bitterness towards Amos Dundee, but it didn't happen. "Crawl," the pastor had said. Twice he had used that word. Over and over it pounded against the anvil of George's brain. Crawl, crawl, crawl. Not only would he and his family be forced to crawl in the presence of Amos Dundee, but all their freinds as well. Ruefully he thought, I guess God won't take away the hate without a little more help from me.

When they came to the spot on the road even with the gravesite, the coach stopped and the honorary pall bearers scrambled forward and crawled through the fence, preparing to receive the coffin. The regular pall bearers then unloaded the coffin from the coach and approached the fence.

It was then that Amos Dundee, mounted on his big black mare, trotted up and around the coach. Dismounting, he gave a tight lipped command. "Wait."

Marching to the fence, he took something out of his pocket. Then, after slowly turning around, he deliberately sought out the face of George Renfro. As he gazed into George's bewildered eyes, his own eyes filled with tears. Turning back to the fence, he flashed the object which he had taken from his pocket and placed it against the top wire. In quick succession the crowd heard four clicks coupled with final whines as the wire cutters severed the taunt wires and sent the two ends flying apart.

Again facing George, Dundee's shoulders were shaking and tears were streaming down his cheeks. He said, "Mr. Renfro..." He tried to go on but couldn't. Taking quick, shallow breaths, he labored for a full minute before bringing his shudders under control. The pall bearers were only vaguely aware that their hands and arms were starting to ache. The crowd watched in awesome silence. Finally, eyes wide, he cleared his throat and tried again.

His voice quivered and even cracked once, but he had his say: "Now Mr. Renfro, I will be greatly honored if you will allow me to witness the burial of your son on your own land."

* * * * * * *

Epilogue

Wim T., the owner of Renfro Oil, is an old man now. He still owns the land where his father is buried. On November 11th of each year he carries on his private observacne of Veterans' Day by returning to his boyhood home. There he recalls the many stories that his mother, grandmother and grandfather told him about his father. He always pauses to re-read the inscription on his father's gravestone. His grandfather purchased the large hunk of pink grantite and painstakingly chisled the message on it himself. The lettering is not professional, but it is deep and will endure forever. Too, its roughhewn quality seems to speak of the love and tears that were behind each banging of hammer against chisel. It reads:

"Royal Renfro, who was killed in France

fighting for his country on September 14, 1918, lies here on his own land. THE LORD WILL PROVIDE."

The End